THROUGH
THE SPACE/TIME SLIP

Some of the stars blurred and streaked like a laser light display, elongating, until all were strips of light. Allis tightened her fingers on the stanchion, her heart beat painfully. The ship shuddered, but Allis's throat was so constricted with fear that she couldn't even cry out.

"The gravity slip is short," Ghyaspur said, easing back. "This one opens close to a red star, a frisky sun with good winds. We'll catch a high wind off a hot spot, and reach planet in ten shifts."

"How long has it been . . . ?" Allis asked softly.

"Back on your world? I don't know—perhaps three or four thousand shifts."

"Years." Allis shuddered. The worst had happened. Earth was in the past, lost to her forever.

There was no turning back now.

The Latest Science Fiction from Dell Books

*denotes an illustrated book

THE SUNBOUND

CYNTHIA FELICE

A Dell SF BOOK

For Erik and Bobby

Published by
Dell Publishing Co., Inc.
1 Dag Hammarskjold Plaza
New York, New York 10017

Dell ® TM 681510, Dell Publishing Co., Inc.

ISBN: 0-440-18373-1

Printed in the United States of America
First printing—April 1981

CHAPTER 1

The dark side of the planet was lighted only by a sliver of moon and the glitter of flickering stars in an odd, purple sky. It was the wind, Senda knew, carrying tiny particles aloft that distorted the steady starlight—perhaps some heat, too—roiling into the air from sun-baked rocks, which made the stars twinkle. She lowered her glance to cracked earth where she was placing her foot. Too late. Senda stumbled over a root and Ghyaspur walked into her heels.

"Sorry," he muttered, dropping back a step.

Senda nodded her forgiveness, but was inwardly angry because her foot felt scraped and probably was bleeding. She knew it was difficult for Ghyaspur to adjust to the irregular terrain of the planet surface after spending most of his life in the smooth corridors and narrow gangways of the ship, but she wished the young man following her would keep his eyes on where they were going, and allow her to do the same, instead of marveling at winking stars, or looking right and left, tracking every strange noise. She didn't understand the fascination some of her shipmates had for coming planetside; one could get lost in an eyeblink without a homing beacon. (Hers was steadily growing warmer, indicating that they were approaching Daneth's camp.) And there always were things to

stumble over on the restricted worlds, even in this
sparsely vegetated desert. And if she didn't stumble,
something dry and whispery would spatter across her
eyes, or a sickening smell would assault her nose. Even
worse were the noises, which buzzed, hooted, and
whistled over enormous distances in the thick atmosphere, heralding the presence of swarming, flopping,
and slithering creatures. Yet, young Ghyaspur had
challenged Bracha, the scheduled shuttle pilot, to
more than a friendly wrestling match, and won the
prize: a few hours on Earth.

With the vast desert stretching seemingly forever
to accommodate the native beasts, something chose to
scratch in a nearby thicket. "What was that?"
Ghyaspur said, stopping.

"A night bird, perhaps a snake or something,"
Senda said, moving along quickly, warily.

"An animal?"

Senda kept walking, turning only when she realized
Ghyaspur had gone to investigate the sound. He was
on his knees, pressing his face into the thicket, sniffing
deeply. "Ghyaspur," she said sharply. "Some of those
things bite!"

Sheepishly the young man withdrew. He brushed
sandy soil from his hands and knees, sneezing in the
dust. She saw him snap some twigs from the thicket
and put them in his pocket before he started walking again, curious eyes already traveling over the
clumps and bent spires of growing things, quick
fingers darting out to touch again, bending to smell.
Impatiently Senda stamped her foot. Ghyaspur took
a few quick steps in response, then stopped again. He
sniffed the night air deeply and with some alarm in
his voice said, "What's that?"

Miffed by his dalliance, Senda walked in the direc-

tion her beacon indicated without answering Ghyaspur. In seconds she could hear his heavy footsteps as
he ran after her.

"Senda, Senda! I smell smoke." He was gasping
when he reached her side, his blue eyes wide with
fear.

"Of course you smell smoke. Daneth has a fire going to keep the wild things away. Don't you know
anything, Ghyaspur?" Secretly she, too, found it difficult to keep her blood from racing when the acrid
smell from the open fire drifted past her nose; on the
Sovereign Sun even a trace of smoke was justification
for mobilizing the entire crew to find the source and
correct the problem. But she didn't want to give
Ghyaspur the satisfaction of knowing that she was
afraid. Senda was a linguist, and linguists went planetside and presumably got over their fear of open fires,
wide open spaces, and beasts that feasted on human
flesh. Senda never had, but no one knew, except
Daneth. He alone could be trusted to keep her secret
and tactfully help her keep her pride.

During the last rendezvous, only a few local months
ago, Daneth had assured her and the pilot that there
were far fewer wild beasts prowling on this continent
than there had been during the last full-fledged call
the *Sovereign Sun* had made to this world, nearly
seventy local years before. But knowing was of little
comfort. Most of the large carnivores might have
given way under the relentless spread of humanity,
but the tiny ones, the ones that made angry welts on
her sensitive skin, adapted to the human onslaught.
At times she even believed insects cultivated humans,
for they were present on every planet she'd ever visited; even the Watchers' sterile world had them.

Senda walked as quickly as she could in the burdensome gravity, eager to be done with the mission. She couldn't see any better than the stumbling shuttle pilot, but her eyes were comfortable with the dim light, more accustomed and more practiced. Now she could see the flickering shadows from the campfire, and the homing beacon was hot. She reached into her baggy pocket to turn it off. Daneth would know by now that they were close by. In her mind she greeted him. She expected no reply. She hurried, then stopped abruptly when the ground before her suddenly dropped along a vertical line.

"Daneth must be down in that arroyo," she said, not attempting to hide her dismay. As she and Ghyaspur stared, a spray of sparks swirled up from behind some brush. The vegetation was thicker below, indicating that water sometimes washed freely through it. Senda shuddered. One more danger to worry about.

"Shouldn't Daneth know we're here?" Ghyaspur said, straining to see past shadows and darkness.

"He may have the agent, that Allis woman, with him again. Help me down this cliff, then conceal yourself somewhere until I return with Daneth."

The side of the arroyo was a real obstacle. Planetside gravity was greater than the pseudogravity of the ship, strong enough to break the bones of the unwary, even in a short fall. Give Senda the sturdy welded rungs of a ship's ladder and she was like a white spider; but she'd never mastered scrambling up and down crumbling rock and mud while being pulled by a planet to three times her accustomed weight. Determinedly, she kneeled to take a firm hold of the pilot's ankle. "Don't move," she warned, then gingerly she let her feet over the edge. She had only inches to drop when she finally had to let go of Ghyaspur's ankle, but the sudden stop that compressed her bones and muscles made her curse.

"Are you all right?" Ghyaspur asked anxiously from above.

"Yes, yes. Go hide like I told you to do." She waited until he backed away, and then she turned to walk toward the campfire.

There were some treelike growths in the wash, and sometimes her eyes failed to distinguish a branch from a shadow. But finally she could see the campfire. As she had suspected, the Earthwoman was there, sitting in the glow of the crackling flames. Her hair, shining with silvery highlights, cascaded like lava veils from her nodding head. As many times as Senda had seen black hair during her planetside visits, she couldn't get used to it; the dark sheen continued to attract her eyes. Senda was very close to the campfire before she noticed that Daneth was sleeping. She almost laughed. Too much spirits again; too long away from the *Sovereign Sun*'s dry galley. He'd sober quickly and return to the ship's routine without complaint, as he always did. But he was another one who vied actively for planetside assignments, and he was more successful than most in winning them.

Allis must have heard Senda, for she suddenly looked up. The Earthwoman had been crying.

"You're too late," Allis said with unmistakable bitterness. "Damn, why didn't you come last night?"

Confused, Senda approached. Daneth hadn't stirred, hadn't drawn a breath. Blond hair curled over his forehead in damp-looking tendrils. She kneeled beside him, watching for his breast to rise. When it didn't, she touched his neck, tense with foreboding. Her warm hand was milky-white against even a death pallor. Moaning, Senda rocked back on her heels, trying to control the sobs threatening to shake her. Her hand fisted as she rapidly blinked away tears. Not now, she thought decisively. There was no time to grieve, this was not the place. But the loss she felt barely could be contained.

Finally she esablished an outward calm. "What happened?" she said. Then realizing that Allis didn't understand, she repeated the question in English.

"He was sick, Senda. Even when we delivered the first batch of diamonds last spring, Dan was sick. He had leukemia. Do you know what that is?"

Senda turned the word over in her mind; it was new to her, but it had roots in an older language she'd once used on this planet. "White blood? Yes, we know the white-blood death, only too well." Then she shook her head. "But Daneth looked well when I saw him last. I know this . . . disease."

Tiredly, Allis nodded. She sniffed and sighed. "He was in remission, that's why you didn't know. We thought it would last a long time, but . . ." Allis shrugged sadly. "I should have guessed when he started sleeping so much, but we were working hard, doing our damndest to get the last batch of diamonds together on time."

Senda understood. Daneth would press to keep the appointed schedule, even if he were dying. But if he were sick with the disease when she last saw him, he should have been dead long ago. She frowned. "I don't understand this intermission thing."

"Remission," Allis said. "The doctors treated him with methotrexate, a chemical that makes the blood and bone marrow return to normal—almost normal. He was fine for months, then last week . . . I should have guessed, but I suppose I didn't want to face it. He was so eager to bring you the diamonds, so damned proud." Senda looked up to see tears streaming from Allis's dark eyes. "Damn you, Senda. What kind of hold did you have on him to make him come out into the desert when he knew he should be in the hospital? He knew!" she said accusingly. "And he . . . he . . . shot the tires so that I couldn't take him away before you got here."

"You think he knew he was going to die?" Senda said slowly.

"No," Allis said softly. "Not until the end." Allis looked exhausted, as if she'd missed many sleeping periods. The circles under her eyes were even darker than her suntan. "He thought it would be like the last time, that an extra day wouldn't matter. But then he had such pain, horrible pain. What could I do? He'd already ruined the Jeep, and I couldn't carry him on my back, could I?"

Senda was touched by the Earthwoman's distress; it was so much like feelings Senda had had when she was younger. Surely, she remembered thinking, surely there was something I could have done to prevent this. But there was nothing, and the child she had borne died; sometimes it just happened. Perhaps these planetbound folk were not so alien after all. She touched Allis's shoulder, her voice sounding steadier than she felt. "If what you say is true, you can be glad that he had the . . . remission. It was more than he expected."

"He expected to live!" Allis said, anger returning.

Senda shook her head. "Daneth knew better; he'd seen the white-blood death. Sometimes a crisis happens, and it's over very suddenly." Allis's eyes were black as the void and just as cold. Senda shivered and withdrew her hand. She didn't feel like being strong, yet she knew she could not fail to remain in control. "You were a good friend to be with him."

"You could have saved him, Senda. If you'd come last night, we could have used your car to get him to Los Angeles."

The accusations were madness. White blood was insidious and always meant death. Senda drew back from Allis, knowing that the woman was too overcome with grief to listen to reason. There wasn't time to comfort her, to wait until she regained her wits, and that saddened Senda. Allis, with her pretty, long black hair, crying over the loss of the man Senda honored above all other men, would be difficult to leave. But the window that provided return to the *Sovereign Sun* with the least amount of fuel expended was rapidly closing. Too bad Daneth wasn't alive to ease the hurt for the Earthling; he'd always been so tender in times of stress. But then, if Daneth were alive . . . Reluctantly, Senda got to her feet. "Where are the diamonds?" She knew it must sound callous.

"In the Jeep," Allis said.

"He paid your fee?"

"Of course." Her voice sounded dull.

Senda walked to the automobile, frame too close to the ground, even to her unaccustomed eyes. The air-filled tubes it normally rested on had been slashed by Daneth's laser. She fumbled with the door handle, realized that it was locked, or they'd changed the operating mechanism again. The window was open and she struggled through. The two sacks of diamonds on the floor were too heavy to jump with, so she dropped them out the window. Good thing she hadn't left Ghyaspur at the shuttle; she'd never have managed both sacks alone. Daneth had done very well, better than the first pickup when he'd said he was just beginning to grasp the local economics and something called "speculating."

Every planet had its peculiarities to take advantage of, but turning paper into diamonds was the best bargain yet. It would take one like Daneth to be successful, though. Once Senda had made very profitable forays on this planet, but the times of pillaging and plundering without being caught were gone. It was more civilized now, even had a few satellites for communication. Senda carried one sack back to the campfire and signaled to Ghyaspur with a wave. She hoped he was watching her and not off exploring the bushes again.

"I'm sorry to leave you alone to deal with this," she said to Allis. The woman seemed dazed, watching numbly as Senda knelt beside Daneth's body. "Just one more thing before I go . . ." Senda reached inside Daneth's shirt, but she found nothing. She pulled back the sleeping bag to expose more of the body. His chest was bare. Alarmed, she looked at Allis.

"Looking for this?" she said. The communicator-stone Daneth had always worn around his neck was in the Earthling's hand. "You get the diamonds, Senda, but this is mine. I've precious little to remember him by."

Senda stared, shocked by the stone's frosty glow. "He gave it to *you?*"

"I can't prove it, but, yes, he gave it to me." Allis laughed, madly, Senda thought. "He called it 'a blessing.' "

"No, not a blessing. *The* blessing. And the proof of his giving it to you is in your hand. The stone is still alive." Senda was confused. Allis, from the baleful bemusement on her face, had no idea of what she held in her hand. In her wildest speculations Senda never had expected to find a living communicator-stone, the treasured artifact from the Quondam Beings in the hand of an Earthling, most especially not Daneth's stone. But there it was. How awful for Milani. Senda shook her head, trying not to think of the ship's captain. "My duty is clear," she muttered to herself.

"What?" said Allis.

"Did Daneth explain about the stone? About us, his people?" She hoped her shipmate had made it easier to do what she must do.

Allis shook her head. "He was in terrible pain. There were a lot of things we never found the time to say."

Senda's temples throbbed. The fool still was worried about things not said when she held a Quondam Being's stone in her hand. What had Daneth been thinking? He must have known he was dying or he wouldn't have given the stone to her. Senda had no choice but to trust his decision.

"He used to make up stories," Allis was saying, "about the stone having occult powers. Sometimes it was easy to believe." Her hand fisted around the stone and she tensed. She was paler now, the stone's power running through her. "It was scary sometimes," Allis's eyes were wide with memories of the past and the pain of the present.

Ghyaspur crashed past a bush and stumbled into the camp; the Earthwoman didn't look. Her eyes, still wide and glassy, were fixed on Daneth's bright curls. Senda's hands reached out for her, then withdrew. Let the Earthling sit in her stupor for a moment—a moment for Senda to think and make plans.

"Ghyaspur, there's a sack of diamonds by the dead automobile. Fetch it," she said.

"But, Daneth . . ." The pilot was instinctively

reaching for the man who had been his guardian, friend, and captain. Senda stayed him with a hand.

"Daneth is dead. He gave the stone to her." She gestured to Allis.

Ghyaspur stepped back, frowning with concern. "But she's . . ."

"I know, but we'll do what we must. Fetch the diamonds, then help me with her."

Ghyaspur nodded, glanced back at Daneth, then ran for the diamonds. Senda went to Allis.

"Come now, come along. Your having the stone changes everything. We can take care of Daneth."

Slowly, Allis pocketed the stone. "We'll put him in your car," Allis said. "With his medical history we shouldn't have any trouble from the authorities, should we?"

"Yes, no . . . of course that will be the thing to do," Senda said gently, helping Allis to her feet.

Ghyaspur returned just in time to put a strong arm around Allis's waist, and they led her between them. A wild beast called in the night; Ghyaspur didn't even glance up.

The grief-stricken Earthling walked placidly across the desert floor between Senda and Ghyaspur, even giving Senda weak smiles from time to time. But Senda didn't know how long the stupor would last. Shuttles did not much resemble automobiles, and sight of it would burn past the numbness of grief. Then she and Ghyaspur would have to overpower Allis. Senda didn't look forward to a fracas in the dense air and tiring gravity.

They were halfway down the hill before Allis saw the gleaming hull and obelisk shape, and she dug her heels into the hard-baked earth.

"Hey, wait a minute!"

There was no mistaking the alarm and suspicion in her voice. Senda nodded to Ghyaspur who drew back to aim his bola at her legs. His first throw was off the mark. Dust was still rising from where the bola slapped at the woman's heels when the second bola ascended, its velocity corrected to account for the planet's strong gravity, felling Allis before she had taken two more fleeing steps. Senda threw herself on the Earthwoman's back while Ghyaspur fought to secure flailing arms and scratchng fingers. Another bola with thongs of leather stripped from the belly of a ravel-beast finally contricted all movement. Allis continued to scream, a stricken wheezing sound, as the bola tendrils enveloped her chest and throat. Breathing heavily, Ghyaspur peeled back the thong on Allis's neck, looking more dismayed than pleased that he'd trussed her so efficiently.

Senda sighed deeply, trying to bring energy back to her fatigued body. It was so hard to be planetside where the air weighed heavily on her chest and stuck in her lungs like syrup. Even worse to have sorrow beating painfully in her heart and the eyes of the Earthwoman wounding her soul with every terrified glance. Taking her was the only thing Senda could do, but was it the right thing? Once she'd brought Ghyaspur a tiny winged reptile from an open port, and together they'd fashioned a gilded wire cage in which to keep it. They'd found it a few shifts later on the bottom of the cage, its shimmering scaled wings like shards of a life broken from beating on its prison walls. How did they feel, these creatures that roamed planets and breathed unfiltered air?

"Senda, I can carry her, but you'll have to open the hatch," said Ghyaspur. He was tentatively hoisting Allis, holding her well-trussed form by the bola thongs. He heaved her to his shoulders with a groan, then straightened his thighs under the load.

With a final sigh and a wish that her heart would be still, Senda hurried down the hill to the shuttle, staggering under a load different from Ghyaspur's, but one just as heavy.

Inside, Senda sat beside the Earthling, carefully strapping her in before loosening the bola thongs. Ghyaspur settled before the controls, checking them meticulously and quietly while Senda finished with Allis. When she passed the bolas to him, his face was stolid.

"Daneth?" he asked gruffly.

"Yes," Senda said, watching her passenger carefully. Allis was calmer now, staring out the portal at the night sky. "And the automobile thing as well."

The power whistled softly, then the shuttle lifted a few feet, turned, and headed back to the arroyo, picking up speed with every second.

"My God," Allis said, alarmed. She strained forward to see.

The shuttle flew over the arroyo and, as soon as the camp was in view, Ghyaspur carefully aimed the lasers. Daneth's body was no more, gone in a puff of vapor, but the dead auto exploded into flames. As the shuttle veered off before the rising inferno, Allis screamed.

"It's all right, Allis," Senda said, touching the Earthling's hand. *Damn, why hadn't Daneth made this easier? If Allis were frightened now, what would she do when—*

But not even Senda could do anything with the gravitational force mounting so rapidly. She barely had time to snatch back her hand before Ghyaspur turned the shuttle skyward and accelerated. Poor Allis was in an awkward position, not even able to

moan any longer as blood pooled painfully in her
lower limbs. I should have told her to breathe carefully, Senda thought, and to move so that her thighs
were parallel to acceleration. Senda hated the fast
breakaways needed on the restricted planets. Damn
the Watchers for that.

Finally sunlight burst through the portal. Senda
opened her eyes, blinking wildly. She reached for the
dimmer and got the portal shuttered, but not before
her eyes were pained and filled with tears.

"Sorry, Senda," Ghyaspur said, half turning in his
seat. "I forgot. How is our passenger?"

"Unconscious for a while," Senda said.

"What are you going to do?"

Senda shrugged. "Explain as much as I can when
she wakes up, if she's not still so grief-stricken that she
can't understand. What else can I do?"

"I don't know. I just hope we don't get into trouble
for taking her off the planet."

"Trouble? With whom? Milani or the Watchers?"

The Watchers were an easy source of terror, even
when there were none near. But Ghyaspur frowned
and thought a moment. "Milani," he said finally.

CHAPTER 2

Dan was dead.

His dying was the only sane thing that had happened in the last few hours, and Allis clung to the memory of his last breath as tightly as she'd gripped his hand. She had loved Dan, but she hadn't expected to go off the deep end when he died. She'd been prepared for his death, though it had happened sooner than it should have and with frightening swiftness. And surely, if she could consider the possibility of madness so objectively, she couldn't really be insane. But if she weren't insane, then . . .

She looked out the portal, first behind, then ahead. The moon and the Earth were of equal size, putting her, she guessed, closer to the moon. This was not the road to Los Angeles. Allis didn't know how long she'd been unconscious after takeoff, but the time she'd spent awake and watching their progress was not enough time to go more than halfway to the moon. Hadn't it taken what's-their-names several days to make the two-hundred-and-fifty-thousand-mile journey?

Allis settled back in her seat, and once again didn't settle in the accustomed fashion; webbing pulled her back against the cushioned chair and her hair drifted before her eyes. Earlier she'd tried to knot her hair, then to lean against it, but the knot untied and there was no such thing as *to lean*. Weightlessness was real enough. Beside her, Senda, with her white hair sensibly cropped close to her head, appeared to be dozing. When she raised one eyelid, revealing a deep-set pink eye, Allis turned away. Again her hair drifted, and she smoothed it against her scalp.

"So, the tears are finished," Senda said gently. "And it is not so bad."

Statements or questions? Allis had little trouble following the lilting quality of Senda's speech, but sometimes Senda didn't form interrogatives correctly. From the first time she'd met the little albino woman more than six months ago, Allis had known she was a foreigner; she hadn't any idea of just how foreign foreign could be. Aliens, if she could believe all that Senda had told her. And Dan, with his Nordic curls and bright blue eyes, was an alien, too. Apparently they'd never read about the improbability of parallel evolution.

The pilot turned to say something to Senda in a language Allis couldn't understand. His skin pigmentation was translucent but normal, and he had ruddy cheeks and lips. His hair was the color of beach sand. The pilot was younger than Dan, but his eyes, deepset and all afire, were disturbingly similar.

"Ghyaspur wants to know if you're ever going to speak," Senda said chuckling. When Allis didn't answer, Senda sighed and exchanged a concerned look with the pilot. For a moment Senda pretended to adjust the sleeves on her pajamalike garment, moving the dun-colored cuff above her elbow. Her skin was milky white, and fine white hairs glistened in the cabin light. Her albinoism was a beautiful quality, in an elfin way.

"You understand that it is the stone," Senda was saying. "We have nothing personal against you, no reason to take you away from your world, except the stone. It has nothing to do with the diamonds; you could do us no harm even if you reported Daneth's activities, which must have seemed strange to you. And it's nothing to do with Daneth either, except that he loved you enough to give you the stone. I don't even know if you loved him; that wouldn't be necessary." Again Senda sighed, frowning and destroying all the elfin qualities with deep furrows in the ashen skin of her forehead and pinched flesh around the pink eyes. "I wish you would give some sign that you understand what I've told you about the stone. Any artifact from the Quondam Beings is extremely valuable, but a communicator-stone is priceless. There are fewer than one hundred of them known in the galaxy. It's a great gift."

It made Allis sick to touch the stone. She turned away from Senda, who was beginning to repeat what she'd told Allis earlier, and she watched the gibbous moon ahead and slightly below the shuttle's altitude. She reached in her tight pocket for the stone, carefully pulling it out by the silver chain she had bought for Dan, so that he could wear it farther down on his chest. It floated above her lap, tethered to her fingers by the chain. As a one-time geology student, she ought to be able to identify the minerals that formed the crystal, but she couldn't. It was harder than quartz, and its specific gravity was greater than most gems— diamonds, for instance. But it absorbed light like a good pearl.

When she touched it the stone came alive, as if her skin energized some hidden power source. She took the smooth pebble between her fingers to watch the subtle glow intensify. The frosty iridescence was easy to look at, but she felt a little dizzy. She hid it in the palm of her hand, as if not seeing the stone would cut off the giddy sensation. The feeling was not so disorienting as the last time she had touched the stone, when Senda had been talking a few hours ago. But the confusion in her mind was definitely related to touching the stone.

Dan had attributed occult powers to the stone, and Senda had expounded that theme, telling Allis that the artifact gave the bearer the power to read minds, a sort of one-sided telepathy. But if Dan had known that power, he was unique, unless Senda and the pilot were consistently thoughtless when Allis touched the stone. She had no idea what her alien companions were thinking. Something physical happened, but she didn't believe it was telepathy. And whatever it was, it was not so sickening this time. Allis put the chain around her neck. The stone floated off her chest, and she laughed in spite of herself. Now she understood why Dan had worn it on such a tight band; the chain wasn't much good in zero gravity.

The pilot said some gibberish to her. Allis turned to Senda in confusion.

"Ghyaspur says that he's glad to hear you laugh. The *Sovereign Sun* is a happy ship, and you'll fit in. He wants to know if you'd like to sit up front with him where there's a better view. He'll be changing attitude and trajectory to rendezvous with the ship."

Allis hesitated, then shook her head. She knew that Senda had not made a completely accurate translation. Was it merely common sense telling her that the pilot's words had been too few to convey all that Senda supposedly translated? Her fingers tightened over the stone; the dizziness increased as she concentrated. There was something . . . something . . .

Allis eventually realized that the alien shuttle was not approaching the moon from the same angle the astronauts had a few years before. They were passing over the moon's north pole, if it could be said to have one, and half the globe was bright with sunlight, a quarter was dark, and the rest bathed in earthshine, making the craters and ridges look soft. When they dipped behind the moon she expected to see more of the dark side, but the far side of the moon was completely lighted. It was strikingly different from the lunar surface she was accustomed to seeing in pictures or through a telescope from Earth. The landscape was heavily cratered; the familiar rills and *maria* were missing. They were, she reasoned, between sun and moon, and the moon, with its uncanny solitude, blocked her view of Earth. She shivered and turned away.

Senda had donned dark goggles, not at all like the sunglasses Allis usually wore, but she sensed their purpose was similar. They fit snugly over the bridge of Senda's nose and clung, seemingly precariously, to her eyebrows, dividing the albino's elongated face with a dark slash. The portals were letting in more light than they had earlier, by the pilot's intention, Allis thought, for she'd seen him working with the controls when the lighting changed.

The pilot was still busy with the controls, and the shuttle turned. He said something to Senda, and Senda said to Allis: "We will begin decelerating now and aligning ourselves with the ship. It will not be so bad as leaving your planet's atmosphere, but I suggest you uncross your legs. That's a bad habit in a shuttle."

The maneuvers were uncomfortable for her already queasy stomach, but not crippling and strangling as acceleration had been. Allis kept her eyes on the portal, on the bright, shining moon. She wondered who would be the first of her friends to notice that she hadn't returned when the weekend passed. If much more time passed they might say that she'd vanished from the face of the Earth, never suspecting how right they were.

The pressure eased and she was floating again. The stone had worked its way out of her blouse, and she tucked it in again, securely between the cup of her bra and her breast. The dizziness had passed, but there was something else now, a slightly heady feeling. It took the edge off her grief and fears.

The shuttle changed attitude again; the scene changed from moon, to black, and then to the sun. At first the bright sunlight prevented her from fully understanding its size, but as the shuttle dropped lower, the ship, a massive rotating disk in the distance, cast them in shadow. They stayed in shadow, ship's shadow, moving closer as her eyes adjusted.

"The *Sovereign Sun*," Senda said, eagerly looking over Allis's shoulder. "It's a welcome sight."

There was nothing with which Allis could compare its size; the sun's and the moon's proportions were meaningless to her since she didn't know how far away they were. The ship might have been the size of a ferris wheel or as big as Connecticut. Its body was rotating within a superstructure that vaguely resembled a child's gyroscope, except that the superstructure was attached by metallic shrouds to a gargantuan, weblike parachute.

"The sails," Senda said, seeing Allis's puzzled frown. "I told you about the sails."

"You told me, but I didn't understand," Allis said. The ship was minuscule compared to the sails. "This isn't exactly an ocean."

"The solar wind," said Senda with a touch of impatience. "The sun has a steady force of particles streaming away from it; the sails catch the wind and pull the ship." Senda shook her head sadly. "Why couldn't Daneth have loved a physicist?"

"I loved an astronomer," Allis said, smiling wryly now. Let Senda puzzle over that for a while; Allis felt inwardly calm. Dan may not have prepared her very well for the stone, but he was an inexhaustible interpreter of astronomy. At the time it had seemed just something else to share, like good food, wine, and lovemaking. She knew that the sun spewed ionized particles at nearly the speed of light. She knew, too, that the Earth's magnetosphere deflected the ions, and that the magnetosphere extended well beyond the moon. Wasn't the great *Sovereign Sun* therefore stuck, like a clipper in a dead calm?

Allis frowned, trying to remember the sketches Dan had drawn on cocktail napkins. No, the big ship wasn't becalmed. Only the tail of the magnetosphere went beyond the moon, and that tail was downwind, on the night side of the Earth. The ship would be well upwind of the magnetosphere, able to take advantage of the solar wind. What difference to her, she wondered bitterly. Had she really expected a rescue mission even if the ship were stuck? That was almost crazier than her being on an alien shuttle, somewhere between the moon and the sun. What the hell kind of mess had Dan gotten her into?

The axis on the rotating sphere was opening, like

a dilating iris, but somehow resembling an illuminated gullet rather than an eye. The shuttle yawed,
and the *Sovereign Sun* stopped turning; they had
matched the ship's rotational spin. The moment the
shuttle entered the gullet there was a metallic *thunk,*
and their forward motion stopped. The iris snapped
shut behind them.

"When we disembark let me help you to the gangway. Freefall is disorienting at first," Senda said, releasing the webbing that held Allis to the cushions.
As the albino removed her goggles and pocketed them
in the baggy pants, Allis followed Ghyaspur to the
hatch, propelling herself hand over hand past the
seats.

Two other shuttles, similar to the one Allis was
leaving, were neatly anchored by gantries, noses
pointed to the rotundalike door. There were lines,
ladders, and equipment Allis didn't recognize bolted
to the sturdy mid-ribs, and as she shoved herself out
the shuttle hatch, she found herself soaring toward
the bulkhead with alarming speed. She tried to twist
so as to meet the impending collision with her feet,
but her body wouldn't cooperate. Somehow Senda got
to the bulkhead more quickly and grabbed Allis,
deflecting her crash. Then she slowed their new direction of travel by gripping strategically placed stanchions.

"Thanks," Allis said, still more surprised than
alarmed by the incident.

Senda nodded. "I should have warned you not to
push. It takes practice, like everything else." She
glanced at the stone, floating free again near Allis's
breasts, as if to indicate that using it would require
practice.

They were floating in what seemed an upside-down

position, even though Allis knew there was no up or down in a weightless condition. Senda braced her feet against the stanchion, almost like a monkey getting ready to leap, and turned both their bodies right side up, confirming in Allis's mind that there must be some visual clues to a local vertical in the axis. Before she could determine what those clues were, Senda expertly propelled Allis to a hatch, which Ghyaspur was opening with a torque tool. When it swung open Allis noticed a subtle change in pressure and felt warm air swirl past her. When the pilot moved out of the way, Allis tried to swim through the hatch. She would have succeeded because there were more stanchions to hold in the circular gangway, but someone pulled her back. She turned. It was Ghyaspur's hand on her leg, and he was laughing. The sound of his laughter was strange, too distant for its apparent heartiness.

"Feet first," Senda said, pushing herself into the gangway to demonstrate. "Otherwise you'll fall on your head when you reach the bottom."

Of course, Allis thought. Rotational spin would provide some kind of gravity as they proceeded toward the outer rim of the ship. She nodded gratefully to Ghyaspur. His blue eyes held hers for a moment—intense eyes, like Dan's. She'd loved Dan and trusted him. But that had been yesterday, and yesterday was ages ago. When he'd spoken of having limited time together, she'd assumed he was referring to his days possibly being numbered by the leukemia. Now she was uncertain. Would he have returned to the ship with Senda, exiting her life as suddenly as he'd entered it?

Senda called to her. "Be sure to take firm hold of every rung, even though it seems like you are floating. It's not very long until you'll feel the tug. Hold on!"

Grimly, Allis followed Senda down the ladder. There was more than the downward tug to contend with; the inertial force of spin pushed her against the ladder and made her head reel.

The outer-rim corridor was tube-shaped except for the flat floor with mossy chevrons pointing in the clockwise direction of spin. The blue-white ceiling was striated, giving the illusion of distant stratus clouds, yet with its dim lights and the closeness of the waffle-textured sides, the corridor had the feeling of a tunnel rather than a proper hallway. Allis was having trouble focusing her eyes. They seemed to want to lag behind whatever she looked at. She felt oddly unbalanced.

"You'll get used to that," Senda said, noticing her discomfort. "The spin is rather fast for a ship this size, but it helps keep us in good physical condition."

Hatches, some open and some closed, pocked the ceiling, and Allis saw faces staring down when she tried to peer into the upper chambers. A few of the crew members dropped lightly into the corridor, and Allis had the impression that they had done so just to have an opportunity to look her over more carefully. She had a good feeling for her oddness by the time they'd passed the tenth person. She wondered if she was catching impressions through the stone, or if it was merely the way they stared at her dark hair and eyes. Like Dan and Ghyaspur, all had light hair, light eyes, and were tall. There was another albino, and others with too few or too many fingers, odd postures, and wry features. There were too many variations to be racial differences, and all were the same or similar to birth defects she had seen or heard about on Earth. It was strange to see so many gene-damaged people in one place.

As she stepped along, she felt that each new step

was less difficult than the last; the lift of her legs was more controlled, the placement of her feet on the mossy chevrons that seemed to cling to the lugs of her boots less clumsy. She sensed that without the additional friction, she'd be bounding off the ceiling, despite her care. Frequently, portals flanked the grainy planking, giving a beautiful view, down and out, of the moon. Ahead, the way curved upward, and she saw the booted feet of oncoming crew members before she heard them or saw their faces. The air smelled slightly antiseptic and was very dry.

Allis had been following Senda, not breaking stride, not particularly disturbed by the crew's curious stares. But suddenly her heart began to pound, as if something ominous loomed ahead. She stopped, frightened by the abrupt palpitations, but conscious enough of her surroundings and companions to hold out her hand to prevent Ghyaspur from walking into her. She felt as if someone had given her a shot of adrenalin, and the results were nearly debilitating.

"What's the matter?" Senda said, looking at her curiously.

Allis couldn't reply. Belatedly she was recognizing more than the fear of her suddenly accelerated heartbeat. Her throat was constricting and her breath shortened. Dark boots appeared at the planking's inverted horizon, growing taller, then sprouting legs. They made horrifying thuds in her mind with every step. Yet her ears heard nothing. Allis stared, frozen by apprehension.

Long, graceful hands swung easily at the woman's sides as her confident gait brought her closer. Her thick, dun-colored hair looked more like a lion's mane than human hair, glorious around smooth skin and impassive features. Allis could see nothing ominous about the newcomer, but she could feel her own body continue to react with fear. Why was she so certain this lion-haired woman had triggered it?

"Milani," Senda said, stepping off the gangway to make room. She turned back to Allis. "Milani is the ship's captain. I have been telling her about you."

It wasn't Milani's imposing height, Allis thought furiously as she looked up. She'd spent a lifetime looking up to most of the human race, and none of them had ever scared her like this before. The electric yellow eyes flashed, and the captain's gaze seared her, making her skin crawl as if it had been burned. But Allis knew that the captain had done nothing physical to her; the sensation had come from within, or perhaps from the stone fastened around Milani's neck, like Dan's had been before Allis gave him the silver chain. It glowed with life.

"What did you do to him?" Milani asked with a dangerous quietness.

"Him? You mean Dan, of course." Allis, trying to match the voice with one equally steely, failed miserably. If she doubted the stones' power before, she didn't now. And if Milani was reading her mind with the help of her own stone, she knew that Allis's knees were weak and her heart about to fail.

"What's wrong with her?" Senda said, stepping between them and looking at Allis with concern. "She's been through a lot, but she'd been very strong until now."

Milani smiled thinly. "She doesn't know how to use the stone."

"No, of course not. Daneth gave it to her only a short while ago. I told you that, Milani. I told you everything." Senda shook her head. "A stone-carrier should know—" she muttered. "What's wrong with her? She looks frightened to death!"

"I don't know. I hear and feel nothing from her," Milani said, crossing her arms.

Senda's shoulders bunched as she looked anxiously from Allis to Milani. "I hadn't anticipated *that* from you," she said to the captain. Then she said to Allis, "Are you all right? What you're feeling is . . . well, Daneth was . . . you would call him husband to Milani, and he was her co-captain, as well."

"What?" Allis said feebly. She began to understand. The captain was jealous and angry about the liaison Allis had had with Dan, and suddenly the adrenaline pumping in Allis's veins was a great comfort, no longer an involuntary response to the unknown fear. "Let me get this straight. You and Dan," she said coldly meeting the captain's dusky eyes, "were married?"

Milani stood silently, unflinching.

"Come on," Allis said. "Answer me. I heard you speaking English just a minute ago."

"The vows they made were not made in a cathedral," Senda said quietly, "but they were just as binding as your marriage ceremony on Earth would be. Perhaps more so. The stones have an affinity for one another; two stone-carriers can share a deeper bond than ordinary people. You can imagine the rapport between two telepaths."

"That rotten, two-timing bastard," Allis said, seething. "I thought he was God's gift!" Every right word Dan ever had said to her was haunting her now. Every gesture, every longed-for touch that she remembered filled her with rage. A hysterical laugh gurgled in her throat. "I thought he was so marvelous-

ly intuitive, always just enough on the wrong side of
my fantasies to keep me from getting tuned off by
encountering them in the flesh. And you can damn
well bet that he never mentioned a wife. He'd have
known that I wouldn't put up with that—the fucking
telepath!"

"Don't speak ill of him," Milani warned, her eyes
narrowing.

"Don't tell me that you don't feel exactly the same
way," Allis said, her voice rising. "You forget that I
have this." She jerked the stone out of her bosom,
brandishing it like a talisman before the aliens. "And
I felt . . ." She stopped, suddenly overpowered by
passions not her own. Milani stood stiffly before her,
looking like a powerful athlete, and her mind was as
mighty to Allis as if it were a measurable force, one
strong enough to draw Daneth back from death itself, let alone from Allis, if she'd only had the chance
to try. And if Milani had that kind of power over
Daneth, who had intimate knowledge of the stone,
what kind of power did she have over a stranger?
But the force Allis knew was there was not pro-
ductively engaged; there was only that heart-stopping
anger that verged on madness.

"Your hatred is all for me, not for him. Oh, Christ."
For a moment she hung her head to blink back
angry and humiliating tears. She'd never been in a
love triangle before; she'd carefully avoided such in-
volvements, knowing they brought certain misery.
But she knew the dangers of being bound to anyone
by force, and instinctively she tried to slip loose.

"Look, I'm sorry. I didn't know he was married.
I admit that it was a whole lot more for me than a
few laughs, and I can imagine that hurts. But with
that stone around your neck you also know I'm tell-

ing you the truth when I say that if he'd told me he was married, I'd never have become involved."

Milani shook her head silently.

"Allis," Senda said. "She cannot read you. Her stone protects her from your thoughts, or you may think of it as protecting you from her having your thoughts. It happens when the stone-carrier hates."

"Then, goddammit, why am I not safe from her thoughts?" Her heart was beating rapidly, still stimulated by the claws of Milani's mind, the wounds stiffening like prison bars, the same bars Dan must have known. "Okay, okay," Allis said, turning back to Milani. "Hate me. Keep your happy memories of Dan. You don't need me around reminding you of bad times. You've had your apology, now let me go home."

"Daneth's stone . . . *your* stone is home," Milani said, "and you must stay with it or it will die."

"Let it die," Allis snapped. "I've gotten along for thirty years without telepathy, and I don't need to feel all that thick crap from your head either." With a sharp tug, Allis broke the slender chain and held out the stone to Milani. The captain took a step backwards, scowling.

"She can't take it from you," Senda said, calmly stepping forward to close Allis's fingers over the stone. "It can only be given in love, the way Daneth must have given it to you."

Allis thought the captain winced when Senda mentioned Dan's love, but no more than Allis did. "I don't know how it happened, but it's not love when a man knocks up a woman and pays her off with a rock. Take the damn thing and let me go home." She stood for perhaps a second, stunned by the cessation of anger flowing into her brain. The thing had shut down, but that didn't cut the flow of her own anger. She flung the stone, and it skittered along the deck at Ghyaspur's feet. She hated the stone and the power it had given Milani over Dan.

For a moment the three aliens stared in horror at the dull stone lying alongside Ghyaspur's big boot. Then Milani spoke: "I don't even understand half of what you're saying anymore, let alone know what you're truly thinking. But I do know this: the stone stays on this ship, and you will stay with it. Neither of us has a choice in the matter. Is that beyond your comprehension?"

"Yes," Allis said. "It doesn't make sense. That stone is as dead with me here as it would be if I were on Earth, because I won't touch it again."

Milani seemed surprised, but she nodded thoughtfully. "Nonetheless, you shall stay." With a final contemptuous look at Allis, Milani turned and walked back the way she had come. Senda trotted after her, talking rapidly in the alien gibberish.

"You'll be sorry," Allis shouted. "You'll rue the day!" But all bravery failed. "Let me go home. Please, let me go home!" And when her plea failed, too, she sank onto the deck, fists pounding with anger, heart aching from betrayal, and tears of frustration running down her face. "Dan, you bastard. I could kill you for dying before I could kill you!"

CHAPTER 3

Confused by arguments that had taken place in a language he did not understand, and finally embarrassed by the Earthwoman's tears and Milani's abandonment, Ghyaspur didn't know what else to do but scoop up the stone and escort Allis to his own cabin.

Once inside, she stopped crying and helped herself to his hammock, and then stared at the ceiling through glazed eyes. She moved only when he tried to press the stone into her hands, flinging it against the ultraloy bulkhead with unmistakable vehemence. He let it lay where it fell the third time, completely confused by a stone-carrier who didn't cherish the artifact in the fashion that Milani and Daneth always had. Half the ship was hers, the stars were hers, if she'd pick up the stone.

Ghyaspur had emptied his pockets of leaves, dirt, and twigs while waiting patiently for someone to contact him in regard to proper quartering for the Earthwoman. Then he arranged his specimens. Still no one called him or came to him, and he began to wonder if Milani was even listening to his subliminal questions. Perhaps she was deliberately not answering him, waiting to see how he would handle the unusual and unexpected.

Another test of his resourcefulness. After all, would

one of the older crew members bother the captain with petty questions such as what to do with an unexpected guest while she was grieving for her dead lover and co-captain? Ghyaspur frowned. But this was not just any guest. Allis was a stone-carrier, and a new stone-carrier should be in the care and tutelage of an experienced stone-carrier, learning the shades and variations of emotional flow, identifying individuals' thought patterns, determining the spatial locations of thought sources, and digging into people's souls.

But there'd been no mistaking Milani's anger with the Earthwoman, stolid as the captain had been during their encounter. He'd expected some ire; how could there be anything else when Daneth had given the stone to someone other than Milani and the giving was good? The stone might be lying inert and dull on his cabin floor just now, but there was no denying that it glowed with life when the Earthwoman touched it. Daneth might just as well have slapped his co-captain in the face; and Milani was an unforgiving person. He hadn't seen a flicker of compassion for Allis.

Ghyaspur arranged the leaves according to their shape, pausing to sniff them and to run his finger over their waxy surfaces. They definitely were different from the hybrid greenery grown in the ship's hydroponic farm. They were more fragrant, yet tougher. After he put the leaves in a specimen sack—a clear glassine one so that he could see their shapes and colors—he carefully sifted the clumps of dirt into a jug, filling it halfway with the stuff from his pockets and the clots that had collected between his boot lugs.

His greatest treasure he saved for last, his eyes straying to it even while he smoothed the cellophane he'd found covering another specimen, a handsome blue and white and silver paper pack that contained remnants of an acrid-smelling brown substance. Finally, he picked up the feather, ruffling the vanes along the central horny shaft, and then smoothing them again. Winged lizards and rodents were common throughout the galaxy; he'd seen many with his own eyes and holos of thousands more. But birds—not quite reptiles and certainly not mammals, with bright plumes, cocky heads, and wings that carried them aloft—were very rare.

His feather was dull brown and black, the shaft bent and some of the vanes broken, but his imagination soared as he tried to visualize the creature from which it had come. A seel eater or an insect eater, or perhaps this was a wing feather from some large bird of prey. Was the whole bird the dull color of this feather, or did it sport red and yellow plumes as well?

He looked at Allis, lying still in his hammock, and he wondered what she knew about birds. She didn't seem much inclined to tell him. Ghyaspur turned back to his specimens, admiring them once again.

Ghyaspur had secured his new collection to the place on the bulkhead of his tiny cabin set aside for that purpose. Each item had to be securely fastened to the bulkhead so that it wouldn't slip and get damaged during ship's maneuvers. The shift had changed, yet the *Sovereign Sun* still spun in stationary orbit over the bright side of the Earth's huge satellite, the moon, not yet moving off to one of the Quondam Beings' gravity slips that would take them away from this solar system. The sails, he knew, were unfurled. They'd probably never been taken in, since the *Sovereign Sun* usually left the vicinity of restricted planets hastily to avoid detection by the Watchers. Perhaps Milani was waiting for a solar flare and the resulting good wind. Yellow suns hadn't much gust compared to the whites and giants closer to the galactic core.

At the halfshift Ghyaspur would be due for sunwatch, but as the time drew nearer he still had not received word on what to do with Allis. She moved once or twice but only to get more comfortable in the hammock. He couldn't leave her alone, even though she persisted in being immobile just now. If she chose to move about and explore when he was gone, she might get herself trapped in the sanitary, or touch his computer console and damage some program. He could of course disable the transmit/receive lines, but that would prevent the system from monitoring the crystal garden he had stashed in the vent. No matter, since Daneth never would see the astounding growth, but he didn't have the heart to end the experiment now.

A dirge sounded from the ship's radio, which was mounted on the near bulkhead. Irritated, Ghyaspur traced it off. He didn't need a funeral march to remind him that Daneth was dead. It was he who had tended to the co-captain's remains, and it was in his cabin that Daneth's stone lay useless on the deck. Not that he wouldn't miss Daneth. Already he felt uneasy because Daneth wouldn't be around to wink when he pulled his mass on the bridge, young and nearly untried as he was. Nor would he be there to warn him when he was about to blunder, like the time when Ghyaspur ferreted out a Watcher study of genetic damage done to gypsies by stellar irradiation and their own nuclear forges. He'd planned to give

the study to Milani. He thought she'd be interested,
since she'd been so heavily irradiated in that sabotaged
salvaging incident, megashifts ago. But Daneth, catching his thoughts and knowing his intentions, had
headed him off and told him the report and, verifying
the extent of damage done to Milani's body, would
only add to her guilt about the accident. Daneth
hadn't explained why Milani felt guilty over something every gypsy sailor could expect to have happen
eventually. It was puzzling.

Ghyaspur would miss Daneth, but he wouldn't
mourn him. He hadn't hibernated while Daneth was
gone this past seventy shifts. He knew that Daneth,
planetside and in a slower time pass, had not spent
the planetary year worrying that his young ward
would not stay out of trouble. Ghyaspur had earned
his shuttle pilot tattoo and had a feather-crystal insignia clipped to his belt for all to see. No one could
accuse him of having special help from the telepath,
for Daneth had not been there to give it and Milani
just didn't use her stone that way, as all knew. Now
no one could deny him the privileges that came with
the rank, despite his youth. And if he could do that
on his own, he could figure out what to do with a
stone-carrier who wouldn't carry her stone.

On the printed labyrinth control face of his console,
he traced a shape that gave access to data in the
ship's computer, specifically to a list containing the
sunwatch assignments. He could trace in a sign that
the computer was programmed to interpret as illness
or emotional distress, which included mourning and
lovesickness, and since he was well within the arbitrary
limit of three such excuses in five-hundred shifts, the
computer would have noted the status-change symbol
next to his own symbol, then replace him without

comment. Instead of altering the list with such a mundane excuse, he simply removed his symbol, which led to an immediate query for authority to make such a change. Blithely he signed the shape for ship's security. He didn't really have such authority, only a select few did. Had there been a real emergency, such as a violated hull that he was on the scene to tend, monitors would have corroborated his need to give the sign and the computer would have branched to a program that evaluated monitor data, assuming some part of the program was constructed to deal with the kind of data received. It wouldn't have mattered much that his hand, which was known to the computer the instant he touched the control face, didn't invoke certain priority or privileged user recognition. But since the computer could detect no danger, and since Ghyaspur was not a privileged user, his communication console was immediately connected to one on the bridge.

Mordon, the first mate, answered the summons. "What's wrong, lad?"

"I have the new stone-carrier in my cabin. She's uncommunicative. I haven't even been able to show her how to use the sanitary."

Ghyaspur saw the pink glow on his screen that indicated Mordon had activated the cabin observation device. Curious? Or checking to see that Ghyaspur was telling the truth? He wondered, and not without some bitterness over being doubted like a child.

"First-touch sickness?" the mate asked, apparently satisfied when he saw Allis lying in the hammock. She'd turned at the sounds of their voices, frowning as if they'd disturbed her.

"No. She won't keep the stone on her."

"Strange, that. Yes?"

Ghyaspur troubled himself to nod, but he didn't comment.

"Tell me," the mate said, his voice suddenly low and conspiratorial. "What happened when they met?"

"I don't know," Ghyaspur said with a shrug. "They spoke the planet tongue and I couldn't understand. But . . ." Ghyaspur hesitated. Rumors were easily started on ship and came to an abrupt halt when they reached Milani's mind—not without reprimand, if they were inaccurate.

"Come on, lad. We've been waiting nearly two shifts to know what happened to Daneth. Did she kill him? Is she a witch? How'd she get the stone?"

"Nothing like that," Ghyaspur said, beginning to feel important. Senda apparently had told them little, if anything, about the woman, which surprised Ghyaspur. Senda and Mordon had been sharing a cabin again for many shifts now. "The white-blood sickness got him. When we arrived he was already dead and the Earthling had the stone."

"And it was alive?" the mate prodded.

"Very much alive. But Daneth hadn't explained its origin to her, nor how it was used. We had to force her onto the shuttle to bring her back."

Ghyaspur's viewing screen brightened now, and he saw Mordon nod knowingly. "The bridge crew knew something was amiss when your shuttle got into Milani's range. She announced that Senda had reported Daneth's death, but nothing more. But nearly everyone saw the woman, and the stone. Last shift crew guessed she'd stolen it and that Senda was bringing her back for punishment, especially when there was such a loud fracas in the corridor. The closest cabins didn't even need amplifiers to hear."

"I don't know what they said to each other,"

Ghyaspur said, wishing that he'd had time to use the language-prep machine before going planetside. For the first time someone was coming to him for data, and that someone was no less than Mordon, the first mate. "But I had the feeling that Milani was not reading the Earthling." There. He'd said it. He believed it was true.

"Not reading!" The mate let out a low whistle. "She must have done something awful big for Milani to hate her that much. Couldn't be just the breaking of the bonds between herself and Daneth, not that it wouldn't be enough to drive an ordinary person mad." He looked at Ghyaspur thoughtfully, as if waiting for his opinion.

Stone-carriers were special to everyone, but some crew members felt that their uncanny abilities, even though they were attributed to an artifact, made them more than human. Who could say for certain that the Quondam Beings were humans? Not even the Watchers, members of the oldest human race in the galaxy, knew for certain. No one had been able to duplicate the Quondam Beings' engineering feats or understand their physics. Those who had what were believed to be communication devices passed down to them, generation after generation, were at least priests and perhaps gods to ordinary people.

It was known that there could have been no break in the giving, from some Quondam Being's own hand to present stone-carriers, or the stones would have died. Not at all like the temperature control packs, which were found from time to time in Quondam Beings' ruins, still warming the nighttime chill and cooling the sunlighted day for anyone who wandered into their sphere of influence. Nor like ultraloy, the backbone of space travel for the entire galaxy, which withstood all forms of decay from rust to spaceweld, yet could be reshaped and reformed by any competent metal worker, even if it could not be duplicated. Even the gravity slips could be used by anyone who had the coordinates to find them and who possessed a counterforce powerful enough to go through them.

The Quondam Beings had left many priceless gifts throughout the galaxy, but none was quite so mysterious as the communicator-stones. Only those had to have been pressed into the hands of eager humans by the gods themselves. Daneth was a good friend to Ghyaspur, guiding him through a lonely childhood into adulthood with love and special understanding. But Daneth was always quick to disclaim the godhead. Milani was different. Always more remote and more aloof from the crew. Maybe *she* was a goddess. It hardly mattered. She was the captain, sole captain now, and absolute ruler of her realm, the *Sovereign Sun*.

"She's not mad," Ghyaspur said firmly, protectively. "Angry, but not mad."

"Not reading," the mate said again, letting the words hang.

"I won't be on sunwatch," Ghyaspur told the mate briskly.

"Yes, of course. I understand," the mate said, recovering some of his professional attitude "But lad, let me know . . ."

Ghyaspur traced out the rest of the request. He suddenly realized how important his responsibility was. He paced, looking at Allis, who'd resumed her watch on the ceiling.

"You can't keep doing that, you know," he said to her. "There are people on this ship who will insist on thinking of you as a goddess no matter what

Milani's opinion of you is. Frankly, I'm inclined to
trust Daneth's judgment in selecting you to receive
the stone."

Her eyes flickered at the mention of Daneth's name.
"Daneth," he said. "Daneth, Daneth." Her head
turned and the eyes glared. She knew whom he meant.
"Daneth would never forgive me if I didn't show you
how to use the sanitary. Your bladder must be aching
by now. No? Well, the time will come, I'm sure. Mean-
while, you can just lie there. I don't care. Stay there
for a thousand shifts, if you can stand my voice for
that long. You're ignorant—the stupidest person on
this ship, and maybe just a little bit crazy, too. When
someone gives you a gift like a communicator-stone,
most people would be grateful. But that's all right.
I won't hold that against you, because you're ignorant
of our customs, beliefs, and language."

Allis closed her eyes and turned away from him.
Her long black hair drifted over the edge of the
hammock.

"You'll have to cut your hair. It's too much of a
bother in soft gravity. Nothing much to hold it down."
When she didn't stir, he said, "Daneth, Daneth."

She opened her eyes and, judging from her tone
and expression, said something foul.

"You're stuck with us, Allis. You have to learn
everything about us. It would be easier if you would
use this." He picked up the stone and held it out to
her. Viciously, Allis snatched at it, as if to throw it
again. Ghyaspur withdrew it from her reach. "I don't
think it will break, but it simply isn't reverent," he
said. He put the stone in his strongbox, carefully
demonstrating the latch mechanism to Allis, who
watched him balefully.

"I think . . ." She closed her eyes. "I think,"

Ghyaspur said persistently, "that you can't close your ears, too, so I'll just keep talking. Eventually you're going to pick up some of the language . . . especially after I set up the language-prep machine. I am your teacher, Allis.

"A good teacher starts at the beginning. That's going to be fun for me. All the history of the gypsy sailors is available from the ship's computer, but it's much more fun to hear the oral tales. We tell them during dull sunwatches, sometimes in the galley. When there was a nursery the really good storytellers would visit and tell the children how our ancestors foiled the Watchers. That's the best story. It may be the only time we had the galaxy in our hands, but it sure was a great one. And I've been so eager to tell someone that story; everyone's told it to me, my being the youngest on the *Sovereign Sun,* and there's been no one for me to tell it to. I've discovered a version that will scandalize my mates, but it simply wasn't all glory for stellar sailors."

Ghyaspur pulled the tumbling blanket from his chest, tossed it alongside where he'd have a good view of Allis and be close enough for her to hear him. She watched him ease his long legs out in front of him and snuggle his buttocks into the cushiony fiber of the blanket. She didn't relax until he leaned against the bulkhead.

"Aha," Ghyaspur said. "I had your attention for a moment there. Did you think I was inviting you for a tumble? That'd be a merry fling, I must admit. I've precious few to play with that way on *Sovereign Sun.*"

The young pilot sighed. Flirting wasn't much fun with someone who didn't understand the language and couldn't indulge or retort. She certainly was attractive to him, though, even if she was rather small.

One never expected complete physical perfection while living the gypsy life; and the grotesque eventually became attractive. He shook his head and then reached over to his strongbox to pull out his ancestor's diary, handling the thin booklet reverently though the pages were very durable.

"This book is as old as stellar sailing gypsies, Allis. So old that the world it was fashioned in is all but forgotten by the entire galaxy—my ancestor's world. It probably was written before your civilization began, but to us gypsies it's only six generations old. This ship has been through so many gravity slips that I'd need the computer to figure out the time dilation. Crazy thing, that time dilation. I met a little Watcher boy at Crossroads when I was still hanging on Daneth's knee. When we called there next, he was a man who'd already gone through two wives and was about ready to put down the third. And Daneth is . . . was my great-nephew, my sister's grandchild. Yet, he'd more shifts than I when our ships matched phase, and he became my guardian. So, you see, I'm *Sovereign Sun*-born, but I was raised by what some of Milani's conservative people call the distaff side of the ship.

"But the book is mine, etched on ultraloy film. You realize how precious it was, even back then. Ultraloy, well, the Quondam Beings left just so much ultraloy in the entire galaxy, and there are some people who would say that using it to fashion a diary was the height of luxury. It tells something of my ancestor's success as a merchant," he said with great satisfaction, which diminished when he realized he was addressing the back of Allis's head. Trying not to feel daunted, he continued:

"My ancestor was a woman of great personal strength and considerable political influence. She sailed the *Sovereign Sun*, this same ship we're in, between planets when we still had a homeworld, calling on colonial ports and orbiting mining operations. But she was unwelcome in visiting Watcher vessels and in their establishments near the Quondam Beings' ruins on the homeworld.

"Oh, yes. The Watchers were around even then—picking trade where they chose and spreading dissension and envy with their profitable interstellar travel and commerce. Ostensibly their ambassadors came to the homeworld to invite us to join the intragalactic chain of trade, since we'd established successful interplanetary travel. But, in the end, they decided our mode of travel, the stellar sails, was too primitive to compete in the free markets. They decided to wait until we upgraded our technology, refusing to help us do it on the grounds that we must develop naturally and at our own pace. They stayed on as supposedly neutral observers. However, not every ambassador was as noble as Watchers claim they are. Many of them had mercantile connections. They exploited our Quondam Being ruins, literally stealing ultraloy off the planet. They traded parts of nuclear-generator plans for ultraloy needed in the colonies, throwing suspicion on the homeworld and creating political unrest everywhere.

"My ancestor cursed the Watchers, the self-designated guardians of the Quondam Beings' seedling worlds. They had pronounced themselves dictators of the galaxy simply by virtue of their having been seeded first and having had longer to develop complicated technology. But these so-called benevolent dictators were the catalyst for our homeworld's destruction.

"The Watchers didn't use their power to prevent the

holocaust. They were, indeed, smart enough to anticipate it and they fled before it happened. That's something my ancestor, and all the gypsies who lived after her, never could resolve. Billions died on the ten continents of the homeworld because of thefts and political policy conceived light years distant. A race of proud humans was incinerated by its own hand, their world forever poisoned, space-borne survivors left homeless, while those who might have interceded, the Watchers who claim the right to intercede anywhere, did not! It was inconsistent. The Watchers must have suspected that we wouldn't continue to tolerate their interference peacefully. Or perhaps they knew that we were further ahead of them in interpreting Quondam Beings' computer logic.

"Resignedly, a thousand and ten stellar sailing vessels' captains calculated their remaining supplies to determine the time when a final shuttle trip to some colonial port must include themselves and their crew as passengers. Spacers—engineers, physicists, stellarians; technicians—starstokers, blacksmiths, and sail-jockeys, all crafters of the finest breed—preparing themselves in their splendid ships to settle on primitive colony worlds where their skills were meaningless.

"But my ancestor prevented the stellar sailing vessels from becoming cenotaphs of the race's ignoble immolation. She led one thousand and ten ships to a place she'd been only once before. She led them through a gravity slip known only to the homeworld's trusted hierarchy. That gravity slip was to have opened for a well-equipped fleet in some future time, for it led directly to the Watcher's solar system. Light years passed in less than a shift of time. And a thousand and ten vessels, each with miles and miles of silver sails, were dwarfed by the Watchers' incredible harbors filled with monolithic ships made of ultraloy stripped from the homeworld. Yet my ancestor's minuscule armada awed the Watchers, for it had arrived years before the ambassador's ships that fled our cinder world were due. Those poor ambassadors were still journeying across the galactic spiral at the speed of light, their bodies in stasis and asleep while their Watcher comrades, the most advanced race of humankind, smugly awaited their arrival and received instead the stellar sailors.

"Had the homeworld not self-destructed, the Watchers might have been dealt with. It might be happening now, in my generation. Clumsy stellar sailing vessels would have given way to ion drive battleships passing between solar systems in an eyeblink. Watcher ships would still be restricted to lightspeeds.

"The secret of the gravity ships' coordinates had been a Quondam Being leaving ciphered from fragments of computer circuitry in the ruins unearthed before the holocaust. We don't even know if they are a natural phenomenon in the galaxy, or if the Quondam Beings built them. If the latter . . . well, perhaps they were gods and not human. I can't even imagine a technology that can warp the very fabric of an entire galaxy. The network of gravity slips is astounding. Look, my ancestor has a print showing the locations." Ghyaspur held up the grid of crosshatches for Allis to see, but she didn't look. He leaned back, contemplating her for a moment. "Well," he finally said. "You'll look another time."

CHAPTER 4

The full evenshift had not passed before the entire crew of the *Sovereign Sun* was whispering that Daneth had betrayed Milani by giving the stone to the Earthwoman. The stone-giving rite had been romanticized in stories more ancient than the beginning of the stellar sailing vessels, but the crew had seen the legends verified in their own lifetimes. However, the more practical among the crew realized the stone was a communication device used by the Quondam Beings on many worlds that modern humankind now inhabited. There was nothing sentimental about stone giving. A communicator-stone belonging to a fallen soldier was as useless to the enemy as hoisting sails before a black hole; thus had they been engineered to prevent their being stolen and misused.

The stones could be given, but not to a mere acquaintance or a casual friend. A love bond was necessary, such as the one between parent and child, lovers, or devoted friends.

The relationship between Daneth and the Earthwoman made the crew wonder as they'd never wondered before. Had Daneth truly loved Milani as he claimed, loudly at times, while the *Sovereign Sun* sailed for thousands of watches along the galaxy's trade routes? It had seemed so then; his deep-set eyes gleamed with pleasure when she stepped onto the bridge, and they clouded with anger if the computer assignments separated them more than one or two shifts at a time. And when Milani touched him, he welcomed the contact, responding with petting of his own, sometimes so enthusiastically that Milani would become embarrassed. And there were always marks of their touching through the stones, sudden smiles, mysterious conversational pauses, and pensive lapses into silence. Yet, the crew wondered, who could really know a stone-carrier's heart? Another stone-carrier, it was said. But could a mere human comprehend the complexities of the Quondam Being's communication devices?

Daneth's behavior, now that they thought about it, had always been ambiguous. True, he made scenes with the computer over shift assignments when they did not suit him, but he also competed with his unfair advantage for planetside privileges. He would leave the *Sovereign Sun* like a hero bound for adventure, and, to hear him talk upon his return, he generally had one. He always returned. Would he have cared for Milani at all if she, too, did not have a stone? Was he drawn back because of the stones' affinity for one another?

As Milani sat in the nearly empty galley, she tried to ignore the crew's careless thoughts. They were close enough to the truth to hurt, but their doubts were too few for real understanding. To them, Daneth was a friend who could be counted on to lend a hand when the work was hard, the co-captain who always had a cheerful word or a compliment on his lips. And when they came to grief, whether from the natural shocks that stellar sailors were heir to or from fretful spirit, Daneth was with them, evenshift and odd, comforting them and soothing their unspoken terrors.

He always knew what to say, of course, and precisely how to say it, and at which moment the listener would be most receptive to him. He was very skilled in using his communicator-stone. Subconsciously they must have known he was a perfect friend because of the advantage the telepathic perceptions gave him, yet instinctively they knew, too, that it was his nature to use his gift beneficently. Even so, they could not understand his giving the stone to the Earthwoman, and in their simple ignorance they thought of the act as a betrayal of Milani, their surviving captain, the only stone-carrier they had left. And it was true that she felt betrayed, but that wasn't as bad as knowing that she had betrayed Daneth.

Once Milani had been certain of his love, but that was before she'd denied him all hope of teaching his zest for life to his own child. She had destroyed his dreams with an unforgivable mistake that prevented her from ever bearing his child.

Crew thoughts flowed soothingly around the hot poker of grief and guilt. Stone-carriers would always be a little mysterious to the crew, a little beyond their ken, even the fundamentally honest and articulate sone-carriers like Daneth. What could crew know of love stripped of secrets until there were only two fragile egos and their tender ids to share and carefully nurture and jealously guard, one by the other? It was a burden that most stone-carriers could not endure, but Milani and Daneth had. At least she thought they had.

The rewards were immeasurable: his sense of adventure to draw upon when her spirits flagged; her filling him with pride where once he used to see the subtle decay of the *Sovereign Sun*, and, indeed, the demise of the gypsy sailors' race. She'd instilled in him a sense of future . . . but maybe that had died during the salvage incident. Painfully, her heart skipped a beat. At least there was his love of the present. To be sure, the stones were a source of their strength, cementing their love. He couldn't have given his stone to the earthworm. He wouldn't have! He must have been mad, or drugged, or—

Milani felt the touch in her mind at the same time she saw Senda's cool white hand cover her fisted one. Milani tried not to cringe. Senda was trying to give her something Daneth would have, but it was repulsive to have anyone's hand on her, except his.

—Are you all right?—Senda said, using the silent talk. She was openly anxious, and there were deeper worries, too.

"Of course," Milani said, withdrawing her hand. Senda had changed out of the dusty garments she'd worn on the planet into fresh ones, soft gray in color with her linguist emblem catching a red sash of mourning like a buckle. Her white curls were shining with cleanliness, her big eyes the only sign of wisdom in her otherwise dull face. She turned away, knowing Senda considered herself a valuable liaison between Daneth's people and Milani.

"You didn't answer me," Senda said.

Milani looked up from the bulb of broth. She didn't know how long she'd been staring at it, nor when Senda had brought it to her. Milani reached for the bulb; it was still warm but beginning to congeal. Senda continued staring in quiet concern. Milani shrugged, said lightly, "Well, you didn't speak, did you?"

"Not aloud," Senda replied, still perturbed. Knowing that she had Milani's attention now, she leaned back in the chair. —I know that you, above all other people, have a clear perception of who your friends are, but it does me good to mention my loyalty.—

Milani nodded, deeply relieved. On top of everything else, she hadn't wanted to become involved in an exercise in penetration to learn if Senda and the other crew members Daneth had brought to the *Sovereign Sun* so long ago would remain loyal to her, their only captain now, or to Daneth's stone and the Earthwoman. It wasn't unthinkable. But since Senda, the oldest among them both with family ties to the dead co-captain and a lifetime of allegiance to his stone, accepted Milani as leader without hesitation, the others would, too.

Senda grieved, and she was as confused as anyone else over Daneth's gift of the stone to the earthworm, but she wouldn't blindly follow Daneth's stone for tradition's sake alone. Yet Senda had doubts. She had not come to Milani to offer whatever comfort her loyalty would bring so much as she'd come to have her own unspoken fears put to rest. Daneth would have done that right away, no matter how personal.

"You want to know about the glimpse I had of Allis before the hate shut down reception of her thoughts, is that correct?"

Senda nodded. Milani was at least partially right.

—Whatever it was that caused you to hate her so instantly and so thoroughly . . . frightens me.—

"She's not a Watcher," Milani said, speaking to one of the thoughts that was deeper than the sentence off the top of Senda's brain. Senda sighed in relief.

"For a while I was worried that I was growing old and my senses were slipping. Space knows I've seen many of them try to slip on board a stellar sailing vessel, though they always give themselves away with their hopeless arrogance. But this would have been a new trick, coming to us from a restricted planet. As clever as they are with rearranging genes, I wouldn't be surprised to learn they aped another racial type, just for the purpose of putting a perfect spy in our midst." The Watchers grew babies in glassine vials, genetically engineered babies who grew up to be perfect politicians, superb merchants, quantum mechanics, geniuses, or whatever they wanted them to be, including cute and lovable, if it suited their purposes. They'd do anything to get a stone, but it wasn't that simple this time. Finally Senda looked at Milani, pink eyes staring intently while her mind dredged up the other question that Milani had not addressed. —Since it wasn't her being a Watcher, then what is she that she could blind your mind?—

Uncomfortable, Milani squeezed some of the warm broth into her mouth, swishing it between her teeth to delay having to answer Senda. It was one thing to probe the mind of another human being for underlying thoughts and the passions behind them; it was quite another to probe one's own. Daneth once had helped her, but Allis had robbed Milani of his aid. Senda still stared expectantly, trying to be patient, but on the verge of angrily demanding an explanation. She was tired and she was worried. If Allis were a threat to the ship's security, she and the rest of the crew had a right to know. Finally Milani swallowed.

"I can give no reason," she said slowly. "A certain loathing . . ." She met the albino's gaze. "A mutual hatred, I assure you."

"This is, then, a personal matter between you and Allis?" she said suspiciously. Only one of Daneth's crew would have voiced such a thought. Milani's people would have considered it bad form.

When Milani didn't answer, Senda sulkily drew her own conclusion. It had to remain Milani's own matter, but she was wise enough to know that nearly anything that affected the captain would also affect the crew. "Still, she's a stone-carrier," Senda said uneasily. "A trust is implied. Daneth knew I was coming, and knew that I would bring Allis and the stone back to the ship. Your reaction would be less predictable, under the circumstances."

Milani frowned sharply. The albino's thoughts were less clear to her now. From years of association with stone-carriers, Senda was skilled at keeping her privacy when she wanted it. The mulling thoughts were not impenetrable, however. "Are you suggesting that I have some obligation to that earthworm?"

"To Allis personally? No, of course not. But to the stone, yes. Don't we all? You know it's easier for one stone-carrier to train another."

A stone, not passed on before the carrier's death, could not be reactivated. When that happened, it was an irreplacable loss to the stellar sailors, even though they had proportionately more stones than any other race of humans. There was little enough advantage over the Watchers. Gypsy sailors kept their stones in space, away from the Watchers' sphere of influence on the planets. Daneth's stone lived on, in space, where it belonged, but Milani didn't care. The wrong stone-carrier was dead.

"Do what you must, Senda," Milani said with forced evenness. "I shall not participate."

Senda persisted. "You have the gift of a stone-carrier's understanding, which gives you insight into even alien minds. Daneth used to say that it was impossible to hate someone he understood. Perhaps in time you could learn to have compassion for Allis."

"I'm tired of understanding," Milani said savagely. Daneth was the understanding one, and that was a fact. Why wouldn't Senda just leave her alone?

Senda sighed and nodded, more chagrined than frightened by the captain's anger. "The sails are still unfurled and ready."

She was prodding the captain tactlessly, plainly worried about a captain who sat mourning in the galley while the *Sovereign Sun* idled in orbit near a restricted planet.

"We're not already underway because I hadn't decided on our destination," Milani said, easily answering something that directly related to the ship. "Now I have. We're going to Crossroads."

Instantly, Senda was as she always was on the bridge, her mental process linear and concise. It was a little early for a complete shakedown on the nuclear generator, but they'd been using inferior fuel in the shuttles for some time now. Senda wondered if it wouldn't be wise to continue doing without the superior Watcher brew, at least for a while. Allis, she was sure, was not going to be a cooperative guest. The Watchers frowned on the gypsy practice of buying talent from open ports where such sales were common, legal at the local level, and where the individuals involved supposedly were volunteers, working off personal or family debts. But the Watchers were not likely to overlook someone taken off a restricted planet. Senda didn't like the risk of going into the hub of Watcher activity with someone like Allis on board.

"We'll confine the earthworm while we're at Crossroads," Milani said automatically. She arose from the slightly adhesive chair and shoved the empty bulb down the recycler in a single practiced movement.

Wearily, Senda nodded; she knew the captain had carried her own thoughts on the matter one step further, which was a stone-carrier's prerogative. But, she realized gloomily, it also meant that Milani had not forgotten how to think in terms of force. The crew of the *Sovereign Sun* had led a fairly peaceful existence ever since they'd abandoned the trade lanes along the outer loop of gravity slips in favor of the faster, more heavily populated inner loop. But there were more Watchers here, too, and news of careless ventures had a way of filtering back to them, even from the restricted planets.

The gypsies had learned to be quite watchful themselves and never to act in a thoughtless or inadvertent fashion, and they had a great deal of time to brood over their feelings between acts of violence. But that didn't mean they'd forgotten how to be fierce. Not even Senda, who'd forcibly taken a woman off a restricted planet, so why should she wish that Milani were any different?

Perhaps it would have been better to leave Allis on Earth. Then Milani would not be so preoccupied with this terrible hate she felt. Yet, Senda knew with certainty that if she had left Allis behind, the Watchers would eventually have come to possess Daneth's stone. They always got the stones that were on the planets, just like they usually got most of the ultraloy left by the Quondam Beings, one way or another. She knew they'd restricted some planets only to protect the rich leavings of ultraloy for themselves. She'd heard that they used drugs and hypnotism to get planet locals to give one of their own Watchers the priceless communicator-stone, but that was ridiculous. A stone-carrier couldn't be hypnotized, at least an experienced one couldn't be. More likely they abducted the stone-carrier just as Senda had done.

Milani was gone by the time Senda reached the corridor outside the galley, and she gratefully headed for her cabin and some well-deserved rest. Like all gypsies, Senda considered her cabin her sanctuary, and it was furnished to comfort her body and decorated with peaceful colors to soothe her always restless and irritated mind. But there were some circumstances when another sailor might vindicate a claim to a sailor's sanctuary. Mordon was there, looking worried.

"What do you want?" Senda said, flopping wearily into her hammock. The pastel fabrics draping her bulkheads swayed slightly as she felt the *Sovereign Sun* drift. A solar wind disturbance had touched the sails. Mordon noticed, too, but he ignored it.

"Answers to questions," he said, moving across the tiny cabin to stand over her. "My captain isn't answering subliminals, my bridge crew thinks there's a Watcher spy on board or that the landlubber is at least a witch, and the *Sovereign Sun* is falling in a forbidden orbit, an easy mark for any Watcher ship that happens to pop out of the closest gravity slip. I'd like to know why."

"Because I brought the new stone-carrier on board. She's not a Watcher, but she certainly must have bewitched Daneth. He gave her the stone, and Milani is . . . angry about it."

"She has a right to be," Mordon said stiffly. "Since the giving was good, it means the sworn bonds between

Milani and Daneth were broken, and it wasn't she who broke them." He looked at Senda thoughtfully. "Bewitched him, you say."

"Don't be stupid, Mordon. It's just an expression. You know there are no witches no matter what the stories say. You'd just rather believe that than see Milani shamed by Daneth's breaking the bonds of his own free will. See how those tales get started? People like you, who put too much emphasis on the old ways and don't know how to change." There were cultural differences between crew members who'd always served Milani and those who'd joined the *Sovereign Sun* with Daneth. They probably had originated from the variety of cultures that had streamed skyward from the homeworld, eventually mutating among the stars as rapidly as their bodies. Crew changes and exchanges were common when the stellar sailing vessels could get together, and one always lived by the ship's captain's preference. But that had not been so easy on *Sovereign Sun,* where there were two captains, especially concerning sexual practices and taboos. Milani's code was rigid, some of it even part of ship's operating procedure, like not allowing copulation between crew members who worked in the same job category, unless they were already bonded before the second one joined the group. Daneth had just quietly asked his own people to be discreet.

Mordon's brow was raised. "You swore to a bond with me and you've never broken it, have you?"

"No, but not out of loyalty to you. One deformed child was quite enough. I won't go through that again."

Mordon looked stricken. "I thought time had eased that painful memory."

"Is that why you've been spending so much time in

my cabin of late?" Senda got up from the hammock, suddenly feeling vulnerable there. "You're mistaken, Mordon. I haven't forgotten. The only reason our bonds appear to be intact is because there was only one clean man on this ship, Daneth, and he wouldn't have me."

"Don't be obscene, Senda. Daneth and Milani swore an oath together before every one of us. You wouldn't have interfered with that, even if you won't completely honor your own."

She'd stopped apologizing to him thousands of shifts ago, for even if she didn't seek out other men for pleasure or for reproductive purposes, she still wouldn't let Mordon touch her anymore. She'd tried to release him from the promises he'd made to her, but he said he'd sworn them for life. The line between love and hate was very thin and difficult for Senda to balance upon. Sometimes she hated Mordon for being a martyr, yet she loved him, too, was haunted by his loyalty, and bewildered by the whole thing. She hadn't broken the oath by playing with men, as she'd done so happily in her youth, let alone with outright infidelity. But she hadn't lived up to the bonds, either, for they hadn't shared a tumbling blanket since the baby died.

"Shouldn't you be on the bridge?" she said, hugging her tired body with her arms.

"No maneuvers, no destination, no nothing. They don't need me on the bridge for that," Mordon said bitterly.

"Milani was headed for the bridge when I left her. We're going to Crossroads," Senda said.

"Good," Mordon said. "We need some good cold jet fuel, and Droganie has been complaining about the nuclear generator's cooling system the last three times through the gravity slips. I know she's a perfectionist, and too meticulous at times, but when I see her standing around the forge during her rest shifts, just waiting for something to happen, I get worried too." He looked at Senda, his little round eyes suddenly taking on a sharpness that penetrated all their gaze beheld. "Now, what about Milani? Ghyaspur says she's not reading the landlubber."

"That's true. And Allis could not possibly be reading her, either. The hatred between them is very intense." And it frightened her, too. But she could not say that to Mordon, for he loved excuses to comfort her. "I've never seen anything like it before."

"That's because you didn't know Milani before she met Daneth. He had a mellowing effect on her, but she's a hard woman on her own. I've seen her force crew members to find their own replacements from other vessels, just to be rid of someone she didn't like."

"Didn't like? Or couldn't understand?" Senda said, troubled.

Mordon shrugged. "It hardly matters, does it? She couldn't get along with anyone whom she considered perfidious or insubordinate. I don't think it's at all unreasonable for a captain to demand complete loyalty, do you?"

"Everyone's entitled to some mistakes, and it doesn't necessarily make them disloyal to the ship not to be overly fond of the captain. The kind of devotion she wants is what breeds religious cults around stone-carriers. Daneth pointed out to her how dangerous that could be."

"There are enough problems even when things are going well without having malcontents on board," Mordon said.

"Well, she can't or won't understand Allis, who I believe is a victim of circumstances. It's Daneth who broke the bonds."

"He couldn't have done it alone. The vixen was guilty, too, perhaps more. She had a lot to gain by winning his love, or bewitching him."

Senda laughed sardonically. "She won't even touch the stone."

Mordon frowned. "That's what Ghyaspur says, too. I don't understand what her reasoning can be."

"That's because you don't have any imagination," Senda said, scowling now. "She walked into Milani's wrath in complete innocence, with no defenses. I'm surprised it didn't knock her out cold; in fact, we're lucky she isn't dead."

"It takes a strong personality and a powerful mind to withstand a blow like that," Mordon said thoughtfully. "And if she can do that, she's probably strong enough to tear this ship apart. Already she has you defending her." He was looking at her critically.

"Oh, come on, Mordon. I'm only trying to be fair."

"There's not always room for justice in a little world like *Sovereign Sun*," he replied.

"There'd better be for a stone-carrier, or we'll lose the stone to the Watchers."

She didn't think Mordon was convinced. He thought like Milani, defensively and quickly, and he'd know the Watchers would have to find out about Allis before there was any risk of losing yet another stone to them. But as much as he might prize the communicator-stone, he'd consider ship's security more important. And poor Allis didn't even realize her life was in jeopardy. Senda, torn, but staunchly loyal to the ship, too, knew she would not even warn her. She didn't dare take the chance that if the need ever arose, Allis forewarned might not be easily disposed of. The loyalty to the ship was nearly instinctive. No one had had to tell Senda not to mention Allis in her report, which she'd dutifully filed in the computer memory.

"Please, go away," Senda said. "I've spent a shift under acceleration, planetary gravity, and trying to talk to Milani. I'm exhausted."

"You forgot to mention that you inventoried the diamonds, made your report, and spent some time in the freshener," Mordon said, smiling one of his rare smiles.

"You've been monitoring me, I see," Senda said drỳly.

Mordon nodded. Tenderly, he reached out to touch her cheek, but Senda turned away. She knew that her refusals to be close to him hurt, but surely it was less painful than the alternative. He was just obstinate to pretend it was not so, too blindly loyal to the customs he'd adopted so long ago. Senda was glad when he left without another word.

CHAPTER 5

". . . were infuriated by the little armada's feat,"
Ghyaspur said with obvious glee. "They couldn't keep
it secret; too many trading and merchant ships had
been on hand during the armada's spectacular arrival,
and people representing most of the worlds in the
Galactic Trade Pact were waiting to see what would
happen next. Watchers ruled most of the galactic
trade planets and all the space between because their
advanced technology, most of which we believe was
stolen from Quondam Beings' ruins, gave them the
might to enforce their will. But they also have a
peculiar vanity. How could the Watchers continue
to claim that stellar sailing vessels were too slow and
primitive to compete in the trade lanes when they'd
traveled across the width of the galactic arm faster
than their own ion drive ships?

"The Watchers saved face by granting trade rights
to the refugees, which reinforced their favorable
countenance in the galaxy. They had to be careful;
they couldn't pull the same dirty tricks with everyone looking on as they did when they were protected
from scrutiny by the inaccessability of the restricted
worlds. They were worried, too. The gypsies had an
aggressive reputation and they feared the armada
would retaliate for the clandestine exploitation of

their world, perhaps even put the Watchers asunder, if given sufficient time and the means. It seemed to the Watchers that the gypsies, having faster-than-light travel capabilities, were a means.

"Getting trade rights didn't end the stellar sailing vessels' plight. They desperately needed to refurbish their sails, take on supplies, and, most important of all, install reliable nuclear generators to produce electromagnetic counterforce, if they were to continue using the Quondam Beings' gravity slips. The Watchers saw in the gypsies' desperation a chance to reduce the threat to themselves, and they took it.

"The Watchers' law said that technology could only be traded for technology, not given away like trade rights, nor bought for common goods. It didn't matter that our homeworld law was different—that never mattered! Left without a choice, my ancestor yielded to their might, finally accepting the so-called Magnanimous Agreement in exchange for the gravity slips' coordinates, the only technical secret with which gypsies could bargain. Nuclear generators would be installed on each stellar sailing vessel in the armada and maintained at no cost throughout time by the Watchers. Stellar sailors could trade only within the framework of the Watchers' law, disadvantaged from the start since Watchers', too, and all their legions in the Galactic Trade Pact could now use the gravity slips. My ancestor did not choose the Watchers' law. It was the only law. It's still the only law."

Allis thought that Ghyaspur became a little hysterical when he came to the part about the Watchers' law. She believed that deep down he thought his ancestor made a rotten bargain and was not the heroine Ghyaspur tried to portray.

"My ancestor's diary tells of the bitterness she felt

in the exchange. But a doomed woman, a doomed race, will grab at dust and, clutching it, dream of building a new race. She saw stellar sailing vessels as wombs of a new kind of human, a race living entirely by technology, unique in their heritage among all the races seeded by the Quondam Beings. A planetless people thriving in a hostile environment, and by necessity . . ."

"Oh, stop," Allis groaned. "It's already up to my ankles."

"Huh?" said Ghyaspur, looking confused and disappointed.

"Ghyaspur, if you tell me that story one more time, I'll scream," she warned. They were sitting in the galley, which was nearly empty, and Allis was more nervous than she'd been in months. The *Sovereign Sun* was beyond the orbit of Mars, nearing a gravity slip orbiting above the asteroid belt that would take her even farther from home. She kept one eye on the hatch that led to the main corridor, watching for Milani to come in for a meal. Ever since she'd learned the language and enough of the gypsies' customs to make sense of what was happening to her, she'd been waiting for another opportunity to talk to Milani. The captain obviously had a knack for avoiding Allis, and time was running short. Allis wasn't going to bother with messages sent through Senda anymore; she was going to meet with Milani face to face.

Ghyaspur nearly had frightened her to death when he'd attached probes to her scalp, run them through a noisy oscillating device, and then to his computer console. The combination, she'd eventually learned, was a language-prep machine that stimulated the language-oriented section of her brain and implanted some root words of the gypsy tongue. Later, Ghyaspur, with his incessant stories, reinforced the machine-induced learning, building her vocabulary by twenty to twenty-five words per shift. For a woman who'd never mastered high school Spanish, she thought she'd done very well, and apparently Ghyaspur agreed, for he'd cut down the time spent on the machine.

Now he shifted in his seat, put his hands on the scarred but still serviceable table between them, and tried to shrug off the flush that was creeping up his neck. "Well, it's your turn anyhow. Tell the one about the Phoenix, the bird that flew from ashes."

Allis shook her head, too irritable to comply. The good-natured pilot had been her guardian on board the *Sovereign Sun* for months, yet she judged him to be only in his late teens. He was tall, graceful despite the gangly appearance of his limbs, and the promise of great strength lay rippling beneath his blouse and trousers. He had a trace of freckles across the ridge of his straight nose, and his fair skin flushed easily when he was angry or embarrassed. When he blushed Allis would laugh at him, and he usually turned away. Finally, realizing how vulnerable a child he really was, she often found herself torn between treading carefully around his feelings and deliberately goading him, just because he was one of them, which satisfied her own perverse sense of justice. Perversity usually won.

"Any good storyteller tells simple tales with just one or two important lessons in the context. And most of all, he sticks to the facts," she said nastily. "Why would your ancestor have traded the gravity-slip coordinates for nuclear generators she already had? You did say that the ships need counterforce to make it through the slips without being crushed in the first place, didn't you?"

"Yes, but the diary isn't too explicit about . . ."

"Forget the diary. Interpret the facts to make a consistent and logical story. Have her trade the co-ordinates for something else, maybe diamonds or pearls."

"But she wouldn't have!" he said, shocked by the suggestion. "Allis, haven't you learned anything?"

"Sure I have. I learned that the Watchers were damn smart to let your world vaporize itself. You brag about war plans being made by the homeworld's hierarchy, and condemn the Watchers for being sus-picious. If the ambassadors had an inkling of it, the smartest thing they could do was to let their an-tagonists grab each other's throats. It's good war strategy and good politics, too. My only regret is that it wasn't enough to eliminate stellar sailors from the galaxy. If they'd been firm about it, I'd still be home, maybe still trying to raise capital for the tool and die company, but I'd be home."

Ghyaspur sat silently, staring at his fingers. Early on in their association Allis realized she could goad him into the most ridiculous arguments, have him ass over curls in short order with her glib tongue chop-ping away at his principles. He was bright enough to realize that he was not necessarily wrong, just out-classed by her age and experience. Usually he wel-comed the opportunity to debate, for even though he didn't like losing no one ever knew that he lost, except Allis. Sound didn't travel more than a few feet in the ship's rarefied atmosphere, so eavesdropping was impossible. And aside from Senda, who occasion-ally sought out Allis to check up on Ghyaspur's tutor-ing or to harangue her about the stone, which was still in Ghyaspur's strongbox, the rest of the crew gave her more berth on the ship than anyone could use.

This time, however, Ghyaspur didn't take the argumentative bait. He sat, completely unresponsive.

"How about getting me another bulb of the coagulated juice, and then we can go sit by a window and drink it," Allis suggested, squeezing out the last of the tangy gel.

"It's *cheros*," Ghyaspur said raising his eyebrows, "a vegetable wine, as you well know, and you know how to get it yourself. Furthermore, it's . . ."

". . . a portal, not a window on a ship. I know, I know," Allis said, nervously glancing at the hatch again. She'd tried to emphasize her contempt for the stellar sailors by becoming a deadweight. However, as inexperienced as her young guardian was, Ghyaspur was not a fool. Once he realized Allis was not willing to starve to death in her own cause, he simply stopped bringing her food. She had to find her way to the galley and learn to dial up her own meals or go hungry. She'd found the *cheros* early on, thank God. It was very mild, but very soothing just the same, and about the closest substance to liquid the ship supplied. The gypsies didn't seem to differentiate much between hunger and thirst.

"Hey," she said, leaning forward and putting her hand on Ghyaspur's. Anger sustained her ill temper most of the time, but it was nice to see a friendly face, too. Ghyaspur could work up quite a frown when he tried, as he did now. "Get the *cheros* as a favor, between friends. Yes?"

He stiffened. The gypsy sailors didn't touch very much. Space on the ship was limited and privacy, especially of one's person, was highly respected. Sharing touches suggested an intimacy that went deeper than the relationship between student and teacher.

"Are we friends, Allis?" Ghyaspur asked, blue eyes penetrating.

Ruffled, Allis withdrew her hand. She hadn't gotten used to his eyes, Dan's eyes. "I'll get it myself," she muttered.

As she pulled herself from the chair, which was as adhesive as denture cream without being messy, she saw Milani come through the deck hatch in a single, gazellelike leap. Allis moved with caution to intercept her at the dispenser in the center of the galley. The inertial force associated with the constant rotation still caused Allis some difficulty with sight-related coordination, such as walking in a straight line. She knew her gait was stilted and clumsy compared to the crew's, and it irritated her not to be able to move with confidence. Her balance, at least, was fine. Her body apparently had made some adjustments even if her brain had not.

Milani wore soft green trousers and a blouse with a red mourning sash around her waist. The stone glowed on her throat, and her tawny eyes glittered with malice as she stared at Allis.

"Milani, I've thought it all over," Allis said, trying not to be intimidated by the captain's eyes. "I think I understand what happened."

"You're doing well with the language," was Milani's reply.

"It's time that we discussed the problem of me and, more important, the friction between us."

Milani reached into the sparkling galley dispenser, which vaguely resembled a cafeteria automat, and took out a portion of high-protein, high-bulk food. There were no savory smells, no sizzling sounds. All the food was high in moisture content, neatly sealed in sanitary glassine containers. "Your accent is odd, but admittedly adequate," the captain said.

Allis frowned. It was strange to be standing nearly nose to nose with the captain, yet feel as if her words were bypassing Milani's ears. "Ignoring me won't help. I'm not going to go away," Allis said briskly, "I've been thinking about what happened, and I've come to the conclusion that Dan didn't break his bond with you, nor his promises, at least not in his mind." Finally she seemed to have Milani's attention, however grudgingly, and Allis continued. "He knew he was dying and he felt that the medical treatment he got on Earth put him on borrowed time. You and the *Sovereign Sun* were light years away, as I understand it, and he didn't even have a way of contacting you. I also know that if he had been on board when the disease struck, he'd have died much sooner; there is no treatment known for the white-blood death on this ship, or on any other stellar sailing vessel. Given the circumstances, I don't think he saw his relationship with me as breaking bonds. Death would have broken them earlier anyway."

"That isn't a very original idea, and it certainly took you long enough to come up with it. Did you think I'd thank you for something my crew has been thinking since you came on board? Or did you believe it was such a new and startling revelation that I'd turn the ship around to take you home?"

Allis shrugged uncomfortably and wondered if Milani were finally reading her mind again. If she were, she'd know it was painful for Allis to accept the probability that Dan merely had been filling in found time with her, a woman who was conveniently available because of their work together at the tool and die manufacturing business he'd set up so that he could buy industrial diamonds without arousing suspicion. "It does make sense," she said lamely. "Dan wasn't the kind of man who'd waste time. Even though his health wasn't what it should have been, he did a lot of things back on Earth that I gather he'd never done before. He rode horses, swam . . ."

"And tumbled with an Earthling," Milani said, shaking her head. "Don't tell me about it, Allis. It would have been primitive compared to what I shared with him." Milani's finger touched the iridescent stone at her throat, as if to remind Allis of its power to bring two stone-carriers to a height of sharing that ordinary people could not hope to attain.

"I'd hoped we could reach an understanding."

"On what? Daneth's plans to stay on Earth with you, or his plans to return to me? None of that matters now. The fact is that you have the stone, and your possession of it eliminates any shred of sympathy I might have had for you otherwise."

"But why?" Allis said, almost tearfully.

Milani didn't answer. Her jagged eyebrows nearly met above the bridge of her nose and cast her face in a permanent scowl and made her gaze icy.

"You say it doesn't matter whether Dan was going to return to the ship or stay on Earth with me, but it must! The only thing the stone proves is that he loved me, and you can't tolerate knowing that. But why has all your anger at *his* betrayal fallen on me? You shouldn't be angry with me. I was as much a victim of his duplicity as you are, even more wronged."

"You say that, but I have no way of knowing if it's the truth."

"You're afraid to know," Allis said, suddenly realizing she was right. "If you didn't hate me, you'd be able to read my mind and know that I am telling the truth, and you can't live with that, can you?" Allis shook her head sadly. "Take me home, Milani. You can't pretend it didn't happen by avoiding me, but maybe you can forget if I'm gone. Take me home."

"No," said Milani.

"Please let me go," Allis said, desperately. She was lonesome and frightened in this alien place, surrounded by people she didn't understand and who didn't understand her. But Milani was unmoved. "I didn't ask Dan for the stone, and if I had known what it was and how important it was to his people, I wouldn't have taken it when he gave it to me. I'm not cut out for this kind of life, and Dan knew it. I've got Earth blood in these veins. I know how to run a business, not spaceships and stellar wind. I'm useless here. Dan must have been delirious."

"You've tried that argument before, and the tears, too, according to Senda. It won't work. Nothing will change my mind."

"You won't know peace until you do," Allis said, brushing tears from her cheeks. She didn't know when she had started crying. "You and your freakish crew can avoid me, but in quarters this close you'll never forget I'm here. I'll become a source of irritation."

"You already are," Milani said. "But we have ways of dealing with straphangers."

"They won't work with me," Allis retorted, too angry even to care what the methods might be. She stepped closer to the captain so that she wouldn't miss a word. "It's impossible to hate a dead man who isn't here to defend himself, though space knows I have reason to hate Dan. I've learned a lot about that stone, even without touching it; Ghyaspur and Senda have told me everything they know about it in an effort to entice me into using it. So I know now that

when I was with Dan I was stripped of all my defenses, all those petty little façades I kept to display to
the world, yet he loved me. Don't you wonder what
he saw there, Milani? I know. And knowing gives
me a tremendous feeling of power and makes me feel
very secure. He strengthened me, Milani. In his deceit,
he made me stronger than I ever was. You will have to
deal with my anger, not Dan. And I almost pity you
because you haven't a grave to hide in!"

Allis remembered to grab a bulb of *cheros* before
leaving the stunned captain. She hurried to the hatch,
past the table where Ghyaspur was still sitting. Ghyaspur, she knew, would look longingly at his mates,
then reluctantly follow her. Even through the intense anger she felt with Milani, a fleeting guilt assaulted her. She had the young pilot trapped by his
duty to her, but she didn't have to command all of his
time. He needed to visit with friends and relatives;
perhaps he even had a sweetheart, or would have if
Allis weren't so demanding. Tough luck, she told
herself sternly. He was one of them, and they all
had to learn that shanghaiing her was a mistake.

CHAPTER 6

Allis dropped featherlike through a gangway to the next level corridor, holding the ladder with one hand and a flask of *cheros* with the other. The bright hue of the mossy chevrons was an instant cue that she was on the habitat level. In the outer-rim corridor, the chevron decks were as dark as shadowy forest moss; as she went closer to the axis, the chevron decks lightened and took on distinctive color casts, blended with green. If she had closed her eyes to the autumnal green tinged with gold, she still would have recognized the habitat level by touching the corrugated walls, patterned differently than the corrugation in any other level. Colored ribs provided more visual clues to identify which segment of the habitat corridor she was in. And if that were not enough, every stanchion and rail had raised patterns of alien code, tactile landmarks, if she could learn to distinguish one code from another. She refused to take the time to learn, preferring to depend on chromatic distinctions.

"And if power is disrupted and the lighting fails, how will you know where you are or how to get where you want to go?" Ghyaspur had asked when she'd become impatient with his relentless orientation lessons.

"I plan to be home before the lights go out," was her usual retort, but secretly she was afraid. She hadn't been inclined to learn a lifetime of ship awareness in a few months; wouldn't learn, for learning was an acceptance of the gypsies' plan for her to share their roving ways.

Ghyaspur would be off sunwatch in moments, and she planned to meet him. She still wore her khaki pants, a fashionable rather than a practical version of real bush pants, and too tight-fitting to put the flask of *cheros* in her pocket. Her shirt was white cotton, midriff-baring and more than adequate clothing on the sunny side of the ship. But with the canned air constantly circulating through the corridors, gangways, and cabins, she usually had her old brown sweater buttoned up around her neck. A few minutes in the freshener kept her clothes clean and comfortable, though the sweater was beginning to ravel from the constant exposure to the sonics and chemicals. There were brightly colored gypsy clothes in the ship's store, which were available to her, but she preferred to remain easily distinguished from the crew, a pariah among them.

The habitat level shared its corridor in part with the huge armory, the segment of the ship that opened to a section of the nonrotating hub where the gypsy crew could soar free to shortcut across the ship. Cabins here had full-sized doors opening to the armory, and hatches in the decks and ceilings to levels above and below. Allis ducked down the part of the corridor that was a true tunnel, which ran under the hydroponic farms and holds in the bilge. That group of less desirable cabins was mostly deserted, housing only ghosts of what was once a large and thriving community of gypsies.

At the end of the tunnel, having circumnavigated the ship halfway, she spied the three-dimensional tangram on the last cabin door before coming again to the armory. She had seen the tangram many times, of course, this least favored route around the ship being Allis's most favored. And she had known a similar brightly enameled tangram in two-dimensional form on the face of Dan's gold ring. She knew now that it was his captain's insignia ring, and that Milani wore one, too.

The crew's cabins were highly personal territory; despite a universal pattern to open doors and hatches, no one entered a cabin without an explicit invitation to do so by the occupant. Even so, Allis impulsively patterned the double circle on the labyrinth control of the captain's cabin. The door slid economically into the bulkhead; indeed, there was no room for it to swing into the narrow corridor.

She expected a monastic and spartan chamber, something in keeping with Milani's no-nonsense mien. But there were colorful cushions and gleaming furniture anchored to the deck, and the deck itself was covered with a scarlet tufted weaving that ran four times deeper along the bilge than did Ghyaspur's cabin. A huge alien carving was suspended from the ceiling in front of a polarized ultraloy portal, looking suspiciously like the swinging couch Dan had installed in the livingroom of the Los Angeles apartment they had shared. Now Allis wondered what he had seen when he closed his eyes and sunk into the frothy cushions back on Earth. A sea of stars, perhaps, or the streaks of light as seen from the gravity slips that looked like tungsten filaments in a light bulb? No earthly scene, of that she was bitterly certain.

Allis realized she'd had some vague notion of startling Milani by being in her cabin when she returned from the bridge. But the sight of the Dan-furnished quarters unnerved her, and she patterned shut the door, never even stepping over the threshold, then nearly leaped into the open corridor along the armory.

The power the woman had over Dan had held him across light years! Dan who was so strong and independent was comforted on Earth by reminders of his bond to Milani. Was it only the stone with the deep sharing it made possible that had made him her prisoner? Or would he have returned to Milani even if there'd been no stone to draw him back? There was little room left for anger with Dan; fear had crowded that out, fear that she was as much in Milani's power as Dan ever had been, and without love to pretend it was all right. She was glad that Milani had not been in her cabin to read from her face what she couldn't from Allis's mind.

As she deliberately calmed herself she saw Senda and Mordon coming from their cabin. Or was it *their* cabin? Even Ghyaspur seemed confused about the relationship between the first mate and the albino linguist, so Allis felt sure *she'd* never get it right. The *Sovereign Sun*'s crew members were not particularly homogeneous. They'd worked out the problems of living in close quarters, not for merely long periods of time but, seemingly, forever. There was that tremendous respect for personal privacy and body space, and there were accepted rules about interpersonal relationships that covered everything from carrying out burdens (the word the gypsies used to describe their jobs and ship duties) to sex.

Half the crew was scandalized by Allis's staying in Ghyaspur's cabin long after she had enough ship-awareness to move out, yet the other half, Dan's half, didn't see it as compromising at all—merely unpleasant, since Ghyaspur had to spend so much time with the despicable and reluctant stone-carrier. She supposed the unscandalized half assumed he was getting something out of it. He was, of course, but not sex. His needs were more complicated than that. The ship's only child was no longer a child, but Allis was the only person who accepted him as an adult.

After touching Senda's ghostly hair, the first mate soared across the armory to a far gangway. Senda impatiently smoothed her hair and looked around to see Allis.

"Ah, this is opportune," the albino said. "I never know where to find you anymore."

"I'm on my way to my favorite portal to get drunk," Allis said crisply, as she headed the way she'd planned. Even the smallest courtesies were against her policy, especially to someone as influential and close to Milani as Senda. She heard the gentle rasp of Senda's gripboots pulling against the planking, which meant she was following Allis closely, but she neither looked back nor slowed down. Up another scuffed gangway and through a hatch, and Allis finally was in a tiny chamber with a huge transparent portal looking out on the wintry constellations. The gypsies called these little chambers "hearths," and while the only energy from the distant fiery furnaces that penetrated the glasslike screen was in the form of light, the hearths did provide a cozy place to relax, not unlike the hearths of Earth.

Allis settled into frayed batting that looked like it was fashioned from the same silky substance as Ghyaspur's comfortable tumbling blanket. She squirmed to make depressions for her bones, though it really was hard to be uncomfortable in the ship's light artificial gravity. She popped the lid on the *cheros*. It was a dry green wine, with a hint of chocolate flavor. Nearly half the gelled contents of the flask went down easily, and though it didn't really calm her nerves, she liked to pretend it did. They'd been in the asteroid belt for days, endless days during which the sun never set, and the end of time as Allis knew it was at hand.

Allis was barely aware of Senda's settling into the batting across from her, for she already was engrossed with the starscape. The ship sailed with the axis pointed in the direction of travel, hauled along by shrouds running from the superstructure out to the miles and miles of billowing sails. There was no sense of motion, though occasionally the ship would sway, pendulumlike, when the solar winds flared. She dimmed the cabin light, the better to see the stars.

Betelgeuse, more magenta than red since it was somewhat obscured by the translucent sails, fixed the hunter in the sky as much as the thrice brilliant points on his belt. Just below the sails Rigel gleamed a brilliant blue-white, and she wondered if the tiny white star near it was its companion.

Until Dan had taken an interest in learning the constellations, she'd considered herself lucky to find the Big Dipper in the night sky. Now she knew three of Ursa Major's stars by name, Mizar, Dubhe, and Merak, and she even knew their colors. She hadn't realized the hues of the stars were so distinctive until she was no longer blinded by the Earth's atmosphere. The familiar constellations were comforting—Canis Major, Hydra, Cancer, Cassiopeia, Triangulum, and Andromeda. She hadn't known she could name them until they were her last link with home and Earth, and then she'd forced herself to remember, pulling their names and placement in the black sky from places in her mind that under ordinary circumstances would have contained only cobwebs. She didn't like to sit on the stern side of the rotating disk. Sol was too small, and the Earth, at opposition, was not even visible.

"Pretty, isn't it?" Senda said.

"Rigel is almost nine hundred light years away," Allis said, looking at the bright blue star.

"And Betelgeuse is only half that far, intrinsically more luminous, too, if it weren't for the sails. And there's Zeta Orionis, the left and lowermost of the three matched gems in the hunter's belt."

"I thought Dan was the only gypsy who knew the constellations. Ghyaspur says they change so frequently that no one bothers to learn them." Allis felt her heart skip a beat and a strange squiggle in her lower abdomen. She resisted an impulse to press her hand against her abdomen, then said, "Anyhow, it's Alnitak, not Zeta Orionis."

"Whatever," Senda said with a shrug. "The hunter has been known by names other than Orion. Orwandil, Germanic if I remember the time and place correctly. A giant to the Hebrews and Arabians, and a war god—Ninurta? That's from Sumeria or Egypt. I don't remember which anymore."

"Menelvagor with his shining belt," Allis said wistfully. "Did you visit Earth back then, too?"

"Menelvagor? When was that?"

Allis shook her head. "Never mind. Just how old are you, Senda?"

"Fifty thousand shifts," Senda replied.

"What's that in Earth years?" Allis asked. She tucked her knees into her arms as Ghyaspur came through the little hatch, making room for him.

"Don't answer that, Senda. She can make her own

conversions," he said, determined as ever to make a gypsy of Allis.

"The answer you're looking for wouldn't make sense, Allis," Senda said, her voice unusually soft. "I saw the pyramids in the Valley of the Nile when I was a child. But I'm not that old. At least, not in real time."

"What real time is depends on your point of view. Those pyramids were built during my world's ancient history. You can't have been a part of that, yet be here, too."

"Time dilation, the gravity slips . . ."

"I know." Allis held up her hand to stop Senda. "Ghyaspur has explained and re-explained. We're getting close to the gravity slip, aren't we?"

From the perplexed look on Senda's face, Allis knew that her eyes must be wide with fear. But Ghyaspur understood her distress. He gestured to the portal. "The sailjockeys are taking in the sails now."

Senda nodded and squinted. "Mordon is out there."

Indeed, Allis could see a dozen pods, which enclosed the sailjockeys and made them look like metallic insects with waldoes and antennas sticking out. They had propelled to the sails, leaving strings of vapor behind. Methodically, the sails began to collapse and furl before the tenders until the films of silver were solid, gleaming pylons of rolled-up sail. Betelgeuse, Bellatrix, and Aldebaran shined true again for the first time in months.

"When I next see Earth, will the Golden Gate Bridge still be there?" Allis asked in a small voice.

Senda chuckled. "We don't range as far under Milani as we did on *Migrant Sun* under Daneth alone.

It takes too much preparation; too much time is lost between. The bridge will be there, Allis."

"But it won't be *now*," Allis said, watching the tenders disappear overhead to stow the sails in cartridges under the superstructure.

"No," Senda said quietly, apparently finally understanding Allis's dismay. "Much time will have passed."

Allis raised her knees and rested her cheek against them, turning away from the two aliens so they would not see her tears.

"What you need," she heard the albino say, "is to stop complaining and become involved in now. You could be making useful contributions to *Sovereign Sun*. Begin with compiling an English lexicon, for instance."

"If I agree to do that, will Milani turn this ship around and take me back?"

"No."

"Then I won't help you," Allis said stubbornly.

"We're bound to return to Earth sometime. Look forward to that," Senda suggested.

"Will she let me off then, whenever it is?"

"I don't know. The stone . . ."

Allis wiped the tears from her cheeks. There'd been few; she was learning to control them. The gypsies looked upon tears as a sign of weakness not sorrow, and she didn't want them to think she was weak. Then, hoping her eyes were not too red, she lifted her head. "Senda, I'd do anything she or anyone asked of me if it would get me home, but I've come to believe that will never happen. Milani hates me, she wants me miserable, and keeping me on this ship is her version of cruel punishment for picking the wrong guy."

"If you continue in this fashion, she may decide you're too much bother and throw you out the hatch,"

Senda said, her pale face screwing up in a ghostly mask of exasperation.

Allis smiled sickly and slowly shook her head. "The stone . . ." she said, letting the word hang. From the flourish of Senda's exit, Allis knew she was right again. No one would harm her as long as she owned the stone. The damned stone. She sat back to wait.

Milani's voice interrupted the quiet, listing vectors and velocity.

"Are those damn speakers everywhere?" Allis said. Milani's voice always was calm, but crisp as a mountain stream.

"Yes, everywhere," Ghyaspur said. He took the forgotten flask of *cheros* from Allis and drank, wiping his mouth with the back of his hand. Allis watched him for a moment. He was trying to be companionable, having nothing comforting to say to her and thoughtful enough not to say just anything. She looked at Betelgeuse again, ruby-red steady light shining across five hundred light years. There were X-rays, too, she knew, and a complete electromagnetic spectrum of rays. She wondered how much radiation her tissues were absorbing. Ghyaspur had told her not to worry, but he didn't know about the baby, now in its second trimester with the bulge nearly up to her belly button.

The ship was heavily constructed with ultraloy, which shielded almost the entire spectrum of cosmic rays. The portals were a form of ultraloy, too. But Allis was not convinced of their shielding effectiveness, Quondam Beings' superior technology or no. Dan's leukemia probably was caused by bone marrow irradiation. Droganie, the ship's blacksmith who worked in the nuclear forge shop, had skin on her hands that sloughed off in thick sheets. There was plenty of evidence of gonad damage; Senda's albinoism, six- and seven-fingered crew members, even Milani's odd hair and tawny eyes. Two crew members had no legs, and they spent most of their time in the axis or near it where they would be weightless, or nearly so. Women outnumbered men, which might point to unseen sex-linked mutations, mutations that were lethal.

What sort of genes had Dan passed on to their child? No way of finding out. The ship lacked medical facilities, had no doctor other than the computer. Allis was not ready to try preprogrammed remedies, even if there were some. Sometimes gypsies used Watcher medical facilities in the various ports of call, but from what she'd learned from Ghyaspur, most preferred no treatment or home remedies, like her own grandmother who ate cherries for her arthritis and comfrey root on general principle.

"Hold on, Allis. We'll be changing attitude with the cold jets to intersect the gravity slip," Ghyaspur said.

There were stanchions and railings everywhere on the ship, even here in the little hearth. Allis selected one and braced as the ship yawed; Betelgeuse seemed to swing left as yellow Bellatrix moved to the center of the portal. Allis looked for the gravity slip among the stars.

"I don't see anything," she said when the speaker beeped, indicating that the maneuver was finished.

"There's nothing to see, yet. This is a very small slip. There, now you can see it encroaching on the stars. See how the gravity wave distorts the starlight?"

Some of the stars blurred and streaked like a laser light display on a planetarium dome, elongating first

Bellatrix, then a nameless blue star, a cluster of three, and finally Betelgeuse, until all were strips of light. Allis tightened her fingers on the stanchion, her heart beat painfully. The ship shuddered and Allis yelped in fright.

"That's only the generator engaging the electromagnetic field," Ghyaspur said. "We'd be crushed, even in a small gravity slip like this one, before we got halfway through without counterforce. The Quondam Beings were mighty engineers." His voice was filled with admiration, but Allis's throat was so constricted with fear that now she couldn't even squeak. Just before she passed out she thought her heart would burst from its furious pumping, and she wondered insanely if Lewis Carroll had ever met a Quondam Being and why her name was Allis.

Apparently, the period of unconsciousness was brief, for the fingers of one hand still were laced in the stanchion, and Ghyaspur was just propping up her knees. He looked worried.

"What happened?" he said, hovering over her.

Not answering, she watched the bulkhead for some sign of its caving in. Nothing happened. The portal, streaked with lantern-show colors, didn't crack. Though she knew they were racing down the galactic arm more quickly than light could travel, she didn't feel any acceleration, or even have the sensation that she was falling. She did, however, feel quite odd, as if she were unevenly proportioned. The generator was keeping them from being crushed in the gravity slip, but its counterforce was uneven. One cheek was sagging, and in trying to move out of whatever had caused it to sag, her head encountered a ripple of gravity. It pulled at the fluid in her ears, then passed through her body like a spasm of weight. But the queerness of shifting energy was nothing compared to the horrible sense of hopelessness gripping her.

"This gravity slip is short," Ghyaspur said, easing back to sit in the batting now that he realized she was all right. "If we wait long enough, we'll be able to see a brilliant light at the other end of the slip. This one opens close to a red star."

Allis couldn't help her alarmed look.

"Not *that* close," he said, laughing at her. "It's a frisky star, though, with good winds. If we catch a high wind off a hot spot, we'll be able to reach Crossroads in ten or twelve shifts, without swinging by one of the planets to decelerate."

"But it won't be *now*," Allis said softly. Ghyaspur shook his head. "How long?"

"Back on your planet? I don't know exactly, perhaps three or four thousand shifts."

"Years," Allis said, but converting mentally, she realized with some relief that it was not many years. She sat up and Ghyaspur offered her the rest of the *cheros*. She accepted gratefully. The worst had happened. There was no turning back now. "You are my friend, you know," she said.

"Sometimes I wonder." Ghyaspur crossed his arms.

"There must be something I can do on this ship," Allis said.

Ghyaspur looked at her suspiciously. "The lexicon."

"Not that," she said, getting to her feet. She swayed and blinked her eyes. "Think up something else." Plans. Already plans were forming. The first gambit had failed, but that didn't mean the next one would. She wouldn't give Milani the satisfaction of seeing her miserable forever.

"Are you serious?" he asked. His face was a little

crooked from a stray bit of gravity passing through the hearth chamber.

"Sure I'm serious. Even if we did go back now, it will be too different. I'll have lost my contacts; they'll all have moved on and grown older."

"If you are serious, take up the stone," Ghyaspur suggested.

"Not that either," Allis said, not really irritated by his suggestion even though he'd made it and been refused a hundred times before. "I want a burden, a real one. What can I do? Steer? Sweep floors? Oh, that's right. No brooms. Well, there has to be something. What about the diamonds? I can sort them as well as anyone on this ship; I was a minor expert, you know."

"If you're serious, let's go," Ghyaspur said, getting to his feet. He swayed against her and grabbed for a stanchion.

"Where to?"

"Back to my cabin to get some prints for lessons on sunwatching."

"Sunwatching?"

"Yes, of course. Everyone on the ship takes a turn at the sunwatch console on the bridge. It's time you did, too."

"I don't know anything about computers," Allis protested.

"You don't have to. The computer isn't much involved. Sunwatching requires a person to scan, choose, interpret, and integrate information from an array of instruments. If the computer kept the sunwatch, we'd have complete integration from different sensors, it's true. But we minimize computer processing by using individual instruments. Even so, those instruments are susceptible to damage and difficult if not

impossible to replace in some instances. Stellar energy
is powerful. But with this method, if the star does
burn out anything sensitive, we lose only one param-
eter. With all the rest, that leaves us enough decision-
making information. Don't forget that stellar energy
isn't just heat, light, and photons. There's heavy stuff,
too. You wouldn't want crew out in the pods replacing sensors during a barrage of protons and neutrons,
and we sure can't be without sundata just because of
equipment failure. Besides, our computer doesn't have
enough memory storage to digitalize stellar images.
If we had one that could, it'd take up too much space
—at least, the ones the Watchers would let us have
would be too big." Ghyaspur frowned for a moment,
probably deciding whether or not to deliver another
lecture about how the Watchers kept wind from
gypsy sails when they could. He must have decided
that the subject had been covered thoroughly, for he
smiled at Allis and said, "Our eyes can do the same
thing sensors and a complex computer can, and we
don't require any extra air conditioning to keep us
operating."

"All right. I'll learn how to watch the sun," Allis
said, trying not to feel uneasy about having to spend
time on the bridge with Milani. "But I want something else to do, too."

The young pilot nodded absently. "The diamonds
are all sorted and stowed by now, but maybe Rezia
can use you in hydroponics. You probably know a
lot about growing things, your having come from a
planet." He started through the hatch. "Hold the
railings in the corridor. You can't tell where the
counterforce is strong or weak until you walk into it."

Allis followed him into the corridor. "Maybe we

shouldn't do it right away," she said when she caught up to him.

Ghyaspur stopped in his tracks. "I knew it was too good to last," he said with a laconic sigh.

"I just meant that I'd like to go to the ship's store first," Allis said indignantly. She gestured at her clothes. "These aren't very suitable for farming." And though the zipper in her pants still closed over the bulge without too much difficulty, it wouldn't much longer.

Ghyaspur smiled, and for the first time he touched her deliberately, running his fingers along her long hair. "And perhaps you'd like to borrow my shears?"

"No."

"Good." He smiled sheepishly. "But you ought to do something to keep it out of your way."

He was slow to take his hand away from her face, and Allis found herself wishing his fingers would linger. But finally the brief and gentle touch was ended, leaving Allis aware of how much she missed familiar contact. "I'll think of something to do with my hair," she said softly. "But first the clothes." Allis brushed past him, just for the sake of touching him, then hurried along the corridor, pretending that the skin along her cheek and arm didn't tingle.

CHAPTER 7

There were no constellations, only foreign stars scattered thickly across an alien spacescape, lacking meaning, which generations of philosophers and myth makers brought to the stars seen from Earth. The sun looked like old Sol would look as it hovered on a tropical horizon, red and bloated to ten times its normal size. But this sun did not slip behind a shimmering sea in the blink of an eye, leaving shrouds of lavender and orange to fade into the crepuscular silence that precedes night. It hung, a ruddy globe with a hazy edge that feathered and faded until there was no color at all, only the blackness of space and the alien stars.

One quarter of the sun's mass was packed into a dense helium core, around which a shell of hydrogen fused with furious intensity, forming even more helium to pack into the core. It also heated yet unused hydrogen gas, lifting it beyond the visible limits of the star, giving it the bright, bloated appearance. A lot of energy escaped from the surface of the star as radiation, much of it as stellar wind that filled the *Sovereign Sun*'s sails on its way to Crossroads.

The Crossroads solar system was the hub of the galactic trade routes governed by the Watchers simply because more gravity slips began and ended here than anywhere else in the galaxy. Aside from the gravity slips, there was only the ruin of a minor outpost on an outer planet's moon to show that the Quondam Beings had been there. If there ever were cities or vast installations, they'd have been on inner, terrestrial-like planets, long since vaporized by the swollen, red sun. It was assumed that if the Crossroads' sun once had warmed the Quondam Beings' homeworld, they'd abandoned it when their sun began to die. The Watchers, however, had swarmed to it like jackals to carrion.

Just below the ecliptic plane and well beyond the tenuous envelope of hydrogen that surrounded the dying sun, gravity slips clustered like tracks in a railroad switching yard. Each slip was a one-way track to another star system, or it was the return track. The gravity slips were not associated with mass, collapsed or otherwise. They were known to be slightly conical in shape, and apparently were gravity waves, but no one knew anything else about them. Nearby, the Watchers had constructed a huge orbital station with everything from stalls for overhauling ramjets to fittings for stellar sailing vessels. The station could accommodate a thousand assorted ships at once, and entertain their crews as well.

Allis was on the bridge, her dark hair neatly braided and securely fastened to the crown of her head. She was at the dual console with the mate, Mordon, helping him keep the sunwatch, the mechanics of which Ghyaspur had been teaching her since the *Sovereign Sun* left the gravity slip, ten shifts ago. There were several display screens on the panel before her, simple optical mirror reflections of the alien sun's disk, and some color-television screens that relayed the same image within specific spectrums. The granular-looking convection cells where incipient prominences formed were faint and indistinct because of this sun's huge envelope of hydrogen. Fortunately, they were already unconcerned about surface activity since any heavy stellar wind resulting from a prominence just now forming would not reach the ship for twenty or thirty shifts, long after they planned to be safe in Crossroads' harbor. They concentrated on keeping track of several hot spots, which were points of runaway fusion reactions within the hydrogen envelope. The stellar wind would become asymmetrical when energy from the hot spots hit them, and the body of the ship would swing like a pendulum on the shrouds, complicating docking maneuvers.

Just now the sails were dragging the *Sovereign Sun* as it fell in toward the sun and Crossroads station, changing the enormous velocity acquired in the gravity slip until it could match orbital elements with Crossroads station. It took every bit of sail capacity the ship had to decelerate, but if they had left the gravity slip at the velocity at which they'd entered, they would have been dependent on their feeble cold jets and the gravitational pull of the alien sun to take them to Crossroads.

The *Sovereign Sun* could not tack in the stellar wind like water sailing vessels tacked. There was no substance like water for the keel to bite and force the ship upwind. For this reason the *Sovereign Sun* was limited to certain convenient trade routes within the system of gravity slips. They could depend on the velocity of the gravity slips to get them nearly anywhere within a solar system in a reasonable length of time; the ship decelerated between slip and destination by using the sails to drag the ship, or they used a torque effect maneuver while swinging by a planet to slow them down. But for the return trip away from the sun, acceleration and ultimate speed depended on the stellar wind, and if the gravity slip they needed was very distant, they might have to spend years getting to it.

When they were hauling huge masses between the colonial worlds of their homeworld system, scouting among the asteroids for minerals, ore, and raw material, they were content with the cheap but slow travel. Now, however, the *Sovereign Sun* was competing with more versatile ships and over distances it was not designed to traverse. Selecting and plotting courses that took full advantage of the gravity slips was essential to their survival, something Milani was reputed to do skillfully.

Allis stole a glance at her watch. She'd been at the sunwatch console for nearly an hour. At precisely one hour and nine minutes, she and Mordon would be relieved from their sticky chairs for one hour and nine minutes. Rotation at the sunwatch console would continue in this fashion throughout the midshift, which was about ten hours long. Ordinarily Allis found that she could easily put in a complete shift of work in the ship's light gravity without feeling the least bit fatigued, but time was already dragging, and the heavy perceptual load was tiring.

She shouldn't be feeling unduly odd at the strange controls, for sunwatching was seated duty, which was gravity and zero-gravity resistant and maintained the body in a fixed geometric relationship to the displays and controls, much like many Earth occupations. But sitting next to the dour mate was not like working with friends back on Earth, nor even with Ghyaspur. She looked out the huge portal that filled one wall of the bridge, being careful not to look directly at the sun despite the special dimmers. Even though that sun was huge and brilliant, it looked more dead than dying.

"Keep your eyes on your work," Mordon grumbled.

Guiltily Allis turned her gaze back to the sunwatch screens. The hot spot she and Mordon had been watching had not changed. She adjusted the phone plug in her ear and fidgeted.

Finally her relief came, a plump woman named Jincala who had the slanted eyes and thick features of one with Down's Syndrome. Jincala was the only other person besides Ghyaspur who smiled at Allis, and she did so now while watching Allis slip out of the console. When Jincala sat down and fastened the safety webs across her shoulders and thighs, she saw the simian crease in the woman's palms. Until now she hadn't been certain that Jincala was truly a mongoloid, or if her peculiar eyes and flat features were some other genetic defect that merely mimicked the syndrome.

Allis retired to the side of the bridge where there was a hatch leading to a sanitary and some room to stretch. She watched to see who would come forth to relieve Mordon, but none of the other bridge crew left their stations, and the hatch leading to the corridor didn't open. In a few minutes Mordon spoke quietly to Jincala, who nodded vigorously, then he vacated his chair. The place beside the mongoloid remained empty.

When Mordon started past Allis on his way to the sanitary, she stopped him with a hand on the crook of his elbow. He pulled away as if she'd hurt him.

"Sorry. That was an accident," she said, regretting that she'd forgotten the touching taboo, even for a second. She'd been trying to get along with the crew, and endear herself to them. Breaking taboos, even inadvertently, wouldn't help. She smiled. That didn't help either.

Mordon stared a moment, his blue eyes still reflexively angry from her touch. Like the other sailors he was tall, but he was skinny and rat-faced. "You're lucky I didn't break your arm, just as accidentally."

"Yes, I know. I'm truly sorry. I just wanted to know if Jincala should be left alone. If your replacement's late, I could take the watch for a while longer."

"Only one reliable sunwatcher is necessary," he said. Grinning, he stepped around Allis and slid open the sanitary's hatch. A few chuckles escaped nearby crew, and Milani looked at Allis from the far side of the bridge where she could not have heard Mordon's words, her eyebrow raised and her lips in a wry smile. Allis flushed uncomfortably, realizing that the captain heard everything she wanted to hear, at least from everyone except Allis. She wondered if Jincala had been especially selected to relieve her on the sunwatch, just to make it plain that even a dull-witted gypsy was more reliable than Allis.

Allis looked at the portal, trying to appear unruffled. A shining spot nearing the center of the portal was growing larger. A planet, perhaps, or the blur of another gravity slip, but Allis didn't want to ask anyone what it was for fear of being made to look foolish. Why was it that the gypsies expected her to know so much? Did they treat their children equally harshly when they first came to the bridge to learn? Unfortunately, Allis had no way of knowing how they treated their children, for Ghyaspur was the youngest person on the ship.

She'd seen the empty nurseries on every level with the environment lovingly miniaturized to fit tiny hands and short reaches. According to Ghyaspur, the nurseries were painful reminders to the crew that the birthrate on the *Sovereign Sun* wasn't just down, it was zero. There was nothing to be done about it until new crew members joined them, hopefully fertile people and, perhaps, parents who would bring their offspring with them. Exchange of crew was commonplace at the open ports and especially at Crossroads, where gypsy sailors from various ships mingled, formed friendships, or fell in love. Others changed ships just for a change of pace. But the *Sovereign Sun*'s crew was more static than most. They didn't move between ships frequently because few other stellar sailing vessels had a stone-carrier at the helm. There was a mystic attachment to the stone-carrier that Allis still didn't quite understand. The best she could come up with was that they *liked* having their minds read.

Milani spoke a few quiet words to the man at the ship's helm, and he nodded. Warning bells sounded and the *Sovereign Sun* changed trajectory slightly. It was like that, hour after hour. The only voice she heard was Milani's, responding to information given silently by her attentive crew. Even when Allis finally realized she was watching a fully developed hot spot on her screens, Mordon, she discovered, had already passed the information to the captain in his thoughts. Allis felt useless.

The last rotation on the sunwatch had taken place, and Jincala was at the console again. Allis and Mordon were required to stay on the bridge until the end of the shift, even though they were not actively involved any longer. The shining spot Allis had seen in the portal had become huge as the midshift dragged on, and finally she'd realized it was not a planet nor even another ship. It was Crossroads station, made entirely of the Quondam Beings' ultraloy. Sunlight curved around the globe, lighting blisters and other odd features, casting hazy shadows in depressions. From the other portal, Allis could see pods racing toward the sails that were already beginning to furl.

Communications began sizzling from a laser graphic device, instructions from Crossroads that were directing them to one of the pockmarks near its north axis, which was to be the *Sovereign Sun*'s berth. Milani's hands were filled with the printouts, coordinating that information with the activity of the crew members in the pods, who were bringing in the sails. Her commands were even-toned, occasionally containing a name to jar someone whose attention was not precisely where she wanted it. Practiced hands moved over the attitude controls, and finally the sailjockeys had hauled the coiled sails to stanchions under the superstructure. It was the first real activity Allis had seen on the bridge, and it had been accomplished without haste or confusion. Yet she knew that maneuvering so close to the giant space station was a critical time. She'd seen ships through the portal, first only three, then twelve, and then a dozen more came from behind like lightning bolts streaking toward the orbiting station. Drones towing freight moved slower, but it seemed as if the *Sovereign Sun* were a rowboat paddling between battleships. Allis began to understand the complexity of Watcher ships, which maneuvered at high velocities close to the station. They turned like helicopters, not at all like the deliberate and calculated long glide of the stellar sailing vessel, nor even the combustion rocket systems of Earth. When there were hundreds of ships around them, Allis grudgingly admired Milani's competence on the bridge.

With a four-month-old wad of Kleenex, Allis wiped the perspiration that suddenly formed on her brow. Any civilization with as much technology as she was witnessing had to be giant steps above the clumsy gypsy vessels. She just hoped that technological advancement went hand in hand with cultural development, and justice.

The voice of the communication console operator changed the monotony of hearing only Milani's even voice. "The Watchers say they will have their medic team ready to take blood samples from us when we dock." She seemed to be speaking for the benefit of the crew. Many looked up at Milani.

The captain nodded, and barely taking her eyes from the portal where the last of the pods were hurrying toward the hatch at the ship's axis, she said, "Tell the axis crew to keep them waiting a quarter shift before letting them in." She paused as the last pod disappeared from view, and then looked at Mordon, who was standing near Allis. "I know what they said the last time, Mordon, and I'm calling their bluff. If they don't understand the sovereignty of a sailing vessel, I shall have to teach them. They'll come on board with their bloodletting kits when I please to allow them on board, and if they dare threaten to refuse us berth and maintenance, I'll claim breach of the Magnanimous Agreement."

Milani took three steps to the communication console. By the shape she traced in the labyrinth connector board, Allis knew she'd contacted the axis. Milani hesitated, apparently distracted again by a subliminal thought. Then she said, "Yes, Droganie. The indicators here show that all the sail mortices and tenons are engaged and operating, but if you've any doubt, go back out and check. I don't want one of those things coming loose when we dock." She crossed her arms and watched the array of colored lights on the consoles. "No telling what kind of diseases the station population has picked up since we've been here last. I'll let them have our blood samples and I'll permit the injections, but I won't pay them dust for it. It's for their protection as much as ours."

Allis saw Mordon grin with satisfaction, and she stepped away from him. Listening to Milani responding to people's subliminal questions unsettled her. Like hearing half a phone call, she had to fill in the pauses. It wasn't difficult to determine that Milani's attitude toward the Watchers was as belligerent as her crew's. Allis had hoped that Ghyaspur had exaggerated, and that all the hatred toward the Watchers was just something to grumble about. With all her heart, Allis wanted a smooth docking and an uneventful debarkation. And now, knowing the Watcher doctors were coming on board to check the crew, she also hoped for a moment of privacy with one of them to explain her plight.

The warning bells sounded, and Allis realized they were about to dock. Automatically she reached for a stanchion, found Mordon's hand already there, and moved to another. The *Sovereign Sun* inched into a blue pit near the pole of the globular station's axis. The handhold barely was necessary; the ship settled as gently as a crystal goblet being placed on a shelf. Lights flooded the docking area as the top of the pit was sealed against the vacuum of space.

The *Sovereign Sun*'s rotational spin continued, and now there was a new motion to contend with. As the Crossroads station rotated on its axis, it carried the sailing vessel's berth along in a minor circle. Precession pulled slightly to her right, and that direction of pull would change as they continued along. Allis held tightly to the stanchion.

The midshift ended moments after docking, and the relief crew began coming onto the bridge to tackle the job of battening down the ship. It was customary, Allis knew, for her and Mordon to wait until Jincala was replaced at the sunwatch screen. But since they were inside the huge orbiting station, the sunwatch was useless, and she was eager to leave. Mordon stood fast until Ghyaspur arrived. Jincala, waiting patiently, saw him and smiled.

"How did it go?" Ghyaspur whispered as the rest of the replacement crew members took their places.

"All right, I suppose," Allis said, glancing at Mordon. He'd not said a word about her performance, and he didn't now. His small face was stolid, as if he hadn't heard Ghyaspur's question, nor Allis's answer.

Ghyaspur caught a warning glance from Milani; he was the only one not in his place. He hurried to the sunwatch console and sat down beside Jincala. When he'd arranged his webs, Jincala arose, prepared to leave.

Allis turned to walk out the hatch when Milani called out, "Wait, Allis." Allis turned to see the captain standing with her arms crossed. "Mordon will escort you to your cabin." And to Mordon she said, "Seal the isolation hatch."

The isolation hatches, built into every cabin on the ship, sealed from the corridor, were a vestige from early times in the stellar sailing vessels' history. Allis realized immediately that she was to be confined to her cabin while the Watchers were on board.

"You seem shocked," Milani said, her amber eyes glinting.

Ghyaspur did too, but he didn't say anything. Allis moved closer to the hatch, but Jincala had stopped there, blocking the hatch, and was watching them curiously.

"I've done nothing to deserve confinement," Allis said.

"What kind of fool do you take me for, Allis? I don't know for certain what's going on in your head, but I can guess. I won't take a chance on the Watchers' learning you're here. I can't trust you to pass yourself off as one of the crew."

"Sure you can," Allis said uneasily. *Move, Jincala*, she thought furiously. She looked back at the captain. "I'm a good actress."

"So we've noticed," Milani said dryly. "Who is the real Allis? The self-centered belligerent who took a free ride the first ninety shifts? Or the willing worker you've become since we left the gravity slip?"

"Surely you understand about that, Milani. I had to try to get you to take me home, but it hardly matters now. Home isn't the place it used to be. I can't go back now, not really. The times will have changed. Home is behind me now." Allis didn't need a stone to tell her that Milani didn't believe her.

Miraculously, Jincala stepped through the hatch, having become bored. Allis leaped after her, blindly wondering if she could reach the exits at the axis before anyone caught her. But the hatch sliced shut in her face, closed remotely by one of the quick-thinking crew members at the consoles. Allis whirled to face Milani, infuriated by her entrapment.

"Allis, stop!" she heard Ghyaspur shout. "Go with Mordon peacefully."

"Sound advice," Milani said. "If you cause any more disruption on this bridge, I'll leave you in confinement until our next port of call."

"You'd love that," Allis said bitterly. She saw Mordon pulling a bola from his baggy trousers, and as he reached for her, Allis shied. "Keep your stinking hands off me!"

Mordon's thick brows lifted in mock surprise. "So you do understand what it's like. Go through that hatch and walk steady, and I won't touch you. I'd not like it any more than you."

Grimly, Allis nodded, knowing that if she tried to run, the bola would catch her as surely as the one Ghyaspur had thrown around her back on Earth. She didn't trust Mordon to be as considerate about loosening the tendrils as Ghyaspur had been. The hatch opened without her or Mordon's touching the control, and Allis dropped through to the corridor with the bola-armed mate close behind.

Jincala was still in the corridor, happily counting gold pieces into her pocket. "I'm going marketing," she said. "I'm going to get a new storybox and perfume. Milani said I could get a storybox and perfume."

"That's fine," Mordon said kindly, but his attention was not on the mongoloid for even a second. His beady eyes were on Allis, waiting to take in one untoward move, and his bola was ready to counteract.

"Jincala, I can't go marketing. Will you get me something at the market?" Allis said.

"You have to give me coins," Jincala said suspiciously.

"Milani will give them to you," Allis said. Jincala nodded eagerly, indicating that she'd do as Allis asked. "Get me some poison."

"What?"

"Poison," Allis repeated firmly.

"Move on," Mordon said threateningly to Allis. And to Jincala, he said, "It's only a joke. Forget about it."

CHAPTER 8

Crossroads was a bustling airdock for the myriad ships cruising to and from the gravity slips, a shipyard where major repairs and complete renovations were made, a manufacturing center that consumed raw goods from one set of solar systems and processed them into products for another, and it was a way station for passengers and freight. Most of all, Crossroads was prized for its marketplace.

Stopover passengers, tourists, and crews on leave were conveyed from the ships that were docked at the poles to the equator of the station where the effects of rotational spin were comfortable to the human inner ear. There a swath of structures rose at right angles to the axis and visitors could walk easily along the equatorial footpaths. They found lodging in crystalline hospices or signed up at chummery lodges that dotted the less desirable industrial district up the inside walls of the globe, near the docks.

They walked through the marketplace, looking through walls glazed only by energized sound-absorbing membranes to see into the slim come-on fronts of breweries, dealers in exotic artifacts and priceless Quondam Being relics, spice emporiums, chapels, haberdasheries, performing-arts vendors, and eateries, often entering to browse or buy. The various human races in the Galactic Trade Pact were well represented in Crossroads, in passengers and crew, in wares-hawkers, and even reflected in the plastic faces of robots. The distinctive flat disk of Watcher faces was numerous.

Occasionally visitors to Crossroads passed structures that did not have open fronts, not even a door or hatch of any kind. These smooth-walled citadels were Watcher establishments, extravagantly built from re-formed ultraloy and prestressed similoy, which was lighter in color and weaker than true ultraloy, but which was as close to the real thing that anyone could produce. The Watcher buildings soared through puffs of clouds to the gravityless axis, sparkling blue towers converging on a maze of pneumatic chutes that moved Watchers and their equipment from building to building in short, convenient runs, unhampered by the drag of rotational spin and the flux of tourists below.

There in the axis, Watcher women and children used Quondam Beings' wings, which weren't wings at all but slender harnesses that propelled the users through the air at moderate speeds. They didn't require as much skill as a little gear- and pedal-driven set of mechanical wings, and they didn't have the inherent danger of a motor-driven propeller. The wings were wonderful in the zero gravity at the axis of a huge space station like Crossroads. Watchers' gossamer garments flowed behind them like lavish trains, and their women and children played shape-making games with colorful streamers on their way to floating, glittering parks. They were perfectly safe.

Even if flyers blundered into the gravity zones, their wings would keep them from two to twenty feet above the ground, depending on the mass of the user. Not even the best-bred physicist among the Watchers

knew why the Quondam Beings' wings worked, nor
what their power source was, but the smallest child
knew how to operate them. Everyone knew that the
wings had not failed to operate, not even once. Never.
Not since the first one was found, and that discovery
was ancient history on the Watchers' homeworld. As
far as was known, only Watchers used the wings. Other
forms of air transportation were expressly forbidden
in Crossroads, which had the effect of keeping their
women and children strictly isolated from everyone
except Watcher men.

Watching the Watchers frolic among the towers was
a favorite activity of most Crossroads station visitors,
at least during their first visits. They clustered on balconies where binoculars and other optical devices
were available from concessions, and stared past the
warm, pearly light of the marketplace to the tantaliz-
ing butterflylike creatures at the rooftops. Milani had
been to Crossroads many times and had seen the
fashion of watching the Watchers from comfortable
reclining chairs come and go, depending on the
Watchers' pretensions of the era. The enforced segre-
gation in Crossroads never changed. The women and
children always remained sequestered from the curious and sometimes worshipful passengers and crews
who passed through Crossroads. But not from Milani.

Watcher thoughts, flowing from layers of admin-
istrative offices, soldiers' barracks, and from the dim
and luxurious dwellings in their tall buildings were
as exposed as the wonderment and joy from the gag-
gles of tourists on the paths. Milani had no interest
in them, except perhaps to notice that there were
more Watchers than ever, and that the swarm of
minds made the ache that was Allis less significant.

She'd hated having the earthworm on the bridge,

where she was accustomed to being open and receptive to the weakest musings. Her crew, skilled and galaxy-wise, produced a flow of useful data. Milani automatically sorted input sprouting from fantasy flashes, guilt twinges, or personal longings from input on how the sails were set and integrated telemetry with efficiency that no captain without a communicator-stone could match. Having Allis close created a numb place that was more distracting than a festering wound. It was good to be in Crossroads, where the fresh input all but overwhelmed the ache. She gave over the place in her mind usually reserved for herself to the onslaught.

Milani hurried past the gawking tourists into a cloistered gangway. Only a few turned to look at her mane of hair, for most were engrossed with the flying Watchers. Passersby avoided the prominently marked air-car track painted on the path where she and Daneth once had walked. She took it to mean that her destination was more popular now. She'd seen that happen before, too. Her long stride took her quickly to a boarding area where she climbed into a waiting car. It whisked her under viaducts, away from Crossroads' equator to a vicinity with low gravity, like the ship.

The bar had been enlarged by the present owners, and attractive conversation pits had been installed with drink dispensers built into the tables. Milani had seen the bar with automat service before, but she'd never seen it so full of people. Either the long-standing preference for human attendants had finally given way, or there were no longer any alternatives in Crossroads. Though the clientele had grown, it had not changed. Watcher insignia, blazoned on the tunics and coveralls of many races of outworlders, was predominant, with splashes of color from innerworlds and the casual-looking togs of stellar sailors livening the scene. Watchers were likely to be wearing any style of clothing that took their fancy, as long as it was made of rare or precious fabric and met their current standard of modesty. Even so, they were easily distinguished from the regular clientele of stevedores and space sojourners by their headgear, no matter how cleverly fashioned to match their costumes. Several turbaned Watchers, all males of course, were present, probably conducting business with people they didn't care to invite to the public rooms of their homes.

The air was thick with the perfumes of intoxicating gases, thoughtfully provided by the management in individual-sized tanks as lavishly as the tankards of ale and globes of gelled wine. Numerous sound-absorbing membranes kept the noise down to a hushed murmur. Milani saw a few of her own crew members already settled down in conversation pits with sailors from other ships. Because of the time dilation of space travel through the gravity slips and the far-ranging habits of the gypsies, seeing familiar faces was becoming uncommon. Milani looked anyhow.

In recent time, more stellar sailing vessels had been squeezed out of their established trade routes in the postern reaches by swifter and larger ion drive ships as the Watchers' influence continued to grow. Such encroachment had forced Daneth's old ship, the *Migrant Sun,* from an outer loop of gravity slips and later Milani's own *Sovereign Sun* to find entirely new places to trade. The only good trading the *Sovereign Sun* had found was on the restricted planets halfway along the spiral arm of the galaxy, worlds closed to them by Watcher law until the natives developed reliable interplanetary travel. Many never would, lacking raw materials with which to support adequate technology, and some simply weren't interested. A few verged on the technology that would be their ticket to joining the Watchers' Galactic Trade Pact, and they were intensely observed by Watcher ambassadors.

The *Sovereign Sun* traded on many restricted worlds now, dealing mainly in staples like diamonds and uranium, and a little in primitive art forms like paintings, jewelry, and carvings. She supposed that other gypsy ships were doing likewise, though last time she'd been in Crossroads *Sovereign Sun* had been the only stellar sailing vessel in port. There'd been no opportunity to exchange information with other gypsies, and no chance to pick up new crew members either. This time there were two other gypsy ships in port, and Milani hoped for a good stopover.

An old gypsy man beckoned to her from across the crowded bar. She didn't recognize his face, but the wry neck and webbed fingers stirred her memory. She threaded her way through the narrow aisles between the pits, ignoring curious stares from spacers who'd heard of but never before seen a gypsy, until she was near the old man. She hesitated, feeling a convivial touch that somehow felt familiar.

"Come in, come in," the wry-necked man urged. He was drunk on gasses and ale, but that merely slurred what was a genuine smile of affection. From his mind, Milani could tell that he knew her, and he was not so drunk that he didn't remember exactly when and how well. In fact, she received the distinct impression that he was less drunk than his swaying torso would indicate.

—Hello, Milani,—he said, reeling from remembered feelings. —Time's played us a dirty trick, eh?— He quaffed half the tank of cinnamon-smelling gas before him, pinching with drunken care the end of the straw before too much gas escaped. The small glimpse he'd allowed of his mind was enough for Milani to remember a boy she'd known named Filoy, misshapen by genetic disaster, but whose heart and mind were sweet to a new and lonely stone-carrier. He was old now, his face deeply lined and his light hair dry and wispy. But his eyes seemed rheumy only from spilled gas, not age. Milani felt a twinge of regret and sadness, and it took her a moment to realize it was her own.

Beside Filoy was a strong-looking woman wearing a captain's tangram in her earlobe. She was younger than Milani, and a relative of Filoy's, judging by her webbed fingers curled tightly around a tankard of ale. Milani saw the unmistakable glitter of another tangram-bearing ring on the finger of the sailor sitting across from Filoy and his captain.

"Do you know my grandfather?" the web-fingered captain said, gesturing for Milani to sit.

Milani nodded and sat down. Suddenly she was oddly uncomfortable, aware of someone's boiling anger. It was not Filoy's, for he was reminiscing pleasantly, the sharp edges of memory blunted by gas and time. His granddaughter was mildly curious about when this handsome captain with the strange but becoming shock of hair had known her grandfather, and under what circumstances. At this close proximity, it left the still unknown sailor to be the angry one.

"I'm Milani, of *Sovereign Sun*," she said.

"Just like you to identify yourself that way." Filoy shook his head. "This," he said in a magnanimous tone, "is Milani the stone-carrier."

"Of course," the woman said, her face lighting up. "The woman in the stories, the one you nearly changed ships to be with. Hello, Milani. I'm Anara of *Bright Sun*." Anara laughed nervously, giving a shake to her blond hair. She'd never met a stone-carrier before, and had only her grandfather's tales of bewitchment to inform her behavior. Still, she was intrigued. Belatedly she remembered the other gypsy captain. "Oh, yes," she said, gesturing to the man sitting across from her. "This is Dacko from *Dowager Sun*."

When Milani looked at the handsome sailor called Dacko, she realized that anger was as much a part of him as the crisp blue irises of his eyes. He wasn't particularly aware of his anger, for he was trying to quell an overwhelming terror that Anara would ignore him with Milani's arrival. Conversely, he was completely certain both Anara and Milani would be his lackeys, and he thought he might use them sexually, perhaps simultaneously. As Milani stared in amazement, he raised a bulb of gelled wine in salute. There was a dead communicator-stone, set in a gold filigreed ring, which he wore beside his captain's signet ring.

"Where did you get that?" she asked.

"What?" he said, puzzled. "Oh, the stone. I took it off the body of a dead colonist in a twin sun system in the outer arm after some local war we wandered in on."

"Not space likely!" Milani said. He'd presented a complete fabrication. Stone-carriers were valued among all the races and rarely put in exposed positions even though they were almost impossible to surprise. An honest explanation of the stone's origin would have been accompanied by vague images of the incident. Yet Milani did not detect a conscious effort to hide the stone's true origin; he'd cut that

off somehow. Now he was furious that she'd in-
sinuated he was a liar; his indignation was as real as
if her accusation were unjust. Milani was accustomed
to the oddness of thoughts that sometimes surfaced,
especially in new acquaintances, who sometimes felt
threatened by stone-carriers. But there was something
bizarre about Dacko's thought patterns that random
musing couldn't explain.

"Still not the most tactful person, eh, Milani?" Filoy
said, his words hurting her until she realized he was
warning her to beware of Dacko. —Something bad
here,—he said when he finally remembered to or-
ganize his thoughts for subliminal communication.
—His crew's a pack of cowards who won't say where
they've been nor what they've seen. A couple of cut-
throats and landlubber demons with him, too.—

Anara put her bare elbows on the table. "There's
a Watcher making his way toward us. The one you
were talking to earlier," she mumbled through her
hand as she lifted her eyes to Dacko.

Dacko smiled thinly and leaned back, as if relaxing.
"It's about time," he said, his mind already far from
the question of the dead stone and anticipating some
triumph over the approaching Watcher.

"Whatever he wants, it must not be legal," Filoy
said, nervously glancing at the Watcher. "You ever
had a Watcher come to you before?"

"Only for blood," Milani said, feeling as suspicious
as Filoy.

The Watcher didn't wait for an invitation to join
them. He sat down next to Milani. He was typical
of the race, compact and muscular with strong slender
fingers that were probably as nimble as they looked
when they weren't laden down with the thick, gem-
studded rings he wore. His neck rivaled Filoy's in

length, but it was perfectly straight and sturdy. The silken turban concealed his hair and ears, and probably his brain-warming wires and communication devices as well. His nose looked like a brown nut in the middle of a plate of baked clay, which was otherwise so symmetrical that his features seemed cast rather than real. The eyes, however, shone like two drops of light, and captured the attention of the small group in seconds.

"I am The Maker of Light," the Watcher said in a quiet baritone.

"I know who you are," Dacko said, his relaxed appearance unchanged. Only Milani knew he was charged with energy, his muscles taut. "I haven't changed my mind about the fee. Seventy ingots of sailcloth silver and twenty of ultraloy for shrouds. Not an ingot less, or I don't take your consignment."

Amusement flashed over the Watcher's eyes. "Is he asking a fair price, Milani?"

"That depends on the cargo and destination," Milani said, feeling uncomfortable. The Watcher was playing with Dacko and had no idea how volatile his toy was.

"You know both by now, is that not so?" The Watcher smiled beatifically.

The Maker of Light had been informed of her impending arrival the moment *Sovereign Sun* had coasted out of the gravity slip. He'd never met her, for he'd been a child in the crèche during her last visit to Crossroads, but he knew she was a stone-carrier, knew her blood type, what diseases she was naturally resistant to, and which ones she was not. He had a personality profile on her compiled by his ancestors and stored in his family's computer. She was precisely the person with whom he wished to deal, and he was willing to pay the penalty of her knowing his innermost secrets to accomplish it.

She wondered what he'd think if he realized how loath she was to know his mind. She was not impressed by the number of females in his household nor with the lavish attention they gave to him. All the females were simpletons, their normal wits altered and suppressed when they were fetuses in glassine wombs. It did not raise Milani's opinion of him to know that the only intelligent Watchers were males. His strength of will did not strike her favorably either, for he wasn't likely to use it for anyone's benefit except his own.

"Dacko should have asked a higher fee to accomplish what you have in mind," Milani said carefully.

Immediately Dacko leaned forward, his eyes impaling Milani. "I'll do my own negotiating," he said sharply. With the same intensity he turned to the Watcher. "The hotwelders have finished installing my new core. I can jump for any gravity slip you specify before the next shift is finished."

"Stellar sailing ships don't 'jump'," The Maker of Light said disparagingly. "They make their way like worms."

Dacko was unruffled now that he had the Watcher's attention again. "Perhaps, but their captains don't question the contents of the shipping canisters, nor refuse any destination that's downwind of the slips. It has to be a restricted planet or you wouldn't have considered a stellar sailing vessel to carry your cargo." Dacko leaned back again, smiling confidently. "Milani's just arrived. Her shakedown probably hasn't even begun. Anara's *Bright Sun* will be down for thirty more shifts. Only *Dowager Sun* is ready to go."

Anara sat back, accepting Dacko's exclusion without protest. Until now she'd been hoping for an opportunity to bid on the run, too, but if time was of the essence, she couldn't take this cargo. She didn't think Milani could either, for ordinarily the gypsy ships didn't come to Crossroads until they needed major repairs, which meant long layovers.

But *Sovereign Sun* didn't need major repairs. Crossroads had been one of two convenient jumps they could have made from Earth. Since *Sovereign Sun* crew members had been making shuttle trips to restricted planets, they'd consumed cold jet fuel more quickly than they would had they been dealing in the open ports where regular freighters shuttled cargo from parking orbits to the planets.

The Maker of Light had made the connection between the lack of fuel and illicit runs, despite the official report that they'd blown a few tanks in deep space. He also had accurate estimates of how long *Sovereign Sun* would need to be in the highbay to have the nuclear generator's cooling system checked. Milani was pleased to learn the job was already nearing completion, and to Droganie's satisfaction, too. Finally Milani realized she had a reputation with The Maker of Light's ancestors for delivering goods safely, albeit slowly when compared to the ion-drive commercial freighters, which he could not use due to the nature of the shipment.

"If I were Dacko," Milani said, "I'm not sure I'd touch that cargo at any price."

"You're not me," Dacko said, scowling as he realized that she was speaking to the Watcher's thoughts. He was angry at being excluded again, terrified that he might be forgotten even as he sat in their midst. "I've a cargo of my own that I can peddle anywhere in the system. I can afford to move out cheaply. My offer still stands, Maker of Light. Seventy and twenty."

He'd deliberately dropped the article before the Watcher's appellation, transforming it from a title to a name. Silently, Milani approved, but the Watcher was far too arrogant even to detect the insult.

The Maker of Light was not interested in Dacko's offer; he hadn't been since *Sovereign Sun* became available. He wanted Milani to take the shipment and he would pay her handsomely to do it. The question in his mind was not how much her fee would be but whether she would do it. Stellar sailors had an aversion to carrying mining equipment to the restricted worlds where it would be used by Watchers to unearth Quondam Being ruins, the deep, rich ruins that the natives did not have the technology to reach. He hoped it would make a difference to Milani that while The Maker of Light was honorbound to deliver the equipment to his brother, who was a restricted planet ambassador, he wanted the equipment delivered damaged, preferably so cleverly sabotaged that it would work for a short time. He was jealous of his brother's careful breeding, of the splendid nurturing he had received, and especially envious of the marvelous opportunities his genetic profile and care had resulted in.

The Maker of Light had been bred to fill a clerking slot in the family's holdings in Crossroads. He'd already risen beyond his intended role to computer master, but that accomplishment had not been enough to offset his brother's magnificent breeding when it had come time to select an ambassador for a new planet that was rife with Quondam Being ruins. Milani was becoming interested. Droganie and Mordon could successfully sabotage the equipment, which would ease Milani's conscience about carrying rape machines to a new world. It might even give her an opportunity to warn the inhabitants about Watcher tactics, if they had not already caught on.

She was aware that Dacko still believed the Watcher was mulling over his offer, certain that Milani's hints at a higher price had eliminated her from the competition. And The Maker of Light, despite his keen interest in settling the bargain with Milani, was enjoying Dacko's appearance of confidence, savoring the moment of revelation with great anticipation. He was also feeling confident, certain that he did not need to keep Dacko in reserve any longer. He had great faith in his computer's analysis of Milani's reaction to his offer, which included enough self-serving possibilities for her to make it attractive in addition to any fee.

"I would want industrial quality diamonds in payment," Milani said, finally. "Twenty thousand carats, synthetic or natural."

The Watcher was surprised. He'd expected to pay in silver sailcloth or ultraloy ingots, both of which were easily available to him. "I'm not sure," he said, angrily aware that even as resources for the diamonds came to his mind they came to Milani's as well.

"Just spacing wait!" Dacko said, his eyes flashing dangerously. "That's my cargo."

The Maker of Light could no longer resist. He agreed subliminally to Milani's demand for diamonds just as soon as his mental computations assured him he could produce the sum before the *Sovereign Sun* left. He didn't even bother to wonder why she wanted diamonds instead of ingots, which suited Milani just fine. He turned on Dacko and spoke in a tone that one might use with a petulant child. "When I have business with you I shall summon you. In the meantime, don't hound me."

Dacko's mind sizzled from insult and rage. He hated the Watcher's authority, his position of power, which didn't seem much different to him than the power Milani's stone represented. He put down his tankard of ale with deliberate calm, wiping some of the foam that had slopped over the rim with his ringed finger. "I don't need orts from Watchers or stone-carriers," he said, his spine stiffening. Milani knew it was not from false pride, which The Maker of Light was silently laughing at. Dacko's pride was real. "I know what went on," the captain said. "If I had a stone-carrier, I'd have had the cargo just as easily."

"What an odd way to put it," Milani said. "Not, 'if I *were* a stone-carrier,' but 'if I *had* a stone-carrier.' Wouldn't the last one cooperate?" She stared pointedly at the dead stone on his finger.

Dacko's eyes were stern and quiet, but he noticed the Watcher's sudden renewed interest. He seized that mote of satisfaction, dwelled on it until it engrossed his entire awareness. "I took it off a dead colonist," he said, blithely smiling. Again the cutoff about origin, his mind merely reveling in the Watcher's envious stare, and quivering with excitement at matching wits with a stone-carrier. Beneath was the pervasive anger, so much a part of him that Milani shuddered involuntarily and fell silent. Impudently, Dacko flashed the ring.

"How much for the ring?" The Maker of Light asked, and nearly bit his tongue when he saw Dacko's smile broaden.

Dacko casually reached into his pocket, pulled out a tiny gem and carelessly rolled it into the pay slot at the center of the table. "A round on me," he announced standing. "As for you," he said to the Watcher, "when I have business with you, I'll send for you." Grinning triumphantly, he spun around and left the conversation pit.

Milani watched him go, feeling confused. He was firmly convinced that he was a totally independent human being, not needing or wanting people in his own social order nor any from outside of it. Yet, he was not like rugged individualists Milani had encountered before, for Dacko also believed there was nothing that could seriously hamper his progress, no challenge too big for him to overcome. No matter to him that he'd just lost a good-paying transport job. The contradictions in his mind were endless, yet he willfully chose each of them. She was amazed at his self-confidence.

The Maker of Light was also making ready to leave. "Your payment will be delivered to your ship as soon as you request clearance from Corridor Control," he said to Milani. "Loading has already begun." He was still miffed that Dacko had gotten in the final word, and she knew that he wanted the dead stone on Dacko's ring. She suspected that if Dacko weren't careful, he might meet with some accident that would somehow part him from his finger, or at least the ring, before he left Crossroads. Then The Maker of Light, too, was gone.

"Whew," Anara said, running her fingers over her hair. "I'm glad they left." She was young and slightly intimidated by Dacko's display of temper and the Watcher's arrogance. And she, Milani thought bitterly, was all too typical of many gypsies, sheltered in smooth-running ships from the realities of the Watchers' tyranny and too distant from her own origins to give them any more thought than she usually gave her grandfather's embroidered tales about bewitching stone-carriers.

"Were you done with them?" Filoy said to Milani, not so drunk that he hadn't known Milani was deeply involved with both men through her stone.

"As close as I'd ever be," Milani replied. "Psyching people has never been my strong point." She sucked in her breath, almost surprised that she'd admitted her inadequacies aloud.

Filoy nodded, accepting her limitations as he always had and with no regrets. "I'll bet you're grand on the bridge. One like Dacko would never see the value in that."

Milani shrugged. Anara looked at her grandfather suspiciously. "You're not very drunk, are you?"

"Not very," he admitted. "Dacko didn't get anything from me, if that's what you're worried about. But I didn't get much from him either. Close-mouthed, that one. Is that the new way, Milani? We've been far-ranging." He easily fell back into the habit of filling in his spoken words with a flood of subliminal information. He briefly described *Bright Sun*'s voyages in the time-consuming outer loops of gravity slips, profitable ones when he was young. And then, like so many other stellar sailing vessels, he described the rapid impingement of their trade by Watcher ships, until the inner loop of slips was the only place left to go.

Milani shook her head. "If sailors don't help each other against the Watchers, we're lost. I think most sailors are trading on the restricted worlds."

Filoy and Anara exchanged glances while they tried to suppress unbidden thoughts about *Bright Sun's* first exploits on a restricted planet. Milani laughed. Alarmed, Anara watched Milani, distrusting her.

Milani's laughter faded and she sipped her ale uncomfortably. Should she speak to the distrust in Filoy's granddaughter, or would the young captain be more receptive to Milani if she pretended not to notice? She was predisposed to like Anara because she had fond memories of Filoy, and she wanted his kin to think well of her. But Milani didn't know how to proceed. It always was so much easier to confront someone she didn't like, for she risked little in doing that. She couldn't help thinking bitterly that it was times like this that Daneth's skill as a stone-carrier was unsurpassed. He'd have known precisely what to say to put Anara at ease.

Filoy sighed loudly. "How is it, Milani, that I believe I know more about what goes on in your mind than you know about mine?" He shook his head. "I thought time with your stone would have changed that."

I never needed to change, Milani thought desperately, guiltily aware that no one could hear her. Space knows I've never even had to try. Daneth always was with me.

If anyone could help her sort out the hurt from the guilt, it was Filoy, who had intuitively understood the anguish of a new and overwhelmed stone-carrier. And she might have asked his help right there in the conversation pit, forsaking all pride before his granddaughter, if a shriek of pain hadn't filled Milani's mind, making her blood run cold. Jincala's thoughts were blissfully simple, even in times of stress, so there was no doubt that Allis was escaping from the *Sovereign Sun*.

Milani leaped from her place, leaving Filoy to believe that once again she was fleeing from him.

CHAPTER 9

Senda didn't know of Allis's escape until the Watcher Communication Center in Crossroads patched Milani through to the *Sovereign Sun*'s bridge. The captain had heard Jincala's terror and pain in the hub of Crossroads while the few sailors left minding the ship could not. Senda didn't waste precious time getting details from Milani; she hit the emergency alarms and ordered complete interior and exterior optics at the same time. A glance at the relayed images on the screens told her it was too late to close the hatch. Allis was already on the gantry that led from the ship's axis to the bay floor, rushing hand over hand along the framework at speeds that should have broken her limbs. Senda hoped she would, then dived for the bridge hatch and raced up to the axis.

Bracha was ahead of Senda, following Allis across the huge highbay where the *Sovereign Sun* was docked, fumbling over the unfamiliar gantry as badly as the Earthwoman. She heard his shouts ricochet off a sound deflector on her right, and then the sounds of her own movements joined the steady rasping of Allis's and Bracha's. She came abreast of Bracha just before he came to the doorway Allis had already darted through.

In the long corridor she saw Allis pulling herself hand over hand along the circuitry of moving ropes ship and dock crews used to move between equipment storage and the highbays when they were encumbered by tools or replacement parts. She ignored the exits to other bays and headed straight for the telpherway terminal. Abruptly, the corridor ended, and Senda nearly flew into the crowded terminal where passengers and crew were bussed from the dock area to the marketplace. With just a little gravity to aid her, Allis had already leaped headlong for the Watcher supervisor, who was easily distinguished by his bored, cross-armed stance from the eagerly moving people surging to the cars. The crowds impeded Allis, and she began screaming for help. A way parted for her with alarm, and people stared. When she reached the Watcher, she ducked behind him.

"They're kidnappers," she shouted, pointing an accusing finger at Senda, who came to a bouncing halt just a few feet away.

The Watcher was more annoyed than alarmed. "What is the purpose of this disruption?" he said roughly to Allis in the deep, guttural sounds of Watcher language. "Get in line and you'll be duly conveyed, just like everyone else."

"Help me," Allis demanded, breathlessly. Her eyes were wide with terror as she tried to keep the Watcher's stout body between herself and Senda. "You must help me."

"Wait your turn," the Watcher said sternly.

"I don't understand what you're saying," Allis said, first in English, then in the gypsy tongue. Getting no glimmer of understanding, she swore, apparently realizing for the first time that the Watchers had a language of their own.

"Did you really believe a Watcher would trouble himself to learn a language that only a few thousand people speak?" Senda said, trying to breathe more calmly. Allis was momentarily stunned to silence, and Senda turned to the Watcher. "She's a bit retarded," she said, reflexively touching her head to emphasize the message.

"I can see that," the Watcher said. Below the facial disk his jaw was quivering with anger. "Inbred misfits. Take her in hand and keep her in control, or I'll do it for you." He looked from Senda's white skin to Allis's eyes, crazed now with fear like a terrified animal.

"He doesn't need words to understand attempted murder," Allis said, half-sobbing as she dodged Senda's first grab for her. "I'm better off in a Watcher jail than in a gypsy ship. At least that won't jump through a gravity slip to space knows where or when!" Allis lunged at the guard, who smacked her aside like a twig before Senda could move again. Senda blinked in surprise. She didn't think anyone would be so ignorant as to move openly against an armored Watcher. Hadn't Allis noticed the power pack on his belt, or didn't she even recognize one when she saw it?

"Sorry," Senda said, quickly bending to hoist Allis up. "I'll get her out of here right away."

"Hold it. She doesn't scan," the Watcher said accusingly to Senda. He moved closer to the stunned Earthwoman so the telemetry unit now in his hand would relay Allis's image to a computer, somewhere in Crossroads. "Is she from your ship?"

"No," Senda said coldly and without hesitation. "We caught her stealing parts out of the highbay. My captain will want to question her."

"Later," the Watcher said. "She's got to go to Disease Control Center first. There's no record of her having any blood tests. She could be a carrier."

"But . . ."

"Have your captain file a formal complaint if he wants to press charges," the Watcher said, dismissing Senda with his tone.

Two more Watchers came from across the terminal, apparently summoned by surveillance devices. They were wearing masks and oxygen tanks to protect them from possible contamination. Allis was beginning to stir when the Watchers brought her to her feet. She swayed and groaned, but didn't resist when they marched her off between them. Bracha arrived in time to see them leave. When he reached into his boot for his dagger, Senda gripped his hand.

"There's time," she said quickly. "They're taking her to Disease Control Center first. The medic staff people are nothing more than breeding mistakes with no more intelligence than half their women. We can get to her there, if we must. You wait here for Milani, fill her in if she's missed anything. I'll try to stay with Allis."

Bracha nodded, and then slipped his dagger into Senda's hand before he left for his post at the incoming cars. Hiding the weapon in her sleeve, Senda followed Allis and the Watchers, her heart pounding with fear.

Watchers had little interest in gypsy sailors as individuals, except where their health was concerned. All the technological worlds had sophisticated genetic laws, which controlled the kinds of genes that could safely be reproduced. The laws made grafting of certain genes mandatory, especially ones that resisted wild carcinogens and virulent disease, which resulted in human races that were highly resistant to almost every known kind of plague. But there was always the danger of something new and exotic being introduced into their bodies by contact with explorers or gypsies.

Even so, the problem would not be with Allis's health, for she was unlikely to be carrying any disease the sailors wouldn't already have caught. The problem would be in explaining her very existence. If they continued to claim she was a thief, there'd be questions about how she got into the highbay, past the Watcher's mechanized surveillance systems, and a simple computer query would end all question of her having come from the outside. If they said she was a crew member, there'd be questions about how and why she missed the medics' bloodletting session when the *Sovereign Sun* first arrived. Senda could easily visualize a Watcher tribune making a case against Milani for attempted genocide, deliberately misinterpreting her insistence of ship's sovereignty as biological conspiracy, and all that even if Allis were completely disease-free. The Watcher tribunals were nothing to trifle with.

But Senda also knew that the probability of a Watcher medic being able to speak English or the gypsy tongue was so remote it could all but be discarded. No one was likely to be concerned about Allis at all, least of all the Watchers, if the Earthwoman would just keep her mouth shut. In that, at least, Allis was not likely to have a choice, which made Senda hopeful that she wouldn't have to use the dagger tucked into her sleeve.

She followed the Watchers into the Disease Control Center, a building near the equator with access via a pneumatic chute. They ignored her presence in the elevator down to a stronger gravity level, and she thought they'd forgotten about her in the maze of corridors until she tried to enter the laboratory with them. One stopped to bar her way.

* * *

Allis had realized there was a risk involved in attacking anyone so violently; she hardly could expect the Watcher to back off and gently ask what could have inspired a nice person like Allis to do such a thing. He must have hit her with the butt end of a gun or a lead pipe, and she supposed that was only fair. Her head ached and she felt dizzy, but it was worth the price to succeed in getting taken into custody. Senda had been able to do nothing except follow helplessly, and then Allis had been strapped into a chair in the center of a huge computer room, and then left alone. No Senda. No guards.

At least it looked like a computer room, with its banks of enameled equipment cabinets, colored lights, labyrinth control consoles, and transparent tubes of liquid coiling around humming machines. She reconsidered. The *Sovereign Sun*'s computer occupied only a double cabin. This place was twenty times that large, and even Allis knew that the more advanced the technology, the more likely that the computers were miniaturized. Yet her chair was jammed in before a labyrinth control screen that was very much like the consoles in the *Sovereign Sun*'s bridge. Perhaps police departments in Watcherland suffered from a worse lack of funding than the gypsy ship, and limped along with ancient equipment.

Her hands were free. Funny she hadn't realized that until she'd instinctively reached for the labyrinth and discovered her fingers on the cool, slick surface. A quick examination of the straps that clamped her thighs and encircled her waist told her there was no way to release them. The restraints ran from her chair through the glossy floor tiles; if there were buckles or snaps, they were underneath. Not even a contortionist could get loose. Her fingers explored the oozing lump on the side of her head. It was egg-sized and tender under a clump of matted hair, but the dizziness was already clearing up and she wasn't having any difficulty focusing her eyes. Her fingers bloodied her trousers when she put her hand back in her lap, and she could feel a warm trickle running down her neck.

The sound of a male voice, monotonous and metallic, surrounded her. Startled, Allis strained to peer over the console, and then looked around. She saw no one.

"Who's there?" she said.

Again the voice spoke, and this time Allis saw speaker nodes on the walls. She'd almost forgotten that sound could travel quite far when the atmosphere was thick enough to carry it. But the sounds hadn't made any sense. The words, if they were words, were foreign.

"I don't understand you," Allis said to the impersonal equipment while looking for something that resembled a microphone, gypsy-style or otherwise. "I speak English and I speak the gypsy tongue," Allis said, switching from one to the other.

More foreign words.

"*Parlez-vous français?*" she said hopefully. "*Habla español?*"

Foreign words droned on, even as she spoke.

Allis sighed. "If this is an interrogation, it's going to be a bit one-sided. Come out where I can see you." If the speaker would appear in person, perhaps she could convey in sign language what she couldn't with speech.

The foreign words stopped and the labyrinth screen lighted up to display two cubes, which Allis happily recognized as preliminary checkpoints like the ones used on the *Sovereign Sun*'s computer. She traced the simple straight line on the labyrinth control, which made the cubes on the screen converge into one. With another remembered pattern, she reduced the cube to a square, and then to a line, and finally to a dot, which disappeared.

A globe appeared on the screen. She'd never seen that before, but she tried the same sequence of commands. Nothing happened. It faded and was followed by a pyramid, a set of circles, triangles overlapping other triangles, leaning cylinders, and finally squares with corners cut out and the corresponding pieces on the other side of the screen. Once the dial pattern she used on board the *Sovereign Sun* to get *cheros* moved a cylinder halfway across the screen, but it wouldn't converge with the other cylinder.

"This is useless," she said in a loud, petulant voice. "I don't know how to run these things. Will someone please come out and talk to me?" She sat back and stubbornly crossed her arms, letting the subsequent geometric images run over the screen without trying to interfere.

Finally the screen went blank. The monotonous voice resumed speaking, and Allis responded at length, first in the gypsy tongue, and then in English. Eventually, she decided, someone was going to get curious and come to investigate. But no one did, and another hour passed. Her legs were numb and her head ached. In frustration she pounded on the screen.

She heard the *whoosh* of air filling space behind her and turned around as far as her restraints would allow. A man in a bright yellow cap with matching tassels walked briskly to her side. Nut-brown hands closed over her fists and firmly moved her hands off the labyrinth screen. He clucked unintelligibly.

"I know it won't break," Allis said peevishly, "but

I sure was hoping I'd knock something loose and get your attention."

His green eyes watched her quizzically from a dish-like face that looked like flawless china. His skin was so smooth that despite the cocoa-colored pigment it seemed transparent. His garments were casually draped veils, secured by a belt very much like the Watcher in the terminal had worn; it also held up a codpiece which, if it wasn't stuffed, was indecently full. He smiled at her gaze, and Allis flushed. There followed some gestures that Allis couldn't interpret. She watched him take a tiny metallic cube from a cabinet and insert it carefully in a nearby machine. Then he fussed with another labyrinth control screen, cursing liberally, she thought from the tone of his voice. Finally he faced her again, smiling proudly.

"Is this better?" he said. He'd spoken in foreign words, but the metallic voice came over the speaker nodes in plain gypsy.

"Much better," Allis said greatly relieved. The double voicing, her own and the male metallic translation, sounded comforting. "Is that a translating machine?"

He nodded. "I wasn't sure we still had one, nor that it would work. I hope you realize that it was quite a bother for me to come all the way over here to put it on line." He looked thoughtful for a moment. "Of course, once I knew your companions were gypsies and of the circumstances of your arrival in my laboratory, I decided it might be worth my trouble."

"I was beginning to think I might be tossed into a dungeon without ever seeing another human being. I'm sorry about attacking the man in the terminal. I have an explanation for that."

"Later, later," he said. "I have already arranged to have that little transgression forgiven. Before we do anything else, I want to get your vaccination in order. You have such an odd lack of immunities, which is what made me suspicious in the first place. Luckily there's no trace of virus or dangerous spores. Are your legs still numb?"

Allis nodded. "Are you a doctor?"

"You could say that," he said, laughing. "But you'd better get used to using my proper title. It's The Maker of Wonderful Bodies."

"I think I'd rather call you Doc," Allis said, but he didn't seem to hear her, for he was consulting the computer intensely. "Do you often make house calls to the jail?"

"Never." He looked up in surprise. "This is the Disease Control Center." The computer buzzed, and he frowned. "Please don't talk for a moment."

As the Watcher continued working, Allis felt slight stinging sensations along her legs. Surprised that she could feel anything at all in the numb limbs, she looked down. Rubbery leggings were growing up over her calves and thighs, and they wriggled and pinched her tense muscles before coming to a halt.

"Is this some kind of therapy for numb legs?" Allis asked, completely forgetting that he'd asked for silence.

The Maker of Wonderful Bodies didn't answer. Nor did he look up from his computer when Allis yelped with pain. She sensed what felt like knife slashes along her calves, but even her most determined efforts didn't budge the clinging leggings. They stuck like glue until the Watcher stepped away from the computer. Allis watched the leggings roll down. Her legs felt black and blue, but they were merely pink, and quite full of life again.

"There, now you won't catch anything horrible for a while," the Watcher said. He came away from his console to her chair. "How long have you been pregnant?" His green eyes studied her and with more than medical curiosity.

"About three hundred and sixty shifts," Allis replied, deliberately avoiding meeting his eyes. "I've been worried about the baby, Doc. I'd like to know if everything's all right."

"Oh, she's doing fine, considering the unsanitary environment."

"The ship seemed clean to me," Allis said. A lump formed in her throat and she looked up at him. He was staring at her breasts, but her worries about the baby were too great to irritate him by staring him down. "Or do you mean the radiation?"

"I was referring to your womb," he said, running an affectionate hand over her head. Startled, he stepped away and stared at his fingers, for a clot of blood had adhered to them. He peered at Allis's head, not attempting to touch her again. "Oh," he said with a distasteful grimace. "That looks hideous."

"It feels pretty bad, too," Allis said. "I think I might need some stitches."

The Watcher backed away from her, holding his bloodied hand as if it were injured. At the other side of the room he plunged his hand into the orifice of a nearby machine. It came out clean. He inspected it for a moment, obviously relieved to be clean again, then went back to the labyrinth control screen, making quick, sure shapes on it with his fingers. The straps fell away from Allis's waist and lap.

"Come here," he said, patting a narrow table. "I'll get you into the bone and abrasion machine and get you cleaned as well."

"In where?" Allis said suspiciously. Her legs were a little stiff from the cramped position they'd been in, but they moved all right.

"I said . . . never mind. You wouldn't understand anyhow," the Watcher said impatiently. "Come over here, right now."

The smile on his face had been replaced by a fierce expression, and his tone implied he was accustomed to immediate obedience. Allis knew her head needed medical attention, but she didn't trust the person-sized cylinder he was opening any more than she trusted *Sovereign Sun*'s programmed doctoring, and she didn't trust any doctor or maker of beautiful bodies who flinched at the sight of blood.

"Shouldn't you shave my head?" she said, hedging as he glared at her again.

"Don't be ridiculous. Your hair accounts for a good number of your beauty quotient points. Now, hurry up."

She looked back at the door, and that bit of hesitation was enough to make him lose all patience. He marched across the room, pinioned her arms as if she were a child, and carried her to the table. He was stronger than a man ten times his size ought to be; all struggling was useless. His arms, she realized, were encased in something hard, like armor. Quickly and efficiently, her body was strapped to the table and her head secured by clamps. He popped her into the tank, table and all, over a wail of protest, and just as soon as the hatch shut out the light, Allis lost consciousness.

"There, that's better," he said. He was smiling affably again, perched on the edge of the table and smoothing her hair, as if she were a child to be comforted. The ache was gone from her skull, and the straps and clamps were gone, too. She knew she must have been anesthetized, but there was no groggy aftereffect. She was wide-awake, quite refreshed.

"I'll tolerate no more nonsense from you," he said, pleasantly but sternly. "If you cooperate, you'll be happier. My household is small, but very comfortable for a man of my breeding, and with this little triumph . . ." he patted her belly, ". . . I'll get upgraded. My breeding is right for it, and recognizing you should be all that is necessary. A bigger household will be even more comfortable."

"You know who I am?" Allis said, sitting up and sliding out of reach of his hand.

"I know what you are, a good package of genes carrying another good package." His smile broadened. "I know you're here in Disease Control Center because there are no records of your ever having had vaccinations. In fact, there's no record of your being anywhere, or anyone."

"Of course not," Allis snapped. "I was kidnapped by the gypsies of the *Sovereign Sun* and brought here against my will."

The Watcher nodded happily. "I suspected something like that."

"I want asylum, and passage back home. Contact the proper authorities."

"Watch your tone," he said, frowning now.

"There must be legal provisions for cases such as mine," she said, beginning to feel desperate.

"Indeed, there are. Idiots become wards of just about anyone who will take responsibility for them.

In this case, I am willing to assume that responsibility."

"I'm not an idiot," Allis said, wondering if the machine was translating the conversation correctly.

"The file the computer began on you the moment you entered this room says that you are mentally incompetent. You failed the intelligence test, and lost any rights you might have had to a tribunal hearing."

"What intelligence test?"

The Watcher leaned over to touch the labyrinth at the side of the table. Cubes, globes, and pyramids flashed briefly on the screen.

"That wasn't fair," Allis said. "I didn't understand the instructions and I don't know how to operate a computer."

He smiled a smile she didn't like. "A certain sign of idiocy."

"You know better. You've been talking to me long enough to know that I'm not simple-minded."

"Obviously you're bright enough to realize that what I'm doing is not completely legal, but you probably don't have wit enough to know that you're going to be happier than you've ever been, if you cooperate with me. If you attempt any of the alternatives that must be occurring to you, I will punish you severely. Now, be reasonable." He reached for her ankle and pulled her along the slick table until they were nearly nose to nose. "If I'm happy, you'll be happy. I don't want to destroy your spunk, but I can't have you misusing it either. I don't want to reduce you into another Petalthighs, so behave."

"Who is Petalthighs?" Allis said, feeling sullen and afraid.

She could feel his breath on her cheek when he unexpectedly stood up and sighed, "A female bred for me, and she was sweet, even if too dull. But I put her down awhile ago, when her vagina lost elasticity."

Allis's mouth dropped open. "Her va . . . hey, look. You don't want me, Doc," she said, swinging off the other side of the table. "I'm already set in my ways, and pregnant besides."

"The fetus is what makes you so attractive. Not that it helps your waistline at all. It's a shame I didn't get you a hundred shifts ago, but we'll get it transferred into a controlled womb just as quickly as I can arrange it."

"No," Allis said, feeling her blood run cold. He seemed so confident, so certain. "No plastic delivery for my baby."

"It's going to be even lovelier than you, and it's not too late to make the proper adjustments on her."

"Adjustments?"

"One full-intelligence female in a household is quite enough to deal with," he said, half-amused. "I'll plan her as a lover, have her sucking on my—"

"Stop it," Allis shouted. "You're crazy. Civilized people don't . . . adjust perfectly healthy babies to . . ." Words failed her. She had a vivid image of a curly haired cherub toddling toward The Maker of Wonderful Bodies, his codpiece open instead of his arms. "You won't do anything to my child. I won't let you." Trying not to look frantic, she edged toward the door.

"Don't be foolish, Ebonyhair. She'll love it, and so will you. I'm saving you from your ruffian captors and giving you a life of luxury besides. I'm not going to be a medic all my life; I've been bred for much better tasks."

"They bred a pervert and a criminal."

He shrugged. "There's no one to help you except me. You're an idiot at best, and a nonentity in addition. You must realize that I've planned this very thoroughly, even if quickly. Such abilities for quick action run strongly in my line. Opportunities like this do not present themselves very often, and I have to face facts. With my breeding I would only be given another Petalthighs, pleasant to look at and very accommodating, but not a very stimulating companion. My genetic makeup is rather high-strung, you see. Not much shows on the surface, but deep inside they know I'm always tingling. So they give me soothing females like Petalthighs."

"They, meaning the better-bred Watchers?" Allis said, summoning as much visible contempt as she could.

"It's kinder to say different, but I'm tired of kindness. Your honesty will be refreshing," he said, looking satisfied. "Don't bother trying to reach that door. It won't open. We're leaving the other way." His head jerked to indicate the far end of the room.

He let her try to open the door, and didn't interfere when she pounded on it and shouted for help. Evading him was useless, too, for when he tired of watching her attempts to find a way out, he grabbed her with ease, one-handedly forcing her to walk with him. Kicks glanced off his shins, hurting only her toes. It was as if he were made of steel. Half-dragging her, he took her out of the laboratory into an antechamber. To Allis's immense relief, Senda and Milani were standing there, barring the way to the outer door with their bodies. The Watcher seemed startled.

Senda was ready, alerted by Milani that the Watcher had finally tired of toying with the Earthwoman and was coming through the door. Milani'd had enough warning from the Watcher's musings to have time to get around the building to the other door, where the man wouldn't expect Senda to be waiting. Allis looked badly frightened.

"Unhand my crewmember," Milani said coldly to the Watcher. She had her hand on a bulge in her pocket, which only Senda knew was nothing more than a torque wrench.

"You must be the gypsy captain," the Watcher said, recovering his composure. "I know the true reason behind this person's presence in Crossroads, and if you know what's good for you, gypsy blight, you'll move aside and forget you ever saw her. The penalty for kidnapping from the restricted planets is very severe."

Senda left handling the Watcher to the stone-carrier, and turned her attention to Allis. "Did you tell him about the stone," she said in English.

"He gave me some kind of test, a totally unfair one. He said that as an idiot I have no rights and that I'm in his custody. Senda, help me," she implored.

"A clever trick," Milani said to Allis before Senda could speak again. "He has me properly figured out, too. He'll have me up on kidnapping charges if I attempt to interfere. As long as you haven't told him about the stone . . ." She cocked her head thoughtfully at the Watcher. "No, you haven't. He couldn't hide it that well. I may have to let him have his way. I assume you will tell him, and you may escape the horrors of his boudoir by doing it. He can't afford to keep a stone-carrier locked up in his rooms, no matter how deep his lust. But I should be gone before you get close enough to another translator to do that."

"They'll surely catch you," Allis said. "Your ship's not as fast as theirs."

"Maybe," Milani said.

"Milani, stop this madness," Senda said. Milani was deliberately using English, apparently confident that she had the Watcher in hand already. Senda thought he looked terribly impatient.

"They'll search the galaxy if they have to to get that stone," Allis said warningly.

"All right, you've had your final words," the Watcher said, starting to drag Allis along.

"Milani, for God's sake, help me!" Allis implored. "I don't want to tell them about the stone, but I will, and they'll come after you."

"Unfortunately you're right," she muttered in gypsy. And finally she turned to the Watcher again, and said in his language, "This person is my crew member. I demand that you allow me to take her back to the ship."

"You can take it to court, if you dare. That's your privilege. But you can't claim her as a crew member; the computer has thoroughly checked and eliminated that possibility. She's officially registered as an idiot, and consigned to my custody."

"Before you do something you're certain to regret, you'd better check your plans with The Maker of Light," Milani said.

"He's my cousin, sure to be pleased for me," the Watcher said, glancing at the bulge in Milani's pocket again. He was probably finally realizing that she wouldn't use a weapon on a Watcher in one of their own buildings, and seemed tempted to shove the captain aside.

Before he could, Milani moved. "Since you're so certain, go ahead. I'll take my pleasure from witnessing your delivery of her to my ship, runneling the ropes like a common dockhand, for that's exactly what will happen after I've called The Maker of Light and told him what you've done." *Careful now,* was the signal shaped in the fingers of Milani's left hand.

"What are they saying?" Allis said conspiratorily to Senda.

"Be quiet," Senda said too harshly. She had no idea if Milani's bluff would work, and the continued warning in the twist of Milani's fingers told Senda that the captain didn't know either, despite her having the Watcher's thoughts. Milani's tawny eyes narrowed at the Watcher and her fingers twisted to a new shape.

Senda felt her mouth go dry. She hadn't seen that sign's shape for half a lifetime, and she'd never seen· Milani use it before. It was from the old ship, from times light years gone. Yet the captain's clenched hand crushed all time as surely as it crushed time for Allis. Senda was breathless from the sight of the sign, from the horror that she was yet again to lose someone she loved, from the imminent danger. What of the consequences of doing murder in a Watcher chamber and before a witness a Watcher tribunal would consider unimpeachable? This could not be. Milani was too young even to know the sign she was giving. Senda tried to breathe, tried to see through eyes that refused to focus on the deadly sign; she had to be sure . . .

"All right," she heard the Watcher say. "There's a communication console. Call my esteemed cousin, if you even know the right pattern," he added with a sneer.

Senda blinked and her heart leaped, beating now as if to catch up with time. She knew Milani could carry the bluff one more step; the foolish Watcher could not help but have recalled the pattern to use on the labyrinth control face, and Milani would know it now. Senda opened her eyes; the death sign was gone. *Careful now,* her captain's fingers said, cool and steady as the tawny eyes. Had Senda really seen the fingers in that other configuration? From the look of Milani as she walked so smoothly to the console and patterned-up a Watcher's image, it seemed to Senda they'd always said, *Careful now*.

Still, it was not over. Senda knew about the consignment from The Maker of Light, and common sense told her they'd deliver illicit goods, even if she did not yet know what kind nor why Milani had agreed to haul them. But she didn't believe one Watcher would interfere with another's bedroom toys. Now she turned away from her captain and the screen to see if the bluff had worked, hoping the Watcher would ask Milani to cancel her call, that it was not necessary, that he was not really interested in Allis. But more than anything, Senda looked at the Watcher so that she could not see her captain's hand.

"Ready so soon?" the Watcher on the screen said.

"Nearly, but it seems that one of your relatives has taken custody of a member of my crew. I can't leave without her."

Still handling Allis roughly, the other Watcher approached the screen. He spoke rapidly and frankly, interspersing his explanation with mocking laughter.

"I see no reason to interfere, Milani," the Watcher on the screen finally said. "Unless, of course . . . are you with me, Milani?"

The captain stood for a moment, and Senda recognized her concentration on some subliminals. "Yes," she said after a pensive silence. "Yes."

"Very good. And now," he said, his gleaming eyes moving from one side of the screen to the other, "my dear cousin, you must relinquish your claim to this creature with haste."

"I have my rights," he said.

"I was thinking of a trade," the man on the screen said. "Any female from my personal holdings . . ."

"Anyone?" the Watcher said suspiciously.

The Watcher's image chuckled. "The Maker of Wonderful Bodies drives a hard bargain, but I agree. You may select the one you want, without exception."

The Watcher released Allis's arm, gave her a wistful glance, and then nodded in agreement. Senda tucked the dagger back into her sleeve, and ushered Allis out the door, not waiting for a signal from Milani nor for another word from the two Watchers.

"I'm safe?" Allis said, walking warily beside her.

"If you accompany me quietly back to the ship you are," Senda said. She heard Milani running to catch up with them. "He must have wanted you to take that shipment quite a lot."

"He made a good deal," Milani said, matching her pace to theirs.

"I'm safe," Allis said, more a sigh than words.

"You just cost the *Sovereign Sun* half of what would have been a king's ransom," Milani said bitterly.

"That's all?" Allis said. "I should think a stone-carrier would be worth much more." Her brown eyes flashed with a lot of impudence for one who'd so recently escaped Watcher custody.

"You're not worth dust unless you pick up that stone," Senda said angrily.

Allis flashed a confident smile. "Milani doesn't agree with you, do you, Milani?"

"You're just lucky that consignment is important enough to make The Maker of Light pull rank on that poor medic."

Allis stopped in her tracks. "Poor medic!" she said, completely indignant. "Do you realize what he would have done to me?"

"Yes," Milani said, calmly giving Allis a thrust between the shoulder blades to keep her walking. "To hear them tell it, every female is happy, and from what I can detect with my stone, I know they're telling the truth. Few Watcher females have enough sense left to be unhappy, and if one does somehow survive the oxygen withdrawal and the drugs, they have other ways of dealing with them, like pleasure-center stimulators or addicting drugs. I suspect, Allis, that you don't know half of what you have escaped from."

Allis was silent as they marched into the elevators. Senda felt that despite Milani's disapproval of how the Watchers treated their females, she'd have left Allis to join them without a twinge of conscience, if it hadn't been for the stone. Allis probably sensed it too.

CHAPTER 10

Milani watched Bracha escort the Earthwoman across the axis of the *Sovereign Sun,* his face tense and grave even though Allis went obediently to the open gangway hatch that led to the keel corridor. Ghyaspur was nearby, cheeks flushed and muscles taut as he tried to make himself look busy by reinventorying cold-jet fuel tanks lashed into place along the bulkhead. His anxiety, assuaged now that he'd seen Allis return safely, was not so much for the jeopardy of the ship's security as it was for Allis herself.

Milani vowed to talk to the young pilot about unwise alliances very soon. Just now there was too much work on the bridge, piling up at the computer terminal ever since Senda left to chase Allis, and not enough crew back from the marketplace to keep the work in real time or to tend the growing number of details. Milani was feeling the effects of Crossroads' heavier than ship-normal gravity in her tired muscles, and the pang of fear knotting her stomach was as intense now as when she'd first heard Jincala's alarm. Resolutely ignoring her unbidden desire for rest in the comforts of her own cabin, Milani shoved herself down another gangway, Senda following like a white shadow.

One glance took in the entire brightly lighted bridge

—showing its comforting array of equipment, most of which was shut down since they were in Crossroads— and three busy occupants as well. Two of Droganie's smiths had been called from the forge shop and were pressed into watching the many gauges that monitored whatever heat-sensitive equipment was still operating, while Mordon sat at the captain's console, pouring over consignment print-outs and bills of lading that had spewed from the computer as a result of Milani's contact with The Maker of Light.

Mordon was still wearing the crisp gray tunic he'd had on when he left the ship to go to the marketplace. From fringe thoughts she knew he was aware of what had transpired; at least he knew as much as Bracha could have told him when he returned to the ship to drop off a package. Of course he'd forfeited the rest of his leave to stay at the helm during Senda's and Milani's absence, cursing himself rather than the Earthwoman for the inconvenience. He also knew that Allis was back. He didn't know how Milani and Senda had secured the Earthwoman's release from the Watchers, but he intended to get all the details from Senda later on.

"Freight Orbit Control wants your acceptance on these delivery receipts," he said, handing a sheaf of stiff print-outs to Milani. "The cargo's waiting in orbit with the ore tenders. I told them we wouldn't sign off until we checked the cargo and got it stowed under the superstructure." He looked at her quizzically to see if she agreed with his decision. When she nodded he made a satisfied grunt and started to move away from her console. Milani stayed him with a hand.

"Post guards out in the highbay," Milani said, "and at least two more in the axis. I don't want to depend on Watcher security systems."

"Allis won't get away again," Mordon said fiercely. "I've already seen to that." He felt singularly responsible for Allis's escape, mentally flaying himself because he thought he should have foreseen Jincala's premature return to the ship, for new surroundings frightened her, even if she did appear to look forward to them. And he should have guessed that Allis would be the only person on board who wouldn't be too busy for the childlike Jincala, and that Jincala wouldn't have understood the reason for an isolation seal across a cabin hatch. He should have warned Jincala to stay away from Allis, should have posted a guard in the corridor beneath the Earthwoman's cabin in the first place, should have . . .

"Mordon, it's not Allis I'm worried about," Milani said impatiently. "She's too shaken to attempt another escape while we're in Crossroads."

"What then?" he asked, his mind blank and surprised.

"It's just a precaution," she said, not completely certain how to express her uneasy feeling. "Is *Dowager Sun* still in port?"

Mordon nodded. "It's berthed at the South Pole near *Bright Sun*." He couldn't imagine why Milani would worry about another gypsy ship, but he knew that she was because her frown deepened.

"The captain of the *Dowager Sun* considered our consignment from The Maker of Light all but his. He's angry, and I don't trust him. Dacko is a peculiar man."

"Dacko!" It was Senda who spoke.

Milani turned to face her. "You know him?"

The albino swallowed hard, trying to force down some unbidden memories. She looked plaintively at Mordon.

The first mate sighed. "It's I who knows him, Milani." He gave Senda an indulgent look, his mind simultaneously wishing he didn't have to speak and relieved that he did. "It was Dacko who bought up my scores on my home planet. I jumped ship first chance I got. He captained a little bucket called *Dwarf Sun* then or I'd have known he was in port. Anyway, I hid from him and his crew, and when they gave up and left, I secured another berth elsewhere. Two ships later I found *Sovereign Sun*. My association with him on *Dwarf Sun* was brief, but I haven't forgotten Dacko, as Senda well knows." He paused thoughtfully. "We'd better post guards at the nuclear forge access plates, too."

He was leaving a lot unsaid and a lot more buried deep in his mind, and Milani knew it. She was shocked and chagrined; Mordon had served on the *Sovereign Sun* since before she'd met Daneth, and if anyone had ever asked, she'd have said she knew all about him. Yet, while she'd known Mordon originally came from planet folk, he'd never mentioned Dacko or *Dwarf Sun*. She'd never had even an inkling he'd been hiding anything during all the megashifts they'd served together on the bridge, yet Dacko was not the kind of person who didn't come to mind, at least sometimes. He'd deliberately hidden his association with Dacko, however brief. And Senda had obviously been less than frank, too. Thinking back to when she'd first met Mordon, she realized she'd not probed much beyond his potential for loyalty to her and the ship. Senda was beyond reproach because that's how Daneth held her, never encouraging Milani to question his judgment.

—You're angry.—The mate's subliminal seemed reproachful.

"Surprised, that's all." It was an understatement, to be sure.

—How in space could I explain jumping ship to the captain I wanted to join?—Anger now. Not an unusual emotion for Mordon, but rarely so bitter. —You knew spacing well from the time we met that I was determined to become first mate and have the mate's share of the cargo. Would you have taken me on if you'd known I'd jumped ship once?—

Thoughtful, Milani sat in the console next to Mordon. "What else don't I know about you, Mordon?" she whispered, not so that the others on the bridge wouldn't hear but because she could summon only that much voice.

"I'll not have you doubting me now, Captain. Listen up, and I'll tell you everything." Mordon spoke loudly. The captain's behavior was distressing to him, but he wasn't going to allow her or the crew to question his loyalty. His mind was set with his usual willingness to take full responsibility for anything he'd ever done, including jumping ship and not telling Milani about it. But he was indignant, too, and just a little worried that Milani would not be as perceptive as Daneth used to be. Knowing that seared Milani like open fire.

"It can't possibly matter now," Senda said, stopping Mordon's ready words by squeezing his shoulder. Despite the albino's touch and its calming effect, Milani knew it wasn't settled between the couple. She wasn't even entirely sure what the problem was, but had decided long ago it was none of her concern. "You haven't cared in all these megashifts, Milani. Why should you care now? His willingness to use what knowledge he has about Dacko to keep the *Sovereign Sun* safe demonstrates his loyalty."

"I'm certain of *his* loyalty, Senda," Milani said, pinning the albino with her gaze.

Milani saw her own accusing stare reflected in Senda's mind, and felt the albino's confusion. Leaving Senda to ponder her captain's sudden shift in wrath, Milani got up to pace between the consoles. The sound of her footsteps in the heavier Crossroads atmosphere that was being circulated through the ship seemed odd, and she halted.

"Mordon, post whatever guards you see fit. Recall the crew. I want the ship ready to leave Crossroads before the end of the next shift."

Mordon's self-satisfaction at being restored in his captain's confidence was momentarily gratifying for both of them. Mordon was quickly about his business again. "We won't be able to find some of the crew," he said unhappily, thinking of the bawdy places and casual, untraceable contacts some of the crew members were certain to have pursued. He traced a quick query on the computer's command screen. "All of them have been required to check with the ship by evenshift, but . . ." He looked worriedly at Milani. —You don't plan to jump without them, do you?—

She shook her head. His concern over Dacko exceeded hers, and she heeded it, just as she always had. "I want to stow the cargo as fast as we can. We'll be taking on ten thousand carats of diamonds when we've secured and have clearance from Corridor Control."

"*Ten thousand?* The contract said twenty." Mordon was about to reach for the laser-seared printouts to check his memory.

"Yes, well, the earthworm cost us some. I had to renegotiate the deal with the Watcher to get her back."

"Spacing witch," Mordon muttered, and there was audible grumbling from the two smiths, too.

Senda collapsed in a chair. She'd just put together her deliberate misinterpretation of Milani's hand signal in the Watcher antechamber with the loss of half the diamonds, and lastly with Milani's accusation of disloyalty. She'd fooled herself into thinking her eyes had played tricks on her because she'd dared to second guess a mind reader. But now she realized she had seen the death signal, and that it had changed only because the stone-carrier had known Senda couldn't carry through. She *had* hesitated. Now she was stunned by her own traitorous behavior. She attached no significance to the memories of the logical results of taking Allis down in that place, and plainly she did not know that Milani had scarcely finished forming the sign when Senda's alarm made her realize it was madness to satisfy her own need for revenge on the earthworm. Milani kept silent.

"Senda, take the forge access plates, and tell Ghyaspur to stay in the axis until he's relieved," Mordon said. Then, as an afterthought, he said, "Better open the weapons locker first. Dacko won't be carrying only a dagger." Usually sensitive to Senda's very presence, Mordon was so enmeshed with his misgivings about Dacko that he didn't notice the woman's stricken expression.

Still stunned, Senda looked questioningly at Milani. Was she to be trusted with guard duty? More likely she'd be ordered out of the ship, abandoned at Crossroads, and then Mordon and everyone would know what had happened.

"Guard the forge," Milani said, turning away so she wouldn't have to see albino's sick gratitude. She tried not to remember the ravages of jealousy when

she'd felt Senda's affection for the earthworm go into
premature mourning and self-pity, tried not to remember the feel of a heated knife blade running over
the burn wounds on Milani's heart. That had been
in the Watcher antechamber; now they were safe in
the *Sovereign Sun,* and the captain was certain Senda's
affection for the earthworm had finally run its course.
In fact, affection for anyone had once again proven
disastrous to Senda, and she was suddenly cold as
space. Milani tried to comfort herself with the knowledge that she had Senda's undivided loyalty once
again.

Loyalty was paramount to the ship's safety; love was
in smithereens, light years gone. But gratitude did not
feel as good as Senda's love had felt.

"Milani, you look as if you could use some rest,"
she heard Mordon say as she watched Senda slip
through the hatch. "I can keep the helm while you
sleep. When just a few more of our crew return, we'll
have enough to go out after that cargo. I'd worry
less about sabotage once we're out of the highbay.
We'll leave word for the stragglers to take a public
shuttle out to our orbit."

Mordon had more firsthand knowledge of Dacko,
and his having slept before going to the marketplace
made him the better choice for the helm just now.
Milani nodded her assent.

"The rest will be welcome," Milani said, and was
rewarded with one of Mordon's rare smiles. "But first
I want to send a message to Filoy on *Bright Sun.*"
She wanted to tell Filoy that seeing him again had
been good for her, and that his very presence during
the meeting with Dacko and The Maker of Light had
been a comfort. But, somehow, saying those things

seemed strange and uncomfortable. Absently she touched her stone, feeling its smooth, warm surface. Perhaps she should say that Anara was a fine captain and a good person, but he'd probably know she hadn't had time enough to make any real conclusions about his granddaughter. In fact, her first impression of the captain had been that she was not strong enough to be in a position of authority, or at best that Anara was merely too young. Dishonesty had a way of coming back to haunt Milani, so she discarded that idea and struggled for something else to say to Filoy. She wanted him to know that she had not run from him again, that knowing he wanted to remember good times with her and become reacquainted had made it painful to leave him there in the bar. Or had it?

"Milani?"

She looked up to see Mordon standing by the communications console, ready to send her message to *Bright Sun*. "Never mind," she said, suddenly turning on her heel to leave. She didn't need to bother herself over an old acquaintance. She needed to rest to be prepared to relieve Mordon at the helm when the *Sovereign Sun* was ready to pick up the consignment.

CHAPTER 11

By the time Ghyaspur was replaced at his axis sentry post by an older crewmate, he'd been on his feet three shifts in a row, and he'd gladly turned over the laser-beam gun. He'd been taught to use the weapon, of course, but he'd never before been expected to use it. Watching the bleak walls and floor of the highbay, wondering if some fiend of Dacko's was hiding in the gantry shadows or slithering unseen along the topside of the superstructure, had produced incredible tension, and he was sweating even though the highbay temperature was quite cool.

Inside the *Sovereign Sun* he'd hurried to the galley to get some food, suddenly ravenous, as if all the stress of guard duty had sapped his energy. He'd sat down with a big hunk of spiced protein processed from hydroponically grown nuts, only to have the computer summon him once again for guard duty, but this time it was only Allis he had to watch. He didn't complain; he knew someone had been in the corridor watching the cabin hatch since Allis had returned, and he realized that assigning even a tired guard to her was probably more concession than she deserved under the circumstances. Mordon could have slapped her in chains, or drugged her. He took the protein, stuffed a few brightly colored bulbs of jellied sweets into his thigh pockets, and returned to his cabin.

Allis was in the chair by the bulkhead terminal, her knees covered with his tumbling blanket. She was tense and her dusky skin looked pale, but she seemed no worse for having been with the Watchers, even for just a little while. Perhaps it was his imagination, but her eyes seemed to brighten when she realized it was he who entered.

"Did you bring some for me?" she said, pointing to the food in his hand.

He hadn't, but he quickly split the spiced protein and handed her a bulb of sweets, too. Then he closed the hatch and sat on it. His fingers tingled from gripping the laser so hard, making it difficult to get the food to his mouth without trembling.

"What's going on?" Allis said, apparently not quite as hungry as he, since the food remained in her lap. "The terminal screen's been flashing like holiday lights for the last shift. Is there trouble with the Watchers?"

Ghyaspur shook his head. "No, the trouble is with another gypsy, a captain named Dacko. Mordon thinks he may try to sabotage the ship because Milani got a consignment he wanted. I was told that we'll probably leave the highbay even before the whole crew is back. The latecomers will have to take the shuttle out to the freight orbit."

"Good," Allis said, picking up the food and biting off a chunk.

Ghyaspur frowned. "Not good. Watcher transportation is dear, and the way I hear it, we lost thousands of carats of diamonds because of you."

Allis chewed slowly and swallowed, her brown eyes somber. "I only meant that we can't get out of this highbay soon enough to suit me. I won't feel safe until there's a lot of distance between me and the Watchers."

Ghyaspur drank deeply of the refreshing gel, then leaned over to put the empty bulb in the recycler. "I don't know why you did it, Allis. I told you about the Watchers."

"You didn't tell me everything," she said with sudden fury. "You didn't tell me they'd tamper with my baby's brain! If I hadn't had to worry about her, I might have been able to make some kind of bargain for the stone and I'd have gotten away safely."

Ghyaspur finished the last bite of spiced protein. He'd been worried about Allis's misadventure while it was happening, and he'd even feared for her life, if not because of the Watchers then because of his crewmates. But he hadn't been too worried about the stone; the Watchers would have had to catch the *Sovereign Sun* before they could get it, and only *if* they had gotten Allis away from the antechamber alive, so only the mention of a baby kept his interest. "What baby?"

The Earthwoman put aside the tumbling blanket and the food before getting up to pace. As she walked she stared at him, seemingly evaluating him in the same fashion some of his elder crewmates did. When she stopped she spread her legs in a stance against the inertia of precession and stuffed her hands in the big hip pockets of her green pants. "I guess it will become noticeable to everyone pretty soon, but don't tell anyone yet. I want to see what the computer has to say about . . ."

"You're pregnant?" Ghyaspur said. Suddenly he didn't feel tired anymore, and his tenseness transmuted into happy excitement. "Are you really pregnant?" he said, standing up. He was looking for a tell-tale bulge under the sashed tunic she wore over the baggy trousers.

Allis nodded uneasily, her loose hair falling across her shoulders as she turned. "Don't tell anyone, Ghyaspur."

Her voice had a warning edge to it. Anyone, he was sure, meant Milani, and he appreciated her insinuation that the captain would not be happy about the news. But he was overjoyed. He started to reach out for her, and then realized what he was doing just in time to stop. Instead he smiled at Allis.

"You're happy about it?" she said, looking confused.

"Of course I am. Allis, do you realize how long it's been since there's been a live birth on *Sovereign Sun?* I think Senda's baby was the last one, and he didn't live but a few hundred shifts. And," he added tenderly, "it's Daneth's child, isn't it?"

Allis nodded. "I wish . . ." The brown eyes became misty as she fought back tears. Then, as if remembering where she was, she stamped her foot and cursed the tears away. "I wish the taboo about touching didn't keep you standing there gaping like an ape. No one does enough touching around here," she said bitterly.

It wasn't what she was going to say, but Ghyaspur obligingly reached out for her. He intended to squeeze her shoulders reassuringly, but she fell against his chest like a feather, and without even thinking, he put his arms around her to hold her closely. *It doesn't mean to her what it does to me,* he told himself sternly as he felt a shiver of excitement. She was from a different culture, a place where even strangers touched and friends cavorted like lovers, according to Senda's memories of Earth. Her soft hair brushed his cheek and he felt muscles bunched up in her back under his hands. Instinctively his fingers massaged the knots, and when they relaxed her torso touched his. He could feel her belly against his hip. The baby? Of course, the baby, he decided. He pressed her closer to him. Oh, this holding was a wonderful thing.

"Space!" Allis said, breaking away from him with startling abruptness. "She'll know from you, won't she?" It was an accusation not a question, with her eyes so dark with concern.

"No. She doesn't have to know. At least I think I can keep it from her. I know how it's done; I've just never had a reason to try before." He was eager to keep Allis's trust, and he didn't see any risk to the ship in doing it.

Allis looked at him suspiciously. "I know she can't get anything out of your mind that you're not thinking about, but you're not going to be able to help thinking about it once in a while."

"There's more to it than that, Allis. We can request our privacy, which stone-carriers normally respect. We're certain Milani does; she'd have to, or lose face. It's just not easy to keep that privacy request going all the time without arousing Milani's suspicion, especially while trying to do ship's burdens where certain information must be relayed to the captain. But it can be done," he said confidently. Daneth had taught him how to treat secrets, even practiced with him a few times, but it had been only a game. From the look on Allis's face he knew it meant a lot more to her. "But, as you said yourself, it's going to become obvious to everyone in time."

"I don't want you to keep it secret so long that you compromise yourself with Milani," she said, craftily sensing his slight reservation. "Just long enough for me to make some computer queries. I don't want old wives' tales from the crew before I have all the facts about what to expect about giving birth on a space ship." She laughed at his sudden frown.

"That wasn't a curse, Ghyaspur, merely a literal translation. *Space* isn't a derogatory word back on Earth. Will you help me with the computer?" She was often frustrated by the computer, which apparently didn't behave the way she thought it ought, though she admitted she'd had no experience with data processors back on Earth, either.

He nodded easily, determined to keep his word until Allis had the data she wanted. He sat down on the hatch again, hoping she would sit next to him. "What are old wives' tales?" he asked, keeping his tone conversational as he folded the tumbling blanket and placed it on the deck.

"They're lies about how babies are born with birthmarks because the mother ate liver while she was pregnant."

"Why would anyone want to eat liver, or any flesh for that matter?" Ghyaspur said in disgust. "As for birthmarks, they're nothing compared to . . ." He stopped abruptly. Yes, he thought. She was worried about genetic damage even though she probably was the most genetically clean person on the ship.

"I want to know what the real possibilities are. All right?"

"Of course you have a right to know," he said, patting the deck beside him.

Allis sat on the hammock, swaying and looking distant.

"Daneth's baby," he said, trying not to feel disappointed that she'd not understood his invitation or had deliberately ignored it. "You can give him the stone when he's old enough."

"It's *my* baby. Dan didn't even know I was pregnant. I have no intention of burdening her with that spacing stone, and it's a girl, if the Watcher is right."

Ghyaspur nodded when she glanced at him quizzically. "They know about such things, though I don't understand how."

"I'd have said amniocentesis, except that those bloodletting leggings he sicked on me never got near my belly. But since they have a machine that can patch up a scalp wound so that you can barely find it again, I guess I'm not surprised that they have a simple test for sexing the fetus." She smoothed her long hair with satisfaction, apparently not even finding a tender spot.

"Allis, Daneth would have known that you were pregnant, possibly even before you knew yourself. He was a stone-carrier."

From the startled look she gave him, she'd obviously not thought of that before. Now that she did, surprise gave way to thoughtfulness. "Do you suppose the baby had anything to do with his giving me the stone?"

Ghyaspur shrugged. "He would have been proud and happy when he learned you were pregnant; it's not much of a secret that he always wanted children."

"Space! How he used me," she said, angry again. "First when he bought out my tool and die company and convinced me to stay on to help him run it, and then when he made me buy the diamonds." The brown eyes flashed guiltily. "No, I can't blame him for that. I knew what was going on and I cooperated."

Ghyaspur was uncomfortable. He stretched out his legs to ease cramped muscles, but that didn't help his

churning mind. Though Daneth was dead, it was difficult to consider speaking ill of him. Still, Allis had a
right to know everything if she was ever to pick up
the stone again. "It must have occurred to you that
Daneth would have known exactly how to use you to
get the diamonds while keeping you certain that you
were in complete agreement with him, perhaps even
causing you to fall in love with him, especially since
you weren't aware of his telepathic privileges at the
time," he told her.

"Yes, I've thought about that. Now I've also considered the possibility that he merely used me as a
caretaker for the stone until the child is old enough
to take over. If so, he made a mistake," she said firmly.

"I am the only person responsible for my decisions.
Telepathic knowledge and unfair influence or not, I
have always been the party responsible for my actions
and I always will be. I knew he was working for some
kind of foreign nation when we took the diamonds to
the desert and Senda came for them that first time.
It didn't make a lot of sense since he was acquiring
them legally and without much discount, which was
not the way a revolutionary on Earth would traffic
in diamonds. I demanded to know if the diamonds
would cause trouble anywhere on Earth. When he
told me that unless the diamonds' unavailability in
the open market could cause harm, neither he nor
the diamonds' use would directly or indirectly hurt
anyone in the world. I trusted him, and even now I
know he didn't lie to me, at least, not about that."

"But you couldn't even have dreamed of what kind
of questions to ask about the baby," Ghyaspur said,
and chuckling, he added, "Not even you could have
gotten it in you alone. Daneth took part."

Allis smiled. "No, but I know it was me who got careless with the birth controls. I take responsibility for that."

"Birth controls?" he said, puzzled. "Is that some kind of law?"

"No, it's what we call the methods we use to prevent unwanted babies from being conceived. I know you haven't heard anything about them on *Sovereign Sun;* you wouldn't need to. The birth rate here is nil anyhow. But I'd toyed with the idea of having a baby and, well, in a few more years I'd have been too old to consider it, else risk having one like Jincala." She looked sharply at him. "Is she all right? I tried not to hurt her."

"Yes, she's fine. But I think you lost your other friend. She'll be too frightened to come near you again. Even Jincala had a better idea of what you were risking than you did."

Allis didn't seem properly chastised by his criticism, but she was thoughtful. "The only risk I regret is the one I took for myself and the baby. I hadn't anticipated that the Watchers could be more contemptuous than shanghaiing-gypsies," she said wistfully. Her eyes swept the tiny cabin as if searching for something, momentarily looking wild. "If I'd wanted to be an astronaut I'd have pounded on doors at Cape Canaveral. I don't like having ultraloy beneath my feet everywhere I walk, and I don't like having my view truncated by a bulkhead every time I look around. I want to smell pine trees and sage, and hear a robin chirp when I get up with the sun. I want to feel rain soaking me and throw snowballs, and go swimming, or at least take a *real* bath. I even want to get back to work and make a name for myself in the tool and die industry. I want my baby to be raised on Earth, and Dan would have known that, too. Wouldn't he?"

Ghyaspur nodded. "Yes, he would, and that puzzles me, unless he knew something about you, or perhaps the baby, that you don't know yourself."

Allis gave him a caustic look, but she didn't ask what he meant. It was just as well. He didn't want to worry her with stories about the wanderlust, a quality Daneth possessed in full measure.

"Well," she said finally. "I think we should get on with the computer queries. Who are the midwives, and which one is best? Is there any information about Dan's genetic background? Can I . . ."

Ghyaspur was shaking his head. "Not now, Allis. The computer's time is pretty well taken up with the emergency. It will have to wait. But you needn't worry. I'll not tell Milani or anyone else that you're pregnant until you're finished."

"All right," she said, sighing. "You look kind of tired. If you want the hammock, I'll go up to the galley and get something else to eat. That spiced stuff tastes like reheated pablum mixed with chili peppers. I'm still hungry."

"No. Stay here. You'll only be in the way."

She looked at him skeptically. "You're guarding me, aren't you?"

"Yes."

"I'm not going to try to escape from here again."

"We're all pretty sure of that," Ghyaspur said, stiffling a yawn. "But we're not taking any chances."

"We? Yes, I guess I forget at times that you're one of them," Allis said, sadly.

"I will always be a gypsy, just as Daneth always was. But that doesn't mean I can't understand the desire to experience the planetary wonders," he said tiredly. "Allis, you talk about snow and swimming as if they were commonplace, and I suppose they were on your planet. But I get chills just thinking about seeing an ocean of a chemical like H_2O, and I can't even imagine what it would be like to submerge myself in it. In a way I am kindred to your planetary soul, and I am your friend. But I will not risk the lives of my shipmates, as you are apparently willing to do, just to satisfy my own longings."

"All right, Ghyaspur," she said, not unkindly. "But you still look tired, and friendship isn't a one-sided affair. Take me to the bridge. I can stay in the extra sunwatch console under Mordon's watchful eye. Then you can come back to get some sleep."

Pleased, Ghyaspur smiled. "I may if Mordon doesn't think of something else a tired crewperson can do. It's worth trying. He just might decide that having one well-rested sailjockey is worth putting up with you on the bridge." He stood up, threw the tumbling blanket onto his strongbox where it flapped. "Are you sure you want to do this? Mordon is not the most tolerant person under the best of circumstances, and with this thing with Dacko . . ."

Allis jumped off the hammock, bouncing a bit too much from the leftover inertia. When she settled she ran her fingers through her hair, making a quick part. "Just give me a second to braid my hair. He'll be crabby enough at the sight of me without my hair adding to it."

He watched her comb the shiny black hair with interest and gratitude, and when she'd tucked the last tendril into place, he opened the hatch.

CHAPTER 12

Milani had been avoiding the games in the ship's armory because she knew that Allis usually was there, watching Ghyaspur compete and occasionally challenging players herself. It was some consolation to know that Allis, though nimble for a landlubber, always lost and that ever since leaving Crossroads no one except Ghyaspur had given her the courtesy of a return challenge. Milani knew from hearing stray crew-thoughts that they were disgruntled over giving up so many carats of diamonds to rescue her from the Watchers, expecially since it was done only to protect a communicator-stone that wasn't being used. A few crew members were trying to curry Milani's favor by being cruel to Allis. Others were confused because Milani had never openly accused Allis of any wrongdoing nor welcomed her as a fellow stone-carrier. Furthermore, they were apprehensive of Allis, doubtful that she was worthy of being a stone-carrier since she came by the device under suspect circumstances. The crew distrusted the Earthwoman's quick smiles as if they were evidence of guilt and treachery. Allis seemed undaunted, determined to be all the more friendly after her brush with the Watchers. Milani suspected that if she could see into the woman's mind she would detect a great deal of hidden misery; no one could endure being rebuffed for so long without losing strength. Milani hoped Allis was suffering a lot.

But Milani's refusal to acknowledge Allis was having another effect that she hadn't planned. The crew was beginning to look askance at Ghyaspur, and however much she hated Allis, Milani knew the young pilot was innocent of everything except misplaced friendship. Still, someone had to keep Allis in hand, expecially since Senda and Mordon had been as busy as Milani herself. They'd gotten out of Crossroads and safely stowed the cargo without interference from Dacko. But they hadn't rested much until now, when the gravity slip that would speed them to an infrequently visited yellow star system was only a shift of fair sailing away, and *Dowager Sun* was nowhere around.

Daneth would have solved the problem of Ghyaspur quickly, probably ten shifts ago when they'd gotten the Watcher's rape machines stowed under the superstructure. He'd have challenged Ghyaspur to arm wrestle or to the poles in the armory, sharing time with him for all the crew to see, openly demonstrating his approval. A frank talk with his communicator-stone, helping him past the young pilot's natural stubbornness—perhaps a word of caution about being quite so friendly with a landlubber—and it would be past and done. Missing Daneth's intervention with the crew on a person-to-person basis was only one of the ways in which Milani felt his absence. It had taken her these ten shifts to ease back from her constant reserve in order to do the job alone, and do it convincingly. Once decided, Milani had instructed the computer to notify her when Allis was absent from the armory; she didn't trust her ability to carry it off with

Allis looking on, as she generally was, right into Ghyaspur's Danethlike eyes. The computer summons had come momeɪts ago.

Milani climbed the ladder in the glittering gangway leading to the armory's midsection, just above the fat bilge. Her hands and feet moved in tandem along the rungs that were polished by generations of solarnauts. As she cleared the hatch she heard hazing and cheering, then the strained grunts of active competitors being relayed through the communication system from the poles at the apex of the armory where freefall games took place to the exercise areas and tables below.

Most of the off-duty crew were up, clinging to the sideline poles, team patches still taped to their chests, reluctant to leave the arena even though they'd been eliminated from the competition. She recognized Bracha's big form wielding one of the cushioned clubs, using the torque from his own body to strike the blow from below at his opponent. Slender Droganie dodged artfully and caught the end of Bracha's club with her gaff and nearly twisted it out of his hands.

For a while Milani watched the two fight, their light-colored garb and gleaming weapons brilliantly silhouetted against the deep-blue ultraloy apex. Light played along the maze of poles as Droganie slipped around Bracha like a hummingbird, easily outmaneuvering the big man, playfully biding time until she could get sufficient leverage to dislodge the club from his mighty grip or place a winning blow. Teammates shouted advice, urging the champions on. Ghyaspur was not among them.

Below the poles, slender webs, which protected vigorous players from tumbling uncontrolled into the gravity area, swayed in the forced air currents be-

tween the apex and the deck. Milani's gaze followed
the webs, stopping at a few idle players, seeking
Ghyaspur. She didn't find him until she looked below
at the balconies of game tables that overlooked the
corridor opening along the outer rim. He sat over a
forgotten game of solitaire, staring up at Bracha and
Droganie, seemingly forlorn at being left out. But
as she dropped to his balcony on a slidepole, she
thought his eyes looked resentful more than long-
ing.

"Care to wager on who will win?" Milani said, sliding into the chair bolted down across the table from
his.

"Droganie," he said, naming the one with the skill
and experience, but secretly he wanted Bracha, the
player usually found wanting, to win. Then Ghyaspur
realized who he was talking to and that his secret was
no more, and he straightened in his chair and said,
"No, no wager."

Milani nodded, understanding he'd not really enjoy
being right, but now she had to rely on instinct.
Ghyaspur was not easy to read when he didn't want
to be. Obscuring thoughts was a skill the more intelligent crew members, like Senda and Mordon, sharp-
ened to a fine art, and honoring their privacy was a
concession stone-carriers usually made. Right now Milani was sorely tempted to practice a few skills of her
own and probe deep and hard. He'd notice her concentration, and even if she succeeded, she would lose
face. How did Daneth begin his talks? While she pon-
dered, Ghyaspur leaned forward, conspiratorily.

"She's pregnant," he said.

"Who is?" Milani said, refusing to be distracted
by a loud *thunk* relayed from the games-players to the
speaker node on the table.

Ghyaspur switched off the node. "Allis. That's what you wanted to know, isn't it? I know the computer's been logging her queries for you, and your conclusions are right. All those queries from my terminal about gene damage and maternity were made by Allis. She finished making her queries, and I don't need to keep it a secret any longer. She's pregnant." The young pilot shrugged and leaned back, his eyes staying with Milani like a hawk's.

Milani fought to keep her face impassive. "Then you have taught her how to use the computer?" It wasn't what she wanted to ask, but she was taken aback by the intensity on the boyish face.

Ghyaspur nodded. "That and other things. We'd spend the rest of our lives nursemaiding her aboard this ship if I hadn't. And, of course, she's got the will to learn now, if only to avoid being caught in a Watcher trap again."

"Perhaps you have been too attentive to your, um, obligations and exceeded what was expected of you," Milani managed to say quietly. She watched Ghyaspur for a reaction.

"That's the first time anyone on this ship has ever said I've done something too well," Ghyaspur said with an ironic laugh. He patterned up two bulbs of liquor, a brew permitted him recently by virtue of his pilot credentials. When the pneumatics delivered them seconds later, he offered one to Milani. She accepted. His lips were pressed together, his mind stormy. Patiently, Milani waited. Perhaps now he would say or think about what she wanted to know. Finally he said, "How come I don't get praise for doing something no one else wants to do?" Bitterness, resentment, and loneliness.

"I suppose it's because you seem to take so much

pleasure in it," Milani said and immediately perceived the disagreement he allowed to slip through to her. He was practicing a great deal of control, more than she'd suspected he had. "You're awfully young to be making an alliance with someone who is so alien to your peers." Ghyaspur's groan was audible and mental; he thought he'd stopped those kinds of accusations when he put on his pilot's tattoo. How many sailors had acquired the required knowledge and skill at his age to pilot the shuttles for orbital encounters *and* in planetary atmosphere? At least now his mind was not so opaque.

"No," he said to Milani. "It's not my taking pleasure in my burdens. It's everyone's displeasure with Allis."

His look was shrewd and penetrating, somehow transforming his boyishly smooth face into the look of a man. Milani had to nod. "How long have you been coupling with her?"

She'd caught him off guard, but her question did not bring the immediate denial she'd feared hearing. Was it bitterness or uncertainty Milani detected? Over what? Had the earthworm taken advantage of his youth and inexperience and made him ashamed to face his captain?

"I don't have to answer that," he said smoothly and then swallowed half the bulb of liquor. "She doesn't work with me in the shuttles," he added pointedly, "so ship's codes are not involved. And since I'm not committed or sworn to any other crew member, I've only myself and her to answer to."

His triumph was unmistakable. "Technically correct, but as you yourself said only moments ago, you've come to privileges earlier than most. I have the right to be concerned for your well-being."

Ignoring her own drink, Milani put her hands in her lap so that he would not notice her trembling fingers. His evasiveness was unexpected and therefore disconcerting.

Ghyaspur shrugged noncommittally, his youthful locks motionless on his forehead as he contemplated the bulb he was twirling between his fingers. "There isn't much for me on this ship. Half the women on board think they're my mothers, and the rest . . ."

. . . were shuttle pilots and therefore forbidden to him by code, or they were involved and committed to someone else. It was a common condition among the solarnauts, as Milani well knew, generally worsening with age and acquired rank and skills, which cut off even more potential partners. Still, it didn't answer her question to know that Ghyaspur felt the weight of his heritage. Was he so unprepared for fatherhood that he was afraid to acknowledge it aloud, or even subliminally? Why hadn't she caught a hint of his pride if Allis truly were pregnant? Unless, she thought outraged, he was not the father and was merely toying with her. *This boy, this insolent child!* Her hands shot out like arrows from the bow, pinning his shoulders against the back of the chair as he cried out in alarm.

"Now you tell me," Milani said hoarsely.

—I only meant to have them take me seriously,— he said, the veil of secrecy instantly parting. Yet he was more concerned with making Milani understand why than with what she wanted to know. She shook him until she felt his pain and humiliation. —A baby . . . to be a father, to have respect and acceptance,— his mind babbled. —If only it were mine.—

Stunned, Milani's fingers slacked. "Whose?" she whispered.

Ghyaspur was smoothing his rumpled blouse, trying to ignore the pain across his shoulders. But he was not so shaken that he did not notice all the crew in the armory cautiously surrounding the balcony. Just for an instant he considered speaking aloud what Milani had already surmised, thereby soiling the legendary love between the co-captains and taking revenge for the embarrassing shaking. A glance at the crew's strained faces told Ghyaspur he had little love to lose with them, and perhaps a great deal of satisfaction to gain in disgracing Milani. They would tear him apart if their captain gave the word, and only if he were lucky would someone ask why . . . later, when they'd vented their anger on him. But the captain's eyes were not angry like her crew's. They were tragic. Graciously he answered her subliminally. —Daneth.—

Only Ghyaspur noticed that the captain swayed slightly, then she caught her breath and reached for her bulb of liquor. Her hand was steady as she raised it to her lips, her features composed, seeming to Ghyaspur more like a statue of a person drinking. When she rose from the chair she murmured the polite words of departure, and Ghyaspur echoed them to her back as she dropped into the outer corridor. She walked straight-backed, tawny eyes looking neither right nor left, until she disappeared under the bulkhead that supported another balcony.

Ghyaspur cleared the game board by shaping a pattern on the labyrinth control, and the playing light faded. He swept the empty bulbs into the recycler pneumatic tube, and got to his feet. A glance stolen at his crewmates told him it would be useless to stretch and yawn, or in any way appear unaffected by the spectacle they'd seen of his being assaulted by the captain. He could only raise his chin and push firmly through their reticent ranks as he headed for the hatch in the bilge.

Ghyaspur took the gangway to the farm level, where he'd be least likely to encounter any crew members and most likely to find Allis. As expected, she was sitting among the hydroponic tanks under a growlight, a sheaf of computer print-outs in her lap. Her black hair glistened with red highlights, and her skin was like the sand of the desert she'd come from. She always wore ship garb now, loose pants and blouse with snug cuffs above the elbow and ankle, over which this midshift she'd draped a leaf-green tunic, belted with blue enameled beads. She'd made few selections from the ship's store and wouldn't turn in the garments for reprocessing the way everyone else did, preferring to tend to the cleaning and mending herself.

As he saw her crease one of the printouts that was curling into her field of vision, Ghyaspur cringed. "Don't do that," he said.

Startled, she looked up.

"Use the holder like you're supposed to," he said, pointing to a discarded canister on the floor beside her. He thought he must have looked very stern, for she didn't argue with him this time, as was her habit. She merely muttered about exchanging her right arm for a piece of paper as she picked up the canister and inserted the printouts for proper display. Usually Ghyaspur liked the differentness of her ways; she seemed a link between himself and the grandeur of planet life. But sometimes her carelessness irritated him, especially now when he'd been so recently reminded of how much her differentness was costing him.

"Who put a bug up your rear?" she asked.

Usually that one made him laugh; planetary humor was more lusty than the wry ship jokes. But he could only shake his head sadly and say, "Milani."

"What did she do to you?"

"Me? Nothing. It's what I did to her. I wish I hadn't. I just didn't realize how bad it would be for her because I was so spacing concerned with myself." He sighed regretfully.

"What are you talking about? Did you beat her at the poles?" Allis put aside the print-outs, and putting her arms around her knees, gave him her full attention. He didn't have to worry about phrasing everything just right; she was patient and would listen until he'd finally said it to his own satisfaction. He sat down beside her. Even the deck was warm in the hydroponic farm.

"She knows that you're pregnant and that it's Daneth's child." He sensed her stiffening in spite of herself. "I know you've been worried, Allis, but you needn't be. Children . . . pregnancies are a special event on the stellar sailing vessels. We rejoice when a woman becomes pregnant, no matter who she is or how she managed to get herself that way."

"Yes, I know. Not hard to understand that a little hanky-panky would be overlooked if it results in a healthy child. But . . ."

Ghyaspur held up his hand. "By comparison to the rest of the crew, you know your fetus has had little chance to be harmed by radiation. We've survived generations in space with worse exposure than you have had." She needed constant assurances.

"Until now," Allis said. "You are the last generation aboard this ship, Ghyaspur, the only one your age. The nursery's empty and no one's pregnant except me."

"The father was Daneth, and he was born and raised in the ships."

Allis nodded. "That's part of what worries me."

"Milani never has been pregnant. It's common enough, as you've surmised, and we can cry about it if we like. But mostly we don't . . . until something happens to prove to an individual that he or she is sterile."

"And now Milani knows it was she who couldn't have children and not Dan. Is that what you mean?"

Slowly, Ghyaspur nodded.

"I imagine she'll live with it, just as I will. You know it would be a whole lot easier for me if he'd *been* sterile. It's crazy enough just being shanghaied and having the curse of that stone hanging over my head without worrying about a child, too. I can't even consider abortion, at least not a safe one."

"I sympathize."

"No one else does," she snapped.

"*I* sympathize," he repeated. "And I also understand, finally, just how devastated Milani is. It's more than her being infertile; she must have suspected that for a long time. But your being pregnant proves that Daneth loved you."

"Well, of course he loved me," she said, clutching her knees tightly. "The stone proves that, not the child. He was on Earth long enough to know I'd receive that kind of gift with mixed emotions at best."

"Yes, I believe you, though I admit it's hard for me to understand why. But the crew . . . no, they won't understand or believe. Milani has convinced herself and probably half the crew as well that any love Daneth might have felt for you was a dying gesture to save the stone. You must remember that they had been lovers for many thousands of shifts.

Fidelity was never a question between them, not with the stones in their possession. It's a rare and beautiful thing the co-captains shared, legends in their own time. Can you imagine what it must have been like for them to make love?"

"Stop it!"

"A history lesson, Allis. Don't take it personally."

She gave him a strange look, then silence.

"What I'm trying to explain is that Milani has suffered a great personal loss. Daneth's dead, and nothing can change that. If he'd never visited Earth, likely he'd have died sooner, for we don't have the skills or the tools to hold the white-blood death in abeyance. Milani is not stupid. She doesn't hold you responsible for his death. There's no doubt more that I don't understand and can't guess about. But I do know that Milani must go on living. If the crew were to learn there was no question that Daneth betrayed her, she'd be scandalized."

"If?"

"I have a plan," he said, looking deep into her eyes. "It will require your cooperation."

"What is it?"

"We'll tell them that the baby is mine."

Her look of incredulity embarrassed him.

"Why not?" he said gruffly. "I've already been accused of coupling with you. They're so willing to think ill of you, and now me, that no one will be surprised."

At least she wasn't laughing at him this time, and he thought her expression mellowed slightly. "You'd do that for Milani?" she asked seriously. "I mean, isn't your reputation involved, too?"

"Yes, but it's a matter of priorities. Milani must be

fit and hale to be captain of the *Sovereign Sun*. I am merely a shuttle pilot, young as well, and entitled to a few indiscretions." He thought for a while, then added, "Likely I'll miss my next promotion, but there'll be others later on."

"No," Allis said sullenly.

Ghyaspur looked at her. The brown, heavy-lidded eyes were moist half-moons in the shadow on her face. "That's all? Just 'no'? I must not have made my explanation clear if that's all you can say. Milani is captain. She *is* the ship."

Suddenly tears rolled down Allis's cheeks and she whirled angrily on Ghyaspur. "What about me? What do I get out of it? They won't stop ostracizing me if they think I seduced their last baby. And if they think I've slept with you so soon after losing Dan, they'll be convinced I'm some kind of witch who stole his stone. And what about Milani? I could stand all the crew whispering behind my back if I thought saving face for her would make her grateful enough to take me home and allow me to have my baby in peace. But she won't. You know she won't." She watched him through her tears, not breathing until he nodded in agreement. She wiped her tears with the hem of her tunic and said through clenched teeth, "I don't owe anyone on this ship one spacing thing."

"You owe yourself the best environment possible in which to survive. All you have now is this ship, and this ship is Milani."

Ghyaspur could tell his words affected her. She slumped as if she'd been stunned by a blow. Then, crying again, she stumbled to her feet, lurching against a hydroponic tank overflowing with vines. "Spacing soft gee," she said, almost kicking out at the tank apparently before remembering what would happen. She planted the soles of her boots against the deck and stepped away as quickly as she could, muttering. "Spacing ship . . . get a madwoman for a captain if I don't lie to the spacing crew."

"Allis?" he said, loud and firm.

She stopped a few rows of tanks away, still in view despite the prolific overgrowth from the tanks. "Yes. Yes. I'll do it," shouting so he'd hear her. She snapped a tangle of leaves from in front of her eyes and flung them aside. The growlights reflected off the sheen of her half-dried tears and red-rimmed eyes. "Just make certain she knows I'm doing it for Dan's baby, the one that's in *my* womb!"

She turned between tanks of green-gold maize and was gone.

Ghyaspur smiled, less happy than he thought he'd be, for Allis's tears disturbed him. Just the same, if she hadn't shown that sign of weakness, he might not have known to press her as he did. He would not, of course, pass on her angry insult to Milani, and he knew that keeping it from the captain wouldn't be hard. He'd had the captain fooled for a while back there in the armory, and even if his then-fuzzy plan had backfired, at least he knew he *could* be impenetrable to the stone-carriers when he wanted. It was a strong and powerful feeling to know that. He'd get a great deal of self-satisfaction from saving Milani from further embarrassment. For a change, no one was showing him the way to make a contribution to the ship's countenance; no one would know about it except Milani, and from her he expected silent acceptance. This must be, he thought, what it is like to be wise and mature. And now, while I feel good and strong and eager . . .

—Milani. Milani,— he said subliminally. —Milani, we will tell the crew the child is mine.— She could not respond in kind of course but she'd give him some sign that she'd heard during the next shift or two.

CHAPTER 13

Allis sat on Ghyaspur's strongbox, using the folded tumbling blanket as a cushion, though the polished wood of the box would have been nearly as comfortable in the low gravity. She'd gotten used to sleeping in the hammock after learning that sleeping on the deck wrapped in the blanket exposed her to inertial force that sent her rolling along the blue ultraloy deck when the *Sovereign Sun* swayed in a gust of stellar wind. She'd become accustomed to getting along with only sparse furnishings—hammock, strongbox, and computer terminal with chair—and to seeing Ghyaspur's planetary collections, which crowded the bulkheads and ceilings of his cabin like posters and pictures of media stars cluttered the walls of teen-agers back home.

Though the Earth collection was the largest grouping, it was a scant link to home, and this day—this *shift*, she corrected herself—it was a bitter reminder of finished past. The jug of sand and the arkoselike rock tethered to the bulkhead by lugs and wire were grotesque against the slick ultraloy. The glassine envelope of leaves she'd meant to press for him, but couldn't for lack of books and proper vocabulary to find substitutes, had gone the way of any alien thing uprooted and handled in ignorance, albeit lovingly.

Withered and brown. An empty cigarette pack and a
flight feather from a hawk were spotlighted by a
chemical light Ghyaspur had rigged, and they were
a source of great joy to him, especially after Allis had
mastered the gypsy tongue well enough to explain
their origins. Allis decided that she fit somewhere between the brown hunk of rock that sparkled with
polished fragments of quartz and the flight feather. It
had seemed a temporary arrangement until now
when she realized she'd rather remain a part of
Ghyaspur's collection and go along with his scheme
to tell the crew that he was the father of her baby
than to face having a barren cabin of her own where
no one, not even Ghyaspur, would come to visit.

Ghyaspur was her only friend, but was he a true
friend or just fascinated by her stories of ancestral
mountains of Earth and the dichotomies of its political machines? He was willing to risk being passed
over for his next promotion to help Milani save her
pride, and the only real surprise in that was Allis's
own shock. First he was Milani's crewman, and then
he was Allis's friend, and maybe only a tenuous one
at that. There was no one to rely upon in this strange
universe except herself. She was committed to the
future, to the ship's future, and to becoming a part of
it until some distant time when the *Sovereign Sun*
returned to Earth.

Discouraged, she sighed and reached for the print-
outs at her side. Best to put them away before
Ghyaspur returned, for if he saw her cache of translations, he'd accuse her of hoarding the recyclable print-
outs and, perhaps, guess what the print-outs contained.
There was no sense in believing that he'd come to
understand that if she handed off to the computer
the painstakingly compiled lexicon of Modern En-

glish, the last slender thread of superiority would be gone. Senda was getting old, and some distant day, perhaps thousands of shifts hence, Allis might have an opportunity to return to Earth by virtue of being the only master of an Earth tongue on board the *Sovereign Sun*.

Too late. Ghyaspur's chestnut locks came into view through the hatch. He'd exchanged clothes at the ship's store, crisp blue blouse and pants with a rainbow of desert tones in his sash. He looked cheerful, the faint trace of freckles across his cheeks thrust high by his smile.

"Finished crying, I see," he said, swinging his hips up to the deck.

He slid the portal door closed so casually that Allis hardly noticed. In the tiny cabin the incoming motion also put him at Allis's side. Kneeling, he rubbed his thumb along her cheekbone, as if wiping away a tear stain, even though Allis had used the freshener before she left the hydroponic farm level. She was surprised. She couldn't remember Ghyaspur ever touching her like that before.

"Your decision was the right one," he said. "You'll know that in time."

"I can see right now; it just galls me," she said, staring at him with amazement she hoped didn't show. He was peeling off his boots. "Ghyaspur, what are you doing?"

The young pilot paused, then tossed the boot in his hand to the octant along the bulkhead where he kept his clothes, leaning across her knees to do it. He didn't lean back, turning instead so that he faced her nose to nose. She felt his hand on hers, not quite shy but not forcefully either.

"Doing?" he whispered. "Touching you. You've

told me you missed being touched, complained that we don't even brush shoulders." The velvety mauve of his eyelids was all that she saw as his arms encircled her. "So let me hold you. I'll just hold you if that's what you want." He'd felt her muscles tense and his fingers softly moved along her spine, soothing her.

His arms held her gently, so lightly that she knew she could break free with only a little effort. But his breath along her neck was sweet and warm, and even the slight touch of his chest across hers conveyed the excited hammering of his heart.

"Allis, the hatch should be closed from time to time like this if the crew is to believe that I'm the child's father."

"This is merely a charade for the crew?"

"Hardly. I've been accused of coupling with you, and will be so accused again. It's not hard to bear that; I wish it were true. I couldn't think of how else to make my wishes known. I don't know how else to tell you how much I care for you, Allis."

The words were manly enough, but they were from a boy's easily won heart. Even so, it would have been easy to stay in the strong arms of this tall pilot and, for a while, forget who she was and where she was. She'd had so little comfort and been so lonely that his closeness seemed heaven-sent, and the pleasure his lanky young body could offer was tempting. But she knew that a few moments' pleasure wasn't what Ghyaspur wanted, and, for all his loyalty to Milani, she knew he'd been as fair and kind to Allis as was possible for a person of tender age and limited experience.

If only he were older or a more ruthless person. Then she could abandon herself to his arms and not care about what followed. Even now she knew she'd hesitated too long; his smooth cheek was turning for a kiss that would be difficult to withhold. She lowered her head to his chest and sighed. She heard him murmur her name in confusion. Already it would be embarrassing for him, but . . . no, she couldn't hurt him more by continuing. She pushed him away.

"Allis," he said, still full of tenderness, reaching for her.

She backed away a few inches. There wasn't much farther to go, and it wasn't enough. He'd felt her respond practically without hesitation. "No," she said quietly, and he stopped instantly, reaching arm in midair. For a moment she was surprised, and then she remembered another gypsy man who'd reacted the same way when she'd said that word. They weren't like men of Earth; they believed her when she said no. She was grateful for their heritage, which assumed such respect. "I'm sorry," she said. "I'm even flattered . . . but Dan. It's too soon for me to consider anyone else."

His lips pursed, but he nodded. He was no doubt disappointed, but hardly shattered as he might have been if she'd told him the whole truth. He was trying so hard to grow up, stumbling heart over mind doing it. It seemed unfair to Allis that he had only mature crewmates—sages with their long, hard years of enlightenment—by which to measure himself. Things might have been different for Ghyaspur if there were other young people and children on the *Sovereign Sun*. Allis resisted an impulse to tousle his hair.

The intercom whistled, and Allis would have turned it off so she could talk to Ghyaspur except that it was Milani's *toot* and she knew Ghyaspur would want to listen. In a monotone the captain listed state vectors and velocity for those who liked to plot the ship's progress.

"Only moments to the gravity slip," Ghyaspur said, spirits a little higher with that knowledge. "It's a short one, if I remember correctly. Let me get the diary from the strongbox."

Obligingly, Allis got up and watched him rummage through an assortment of hand-wrought and machine-made decanters, daggers and darts, scarves and other bits of beautiful cloth and lace past the case that contained his many bolas until he found his ancestor's diary. He turned to the page of grids, quickly pointing to one of the crosshatches. He laughed.

"It's so small that a Watcher ship couldn't get through," he said. "Look at this, Allis. A big ion drive ship would have to make three jumps to get to the same place from here. There aren't many like this . . . not that the Watchers don't have some ships small enough to fit. Eventually we may not fit either. It seems that all the gravity slips are getting narrower as the star clusters pull apart, although they are being stretched in time." He looked up at her, his eyes sad and beautiful, even as he smiled. "Come on, Allis. Sit down. You might as well be learning some of the intricacies of the galaxy and how they affect a stellar sailing ship while the hatch is closed."

"All right," she said, sitting beside him.

"Are you trembling because of me?" he asked quietly, "Or because we're about to go through a gravity slip?"

"Both," would have been the honest answer, but she said, "I know the *Sovereign Sun* has made many jumps through . . . what are they? Gravity slip isn't much of a description. Are they intrusions in space? Black holes?"

"What's a black hole?" Ghyaspur said.

"It's what results when a star collapses in on itself so much, creating such a powerful gravitational pull that not even light can escape it."

"Oh, I've heard those called disappearing stars, but I don't think anyone considers them anything more than a philosophical curiosity. And if they do exist, I don't believe anyone would want to get near one with a ship. No, a gravity slip is not like a disappearing star or a black hole. There's no mass involved, at least, we've never encountered any."

"How can there be gravity without mass?"

"Ah, now that is the question," Ghyaspur said, apparently somewhat surprised that she'd asked it. "Answer it and you'll be above the Watchers in knowledge, right up there with the Quondam Beings themselves. Your idea that it's an intrusion in space is probably closer to the truth than anything, though we've no idea of how or why a gravity slip results from the intrusion. There are no gravity generators at either end of the slip, so far as we know." He gave her a wry smile. "Who knows what a gravity generator would look like? Maybe it looks like starlight, and we've overlooked it. We don't know much about gravity slips, except where they can be found and that's above or below the ecliptic plane of a star in a stationary orbit, which means that *when* you're looking for it isn't quite as important as *where*."

A warning whistle sounded to alert the crew that the ship was coming about and that they had about sixty seconds to find something to hold onto or risk being jostled by the maneuver. Ghyaspur generally held on, prudent lad for all his brave bearing, but he made no move for the cabin grips just now. Resolutely, Allis followed his example.

There was a sound . . . no, a feeling, a gentle vibration, but no sway or other detectable change in the ship's motion. She realized the nuclear-powered counterforce had come on, and that it would prevent the ship from being crushed in the gravity slip in the same fashion that an electromagnet could prevent a metal bar from falling back to earth if the counterforce were properly balanced. Another bell and she began to feel the slight unevenness of pull in her muscles. They were in the gravity slip.

"Now, if you had studied this map," Ghyaspur said rather majestically, "and if you knew where we were and what our course was, you'd have known that we were heading straight into the gravity slip and that the maneuver bell was more customary than necessary this time."

Milani's flat voice cut off Allis's response:

"A happy event will occur aboard the *Sovereign Sun*. Allis is pregnant with Daneth's child. You will forgive me if I do not partake in any celebrations."

The intercom node deadened and Ghyaspur paled. He looked as if he'd been struck. "Why?" he whispered in a strangled voice.

"It's not you, Ghyaspur. Don't you see that it's my part in this scheme she's rejecting. She can't . . ."

Allis stopped. She suddenly wasn't certain that he'd addressed the question to her, that he wasn't at this moment talking to Milani, silently. It was too much like watching a person pray to his god with his head bent over the blue book and his face so intense. Allis grabbed her print-outs and leaned over to open the hatch, slipping through just as quickly as she could, leaving him to await the voice of god from the intercom.

CHAPTER 14

Senda had chosen a secant in the armory on the first balcony above the outer-rim corridor as a convenient place to strip down a troublesome language machine. The device was old, probably older than she was, and ought to have been replaced by a more recent model gigashifts ago, but the ship always had more urgent needs, like a new communication system that would interface with equipment the Watchers used or sails to replace the ones that were space-welded to the shrouds by the bombardment of hard radiation that caused subatomic changes, even in metals.

Usually Senda tore into a language machine only far enough to erase dead and unused languages to make room for the dialects and neologisms that sprang into use on Watcher-dominated worlds and for the totally alien languages uttered on the restricted planets. The ancient device was looping between basic root words from language to language, making crazy semantics of its own, and Senda was into the confusing and complicated heart of the machine to find out why. Sensibly, she was on line with the ship's computer, which contained the maintenance and repair manual in a dead language.

It had been less time-consuming for her to spend two shifts plugged into another language machine—to jog her memory of the ancient language enough to work directly with the data stored in the computer—than to sit down somewhere and work out a translation program for the computer. She always did believe that the human brain was much more efficient than the computer's, and this incident confirmed her beliefs. Yet as engrossed as she was with the array of memory bubbles, laser-carved circuits, and capacitors before her, she'd easily been distracted by Milani's announcement that Allis was pregnant with Daneth's child.

Senda could feel the armory filling up with crewmates above her, but she didn't look up. She sat with her slender white fingers curled around the glowing edge of the laminar-flow board that held the colorful guts of the language machine firmly in place while she worked. She tried to concentrate on the tiny parts before her, but she kept thinking of her crewmates. They hadn't come to exercise; the fluctuating energy that ran amok in the ship during a gravity slip jump could be dangerous if one were struck while dodging a blow from a gaff or in the midst of an intricate freefall arabesque. Likely they'd come together to gossip about the landlubber's bewitching of Daneth and his subsequent betrayal of Milani. Neither was a topic Senda enjoyed, for she'd known right from the beginning that Allis was not a witch and she had little difficulty believing that Daneth could betray his cold and rigid co-captain for Allis, just as Senda would have if Milani had not interfered. Remembering the incident in the Watcher antechamber still made Senda cold and raised bumps on the back of her neck. She'd never come so close to compromising the ship's security, indeed, betraying the entire gypsy race by hesitating to prevent leaving a stone-carrier in Watcher control. Senda wasn't confused about Milani's hate for the Earthwoman any longer; anyone who could sow treason among loyal gypsies deserved nothing but scorn. Milani must have sensed that potential in Allis right from the start.

The computer cut in to advise Senda of the next step in reassembling the language machine, but Senda had missed performing the last operation. She instructed the computer to go back, then listened carefully so as not to miss the step again. Aside from the strand of hair, the long black one she'd found under the supposedly air-tight case, she'd discovered nothing amiss, and she was forced to hope that taking it apart and putting it back together would correct the problem. The medium in the laminar-flow board would trap any other foreign particles that might have worked into the circuitry; maybe a good cleaning was all it needed.

Someone tapped her shoulder and with great irritation Senda halted the computer and pulled the sound node out of her ear. Mordon sat down next to her on the cushioned bench, his thin blond hair rippling along his pink scalp as a wave of stray energy passed through the secant. Senda's stomach flopped, but the medium in the laminar-flow board didn't react. Someone had brought the first laminar-flow board to the ship as part of a game board. Everyone had quickly discovered the boards were perfect stations for work with small parts that practically defied the strongest pseudogravity the ship could provide. Bits and pieces placed in the laminar-flow board didn't drift away and came out of the medium free of dust.

Mordon glanced at the board. "You have a bad capacitor," he said, reaching through the medium to pull one out.

The capacitor looked like a purple bead; the others were dark red. Senda had already checked all the capacitors to see if each was holding the proper charge. She'd missed the burned-out one. "More spacing interruptions this shift," Senda muttered, taking the capacitor from him and looking in the repair case to see if there was another just like it, only red.

"It's rather unusual for you to do something this intricate, isn't it?" He gestured at the gutted machine.

Senda hunched over the repair kit, frowning. "Housekeeping is no one's burden anymore, or everyone's. Too spacing few people to do everything that needs to be done. How long do you suppose I'd have to wait for this machine to be repaired if I waited for a housekeeper to get around to it?"

"I only meant that you could have asked me or Droganie to have a look at it. You've probably overlooked that capacitor three times or more not knowing what you were looking for." He and Droganie were renowned for their skills in repairing old gear and jury-rigging anything. Since the last housekeeper had left the *Sovereign Sun* to join a new-found lover on another gypsy ship, it had been common at least to ask the blacksmith or first mate to point out the problem, for doing that generally saved time.

"Droganie won't leave the forge shop when we're in a gravity slip, or haven't you ever noticed that?"

Grimacing, Mordon shook his head. "And asking me would have put you in my debt, and even though that would be only a tiny burden, you couldn't bear it." He looked at Senda from the corner of his eyes and she flushed. She saw the hurt in his face before he turned away. "I am a patient man, Senda, and I waited for time to heal your hurts, just as it healed mine. I watched you confide in another man . . . oh, yes. Don't look so surprised. I know Daneth was your confidant. When he left the ship for Earth, I'd hoped you would turn to me, and something was gained; at least you tolerated my presence for a while. But now this mantle of seclusion you've cloaked yourself in is thicker than ever. What is it that you could tell Daneth that you can't tell me?" He looked at her slyly.

Feeling miserable, Senda gave an almost imperceptible shake of her head. There weren't even any shadows for her to move into, away from Mordon's gaze. Second only to Milani, Mordon would be most unforgiving about anyone, even his beloved Senda, hesitating to shoulder a burden, even if that burden meant killing a loved one. Mordon simply couldn't imagine loving someone whose interests were not exactly like his own. To him, Allis was nothing, an alien and an ignorant one, worthy only of his scorn because she was not a productive crew member. Mordon was a harsh man with a rigid code.

Sometimes Senda wondered if he'd felt anything at all for the baby, his own flesh in miniature, yet a traitor to Mordon and to the ship in death. It was an unfair thought; she knew he'd grieved awhile. But for a man who'd come to the stellar sailing vessels from a planet where a child normally lived to become a productive adult, he accepted the gypsy heritage without bitterness. He was even stronger than other gypsies. She couldn't picture Mordon being terrified of having to face planet life again with its big and endless skies and bludgeoning gravity. There could be nothing else for Senda if she failed Milani again, for abandonment at the first port of call was punishment for disloyal sailors. Her fear of going planetside was something she had been able to overcome with Daneth's help, at least for periods long enough for her to carry her burdens. That fear had been different from the dread that made it impossible to return Mordon's love, the dread of losing his love just like she'd lost the baby.

With Allis's arrival, fear and pain jumbled together. Since Crossroads, only one thing was clear to Senda; she needed the security of the ship with its scuffed but sturdy bulkheads and its gentle lights that never made her wince, and she needed all that more than she needed anyone's love. Besides, Mordon wouldn't love her at all if he knew she'd risked the security of the *Sovereign Sun* back on Crossroads. She shuddered. When Mordon touched her and looked at her with concern, she glared until he removed his hand from her arm.

Eyes lowered, he took the repair case from Senda, selected a new capacitor, and without the aid of the computer he began reassembling the gutted language machine. After a while he said, "I've shared secrets with you that even Milani didn't know, and I knew you would keep them. Why do you trust me less than I trust you?"

"There are some things you can't understand," she said, watching his strong fingers replacing tiny memory bubbles and fragile wires in the helmet of the machine. If it was mechanical, he never was confused. An unusual sequence of capacitors and resistors was nothing more than an intriguing puzzle; they had to come together one way or another to provide the desired result.

Mordon hesitated over the work, turned to look

at Senda; his eyes were wide and moist. "Were you in love with Daneth?" he said hoarsely. His pointed chin was quivering, his lips pale and thin.

"No," Senda said, sincerely and emphatically, for despite her resolve to feel nothing for Mordon, his fear had touched her.

He sighed and ran nervous fingers over his hair. "I couldn't think of anything else you wouldn't tell me," he said, unsure of himself yet sounding relieved. "Especially after you said . . ." He seemed embarrassed. "Sometimes you say things to hurt me, don't you?"

It was true. She used innuendoes and shocking suggestions to keep him at bay. This was the first time he'd given any sign that he took her seriously, that her barbs had done their work. It ought to have made her glad, but she only felt discouraged and alone.

"Well," Mordon said, suddenly gruff, "at least your tongue is not caustic as it usually is. I don't know if that's a good sign or bad, but it's a change." He bent over the work again, leaving Senda to stare at his nearly bald head. His muscles stretched as he reached for another part, then bunched.

"What are you doing?"

Both of them turned to see Allis standing behind them, hands in her pockets, perpetual smile on her lips.

"Repairing a language machine, which apparently blew a capacitor when you used it." He hadn't overlooked the hair. It was still in the laminar-flow board and his fingers traced it as he reached for another part.

"I'll help," Allis said decisively as she sat down beside Senda. The bench was small and Senda inched away.

"The burden already has two more hands than it needs," Senda said pointedly. Mordon pretended not to hear, but Allis was immediately put off. She looked helplessly at the crew members at nearby tables, who gave her nothing in return except penetrating stares.

"What do you want from me?" Allis said, her voice so vicious that Mordon sat up. "I've learned the language, kept working in the hydroponic farm and on the sunwatch, even kept customs I don't believe in." She tugged at the green bracelet that gypsy women wore so that everyone would be aware of pregnancies even before their conditions became self-evident. The bracelet was too large for her small wrist and it came loose in her hand. "If I knew what you wanted, I'd give it."

"Try allowing us privacy from your alien presence," Senda said, eyeing the Earthwoman with disdain. "We know your smiles are a mockery, your special kind of deceit used to put us off our guard. You care nothing for this ship nor for anyone in it. You're obsessed with returning to Earth at any expense, including ours."

"Even you," Allis said, her eyes narrowing to slits. "The others mimic Milani's behavior as if they didn't have brains of their own, but I didn't think you were an automaton, too. I thought I could depend on you to be fair." Her dusky skin was especially dark around her eyes, setting off the whites like flame.

"Did you think the veil of suspicion would lift just because you're carrying Daneth's child?" Senda shook her head. "There won't be any celebration for you, Allis. Not for this child."

Even though gypsy clothes were too large for Allis and made her look a little out of place, she certainly did not seem waiflike with that much hate on her face. "Is it too much to ask for you to believe that your one-time captain and god fell in with a mere mortal? Can't any of you get him off the pedestal? He was a man, after all, first and always. Or does the remaining god have you so tightly controlled that you can't get past your prejudices against planet people?"

Mordon snorted, no doubt thinking of his own origins, but he didn't comment. Allis's look of impatience suggested that she knew he was leaving something unsaid.

"Dear Jesus," she muttered in English. Suddenly her spine straightened, bringing her head erect. In gypsy tongue she said, "Milani isn't the only spacing god on board the *Sovereign Sun*."

"Ask your god to save you then," Senda said.

"She will," Allis said with determination. Abruptly she got to her feet and leaped from the balcony down to the outer-rim corridor. She overbent at the knees to absorb the shock and leaped carelessly along until she disappeared from view. Satisfied that she would not return, Senda turned back to Mordon. He was staring at her in amazement.

"I thought that hurting tongue of yours was reserved for me," he said. "How does the Earthwoman rate it as well?"

"I'm just tired of her hanging on to me. I don't have time to listen to her whining any more than yours," Senda said sharply. "And speaking of time, we should be on the bridge. The shift is about to change."

"I am a patient man," Mordon said, probably more to remind himself, Senda decided, than her.

She left the laminar-flow board where all the language machine parts would be safe until she returned and followed Mordon along the balcony toward the hatch at the far end of the armory. Other crew members, also mindful of the imminent shift change, were making ready to leave. The straying energy was erratic and strong, causing some jostling along the rails; spaces between bodies immediately increased and hands reached for stanchions. The end of the gravity slip was near.

CHAPTER 15

Allis had the stone in her hand the moment danger struck the ship. Later she realized the simple motion of palming the artifact saved her life.

She'd picked it out of Ghyaspur's strongbox for the first time in nearly four months and was rewarded with a mind-blast of fear equal only to the horror she'd known the last time she'd held the stone and faced Milani. Only the instant awareness that the fear came from the bridge crew saved her from throwing it aside as she'd done the last time she held it. She bolted from Ghyaspur's tiny cabin and hurried up-spin toward the bridge hatch before she had time to think of why.

Allis's hand was on the ladder when the ship lurched violently. Her arm wrenched as her grip boots sprayed sparks, contact surface ripping from the chevron-coated deck. Only holding onto the ladder despite the sudden and awful pain in her shoulder saved her from being dashed against the far bulkhead. There'd been no signal that the ship was coming about, and even Allis knew that was not normal procedure.

Hastily she pocketed the stone and reached for the ladder with her good arm, awkwardly hauling herself to the bridge hatch. She wrestled with the latching mechanism, but had no leverage now that the ship's rotational spin had stopped, and she was unaccustomed to weightlessness. Somehow her body grasped the problem, for she planted her feet against the jamb and slipped the lever aside with her good hand. The hatch slid open as the warning to abandon ship began to hammer from the communication system.

That command struck terror in the hearts of sailors on Earth since time began, but to the sailors of the stellar winds it held a special horror. No one could swim in the *Sovereign Sun*'s ocean.

The bridge crew were abandoning their control stations. Senda and the other albino swam above the control panels, flashing lights from the display screens reflecting a weird array of color on their pale arms.

"Pods!" Allis heard Milani shout. "The shuttles have taken a direct hit. Use the pods."

The pods were the aliens' equivalent of life jackets or space suits, and knowing this made Allis's fear heighten. She had no idea of how to open a casket-shaped pod, let alone operate one if she got in. Her panic must have showed, for Senda grabbed her belt, towing her after Mordon and Milani, who'd already flowed past them into the outer corridor.

"Do you have the stone?" Senda asked as her lithe limbs propelled them to a nearby gangway.

"Yes," Allis said, wondering if she'd have been dropped if her reply were negative.

She saw Milani give Senda a quick nod as she entered the gangway, and just for a second Milani's angry yellow eyes met Allis's, making her aware that Milani loathed giving that nod of life. She'd done it to save the communicator-stone. Without it in her pocket, Allis would have been left to flounder helplessly in freefall.

Other crew members were squirming into the gang-

way from other levels. She saw Milani brace herself
to pull one of them through—Ghyaspur, Allis realized
with relief. But others who had been on the bridge
had gone, she knew not where. At the pod-ejector
chamber in a cargo area a level below the axis, they
numbered six of the crew and Allis of Earth.

Senda pushed Allis into one of the cramped pod
cylinders and nearly sealed the hatch on her fingers.
Almost immediately Allis felt the thrust of being
ejected into space. She prayed that Senda had remembered to turn on the life-support system. When
she realized she was breathing comfortably, even if
too quickly from fear, she hoped Senda would retrieve
her pod. She couldn't operate the cold-jets, and was
too panicky to trust herself to correctly decipher the
markings on the dimly lighted controls. She'd probably propel herself away from the other survivors who
were being ejected from the floundering ship. She
hoped to hear the telltale clunk of a waldo as it
grasped the silent coffin. But nothing happened. She
could no longer tell if her pod was moving or motionless in space. She didn't even know where that
space was in relation to her own solar system.
Drenched in sweat, she waited, measuring time by the
beat of her heart.

Allis was hot. She suspected her excessive perspiration was overloading the life-support system, but her
fear would not subside. If only she were not alone.
Reflexively she reached for the stone and cried out in
anguish as pain fired along the nerves in her shoulder.
The resolve to touch the stone was bitter and painfully ironic; it had brought nothing except agony, but
she would not be alone, if only she would touch it.

When her fingers were firmly around the smooth
stone, her mind rebelled against the influx of emo-

tions. She could not separate the feelings from her own, nor identify whose they were. Yet sensing there was life beyond her coffin walls was a comfort in a torturous way. She hoped someone, Ghyaspur perhaps, would remember her plight of ignorance. Moments of eager anticipation passed before Allis began to wonder what would happen even if someone did snare her pod.

Even if there was a planet nearby, she knew the little pods would not withstand atmospheric re-entry. They were designed for use in frictionless space, for repairing sails and maneuvering cargo, and little else. Did these alien gypsies have SOS signals? She wished she'd heeded Ghyaspur's advice to pay more attention to ship's operations. She might be able to answer her own questions if she hadn't been so stubborn about remaining a deadweight for so long. Her only comfort now was grudging acknowledgment that Milani was an efficient commander and that if the gypsies had an SOS system, the woman had activated it.

When the tap of a waldo finally came, Allis said a prayer of thanks to the God she thought she'd left behind in Sol System. She sensed she was being towed or drawn, then distinctly and abruptly decelerated. When she heard the hatch screw, she put the stone back in her pocket. She said one more prayer of thanks that Milani hadn't had her ultimate revenge in the vacuum of space, then stuck her head out and breathed foul air.

Allis pushed herself out of the pod, grasping the lid to prevent herself from crashing into the bulkhead. She was in the axis of another stellar sailing vessel. Though larger, it was similar enough to the *Sovereign Sun* that she knew she was not mistaken. The decks and bulkheads were seamless blue, the faint but telltale glitter of ultraloy beneath a film of oil. The doors were oval hatches, built to slide into the bulkheads with a pull of the lever. The launch facility for the shuttles was larger, and the look of the planet-fall vessels kept Allis's attention for quite a while. Allis had some concept of how much volume the life support and thrust systems occupied, and even allowing generous proportions, she realized the shuttles were huge, capable of carrying at least thirty people. Then she noticed the armament; no mistaking the barrels of ballistic projectors after she identified the warheads of the missiles loaded under the belly.

Finally, as Allis turned to watch the rest of the survivors from the *Sovereign Sun* push out of their pods, she confirmed her first impression that this vessel stank. The air was foul with common, everyday body odor. She knew water was more precious than gold on the stellar sailing vessels, but Milani's ship had sonic fresheners that were regimentally used. The *Sovereign Sun*'s air had been as sweet as canned air could be. Either this new ship didn't have a freshener, or the crew didn't use it.

The pressure gauge near one of the hatches lighted, the cover slid aside, and armed warriors swarmed in, surrounding the *Sovereign Sun* folk in seconds. They were dressed in a variety of fashions. One could have been a Cossack with his fur cap, another Fidel Castro, complete with dark beard. Their belts were studded with gems, fingers clasping weapons gleaming with precious stones. Ironically, most smiled, but they were grotesque expressions. Involuntarily the contrast between the gypsies Allis knew and the rescuers made her shiver.

Suddenly half the bulkhead that should have been separating the axis shuttle-hold from the armory slid aside, revealing a vermillion-draped chamber that, despite the alien furnishings, reminded Allis of a baroque boudoir. Rich colors curved, using the natural line of what was once the bilge in the armory, but the glitter of the ultraloy was blurred by veils and golden tassels. She recognized a hammock, luminescent webs anchored in golden filigree, and zero-gee decanters etched in breathtaking colors. Streamers of gems, purposeless except to fill a secant or break a radius into a curved line, glowed. But most awesome of all was the tall man who swirled from below her line of vision through the open bulkhead and into the hold, plum veils of sleeve and hem trailing behind. He moved gracefully, not touching the zero-gee poles. He was propelled, by what means Allis didn't know, but she had seen enough natural movement in zero gravity to know that his was impossible without artificial means. He was light-haired, like all the gypsies, and had a smooth oval face, handsome in a rakish way. His eyes were gray-blue and sparkling.

"Milani, your ship is dead. We'll salvage what we can, though I regret your cargo has been destroyed." His syrupy voice held no sympathy for the death of the ship and crew; only contempt for the survivors.

"Maker of Light didn't want to take any chances, did he?" Milani said. She'd barely freed herself from the pod, still restraining the tendency to float away by holding the lid. "We have the right to check damage first. Survivors might be trapped and unable to help themselves. You had no right to haul us in." Her mane of blond hair was damp, her forehead glistening as she faced the opulently clad man.

He smiled. "My bridge crew evaluated the damage. The ship's dead. You're the only survivors."

"How'd he beat us through the slip?" Senda muttered under her breath.

Dacko, Allis thought.

Milani's crew was gathering around her, their faces tense and angry. Instinctively Allis joined them. She was frightened of the strangers.

"I should have thought of his buying a tow," Mordon said.

Milani's lips were a tight line, her teeth clenched until she spoke again. "At least allow us to tend our dead."

Dacko burst out laughing. "To be sure, Milani," he said sarcastically. "And first port of call for the survivors, too." His crew chuckled until Dacko stopped laughing. "But first, give me the stone. I'll keep it safe for you."

Allis imagined that her own face paled as visibly as Milani's. She realized the *Sovereign Sun*'s crew members were reaching for the daggers and tools they kept in their belts, ready to wield them in their captain's defense. Allis sensed that the ominous things packed on their captors' hips outclassed such primitive weaponry. Milani apparently came to the same conclusion. She handed over her stone wordlessly.

"You're wise to take me seriously . . . better late than not at all," Dacko said, rubbing the stone between his fingers. It had dulled away from Milani's flesh.

"Will you check for survivors?" Milani asked. She must have known the answer. The stone would have revealed Dacko's intentions before she handed it over. Perhaps, Allis thought, Milani hoped for a change of heart.

Dacko grinned. "Of course."

Allis didn't need to touch her own stone to know it was a lie.

"And we will receive first port-of-call landings in exchange for what you can salvage from the *Sovereign Sun?*" Milani said, as if she believed the first answer.

"You'll have to work passage. The *Dowager Sun* has no space for deadweight. You'll work our ship's forge." His grin widened. "All of you."

Milani nodded grimly, then without further comment pushed herself across the axis to the gangway. Armed guards scrambled to follow; Allis thought Dacko looked surprised, but he gave no order to halt Milani's exodus. Guards roughly pushed Allis and the others along. Because Allis cried out when her injured arm was touched, no one thought it strange that Ghyaspur helped her along through the axis to the gangway. Midships, they ducked into a narrow corridor, and though pseudogravity was evident, it was weak and difficult to move through without both her arms to propel her along. Ghyaspur stayed close, boosting her when she lost momentum. Shortly, the guards deposited them in a filthy forging shop, and then a heavily shielded hatch slid closed behind them.

The forging shop was huge, rimmed in dirty ultraloy and wainscotted with what looked to Allis like sealing wax. Metal presses, slitters, and extruders lined the torus along the bilge, and a few ingots of silver and other shiny alloys that would eventually become sailcloth were chained to the deck. In the center of the shop Allis believed she was looking at the white heart of the ship's nuclear forge, separated from them only by a transparent wall.

"Murder," Droganie said looking at the glow.

Milani shook her head. "See how bad it is," she said

to the blacksmith. To the others she made a soundless gesture. They separated, searching the shop for hidden listening devices while inventorying the contents. All except Allis, who stood dumbly, holding her bad arm. Milani ignored her.

"They didn't disarm us," Allis said to the captain.

"It emphasizes their contempt," Milani said.

"I mean that they didn't disarm *me*," Allis said, fumbling in her pocket with her good hand. Hastily Milani stopped her, pretending to be concerned with Allis's injured arm.

"I haven't forgotten what you have," Milani said in English, low-toned, only for Allis to hear. Her tawny eyes still held the sick anger they always had when she looked at Allis. "Keep it hidden from that pirate; you are my ace-hole."

"Why should I?" Allis hissed back. "I'd just be trading jailors."

"There's a difference, earthworm, between being a reluctant passenger on a law-abiding vessel like the *Sovereign Sun* and the slave of a pirate. With you in Dacko's hands, havoc could come to entire trade routes. I'll kill you before I let that happen."

"Since Dacko already has your stone, suicide seems the only honorable path open to you," Allis said sweetly.

"I know with whom I deal. I'm experienced in using the communicator-stone. You know nothing, neither about the pirate nor about using the stone. You'd be worse than a child playing with the control rods in the forge."

Milani's fingers were running experimentally over Allis's arm. When she found the separation in the shoulder, Allis winced. Even so, she was surprised by the woman's gentleness.

"Ghyaspur told me that it takes years to learn how to use the stone," Allis said.

Milani nodded.

"Since I can't operate it, how can I be your ace in the hole?"

"It may be years before we have an opportunity to escape," Milani said grimly. "By then you will know how to use it. But I promise you, if I even suspect you'll become Dacko's tool, you will die."

Allis nodded solemnly. The differences between the ships had been enough to unnerve her in the first moments, and she'd instinctively sided with the *Sovereign Sun*'s crew, even though it meant following a woman she hated. Now, having established her worth with Milani, her stone's worth, she reminded herself, she felt safer, despite the threats.

Mordon joined them, whispering, "One listener is by the slitter, Milani, another by the hatch. Nothing will carry that far. A slovenly job, probably more for amusement than security."

"Disconnect the one by the hatch, but let them think we've overlooked the other."

Mordon nodded and moved away, and Droganie filled the place beside the captain. "It's bad," she said. "We should stay behind the ingots as much as possible. I'm going to rig another shield over the furnace, but it won't help much. The magnetic shield's been tampered with; maybe Watcher work."

Milani merely nodded, calmly retreating to the closest stack of ingots as Droganie went to work. Allis followed, wondering what kind of hideous rays were pouring into her body, into her womb.

The search over, the crew rallied around the captain. Their faces were long with anger showing through. Milani offered them no reassurances and didn't even bother to assess their plight. No doubt they were fully aware of their predicament; all seemed to have some knowledge of Dacko, but Allis was still going on intuition.

"Did anyone find something to fashion a splint? Allis has injured her shoulder."

"We can cast it to immobilize it," Bracha said, moving forward to examine the damaged shoulder himself. "There's some gel that will do."

Milani nodded, adding in English, "Slip the stone securely against your skin before Bracha hardens the cast. It will not be found in anything but an extensive search."

"You're crazy," Allis said. The thought of the stone feeding the soul-searing thoughts of her shipmates and the pirates without being able to break contact made her sweat with fear.

"Coward! You were given a gift others would trade their lives for, and you tremble to take it up. Daneth misjudged you!"

Allis did tremble to take it up, but she held her arm out to Bracha and nodded to Milani at the same time that she would do as she had been asked. It was more a gesture of defiance than sudden bravery. Deep inside she knew she'd gladly give the artifact to any one of them to avoid the anguish the stone could bring. But it would be fruitless, for Allis loved no one here except herself. And for herself alone she would learn the stone's secrets.

She nearly passed out from the pain. Bracha had accepted her limply held arm as an invitation to realign it. Moments later, as Bracha put batting around her shoulder and arm, he also slipped the stone next to her skin. She looked at Milani, and despite the captain's nod of approval, the hate in her eyes made

Allis grateful that her own anger still effectively blocked out the captain's thoughts. The feelings and overboiling emotions from the rest of the crew were bad enough, and she broke out in a cold chill. Fear, anger, distrust, humiliation, were being fed into her brain by the stone.

She wanted to scream. She cursed the Quondam Beings who had fashioned the device. Feeling the terrors of six people as if they were her own was too much to bear. Then something gentle broke through the anguish. Allis's mind eased and she tried to relax. Bracha's fingers were lingering at her neck as he adjusted the sling. Were the tender feelings his? Or were they from Ghyaspur, who was standing to the side, trying to look brave. But she couldn't distinguish personalities amid the emotions. She knew Ghyaspur could be compassionate, but Bracha? She couldn't be certain. Milani, she noticed, was studying her critically. She was the one person Allis was certain the gentle thread of warmth did not come from.

"What do you feel?" the captain asked her.

"One of you is being kind," Allis said, her tone sarcastic.

"Which one?"

Allis shook her head. "If I could identify him, would you have him stripped and lashed?"

Frowning, Milani shook her head. "One time, Allis, we'll have it out between us. But for now I need you, and I will guide you in learning to use the stone. All our lives depend on it." She gestured to the men and women around her. "Let there be a truce for now," the captain suggested.

Milani must not have realized how affected Allis had been by the crew's behavior toward her, their unrelenting rejection, or maybe she thought Allis was too stupid to notice. Even now they didn't look regretful. "A truce," Allis agreed reluctantly.

Milani nodded, satisfied, and turned to her crew. "You must each identify what you feel, tell her your emotions, and later confirm your word-thoughts, until she learns to recognize them and read for herself. Hold back and it will take her longer, lie and she'll become confused. Cooperate and she'll read us out of here when the pirates least expect it."

It was Droganie who objected. "Stone-carriers are on their honor not to listen where they are not bidden," she said sourly. "Allis can't claim respect from us, yet you want us to go naked in front of her."

"Tough shit," Allis said. "It's my neck, too!"

Not without misgivings, the others nodded their agreement. Neither they nor Allis had much choice in the matter, but it was obvious their cooperation was not going to start now. No doubt they wanted a less public time to begin, a moment with Allis alone.

"What happens next?" Allis asked, hoping for a better picture of what she was up against. As Milani had said, she was practically ignorant of pirates. At best she knew there'd been some trouble with Dacko on Crossroads; beyond that she knew bits of what she'd thought were folk tales told in the armory over mulled wine.

Milani shrugged. "The report that I will have to sign, if Dacko even pretends to follow conventions, will probably say his ship collided with ours as we came out of the gravity slip. It's not a common accident, but not impossible since there's no way to detect a ship through the slip. In reality, of course, a missile hit us aft when we came out. Dacko had been waiting for us to poke our nose through."

"With seven of us to testify in Watcher court about what really happened?"

"Make no mistake, Allis. We'll never live to see tribunals if Dacko has his way. We've been rescued and allowed to live only because I am a stone-carrier. With hostages, Dacko can force me to do his will. I suspect I'll make some shrewd bargains for him in the trade ports before this is over. Normally, there are no survivors in a pirate raid, no one to tell the Watchers what happened."

"Since he knew of your stone, won't he look for Dan's?" Allis asked, shivering. She didn't like what she was hearing, and she didn't like what she was feeling.

Milani's smooth face darkened at the sound of her co-captain's name. "Perhaps, but if he did know about it, and finds only dead in the *Sovereign Sun,* he won't cry over it. A dead operator cannot use the stone for him, nor pass it to another person. It's dead forever. He'll concentrate on the live one."

"Could there be survivors besides us who might tell him about me?" Allis asked quietly. She was feeling weak with the weight of the stone on her arm. Her stomach felt queasy, but she watched Milani closely. This was the first time the captain ever had paid attention to her.

Milani was shaking her head. "The possibility of survivors was remote before we ever ejected ourselves. The axis took a direct hit, the keel another. The life-support system was out from the start. No one could get to the emergency . . . I know by my stone that they were dead. We were lucky to be close to the right gangway. Had it been any other way, we would have given our lives in the locks in an attempt to get to the rest of the crew."

Callously, Allis tucked away for future use the knowledge that if anything did happen to Milani before they were able to escape, she had a bargaining stance for her life, even if the others had no such hope. Then she collapsed, sick and weak.

CHAPTER 16

Milani excused Allis from working along with herself and the rest of the crew in securing the ingots and equipment in the filthy forging shop. Even if the pirates were spying on them—and Milani had no doubt that they were—they wouldn't think her inactivity strange, because she had an injured arm. Actually Allis was incapacitated by the stone, emotionally exhausted by the steady flow of confusing data, and somewhat dazed. Milani knew it would happen since Allis hadn't the slightest control over the input, but she also knew that eventually Allis's brain would begin to shunt the overload to short-term memory in self-defense, with only a slight chance of her going insane.

As Milani piled a second row of ingots between the forge and the bulkhead where Allis was sitting, she couldn't help looking at the little woman. Allis, she knew, was small even among her own kind. Small, but well proportioned. Not wiry or tough, but strong in a compact sort of way. Her hair was black as space, tightly braided over the crown of her head, an alternative to cutting it that worked satisfactorily. Her eyes were light brown, close enough to the yellow irises that sometimes occurred among stellar sailors that they wouldn't attract undue attention. Allis looked much like an ordinary sailor, even to adopting their dress of cuffed blouse and pants. She was set apart only by her small stature, but not greatly so. Beyond her physical appearance Milani knew nothing about the woman. Not her character and not her morals. She'd avoided her, hating her, sickened and reminded of searing pain by the very sight of her.

Now Milani regretted shunning Allis, for she couldn't be certain it was wise to let her live. She was an unknown with the potential power of a communicator-stone in the ship of a butcher. Deep inside it was Daneth's judgment Milani trusted, but she was unable to reconcile that faith in her co-captain with the betrayal by the lover. Sometimes, like now, she sweated, and wondered if she was doing the right thing.

There was little to be done about the filth in the forge. Droganie had changed the clogged air filters. As the particles of dirt became airborne and were trapped in the filters, they would help, but until then the prisoners would wallow in the filth. The air was heavy with the odors of lubricants, hot metal, nutrient dust, tobacco, and above all, the overpowering smell of unclean bodies, and those were probably eternal. Dacko and his crew were immune to their disgust. It was not the first time Milani had experienced the stench on a sailing vessel. It was common on ships whose crews never stayed planetside long enough to sense the treat of clean air and wonder how to provide themselves with the same. Dacko's kind, pirates, made few planetside visits, preferring to live off the profit of honest traders. But his thick perfume that Milani had smelled back in Crossroads was not enough in itself to alert her to his evil intentions; indeed, not even his angry and wayward mind had given her warning of attack and capture. But the dead communicator-stone was gone from his finger, and she could guess the price The Maker of Light had paid.

Milani noticed the screw of the hatch begin to turn and she signaled the crew to stand alert. Secretly, she ordered Mordon and Senda to stay at Allis's side, daggers ready. For now they merely helped her to her feet, propping her good arm on the stack of ingots so she would not slouch too badly. Dacko wasn't likely to recognize the signs of first-touch sickness, especially in someone who was otherwise injured.

Several male guards stepped through the hatch, weapons drawn, eyes scanning the little group of prisoners. Satisfied, they stepped aside to reveal Dacko. He was unarmed, but probably heavily armored because he moved sluggishly, despite Quondam Being wings.

"There wasn't much to salvage, Milani," Dacko said, "One sack of industrial diamonds isn't enough to cover the passage of seven people to our next port of call."

Milani stiffened and wondered if Dacko's crew truly had overlooked the bursting secret hold. The cargo areas were nearly empty, the industrial diamonds from her own strongbox. He'd have no use for the mining equipment stowed under the superstructure, even if it were salvageable. But in the hidden hold was the cache of diamonds Daneth had secured on Earth, and more. Much more. She'd have traded some to have her stone to know if Dacko was telling the truth or merely toying with her.

"What did you plan to do with only ten thousand carats in this sector of the galaxy?" the pirate asked her. "A trading vessel can't survive long on that paltry sum."

"You thought it was handsome enough back in Crossroads," Milani said.

"Then it was twice the amount. Where's the rest?"

"Same place your dead communicator-stone is; in The Maker of Light's strongbox. I think you made the better bargain, Dacko. A tow from Crossroads to the proper gravity slip, and now you have my fee and the consignment as well, if you have any use for it. That's a good exchange for a stone that's dead and useless."

Dacko smiled. "He hopes to activate it; it seems there've been some breakthroughs in Quondam Being engineering."

"I've heard that before."

"Don't think you can put me off, Milani. The diamonds. Where are the rest of them?"

"I told you. The Maker of Light has them. You must have noticed our crew number was below normal. We have been trading for talent rather than profitable cargo. I made some shrewd buys from the Watcher."

"There's nothing recorded . . ."

"Dacko, you're dense," Milani said, cutting him off. "Watchers can't deal in flesh out in the open. Did you expect me to record it in the ship's computer where any spacing bureau that has a few splicers could siphon it off? Of course it's not recorded."

"A stone-carrier should have a good cargo and a full crew. And with two stone-carriers on board . . ." He let his accusation form unspoken.

Milani froze and saw Mordon and Senda edge for their daggers. "Our other stone-carrier died at our last port of call without bringing out the trade goods," Milani said carefully.

"Mmmm," Dacko mused. "Died planetside, eh? He was your co-captain and mate, wasn't he?"

Milani's fist tightened. "He was."

"Did he pass his stone to you?"

"He did not. He died planetside as I said. I was aboard the *Sovereign Sun* when it happened."

"Search her!" Dacko snapped. The guards leaped to obey. They stripped Milani down, checking and rechecking all places of concealment in her garments and on her person. Milani stood proudly, enduring their prodding fingers, confident they would find nothing. She'd gladly endure any humiliation to preclude a search of the rest of the crew. That would result in Allis's death, and end the only hope for escape.

The guards came away from the naked captain empty-handed. The leader shook his head at Dacko. "It's not there. The computer log must have been accurate. The co-captain died planetside without her being there to accept the stone."

"Missed your chance to be a double-stone-carrier," Dacko said to Milani. "No matter. It wouldn't make your work any easier. And since the salvage was so poor, we'll have to get you working quickly to repay all this hospitality." He paused a moment to stare at Milani's breasts; her eyes fell to his crotch and she sneered. Angrily, Dacko turned. "We'll be calling on the miners of Thang very soon. You'd best prepare a proposal . . . your diamonds for enough ingots to double my sails."

Inwardly, Milani cringed. Most of the Thang hierarchy knew and trusted her, for she'd been buying sailcloth from them for half a lifetime. Partly she'd allowed herself to be persuaded to take The Maker of Light's consignment so that she could warn the gentle miners of their Watcher ambassador's plan to do some mining of his own. She was unlikely to get an opportunity to tell them anything, but they'd no doubt learn a thing or two about Dacko and perhaps be wary of any spacefarers for a while.

"You can do it, can't you, Milani?" Dacko said.

"Double your sailcloth? I won't know until I sit in their presence with my stone," Milani replied quietly. "I can't foresee."

"You will succeed, Milani, or suffer the consequences."

"I'm sure you have plans to ensure my enthusiastic cooperation," Milani said dryly.

"Of course I do," was the cold reply.

The pirate turned and left in a swirl of crimson silk. His guards filed out and closed the hatch. Milani's crew averted their eyes while she dressed, all except Allis who was no longer holding the ingots for support. She stepped over cables to reach Milani's side.

"You ought to make the worst possible deal," she said, looking angry. "Don't give him what he wants. He's nothing but a jackdaw in peacock feathers."

Milani blinked at the Earthwoman. "You would resist?" she asked in surprise.

"Yes," Allis said firmly.

Milani adjusted her sash. "Noble," she said. "But then, you are not yet aware of the stone's burden. Dacko knows how to turn it to his advantage, I'm sure. I suspect he's had some experience in coercing stone-carriers. I'll not resist him very much."

"Coward!" Allis accused.

Milani was nonplused. "You have much to learn," she said quietly, speaking in English now. "The stones are a blessing and give the operators an almost divine insight, which can be the biggest advantage over one's fellow humans in almost any situation. But the blessings are balanced by a burden. Physical pain and anguish are as much a part of the human mind as the things we like to encounter, like love and truth. I can control my responses to what I feel through the stone. I can channel and store the ugliest sensations without being driven insane, detach myself, so to speak, emotionally. That ability can be learned and is, in part, what you lack in using your stone. Still, detachment is constrained when loved ones and friends are involved. A proclivity exists to be with them, an overwhelming urge to share. It's impossible to store the emotions of friends and lovers like computer data. That is what Dacko knows and will use.

"He could torture some innocent stranger and I could watch, and even feel the throes of death like a dispassionate woman made of ultraloy, then tuck the experience away like a bad book just read. But touch one of my crew and instantly I would be with him, crying with his pain and suffering his anguish exactly as if it were being inflicted on me. Such trials are worse for the stone-carrier than the victim. There's no hope in fantasizing that perhaps the pain is not so bad as it looks. The stone-carrier knows exactly how bad it is, and if you know you are also responsible for causing it, your own misery intensifies." Milani glanced over at her crew, wondering which of them Dacko would use to hold her. When she looked back at Allis, the Earthwoman was frowning and wordless, apparently considering what she'd been told.

"I couldn't stand that either," she finally admitted. "I'm suffering enough now."

"You're far from my degree of control," Milani said, sympathizing. "I'll help you as best I can to get that load in your head properly stowed. Perhaps we should have another session now. You seem less pale. Anger apparently strengthens you."

But the session was fruitless. Allis didn't perceive

raw emotions as Milani did, nor was she able to follow
directions in how to channel the data. They simply
didn't have the same reference frames, one being
from the spacelanes, the other from planetlock. She
left Allis slouching against the stack of ingots, and
crossed the forge to the other stack where the rest of
the crew waited. Senda looked at her expectantly.
Milani shook her head.

"If only it were someone else," she muttered, sinking
down between Senda and Mordon.

Ghyaspur leaned forward as if to speak, but he only
stared at Milani. His eyes were bright as stars and as
intense as the biggest blues in the galaxy. It was as if
he were speaking to her subliminally, and finally Milani realized that after a fashion he was doing precisely
that. If anyone could receive the stone from Allis, it
was Ghyaspur. If anyone knew her well enough to
persuade her to give it, that, too, was Ghyaspur.
Milani barely nodded, but Ghyaspur smiled wryly.
There was no mistaking both their intentions. Even
Senda and Mordon seemed to understand. A moment
later Ghyaspur left the crew to go to the Earthwoman.

CHAPTER 17

Allis stared at the dirty bulkhead, her mind in a turmoil of alien sorrows despite most of the *Sovereign Sun*'s crew being asleep and supposedly relaxed. There'd been no sign of movements from the barrier of ingots across the shop where Milani had ordered everyone to stay whenever possible to minimize exposure to the radiation escaping from the forge. But for Ghyaspur, Allis sat alone behind a second stack of ingots.

Only the young pilot seemed concerned that she was uncomfortable with the stone pressed to her flesh, infusing her with unnamed fears that alarmed her brain and knotted her stomach. She suspected it was the prisoners' grief she was feeling. They'd not spoken of losing their shipmates, friends, and lovers, in keeping with their custom of reserving mourning for the privacy of their own ship, at a time when Milani would indicate it was appropriate. But Allis knew such feelings could not be shunted aside until ship's burdens were all satisfied and the sails filled with a steady wind. If it was sorrow she was sensing, it was a hot and sharp form.

Sitting was the worst of it, she decided. Not that it was uncomfortable in the low gravity, but the monotony made it hard to think of anything except the acid in the pit of her stomach and why it was there. She'd had few thoughts of her own since she'd taken up the stone, and she was sorely tempted to tear off the hardened gel cast and rid herself of the alien device. From Milani's obvious disappointment after the last session, she knew the flow of moody stuff in her head would not end soon. Somehow it was up to her to end it, but not even Milani had been able to show her how.

Circles, Milani had called the stuff in her head. Like colored circles. Find one circle of color and pull it straight, like you would a ringlet of hair.

But her mind was like a black murky globe atop her shoulders. Colors, if there were any, congealed to black. She couldn't find a circle to save her soul or her sanity, and Allis sensed that her sanity would be in peril if she didn't succeed soon. Milani had said that the burden could drive an experienced stone-carrier mad. What it was doing to Allis's mind, so inexperienced and so vulnerable, she could only guess. Perhaps in the next moment synapses would fire wildly and she'd lose what little control she had. Even now her head was pounding, adrenaline was flooding her body, but there was nothing to be done with the excessive energy, no place to run, nowhere to hide. Nothing even to flee except the elusive circles somewhere in her mind.

Next to her, Ghyaspur's head dropped to her shoulder and for a moment he snuggled against her. Something warm glowed briefly in her mind. Then, apparently less asleep than she'd thought, he sat up, resting his head against the ingots again. The warmth cooled.

"Do that again," Allis whispered.

"Huh?" His eyes blinked and opened.

"Your head on my shoulder felt good," she said.

She moved closer to him, thigh against outstretched thigh, shoulder against shoulder. The warm spot returned and swelled as she relaxed against him. She felt the ruddy glow of his mind soothing her as he moved his arm to encircle her, hesitantly at first, then firmly as he realized that was what she wanted.

"Does it hurt very much?" he asked. Even though he touched her cast, she knew he was alluding to the stone. He was right not to speak of it. One listening device was known to be operating, and there could be other devices spying on them, much more refined by an alien technology whose limits she did not know.

"It hurts," she said grimly, but the pain was softened by the warm glow in her mind, brought about, she was sure, by Ghyaspur's closeness. His eyelids were fluttering closed again. He didn't seem worried that she'd misunderstand his sleepy but reassuring squeezes, nor did it seem that he'd forgotten the incident on the *Sovereign Sun* since he held her lightly but comfortably.

Allis lay against his chest, listening to his heartbeat and feeling the warmth in her mind pulsate like an echo. A sudden change in the ship's vibration accelerated his heartbeat and disturbed them both. Allis stirred.

"It's nothing," he whispered. "A power surge in the air blowers."

His heartbeat slowed and leveled at a reassuring pace that Allis's own heart seemed to match. She concentrated on the warmth in her mind, idly wondering if in exploring it she would find the circle of color Milani spoke about. She didn't think about it too deeply, however, afraid to break the soothing spell. The weariness of her body tugged at her brain, the dull ache of her shoulder became remote. The last

thing she remembered before she fell asleep was knowing that Ghyaspur's thoughts were like a circle of
orange feathers.

Allis was awakened by the absence of Ghyaspur's
arms. He'd just stood up, leaving her slumped against
the ingots while he stretched. Seeing Milani's hand
signal from across the shop interrupted Ghyaspur's
stretch and brought Allis fully awake.

"We're coming about," he said, hastily grabbing
Allis's good arm and half-dragging her to the bulkhead, where there were ample stanchions. The rest of
the crew made way for them, then all braced for the
maneuver. The ship swayed, but did not come about.
They looked at Milani, her face haggard and eyes narrow from sleeplessness.

"You spoke as if you were reading their bridge with
your stone," Senda said hesitantly to Milani.

"No," Milani said tiredly. "It's just that I got a
look at the size of his sails when we were in the pods
and I know the distance from the gravity slip to the
planet. The timing was right for a good parking
orbit."

The ship lurched mightily. Ghyaspur had caged
Allis against the bulkhead with all four limbs or she
might have been ripped from her single handhold.
Nothing stirred in the battened-down forge, but tell-
tale clinks echoed from the closest airduct and there
was the feel of objects not properly stowed battering
against the bulkhead they were holding.

"A careless master," Droganie said. "A wonder he's
lasted this long."

Mordon scowled. "One like him has no respect for
the cost of raising goods off-planet. He swindles or
steals whatever he needs to replace them."

When the impetus of the jostling maneuver ended,

the crew began releasing themselves from their grips along the bulkhead to return to the barrier of ingots. With his hand still on her arm, Ghyaspur guided Allis along after them, sensing, no doubt, that she would have returned to her solitary place otherwise.

"You look as if you slept," Milani said as she sank down behind the ingots.

Allis nodded, glancing at Ghyaspur.

"That's a good sign."

Ghyaspur was looking intently at his captain, wry smile on his lips, reverence in his eyes. Milani did not meet his eyes, deliberately avoided them. When Allis looked again, there was nothing special about his expression, and Milani seemed merely weary.

"Sit down," Milani said, speaking English now. "Tell me how you got to sleep for the shift, and we'll start from there."

Allis sat beside Milani, pretending to be deep in thought, as if what she remembered was hard to understand. She still had Ghyaspur's orange circle, so ruddy and sparkling when Milani'd given the warning to prepare for the ship's maneuver that Allis had been alerted, too. It was wispy now, as if he hadn't a care in the world. And how could that be? He was a free soul trapped in the pirate ship's prison, life in constant jeopardy, if she could believe all that she'd been told. Of course there was the closeness of having spent the evenshift nestled with Allis. Had it meant more to him than comforting a friend? And if it did, why would he want Milani to know? Perhaps she had misread that look. Ghyaspur was, after all, alien, and she'd never been able to figure out the rest of the crew even if Ghyaspur had seemed transparent. Perhaps she'd never really understood him either.

"Come on, Allis," Milani said impatiently. "I

couldn't read you if I had my stone, so you'll just have to talk. Tell me . . ."

"Shhh," Senda warned, putting a hand out for silence and inadvertently touching Allis's knee.

Another circle gelled into cool blue as they looked at the albino. Senda gestured toward the hatch with her pink eyes, crepy lines in her face deepening as she frowned. The hatch screw turned.

"He's not wasting any time," Milani muttered, getting to her feet. She put her hands out to the sides, palms forward to indicate their emptiness, and went to the hatch unbidden as Dacko's guards burst in, weapons raised. They parted to make way for the pirate leader when they were certain all their captives were in view.

Dacko wore common sailor garb. The blouse and pants were cut from velvety blue cloth and the sash from yellow linen, but he was unadorned by jewelry. Somehow the restraint in his attire made him appear all the richer, and Allis was surprised he had the taste to know it.

"How thoughtful of you to be ready, Milani," he said, brushing past her. Milani turned to watch him hover before the rest of the prisoners. "You'll need a companion, of course."

For a moment Dacko regarded the *Sovereign Sun*'s crew, chin in hand propped up by an arm. Each met his eyes with a chilly gaze, which the pirate neither acknowledged nor seemed to care about, until he got to Ghyaspur. Dacko's thick brows raised in appreciation, gray eyes glittering, then laughing with delight as Ghyaspur finally blushed.

"I overlooked this child last shift," the pirate said. "How do you suppose I managed that?" He looked back to see Milani's expression. She was impassive.

"But maybe we'll take the one who's not full grown," he said, turning abruptly to Allis. Dacko beckoned with a finger.

Allis stood up uncertainly. "I'll be of little help. I'm injured."

"How convenient. A tingler in your neck muscles ought to keep that bad arm burning. Think you'll pick that up easily enough, Milani? Don't want you to strain yourself." His grin was hideous.

Allis began to understand, and understanding made her tremble. She saw Milani's eyes widen and for a moment Allis thought the captain would laugh out loud. The captain's amusement stopped abruptly, for Dacko turned toward the hatch and had her in view again.

But for her foreboding, Allis would have rejoiced at suddenly knowing there were several colored circles spinning in her head along with Ghyaspur's angry orange and Senda's cold blue. She had no idea of whose they were, pirates or shipmates, since this time no one had touched her when they appeared. Feeling tense, Allis followed the angry captains out of the hatch.

Allis and Milani were given overcoats, thick shiny ones. Allis was fitted with a tiny leachlike mechanism that pierced her skin and gripped the tendon that ran from her neck over her shoulder. Relaxed, it was merely annoying once the first sting of the puncture abated. But judging by Dacko's satisfaction, Allis had no doubt the device held tremendous potential for pain. Milani watched the tingler's placement in silence.

"That is only an on-the-spot reminder," Dacko said, watching one of the guards wipe away the last drop of blood from Allis's skin. She'd gained another circle of thought, but it was pretty empty, as if its owner were dull-witted. "If I'm not satisfied with your bargain, we'll have a real session in pain when we return to the *Dowager Sun*."

"Do you think I'd risk facing the burden?" Milani asked scornfully.

"Stone-carriers take any risk they think they can get away with," was his matter-of-fact reply. "If you don't exceed my highest expectations, I will strap that stone to you and watch you experience the burden."

Milani's expression was unfathomable as they were hustled to the axis and into one of the huge shuttles. Allis suppressed an urge to scream. Milani faced no burden carrying her stone with Allis as the load. The hate the captain felt for her prevented her from feeling even the slightest discomfort from Allis. Milani's insane smile mocked her. She had visions of torture, something unknown flailing at her body, and Milani, woman of steel, looking on with an insidious grin. It smacked not of ludicrousness but of a strong reality. She'd never thought of torture before, but then she hadn't imagine stellar sailing vessels, aliens, or pirates either. Suddenly torture was easy to add to the strange list of realities.

Obsessed with fear, Allis couldn't even attempt to examine the increasing number of colored circles in her mind let alone to identify whose they were. She barely even noticed the awesome sight of the ice-sheathed planet growing larger in the viewplate, reflecting light in blinding flashes until someone turned on the dimmers.

They were met by a small groundcar, a sledge of sorts that was silently powered and slithered through the snow covering a barren countryside. The amazement Allis felt at being the first Earthling to visit an

alien world was only a little less strong than the
shock of having a pain-making device clamped to her
body. It was dim, cold, and cloudy, she realized, with a
green glow that did not fit the winter season. Seemingly the snow itself cast the color, moss bright in
shadows, limelike in the light, crystalline and shimmering in the air. Lichen, she guessed, and the squat
crimson silhouettes at the side of the track they were
following must be slumbering trees, their thick limbs
heavy with green snow. Ahead, through the cab of
the sledge, she could see a cluster of snow-covered
structures that had the vertical angles of humankind's
touch to them as well as the haunting glow of ultraloy.
Parts of the structures were protruding from a glacier
that ran in a deceptively soft rise to distant, green-
capped mountains.

The sledge halted before the buildings. Dacko
sighed and turned to Milani.

"You'll be wasting your time if you try to read me,"
he said. "Or did you already know that?" He held her
stone between his thumb and index finger. "Concentrate on the bargain you must make."

Milani grinned slightly, held out her hand to receive her stone from Dacko. "I stay out of mires as
much as possible."

"Just remember the child here," Dacko warned,
withholding the stone from her. He frowned. "Or is
she a child?" His gray-eyed stare penetrated, and Allis
looked away. "Mutant-small?" he asked Milani. When
she didn't answer he shrugged. "No matter. She's one
of yours. Just remember that if I'm not pleased . . ."

As the pirate's voice trailed off, he handed Milani
the stone. Immediately Allis felt her shoulder twinge,
then ache with pain. A moan escaped her as the pain
increased.

"Enough," Milani said quickly.

The pain eased and Allis looked up to meet Milani's steady gaze. There was nothing in it, no sympathy, no hate—nothing to give her a clue to her fate in the woman's hands. Milani had merely mind read Dacko's touch on the controls of the tingler and she'd spoken quickly to keep him believing he had her in his control.

The door of the cab burst open and two small furry-faced men bundled in fluffy coats stood atop the waist-deep snow.

"Welcome, Milani," the wider of the two said in slurred gypsy tongue. He nodded to the pirates and to Allis. "I am Tamas, your host and guide while you are at the Northern Glacier."

"I remember a child named Tamas who greeted me in the company of his father, Klaas, the last time I visited your world."

Tamas smiled, revealing a row of sturdy yellow teeth. "I am that child," he said. "I have brought my son, Theas, to see the woman from the stars who never grows old."

The other miner beamed, but, except that his eyes were more limpid and curious, there didn't seem to be anything youthful about him. Milani reached out to accept the snowshoes he handed up, and slipping them over her boots, she stepped into the snow. "Have you had sledges like this very long?" she said. "They look off-world in design."

"Are they not fine?" Tamas asked, obviously proud. "The stellar sailors are no longer the only star people who visit us. We exchanged this sledge for a glacier even farther north." He chuckled, amused by the exchange. "It's miles thick, which the star people claim to approve of. Can I interest you in a river of ice, Milani?"

"Not today," she said quickly. "Where are they, these other star people?"

Tamas shrugged. "They keep to themselves, appearing in their flying machine as mysteriously as you do, although more frequently."

"They're stuck in a blizzard," Dacko said, jumping into the snow. His feet made no impression there. They stood back to allow three guards and Allis also to alight. Even though the air was windless, cold bit through her garments as they followed the miners to the buildings. The gravity made Allis's breasts bounce and ache, and it tugged on her womb, making it feel so heavy she thought it would drop out of her body onto the snow. At first she had believed her pregnancy made her especially sensitive to the gravitational pull; then she saw Milani was breathing hard, exhaling great frosty gasps after only a few steps. Of the off-worlders, only Dacko seemed untroubled by the planet's pull. He barely touched the snow, leaving only childlike impressions in it, propelled by some concealed gravity-defying device, no doubt the same device he used in the ship. The little miners didn't stare; they must have seen such feats before, and the pirates took no special notice of anything. It was ironic, Allis thought, as she trudged through the snow, to know she was the first Earthling to set foot on an alien planet and to be in the company of beings of two alien races, about to enter what she believed might be the ancient dwellings of yet another race. How ironic that of all these, she cared only that she wouldn't have to walk too far.

Inside it was less cold, but though the two miners

shed their coats, the sailors did not. Green snow lay unmelting in corners, green icicles grew from low ultraloy ceilings, making Milani and the taller guards duck or break them with their heads. They were led through a maze of ice corridors and barren rooms of ultraloy until they reached a great hall where a fire blazed in an open hearth. Water ran before the fireplace in rivulets, flowing to a low corner where it froze into a sheet of ice.

A table was arranged before the fire. Two more small men sat there, eyes limpid. On looking closer, Allis realized their torsos were bare of clothes but not of hair. On their heads and chins their hair was coarse and curly, but the remainder of their faces and bodies were covered with flaxen fur. Even their eyelids were covered with the deceptive down. She glanced back at Tamas. His eyes seemed less limpid when she realized their depth was an illusion caused by the deep fur.

Dacko hovered next to Milani's chair; Allis was guided opposite them by Dacko's mates. She was suddenly aware that she'd been ignoring the whirling circles in her head. Pleased with her ability to do so but cursing herself for overlooking possible data, she tried to identify Dacko's circle. Tamas, she noticed, was ready for business, leaning forward and eager but somehow not looking particularly small amid his tall companions. The boy had moved off to the side of the parley table to tend the fire, feeding the flames with dark stones.

"What do you wish to trade?" Tamas said, not offering to introduce his companions.

"That depends on what you have to trade," Milani said.

"Metal ingots, of course," Tamas said. "There's copper from the deep digs where we found more Quondam Being machines, some silver, and ultraloy, all processed into ingots for convenient handling."

"And the threads of the ice-worm cocoons?" Milani asked.

Allis looked at her curiously, wondering what an ice-worm might look like and if the thread from its cocoons were finer than silk. Yet without having heard of the creature before, she was positive they fed on the lichen in the snow and ice. It was logical, of course, yet she felt as if it was knowledge acquired in the past second or two.

"No skeins of thread are offered this year. We have only enough for our own needs. The snow was scant, the crop poor."

"A pity," Milani said. "It's thread we came for. Our forge is well supplied with ingots for sailcloth."

Allis's shoulder was growning uncomfortably warm as Dacko looked sharply at Milani. Allis grimaced, her curiosity about ice-worms melting rapidly from the heat in her shoulder, but Milani was not looking.

Tamas shrugged. "A bargain depends on mutual need, star person. But since I cannot offer what you want and you do not require what I offer, we have no need of each other this winter."

Allis thought the little man moved back a bit, readying himself to rise and leave. Apparently Dacko thought so, too, for he was causing Allis's shoulder increasing discomfort.

Milani grinned at Tamas. "As you say, one must have the goods, the other the need. Perhaps you have need of these." She took a fistful of diamonds from the pouch at her belt and placed them carefully on the table.

Immediately three dull circles in Allis's head brightened as the miners looked at the diamonds with interest, then at each other.

"We always are pleased to consider diamonds, which we require for our drill bits. What would you have in exchange?"

"Thread," Milani said simply.

"I told you we have none to offer," Tamas said. "But we have ultraloy ingots for your sails and fine-quality silver with which to plate them."

"I can get sailcloth anywhere. It's thread I want."

"But you do want the sailcloth, too," Tamas said shrewdly.

"Without thread there'll be no deal," Milani said, starting to gather up the diamonds from the table. "I'll have to save these to bargain with elsewhere."

Allis rubbed her shoulder uncomfortably. It was difficult to concentrate with the pain distracting her, but she thought she sensed something like lust coming from the three little men. More likely it was their need for the diamonds; even if they occurred naturally on this frozen world, they'd be hard to find. Allis had sat in contractors' offices often enough to realize Milani's perception of the situation was acute and the negotiations were going well, but Dacko didn't know. There was a growing impatience in the circle of thought she believed was his.

"How much thread would you want?" Tamas said more calmly than he felt. "And how many ingots of ultraloy and silver?"

Milani sat back, playing with one of the diamonds between her fingers. "I could use forty ingots of silver and four hundred of ultraloy." The little man smiled. "But unless I get five hundred skeins of thread, I will have no need for the ingots. I can make a speedy jump with the extra sails to Sodan and trade the thread in time for the new season's fashions."

"Two hunderd skeins," Tamas said, "is all your pouch of diamonds will buy."

"Four hundred and double the sailcloth," Milani said.

"Two hundred and fifty," the tiny man countered.

Milani hesitated. Allis sensed from the satisfaction in her own mind that the little men must be feeling a fair point had been reached in the negotiations. Milani had to be even more keenly aware, for with her stone she'd have the miners' deepest thoughts. But Allis's arm was twitching under the coat she wore; Dacko was not satisfied. Allis frowned at Milani and coughed to get her attention, but the captain had eyes only for the small furry man. He was worried, prepared to give more, if Allis understood correctly how strong his need was for the diamonds. Milani must know this too. Allis's shoulder was aching now, so inflamed she could hardly keep back the tears. Would Milani never satisfy the pirate?

"Four hundred skeins and triple the sailcloth," Milani finally said.

The little man was infuriated, but Allis sighed with relief as Dacko eased the pain in her shoulder. Her relief was only physical and very brief as fearful anticipation filled her mind. Tamas still was angry, so angry that Allis believed he'd break off the negotiations without agreeing to Milani's last offer. She knew she'd get more than a jolt of pain if he did; she'd be murdered with pain that Milani wouldn't know. A spasm of belligerence shot through her, Tamas's, and a horrified Allis met it with a mind-thundering *No!* His circle of thought skittered in confusion, sparking like an ember in the fireplace jabbed by a poker.

"Three hundred skeins and triple the sailcloth." Tamas seemed embarrassed as the other two little men stared. Milani recovered from her own surprise by nodding.

"Three hundred skeins, one hundred twenty bars of silver, and twelve hundred ingots of ultraloy," she said, talleying the final count.

"Done," Tamas said, breathing a relieved sigh. He was disappointed by Milani's behavior; she hadn't lived up to her reputation of being a fair customer, and he was more than a little confused by his own impulsive acquiescence. But he said graciously, "Shall we have a drink of warm ferments to celebrate and to bring some warmth to our veins? Your friend here especially seems to need one."

Milani glanced at Allis who was shivering not with cold but with the aftermath of pain tremors. "My friend is not well. I'd better get her back to the ship."

"I will stay," Dacko announced. "Bring on the drinks, Tamas. A shift planetside is something I don't want to miss." He winked, and Allis was certain she had his bawdy circle of thought isolated now. It gloated more than it glowed.

"Smooth tunneling," Milani said tiredly to the miners as she rose from the table. Allis rose with her, and so did the pirate guards.

"The delivery . . ." Tamas said, obviously disappointed to see her leave so soon. There was a mystery in his mind, one he might solve if only Milani would stay.

"I'll take care of that," Dacko said, dismissing Milani with a wave.

The boy stepped forward to guide them through the icy maze to the outer door. That he opened silently and let them out into the thick, green snow, falling heavily now. Theas, Allis was certain, was disenchanted by the visitors from the stars, something Milani seemed aware of too. The captain stared at the boy with concern, looking as if she was about to speak. Then the door closed and Theas was gone.

"Hand over the stone, Milani," one of the guards said to the captain. Milani unpalmed the stone into the pirate's waiting hand, then she struck out for the sledge in long, sure strides. Allis hurried to keep up.

Back at the shuttle, Allis and Milani were trussed to chairs with built-in manacles in the rear of the shuttle. The two crewmen went forward to drink and talk in the comfort of the cockpit.

"Why aren't they breathing hard anymore?" Allis said, painfully aware of her spine and hips holding up her whole tired body.

"Drugs," Milani said. "Some prefer putting off the pain until they're back in the ship where there's less strain. Or maybe these people never pay the price, just put it off by taking more drugs."

Allis might have welcomed a bit of something to take the edge off her pain. Her shoulder throbbed, but the manacle around her wrist was tethered so close she couldn't reach far enough even to touch the afflicted area. She could, however, reach her belly, and she spread her fingers over the bulge. Her womb seemed to have grown tenfold since they planeted. She saw Milani look away sharply when she realized where Allis's hand lay, instantly uncomfortable.

"I know you made the best bargain you could," Allis whispered.

"Not for you," Milani answered in English, her

voice sounding strained and bitter. "Make no mistake about that, Allis of Earth. I would have taken great pleasure in seeing you suffer if the rest of my crew was safe from Dacko's vengeance."

"You were tempted, but you didn't abuse the power you had over me," Allis said. "I only wish you had exercised as much restraint with Dan."

Milani laughed ironically. "You're attributing powers to me that I never had. If I could have controlled Daneth, he never would have left the ship, and you never would have come to it. I can control only those who give me control; Daneth gave me little and you give me none."

"You seemed in perfect control of the miner, Tamas," Allis said.

Milani hesitated, then said, "Luck." The bitterness in the single word was unmistakable. Her breaths shortened, whether from the constant struggle with the gravity or from anger Allis could not tell. But instinctively she knew Milani was telling the truth. Some quirk had caused Tamas to finalize the bargain at the last moment; it had nothing to do with Milani's control over the situation. Milani couldn't have depended on luck to keep Dan with her, and she knew Dan wouldn't have been easy to control under any circumstances. He'd have fought for his freedom, even, Allis admitted reluctantly, for his freedom to return to Milani. Allis remembered the last weeks on Earth, Dan's pensive silences when Allis thought he'd slipped into brooding thoughts of his illness but which she later interpreted as sadness when he realized he must leave Earth.

Remembering had made Allis angry, as much with Dan for being so weak he would not break his ties with the gypsies to stay on Earth as with Milani for pulling him back to her with her stone. Of course Allis had told herself that Dan was going to stay, that he'd give up the gypsy life to share Allis's love. She'd even made excuses to Milani for him, telling the captain that Dan was simply being practical to stay on Earth where his life had been prolonged once and perhaps could have been prolonged again. Milani hadn't believed a word of it, and Allis didn't either. That would have meant Dan had handed over control of his life to the doctors on Earth, and Dan hadn't. He died in the desert, refused any hope of rescue. The truth was that Allis would never know for certain if Dan intended to go or to stay. She could admit that now, but she didn't know if Milani could too.

Allis brooded awhile, then she actively tried to touch the two pirates. With nothing around to confuse her, she succeeded, finding them in a deep, drugged sleep with their thought circles sluggish and lopsided. And as she toyed with those circles, she realized how odd it was to have another living being even closer with only the sound of Milani's ragged breathing to make her presence known. Allis was growing accustomed to the stone, and the knowledge pleased her. Her pleasure was short-lived.

She thought of the path the sledge had taken through the snow, experimenting in that way with spatial orientation, and suddenly she was confronted with thousands upon thousands of circles in her head. She gasped for air like a smothered person, opened her eyes to see Milani straining at the ends of her manacles to reach her when she finally got a breath of air. The captain was alarmed.

"Where do all those people live?" Allis asked, bewildered.

"What people?"

"The miners. There must be half a million or more."

Milani looked at her strangely. "Their homes are underground, in the ruins of the Quondam Beings' city. It's warmer there than on the surface, well protected from the frequent blizzards, so they chip the ice away from the walls and burrow. Often as not they chip away the walls, too, melt them down and sell the stuff to those of us who come from the stars. How do you know their number? Do you read that far?"

"Well, I can see their thought circles."

Milani grunted. "Thought circles won't get us very far, but I suspected you had organized the flow that much when you got some sleep last shift. What other accomplishments haven't you told me about?"

"None," Allis said, still unwilling to trust the captain. She would have liked to know if Milani could confirm that the bawdy circle she'd found in the crowd was Dacko's, but such singling out would have given Milani more information about Allis's abilities. She couldn't prevent the fear that made her keep silent.

CHAPTER 18

Ghyaspur had never seen Milani haul cargo before, but she handled the tote sacks filled with ingots as easily as she did the skeins of worm thread, shinnying down the gangway pole without getting hung up on the stanchions the way Ghyaspur and other broad-shouldered men often did. Her gaze took in more than the work. He noticed her glance darting down corridors forbidden to the working prisoners, subtle appraisals of their pirate guards, their weapons, and the attention or lack of it paid to their duties. Ghyaspur, too, began a circumspect examination of their prison and guards. There was no doubt in his mind that he and his crewmates would be called upon to turn these ingots into proper sails for the *Dowager Sun,* and he hoped, as he assumed his captain hoped, that the additional activity would provide an opportunity to escape.

At the moment, Ghyaspur didn't know how they would escape. They were outnumbered so many times that overwhelming the pirates in hand-to-hand combat was not even a remote possibility. He'd noted the locations of enough airducts to surmise that a sneak-out was more plausible, but the ducts would only accommodate slender folk like Droganie, Senda, and Allis. And such a move would have to be carefully timed so that if those three could make their way to a shuttle in the axis undetected, there would be somewhere to escape to—a Watcher space station, another ship, or a planet with a hospitable atmosphere. Even so, getting three out was better than none, and if it was done at the right time and at the right place, the escaped prisoners might be able to bring help to those left behind.

Ghyaspur loaded another ingot into his tote sack and started back down the gangway to the forge. The information necessary to make a sneak-out work was tremendous. They'd need to know when the listening device was untended, the location of tools to take off the duct covers, and to know when it was safe to steal them. They'd have to know where the pirate crew congregated and when most of them were sleeping or simply off their guard, and that was aside from knowing the state vector and orbital elements of the *Dowager Sun* so that a course could be plotted for the shuttle the fugitives would use. A stone-carrier could know all those things and coordinate a successful escape, but it would have to be a stone-carrier who understood the workings of a stellar sailing vessel. Milani was right. Allis would not be able to do it. Ghyaspur was certain that he could, if only he had the stone.

He had his peers' support; none of them had missed Milani's nod of approval, and while Milani and Allis were gone with Dacko planetside, his crewmates had offered suggestions of how to seduce the Earthwoman into giving him the stone. They repeated rumors, or firsthand experience passed off as rumor, about landlubbers' sexual proclivities, and even suggested preying on her fears for a safe delivery of the child she was carrying. He began to doubt his lifelong precepts that all his elders on the *Sovereign Sun* were somber, clean-living sorts. Thinking of ways to cause Allis to love him enough to give him the stone was a serious job to him, but not an easy one. He was fond of Allis, and he didn't want to hurt her. But the safety of his captain, crewmates, himself, and even Allis depended on his success, and with stakes that high, any embarrassment he felt over the duplicity he planned to perpetrate was minor.

When the ingots were safely stowed in the shop and the prisoners secured once again behind the thick hatch, Droganie rigged yet another shield, one behind which the crew would hide while she inserted the ingots into the forge for softening, a process which violated the already malfunctioning magnetic sweepers. When that was done, Milani called a halt to the work and the crew drifted back to the ingot barriers to rest. Ghyaspur and Allis were left alone.

"I thought I had it figured out," Allis said, sitting down beside him. The pirates had not taken away the coat she'd used on the planetside trip and she pulled it up over her knees like a blanket.

"Figured out what?" Ghyaspur said. He was tired from the work, but was grateful that he and his crewmates had been allowed to do it. Muscles atrophied quickly without proper exercise in low gravity.

"I thought the crew was angry with me because I wouldn't carry the stone, but now that I'm carrying it, they still won't have anything to do with me." Her nose wrinkled as she gestured at the empty space between them and the other barrier of ingots. "I admit I wasn't happy when Milani forced it on me, but I *had* gone to get it of my own free will when we were still on *Sovereign Sun*."

Ghyaspur glanced uneasily in the direction of the

listening device. "I suspected something like that, since you had it when we got here. I'm sure all of them realize you had a change of heart," he said sympathetically.

"I can understand Milani's continued anger; she has to have a scapegoat because she doesn't believe she's capable of originating feelings of her own. But why does the rest of the crew continue to ostracize me?"

Ghyaspur chuckled deep in his throat. "You haven't been banished, Allis. You must have noticed that my people are very perceptive and that they practically ritualize privacy at certain times."

"They think you and I—?" Allis stared at him, first with amazement and then with such perturbing concentration that Ghyaspur had to turn away. He felt his face flush. How much was she reading with the stone? She certainly seemed more comfortable with it now, but she couldn't be getting much information from it in this short a time. Surely if he could willfully deceive Milani, an experienced stonecarrier, he also could fool Allis, who was a rank beginner.

"Do you mind terribly?" he said, hoping he sounded more shy than embarrassed. Lies were difficult for him, even a little one like the deeper motive for the crew leaving them alone. She didn't answer; Ghyaspur's heart began to pound. He concentrated on her eyes, soft brown eyes with bright flecks of yellow practically boring holes in his temple. He was uncertain of what to make of her continued concentration.

—Allis,— he said quickly and concentrating equally hard, —you're so exotic with your Earthy ways. You move like a forest creature, alert and cautious, your dark hair is like a shadow of mystery around your face. I like being with you. When we're alone I imagine we're two feral creatures, important only to each other . . .— He kept the words coming, fairly certain she could not understand them yet, but certain she would feel the overboiling emotions through her stone. He believed she could sense his sincerity, perceive the genuine lust he felt for her, and never guess that he was deceiving her, too.

Finally he noticed the glistening of tears in her eyes and heard her choke back a sob. She buried her face in the coat, overwhelmed and shaking. Surprised, Ghyaspur touched the nape of her neck, knowing that he'd moved her deeply, but uncertain of how to deal with her tears. Perhaps, once again, the weakness they betrayed was a good thing. He felt very strong, which reinforced his countenance, and he felt certain the comfort he offered Allis was for the best.

"Well," she said, muffling a final sob, "at least I finally understand."

"I'm glad," he said. "I wouldn't want you angry with me for . . . persisting." Tentatively, he put his arm around her. He'd not forgotten her refusal on board the *Sovereign Sun*.

Allis shrugged, then dried her tears on the lining of the coat and laid a still-damp cheek against his hand. "The question is, will you be angry with me?"

"Why should I be?"

"Because you're so young"—he stiffened at those words as he always did—"and I've never taken advantage of a young man before." She moved closer to him and he encircled her with both arms, breathing in the scent of her hair and feeling her breasts against him. He forgot his brief anger.

"I'm not so young that I don't know how to love a woman and how to hope she'll love me in return," he whispered.

"I know."

She kissed his collarbone and his skin tingled. Ghyaspur's hand moved around to the front of her, avoiding the hardened gel on her shoulder, tracing a line over her breast, her ribs, and finally to her pelvis. He felt the firm mound of her enlarged womb above the bone, startling him at first, then filling him with awe and joy. "I want to make love with you," he said tenderly. In his young life no one had ever said the ritual words to him, and he'd only said them a few times, usually choking on them in fear of being refused. But they came out smoothly this time; he'd never been so certain of an affirmative reply as he was now, with Allis touching him so intimately.

"Yes," she said dreamily, "but will you respect me afterwards?"

It was, he knew, to do with some Earthly courting ritual, an oddly timed jest. She knew she was with a gypsy now, and she'd been with one before, too. Had Daneth loved her because she made him laugh even when his penis swelled and nearly was ready to be enveloped by her? Or was it her mouth, first bestowing kisses on his lips with tender touches, and then, *space*, the jolt of her smooth strong tongue teasing his lips open. He'd never kissed that way before, knew that if he gave a thought to what he was doing he'd condemn an oral exchange like this as extrinsic and probably obnoxious.

He didn't think about that. He enjoyed the feel of her tongue in his mouth as much as she would soon enjoy the feel of his manhood inside her. Ah, yes, he would repay pleasure with pleasure and . . .

Space! Was Allis built the same as gypsy women? She was, after all, alien, and perhaps this weird and passionate form of kissing was more intrinsic to Earthly lovemaking than he knew. Perspiring now, Ghyaspur's hand came over the round of her rump until it found the waistband of her pants and slipped underneath. Her hair was like coarse silk, her thighs damp and silky, but he found the classic formation, so right as he gently swung his pelvis toward hers. Mind relieved, body ready, he kissed with those strange but wonderful tongue-filled kisses, then he consigned himself to ecstasy.

Allis dozed from time to time, lulled by Ghyaspur's peaceful and contented sleep, then disturbed by her own dark and drifting thoughts, which she refused to pursue. At least for this shift she was not alone, and she clung to Ghyaspur who moved sleepily to accommodate her. His eyes moved rapidly behind mauve lids and his cupid's-bow lips curved slightly to smile as he dreamed of loving her yet again. She tried not to see what he saw and not to feel what he felt, but it was too easy to join the goodness, too difficult to stay away and alone. He'd been clumsy as a puppy but as sincere as a stallion. In his dream he was a hoary man of wisdom. She hated herself for using him so badly, and wished the shift would never end so he'd never know.

But it did end. In her mind she felt the crew stirring behind the other barrier of ingots. Ghyaspur awoke, too. He slowly extricated himself from the tangle of her limbs and the coat, smiling and kissing her.

"I used to dream of being loved by a stone-carrier," he whispered.

Who, Milani? she thought wickedly but said kindly, "Was it so special?"

"It was wonderful," he said sincerely.

"Yes, it was wonderful," she echoed softly, remembering Dan during their happy time on Earth. But the joy was brief, for the reality of being pregnant and in a pirate ship was too harsh to ignore. In the end there was only herself to care for and to trust. Allis sighed. "I wish I could take this cast off. Maybe I can . . ." She eased her fingers inside the hardened gel, probing and stretching.

"What are you doing?"

"Trying to reach . . . I want to give it to you."

Ghyaspur's blue eyes widened. Milani's plan carried out so soon? He hadn't thought it would be so simple; he was wild with joy and bursting with pride. Endless rewards were in his mind even though he was not a greedy person. He simply understood gratitude and knew Milani would be grateful to him for not having to deal with Allis anymore. When Allis handed him the stone solemnly he barely contained his triumph. He leaped from the ingot barrier and across the forge to show Milani.

Allis followed to watch. Ghyaspur was afraid to speak because of the listening devices so he opened his hand to let Milani glimpse what lay within. The captain's tawny eyes widened in amazement, and she smiled until she turned and saw Allis's frown. Milani stood up to whisper in Ghyaspur's ear. His sunny locks of hair bounced gently as he shook his head. The color in his face drained until it was as white as Senda's, as he finally realized the stone was dull and useless, dead in his hand.

"What is this, Allis?" Milani demanded in English. "What manner of fool are you?"

"You had a hope," Allis said calmly. "It needed to be crushed. I don't want you or any of the crew hoping I'll fall for one of your dogs when you command them to set their sights on me. You needed to know that I'm not a woman to trifle with, that I'll do what I have to do to live through this imprisonment. You've had an advantage over me since I stepped on board the *Sovereign Sun,* but it's gone now. I have a stone and you do not."

Milani's eyes were slits of amber as she drew herself up to her full leonine height. "If you've crushed that boy with your cruel games . . ."

"If he's ruined, it's on your conscience, not mine. You put him in the middle of a private war, one I didn't ask for either, but by space I'll take it on and win!"

"You have no soul," Milani said scornfully. "You're loveless and empty."

"You'd like to believe that of me, but it's Dan you disparage if you do. He gave me the stone with complete knowledge of what I am—demon, or woman, do you suppose?"

Milani's hands clenched, her knuckles turned white. "I should have gone with him. Somehow that stone was given without love," she said firmly.

Allis wondered if Milani believed that lie, supposed that she did. Allis's own sanity was based on anger with a dead man, and that was just as stupid as feeling guilty about his death. Certainly she was beginning to feel stupid at being faced off with Milani like a pair of enraged cats, especially with Ghyaspur looking on so balefully. She'd sacrificed the young pilot, her one and only friend, as a means for ending the confusion in Milani's mind over her value. She didn't want to spar with the captain about Dan.

"I think you were honest in your attempts to help me learn how to use the stone until you saw another way," Allis said, glancing at Ghyaspur. "Now you know there is no other way, so where do we go from here?"

"Forward rapidly, I suspect," Milani said. "You must be reading word-thoughts to have caught the plan from Ghyaspur."

Allis nodded. "Ghyaspur's anyway. Enough to understand that he was pulling a con and why. It wasn't hard to figure out."

"I wouldn't have allowed him to try if I'd known you'd progressed that far. He doesn't deserve your ill will," Milani said.

Allis refused to consider Ghyaspur, tried not to remember the shocked look on his face when he realized he'd been duped. He was a pawn between queens, nothing more. Allis looked squarely into the amber eyes. "Do you accept me as your only hope for salvation from this hellship?" she said.

"Yes," Milani said simply. Without turning she beckoned to Ghyaspur to give the stone back to Allis. He moved slowly from the cluster of crewmates, none of whom, except Senda, had understood the exchange between the two fierce women. Yet, instinctively they all understood, especially Ghyaspur, for he handed over the stone like a beaten dog, and they all lowered their eyes. Allis felt his humiliation even before the stone touched her fingers.

It doesn't matter, she told herself sternly. No one matters except yourself. They're aliens, and even the best of them are completely loyal to Milani. Even though she's a ruthless bitch, they'd follow her to hell, an appropriate kingdom for a goddess like her. Allis had to stand up to Milani, take command or lose her life. Yet she wondered if she or Milani would ever be able to look into Ghyaspur's eyes again.

CHAPTER 19

For a few breaths Senda stood frozen, watching her captain and the Earthwoman. Their eyes glowed in the dim light, amber yellow and amber brown, like the eyes of feral beasts meeting over a fresh kill, and Ghyaspur, looking suddenly more dead than alive, the stunned meat. But these wild humans weren't fighting to fill their bellies any more than two animals fought over a carcass. A crude battle for supremacy, and unthinkably her captain had lost. Senda couldn't bear it, knowing that it might not have happened if she had done her duty when Milani had called upon her.

"This looks bad," she heard Mordon whisper in her ear. "There could be other eyes watching."

Her heart suddenly raced furiously, thawing her body and bringing her rapidly into the scene. Once again she stepped between the two stone-carriers, forcing calm that she did not feel.

"Stop this spectacle at once," she said, speaking in English. "You cannot know what spying devices may be here. We were in and out of this forge most of last shift, stowing the ingots, and we made no search to detect anything they might have installed during our absence."

"It would not be wise for the pirates to suspect we are fighting among ourselves," Allis said.

"You're wrong," Milani said, "but this is not the time. For now, we have work to do. There is sailcloth to be made, for that's the only way to keep the pirates from bothering us while we make plans."

"What use are plans without a stone-carrier?" Ghyaspur said, speaking for the first time.

"Allis's cast needs attention," Mordon said, a trifle too loud, and he edged past Ghyaspur, as if he intended to look at Allis's arm.

Senda glared at him, for her hands were already on Allis's shoulder, as if just discovering a weak spot or rent in the hardened gel that kept the supposedly broken arm immobile. But at least the circle of crew behind Milani was distorted now, and if there were any new observation devices and pirates using them at the moment, the scene in the forge would look less strange.

While Milani and the remainder of her crew turned to the forge and slitters, Allis allowed Senda to lead her behind the stack of ingots where she'd lain the shift before with Ghyaspur.

Senda hurriedly fetched a pot of gel from the locker beneath the slitter, then returned to Allis. "You had no right to use Ghyaspur that way," the albino muttered.

"Don't talk to me about using people. I've been nothing more to you than a receptacle for the stone since the moment you found out I had it."

"Not for myself," Senda said stiffly. "There were other people to consider, the rest of the crew, even Daneth's wishes."

"There was a time when I almost believed that, or at least believed you thought it was true. But there's something else . . ." Allis was staring at her. Someone had removed the cover from the light, and the forge was bright again. Senda flushed and turned away to wipe the oozing gel on her already soiled tunic. With her good arm Allis touched Senda's bended knee, smiling suspiciously. "I can find your thought circle easily when I touch you."

Startled, Senda drew back. How much did she already know? Enough to learn Ghyaspur's plan, and that had never been spoken aloud either. In a panic she pulled in her thoughts, privacy assured, unless Allis had no qualms about not honoring the ancient trust. And even at that, pulling apart a privacy request took interminable time to learn.

"What did you do?" Allis said, looking puzzled. "One moment I could at least feel something, now there's nothing but nothing."

Senda concentrated on sealing the place where Allis had forced the stone out from behind the cast. "There's nothing you can do about it, Allis. I simply won't let you have my thoughts," Senda said quietly. Not even Allis must know how afraid she was.

"I'll do it without you then," Allis said. She slipped the stone behind the gel in a deft movement, and Senda quickly applied more gel.

When Senda didn't comment, Allis spoke again. "Make the cast looser below the elbow so I can exercise my arm." Senda shot her a glance and pushed stray hairs off her white forehead.

"It has to be a real cast to be convincing," Senda said. "Those pirates are not idiots."

But the albino already had pulled a knife from her tunic belt and began paring the cast at the elbow. Allis smiled to herself. Senda never had done her bidding before, and with her thought circle so cool and impenetrable, she could only guess what the albino's feelings were. Strange how quickly that had happened.

She'd sensed Senda's alarm and knew the albino was truly worried, even though Allis could not tell how deep the worry went. She'd assumed it was about Ghyaspur, or even the pirates, yet somehow those ideas did not fit. Now there was no hope of knowing. She really couldn't get past the frigid circle, and only some sense of movement and maybe the knowledge of a sore muscle escaped involuntarily. If the others behaved like this, learning to use the stone was going to be an impossible task.

As soon as Ghyaspur had given her back the stone, the influx of feelings began again in her brain. None of it was friendly, but it did not sicken her or make her tremble. She didn't think it ever would again. She could deal with it in a clinical fashion, separate herself from the flow. The visual aspects of thought circles were beginning to make sense, too. The colors and textures were not a conscious or arbitrary assignment of hue to an individual's thought, but a subconscious interpretive aid that simply happened as other people's thoughts were filtered through her brain, somehow becoming associated with colors during the process. More and more the conglomerate of thoughts was congealing into distinctive circles of color, no two quite the same. The problem was that she only recognized two of them, Senda's and Ghyaspur's, the two people she had touched.

The circles were not auras haloing a subject's head, but colored disks whirling somewhere in her own head, lacking any spatial relationship that she could identify. Now, sitting close to Senda, she concentrated on the albino's thought circle. She wondered if it was a subconscious interpretation of gestures, even eye

movement, that helped her feel Senda's hands, the very
touch sensations that Senda had as she re-formed the
cast. It was as if physical action and responses were an
open area of Senda's brain, different from thought
processes, or even emotions, neither of which Allis
could detect in Senda just now. The fact that Senda
was interacting with her helped her make the identification, she was sure. Milani had alluded to being
able to recognize where a thought was coming from
spatially, but for now Allis decided to concentrate on
this method she'd just found. Perhaps it was limiting
and slower to have physical contact in order to identify
each thought circle, but it was sure, even if she had
to kick each crewmember in the shin to do it.

"There," Senda said finally. "It's finished." She
stepped back to look at her work critically, decided
it was convincing enough as long as Allis was not so
stupid as to use the supposedly broken arm when a
pirate might see. Allis did not respond to Senda's suddenly exposed and disparaging thought, for the privacy request re-engaged so quickly that she realized
Senda had deliberately scolded her.

"Send Milani to me," Allis said as Senda gestured
that they should join the others who were already
working at the forge.

Senda's eyes widened, surprised, Allis guessed by the
lurch in her thought circle, that Allis would consider
giving Milani an order. Then the albino sighed.

"You should at least consider that the pirates will
think your giving Milani orders unusual. They know
who is captain," Senda said.

Allis nodded easily. She had no doubt that Senda
would have delivered the message if she'd insisted,
but the albino also knew it was nothing more than
another test. There was time to reconfirm her new-

found power. For now she turned to follow Senda to her working comrades.

Allis sensed some grumbling about empty stomachs and cramped muscles, but nothing was said aloud. She noted which thought disks in her mind had emanated these feelings and assumed the other disks crowded around them must be the well-fed pirates scattered throughout the ship. Allis was hungry, too. She'd had only one portion of the unappetizing gruel since returning to the ship from Natarro. It was comforting to know that she was not the only one who'd be grateful for more of the gruel right now, but when Dacko and two of his men opened the hatch and entered the forge carrying rations, she knew it was merely coincidence.

The pirate looked like an Oriental emperor with his embroidered silk robe, though he was too blond, and even Orientals would consider the embroidery of stylized dragons alien. Allis realized the pirate was floating, an aberration even in the low gravity, and she recalled that she'd intended to ask her crewmates how he did that.

"Ah," Dacko said, looking around the forge shop with some approval. "Let it not be said that Milani's crew is not industrious."

Allis looked for a thought circle emanating an element of surprise at finding them working, but as distinctive as Dacko's thoughts had seemed when they were on the mining planet, she couldn't find them now. Her only consolation was that she felt no immediate danger anywhere, even though the pirates had dropped the rations sacks and made no move to leave. Dacko was surveying the silent prisoners, his eyes roving until he spied Ghyaspur standing alone by the extruders.

"You," Dacko said pointing at Ghyaspur. "Come with me. I have . . . other work for you, more suited to your tender age."

Allis had been avoiding Ghyaspur's mind. She hadn't wanted to share the humiliation he must have felt when she'd fooled him into making believe she loved him enough to give him the stone. But involuntarily she now shared his sinking apprehension. From someone else she gained certain knowledge that Ghyaspur's smooth cheeks and high color made him a tempting morsel for Dacko's bizarre appetites.

The last was not Dacko's thought, for he'd only waited long enough to see Ghyaspur take one hesitant step before ducking back through the hatch, a train of frothy green silk flowing behind. Dacko's thoughts might have the floating sensation that Dacko must be experiencing, and perhaps, Allis thought, she could recognize that in one of the many circles in her head. But she didn't. Instead she sensed the rhythm of Ghyaspur walking with mock pride. He looked neither right nor left, nor did he display any outward sign of fear.

Whatever lay in store for him, he'd not give the pirate the satisfaction of knowing he was afraid. Only Allis knew how quickly his pulse raced, his heart pounded, and his mind reeled. He wondered if he was to be the victim of some vile experiment, some horrible endurance test, or maybe, he thought hopefully, some contest of skill. He didn't consider the possibility of sexual abuse, and Allis realized that was because the gypsies would not consider bedding a person they disliked, let alone an enemy. The pirates were gypsies, at least some of them were. And the one who knew Dacko's proclivities and had inadvertently passed them on to Allis considered them odd. But there it was, and Allis alone knew what Ghyaspur was going to face.

An impulse to shout and fling herself against the pirates was aborted before she even moved; their hands were dangerously close to the weapon packs on their hips. She'd never even seen those guns fire, didn't know if they hurled projectiles, focused laser beams, or spewed chemicals, but she was certain they were deadly. Then, before she had time to be appalled by her hesitation, the hatch closed behind Ghyaspur and the two pirates. All she could do now was to pray that she was wrong, that she'd misinterpreted that fleeting thought from the pirate guard. Hadn't Milani said that thoughts were often misleading?

"Why do you suppose they wanted Ghyaspur?" Droganie was saying.

When Allis turned she realized all the gypsies were looking at her and that Droganie's question had been addressed to her. She hesitated. "I don't know."

Disgusted and disappointed, Droganie reached for the brown ration sack, and the others joined her in various degrees of discontent. A stone-carrier ought to have known the answer to Droganie's query. Plainly they had no faith in Allis.

The crew ate in silence, and Allis, suddenly without appetite, had to force herself to swallow the bland gruel. She'd lost Ghyaspur's thoughts only moments after he left the forge, the distance between them playing tricks on her now. How was it that she'd been able to identify Dacko's thoughts when she was resting in the shuttle and he was miles away and deep underground in the miners' city? Was reception distance with the communicator-stone less in space than it was on a planet's surface? Or had she been mistaken about sensing Dacko's bawdy thoughts on the planet?

Milani put a half-eaten ball of gruel back into the sack and took a final slug of congealed broth from a glassine sack. "Save some of the food," she said. "They may forget us again."

"They ought to put us on double rations," Droganie complained. "Sailmaking is hard work."

Milani shrugged and stood up surveying the shop. "I'll work with Allis," she said.

"What can I do with a broken arm?" Allis said, suddenly belligerent.

Milani glared, and Allis didn't ask again. She ought to have given that order herself, before Milani had a chance to think of it. She followed Milani to a stack of silver alloy ingots, knowing that the two of them would help very little with the sailmaking. They had other work to do.

Drained by the incessant demands Milani had made on her, Allis fell into a deep sleep just as soon as they'd finished the last of the rations. It seemed only moments later when she felt a gentle hand on her shoulder. She sat up with a start when she saw it was Milani who had touched her.

"You've joined someone's dream," the captain explained. "Who is having such sleep terrors?"

Allis felt tears on her face and heard a sob escape from her own throat. Only then did she realize that she'd been roused not from her own dream but that someone else's nightmares had gripped her through the communicator-stone. She huddled, wiping away tears. The lights in the forge had been covered by fabric torn from the coat Milani had worn on Natarro, but enough illumination escaped for her to see the shiny new roll of sailcloth near the sleeping forms of her crewmates. She sat, trying to identify the dreamer.

"Who?" Milani asked again in a whisper, "and I'll waken him." The captain looked at her through tired tawny eyes, eyes that Allis was certain had not closed in sleep for a long time.

Allis shook her head in confusion, knowing that this was just a continuation of the lessons that had exhausted her during the workshift. There was not just the identification of individuals' thoughts, the probing of what was beneath when Milani was hopeful that Allis had zeroed in on one of the prisoners' minds from the descriptions Milani gave her, and then *listening* for word-thoughts that never had come, but also the more subtle lessons of a stone-carrier's burden.

It was clear to Allis that Milani was insisting she accept responsibility for her crewmates; yet Milani had been incompetent in describing what that responsibility was. It was as if she didn't truly understand it herself. Allis guessed that because one among her crewmates might be suffering, and it was her duty to alleviate the pain if she could. What was so difficult to convey, if that was the lesson? She concentrated, tried to touch each one of the sleepers, and found she'd counted four contented dreamers, the number of prisoners less Milani, Ghyaspur, and herself. Slowly she ventured a reply. "It's not a dreamer . . . he's wide-awake." She struggled to find a point in the dizzy circle of emotion that spun in her mind. She did and drew it out. "Oh, no . . . Ghyaspur!"

"What's happening to him?" Milani said with alarm. "Allis, please try . . . is he hurt?"

"Not the way you mean," Allis said, trembling now from shared disgust and anger. "He's . . . being forced to have sex with Dacko."

Milani's grip on Allis's shoulder tightened. "Is this happening right now, or is he remembering?"

"Now," Allis said, nodding dully. She could feel Ghyaspur's tremendous urge to flee, but the silken bonds on his wrists were firm. He was tied to stanchions that were practically invisible along the bulkheads draped with fleecy padding and soft silk. Through Ghyaspur's eyes, Allis recognized the baroque scene of the converted armory, Dacko's den. There was the taste of strong wine in his mouth and a trace of something bitter—a drug, he suspected, that was to have made him relax. But the adrenaline surging through his body had muffled the intended chemical effect, and he tried to turn enough to see Dacko, screaming with fury that the pirate apparently found amusing.

"You've not had anything but thought circles beyond the shop bulkheads before," Milani said urgently. "But you remember I've told you of the impelling force to be with friends during times of trial. Listen carefully, Allis. There is a spatial relation between Ghyaspur and Dacko. He is under him, atop, aside, but Dacko is close. A small move in your reception and you can read him. If you can identify Dacko, get a firm grip on his thought circle, we'll be farther ahead than I'd hoped. Try to move your reception from Ghyaspur to Dacko."

"But . . . Ghyaspur," Allis said, shaking her head with great agitation. "He . . ." His genitals were being stroked and admired, his spine was rigid with horror.

"We're powerless to help him, and his life is not in danger," Milani snapped.

"You'd have me use him again?" Allis said. She was shaking with anger, outraged by what Milani wanted to do.

"Stop it, Allis. Do you think I like seeing my crew

humiliated? Give me a practical solution to save that boy. Come on, earthworm. Tell me what to do. You're the one with the stone!"

Allis sat stunned. They could beat on the hatch until the end of time and never beat it down. If they could, armed guards would level them in seconds. "I have no answer," Allis whispered.

"Then do what you're told, stone-carrier. Move from Ghyaspur to Dacko."

Allis thought the order was impossible. She knew, vaguely, what her receptors were, understood the concept, but had been unsuccessful in selecting whom she'd hear unless the person were physically near, preferably touching her. She tried though, and felt a multitude of circles swirling in her head. "It's no use," she said.

"What happened?" Allis shrugged. "It's a familiar pattern, almost like when all our crew are awake," she said.

"You've broadened your reception instead of moving it. You're probably picking up the whole pirate crew. Do you still have Ghyaspur?"

Allis nodded. She'd not be able to leave him, and he was tearing out her heart with his anguish.

"Then just wait. When Dacko climaxes his circle will burst momentarily. Watch only that one, and when it re-forms, you'll have him."

There was no way to pretend that she was a clinical observer; she could not even distance herself to being a voyeur. She felt Ghyaspur's buttocks being spread as if they were her own, gently at first, and then with increasing ruthlessness while he tried to squirm out of the pirate's grasp. She waited, sweat building on her forehead and under her arms. She felt the first violating thrust as vividly as the last. Then one circle nearly pushed the others aside in a flame of eroticism and, as Allis watched the parts regroup, the intensity of the moment allowed her to focus on the single reassembling circle. She found the ragged point there and drew it out. "He's satisfied. Like a dog that's just glutted itself," she bitterly told Milani.

"Stay with him," Milani urged.

"He feels powerful . . . I mean, he really believes that. It's as if he has completely blanked out the fact that Ghyaspur is tied up. And he's angry . . . not with Ghyaspur and not with anything in particular that I can understand. Perhaps I'm misinterpreting, but he's not really aware of his anger."

"I think you have it right, Allis. It's his mental state, and it's most dangerous when it boils within. I've had few opportunities to read him, but I know his thought patterns are different from anyone else's I've ever met. The cutoff you mentioned is typical of him alone. It's as if he has no conscience, and I've never seen that before."

"He's sending Ghyaspur away," Allis said. "He doesn't trust him, even tied up, while he sleeps. Too bad; I think Ghyaspur's angry enough to kill him."

Milani nodded absently. "The fear is a part of him, too. Allis, I can't understand that man, yet I must if we're ever to get out of here."

"That's why I have the stone," Allis said.

"What?" Milani took her hand off Allis's shoulder. She'd not been aware it still rested there.

"You never did understand people . . . not Dan and not Dacko. I don't think you even understand your own crew. That's why it is I who will lead us out of here."

Milani's amber eyes were glazed, her shaggy hair giving her a wild appearance. Allis thought they could have murdered each other, but the time was not yet. And somehow both had enough sanity to know that.

CHAPTER 20

Many shifts had gone by since Ghyaspur had been taken from their midst, and Milani knew from Allis's face that the boy had been abused by Dacko time after time. It was strange to see a stone-carrier's kind of pain on the earthworm's usually smooth features, she with her black tresses still defiantly long and braided like a frame around her pretty face. She wore gypsy garb and moved with an acquired grace in the low gee of the ship's forge, and she worked alongside the crew when she wasn't working alone with Milani, but she still was alien. Not gypsy.

A witch who'd stolen a man's heart and his stone could never be a true gypsy, and it was becoming painfully evident that she'd never be a good stone-carrier either. For all the stars Milani genuinely wanted Allis to learn to operate the stone with some degree of competence, yet the only phase she'd mastered was finding close up thought circles and identifying emotions. Hate, anger, disgust, and embarrassment were the ones she'd learned fastest, for in the *Dowager Sun* that was what the captives experienced most often. Love, joy, and even complacency were only recent learnings, and, even knowing this, Allis was rarely certain who those emotions came from. Bracha and Droganie were gentle souls, and Allis claimed she could not tell one from the other. Senda and Mordon were practical, ruthless people, and Allis complained they were a monotone of grimness.

Milani worked with Allis for shifts on end, helping her read while the others worked all the harder at the forge to cover for them. Allis would tell Milani in English what swirled in her head. Patiently, Milani would slow the circles down, describing the process used to find a point on the circumference that would allow her to delve into the real thoughts within. With her remembered knowledge she could identify each of the crew from Allis's verbal descriptions. But even so, without Milani standing by, Allis had little success of her own. Worse, she'd not been able to catch more than fragments of word-thoughts, not even from Ghyaspur in his worst moments. Word-thoughts were the knowledge that was essential to any escape plan. Milani was strained, but she could not afford the luxury of impatience. The truce between her and Allis was a shaky one, at least it was on Milani's part. She didn't trust Allis to feel a gypsylike honor about the agreement, and that distrust frayed the tie. It seemed that she, Milani, must bear the greater weight, steady it more, for Allis might shrug at any time under the unwanted burden.

"Ghyaspur," Allis said, suddenly looking up from the stack of softened ingots she was moving to the extruder. She was looking at the hatch, and Milani followed her gaze.

Ghyaspur entered under guard, apparently unharmed but moving so slowly that one of the guards gave him a shove. Senda, closest and quickest, caught his arm and helped him regain his balance. He responded to the older woman's welcome hesitantly, but he seemed relieved to be back.

The guards had followed Ghyaspur into the forge. "Dacko wants to know how much longer until the sails are ready," one said to Milani. He didn't wait for her to reply, but instead went to inventory the bolts of completed sails himself. His companion lounged at the hatch, laser in hand. "Not enough," he finally said, looking very dissatisfied.

Milani shrugged. "We can't work longer shifts without more food. What you've given us is barely children's portions."

The pirate nodded, taking in the gauntness that was beginning to show on the captives. "I'll see what I can do," he said, sounding surprisingly sincere. He left with his companion, and everyone looked at Ghyaspur.

"Are you all right?"

"What happened?"

"Where have you been?"

"I'm all right," Ghyaspur said, not raising his eyes to meet the others'.

"But we want to know what happened," Senda said sharply.

His long arms were dangling uselessly at his sides, and Milani could see that his wrists were raw. There was some color in his cheeks as he finally looked at Senda. "I . . ." He looked at Milani helplessly, his blue eyes full of hurt. "Shouldn't we get to work or something?"

Milani nodded. "Yes. Back to work, all of you," she said briskly.

Ghyaspur headed straight for the forge to feed ingots into the extruder, the hardest and most exposed work of all. Droganie seemed about to protest until Milani caught her eye and shook her head in warning. Ghyaspur set a fast pace, perspiring quickly in the white heat from the forge. All were hard-pressed to keep up with him.

At the end of the workshift, the pirate guard returned with full rations for all of them. The *Sovereign Sun* crew shut down the forge with haste and retired to the safety of the dwindling ingot barrier to eat.

"They must have decided they need us for a while longer," Mordon said just before stuffing his mouth with food. There were fibrous foods and glucose along with the monotonous gruel they'd been eating.

"There's some talk of having us set the new sails," Ghyaspur said, speaking for the first time since his shaky words to Senda when he returned.

"What else?" Milani asked, taking a generous portion of food for herself and sitting next to him.

"Nothing," he said glumly. "That's all I know."

"Twenty shifts out there with them and that's *all* you learned?" Droganie said with astonished disbelief.

"Yes, that's all," Ghyaspur said, suddenly angry.

"I think you should tell them why," Allis said quietly from a secluded place in the shadows.

"Allis!" Milani said sharply.

Ghyaspur sat numbly for a moment, looking from Allis to Milani, apparently just realizing the one stone-carrier knew almost as well as himself what he'd been through, and that she'd probably told the other. His lips thinned and he hung his head, shaking it slowly.

"Ghyaspur, it's not your shame," Allis said, moving forward to sit near him, too.

"Allis, leave him alone," Milani said in a threatening voice. Milani wanted to forget what had happened, and she only could imagine that Ghyaspur would prefer to forget, too.

"I know what I'm doing," Allis said, switching to English. Her voice had a calm and deadly quietness. "He's ashamed and miserable and so damned confused he can't even trust his friends to continue loving him if they knew what happened. I won't leave him that way."

"Let him forget," Milani insisted.

"He can't forget Dacko any more than you can forget me," Allis said. "But he's not built like you, Milani. If he has to live with that much pain and guilt inside like that it will tear him apart."

Milani was stunned into silence for a moment, and by the time she regained her composure, Allis was again talking to the boy.

"Trust us to love you no matter what's happened, Ghyaspur," she was saying. "Yes, all of us."

Alarmed, Milani realized Allis was speaking to Ghyaspur's subliminal thoughts. "Senda," she hissed. "The listener . . ." How long had she been able to do that? She knew she should feel pleased that the lessons had been successful . . . or was it only Ghyaspur she could read?

Senda melted out from the barrier of ingots to distort reception, if the pirates were listening. Even people unfamiliar with silent talk would recognize what was going on after a while.

"If it had been Droganie or Milani who'd been taken in your place, would you have been ashamed of them? . . . Yes, maybe it is a misfortune this time that you're young and so handsome, but you're certainly not to blame for that either."

Milani watched Ghyaspur closely as he picked up

his head to glance nervously at his curious crewmates, as if trying to determine if Allis was right. "It was so humiliating," he said slowly.

"That was Dacko's intention. It gives him a surge of power to demean one of Milani's crew. He'd have done it to her, but he's afraid of her."

Milani leaned forward to listen more closely. Did Allis *know* what she was saying, or was she merely guessing, trying to comfort Ghyaspur?

"Power comes from respect, not . . . not what he did," Ghyaspur said, confused.

"Not with that one," Allis said. She paused to reach for a bit of food, then chewed thoughtfully, perhaps listening to Ghyaspur, perhaps forming her own thoughts. "No, he's not mad. He's as sane as you and I. But he thinks differently . . . and no, I'm not saying that to make you feel better. Ask Milani. It was she who put me on to him. Dacko is abnormal, but he's not insane."

"It's true," Milani said, shifting her long legs. "He's very complex and different from any other person I've ever met. He can cut off inhibiting thoughts that would prevent you or me from doing the things he does. As far as I was able to determine, he has no ties with any other person, feels no need for people except as objects for his scorn, or perhaps as obstacles to overcome."

The tautness across Ghyaspur's shoulders loosened, and he looked at his crewmates. "You still want to know what happened, don't you?" he said, a bit nervous but almost eager to tell them.

A few nodded, but Mordon scratched the stubble of beard on his chin, then shook his head. "No need to tell. Your wrists are sore, your ankles are raw. I've been planetside enough times to know when someone's been bound and violated. Dacko's more Watcher than gypsy, and that's something I know from personal experience, too."

The others finally understood, and their expressions ranged from amazement to anger. None, Milani was pleased to see, was embarrassed. Milani had thought that Ghyaspur's telling would mean revealing the sordid details that even she, with all her experience with the stone and knowing equally inhumane acts, didn't want to hear. Perhaps Allis had been right to persuade him to talk about it. The little Earthwoman was silent now, letting the crew take over her task. They condemned Dacko for the blackheart he was, and sympathized with Ghyaspur. Not a word of condemnation or shame was spoken, and Milani began to realize how skillfully Allis had handled the situation. Even if Milani had had her stone, she would not have known what to do with Ghyaspur's shame; it was almost like having Daneth.

She stopped. Allis wasn't like Daneth. She was an earthworm, simply well equipped to deal with this particular situation because, as Mordon had said, it happened all the time planetside.

"Do you suppose," Allis said, interrupting the commiserating crew, "that you might be able to use your . . . presence with Dacko to our advantage?"

"Information?" Ghyaspur said, then immediately shook his head. "Dacko doesn't trust me."

"No, I imagine he does not, and I really ought to know for sure by now." She turned to him conspiratorially. "If you appeared to be . . . broken, or at least passive . . ."

Ghyaspur stared at her. "I couldn't!"

"Remember that I can't get anything he's not thinking about," Allis said in a rush. "There's so much information we need. If you asked the right questions, well, even if he won't answer you, *I* might be able to get the answer."

Allis was right. Engaged with Ghyaspur, Dacko might not cut off those filmy fringe-thoughts that so often led to true motives and intentions. She might learn just how much time they had before Dacko planned to dispose of them, and how he planned to do it. Even practical knowledge like course settings and state vectors could be brought out of an unwary subconscious with a well-turned phrase. The pirate couldn't know· that anyone was listening to him. But Ghyaspur seemed horrified, and Milani could not add prostitution to what he'd already been through.

"Enough," she said to Allis. Yet she had to admire the Earthwoman's resourceful idea; she was beginning to think like a stone-carrier after all.

"No, I can't stop now," Allis said calmly. "Ghyaspur, you've been around stone-carriers all your life and you know how the device works, what I can do with it and what I cannot. You'll know what to say to make him think about what I need to hear. You also know what information we need to know better than I do, and . . ."

"Let me think about it," he said, so abruptly that Milani knew he was merely putting Allis off. The Earthwoman knew that even better.

"There's no time," Allis said. "He'll be sending for you again soon. Very, very soon."

Only Ghyaspur's eyes moved. The screw in the hatch was already turning, and as the boy watched, one of the pirates stepped through. Ghyaspur looked as if he'd been struck, but he started to get up. Milani stayed him with a hand on his knee, felt his muscle quiver beneath her touch. "Don't move until you're called," she whispered, warning him not to respond to information he wasn't supposed to have. "And remember, you won't be alone."

"I think that's the worst of it," he whispered as he rocked back on his heels.

"Hey, white one," the guard called to Senda. "Eat your rations somewhere else." Senda shrugged and moved away from the listening device, still chewing the crisp crackers. The guard turned to the group of huddled prisoners. "And you, Ghyaspur. Come with us."

Ghyaspur moved like an old man to the hatch.

CHAPTER 21

Stacked along the bulkheads of the *Dowager Sun*'s forge were bolts of silvery sailcloth, annealed and ready to be unfurled before the stellar wind. They were only a few mils thick, yet polished to a mirror finish so bright that light reflected off the bolts hurt the eyes. Allis couldn't help but marvel that the processing from arm-sized ingots to the finished bolts of sailcloth had been accomplished in a metalworking shop not much bigger than a good-sized silo. On Earth a mill of gargantuan proportions would have been necessary to house the furnace, rolling mills, and extruders, but it seemed that off-world advancement of the arts had led to miniaturization and effective use of wall and ceiling space that would have been impractical in Earth's heavy gravity.

The rolling mill looked like the van of a truck standing on its end; it contained more than a mile of rolling surface, which squeezed the silvery ingots thinner and thinner. During the later stages of rolling, a layer of ultraloy was bonded to the sailcloth, resulting in an extremely durable finished sail. Silver alone would have been too fragile to withstand handling.

The bolts of sailcloth were stood on end and reached from the deck to the middle of the bilge, where they were secured in stanchions designed to hold them. When the first bolt had been put into place, Allis thought Dacko would have the same problem as weekend sailors on Earth who built boats in their basements. The bolt was too large to fit through the hatch. But Droganie had explained that the forge would be depressurized, the bulkhead behind the stanchions removed, and the bolts of sailcloth would be maneuvered into place by sailors in pods at the masts or stowed under the superstructure. It remained to be seen if the captives would be removed from the shop before it was depressurized. It seemed to Allis that a slowdown of the work would at least delay such an end, but Milani insisted that they work at a normal pace. Anything less, she assured Allis, would result in immediate retaliation.

The sail that would fill the last stanchion was being hoisted from the rolling mill by block and tackle, with Droganie pulling the slender chain. Allis was at her assigned work of restacking the unused ingots, idly wondering where they'd put more sails in the forge, when she heard her first clearly formed word-thoughts. They were directed at her, not like the eavesdropping on thought processes she'd been doing to Ghyaspur and the others.

—You've learned to read faster than I've ever seen any stone-carrier learn,— it said.

The words were like crystal in a geode, instantly sharp and clear once the rock encasement had been penetrated. From the dour overtones, Allis had only a slight doubt that it was Mordon, the mate. She looked for him and found him by the slitter, watching her.

—You hear me well?— he asked, his brows raised quizzically.

Allis nodded and grinned. He might just as well have been whispering in her ear, the words were so clear.

Mordon smiled. Allis thought his face would crack with even such a small smile. If possible, Mordon was more austere than he'd ever been on the *Sovereign Sun*.

—I've been with stone-carriers half my life, and it's always been by choice. I use the silent talk easily. I'll help you, Allis, for if you still cannot read Milani . . .— His glance shot up at Allis for her to confirm or deny. Allis shook her head. —Then she cannot tell you all you need to know. Those of us who work the bridge are experienced with the silent talk and can communicate clearly. We make it easier for even a good stone-carrier.— Allis was certain he meant that she was not a *good* stone-carrier. —When I communicate directly with the silent talk, it's to be taken as an open invitation to read what is there, the words, the underlying emotion, everything. But when you meet this . . .— His circle of thought twirled abruptly, like a wobbling top, like Senda's thought circle always whirled. The geode had snapped shut. When it burst open again it was as if the crystalline thoughts had willed it. Certainly Allis had had no influence upon the return of thought flow. They flooded her like an undammed stream. —. . . it means I'm requesting my privacy. As I understand a stone-carrier's abilities, there's no way I can enforce the request but I'd like to know it's respected. The captain honors our privacy, every time, without fail.—

Allis nodded without looking up. There was no way she could assure him, and besides, she already knew Mordon would not believe her if she did. He was right. The silent talk peeled him bare, right down to his crusty heart. To him, Allis was merely a tool to be used in springing the jail door, a tool, like a computer, that only would be useful if programmed properly. And yet there was something good about him, something he hid . . .

—So, you don't like what you've found in my mind. Does it matter? There's nothing you can do without our aid. You can't trim a sail, nor even keep a proper sunwatch. Without us you'll never see your homeworld again. Without you we'll rot in this stinking whore of a *Dowager*.— His words seemed to carry spit with them.

The hatch of the forge shop opened and three of Dacko's pirates entered, guns in hand. Allis dropped her contact with Mordon to try for the pirates. Her directional perception was becoming more accurate, especially when the subjects were in view. She found them on the second try and sensed that despite their drawn guns, there was no immediate danger. The pirates had a healthy respect for treachery, it being common among them, but they would not use their weapons unless the captives forced them to by action or inaction. They were not merely dropping off food this time; something was different, and hence the drawn guns.

"Batten down in here," one said. "You will furl the sails and haul them in. The new sails must be stowed under the superstructure."

He meant that the captives were to go out in the pods to do the work. It was dangerous work, Allis knew, and the pirates had no intention of risking their own people when the captives could do it. Allis knew, too, that they were fast approaching a gravity slip. There could be no other reason to haul in the sails.

—Put everything in the lockers that isn't bolted to the decks. Anything that's loose will be lost when we open to the outside.— It was Mordon again, himself already checking the stanchion clamps with Droganie so they would release without a hitch. He wanted Allis to look as busy as the rest of the crew, who were battening down the forge according to a set routine under the unusually alert gaze of the pirates.

—The coats and the food . . . into the lockers . . . anything loose . . .— He was a clear thinker, and Allis realized that at least part of the reason she was having trouble understanding the crew was because they weren't talking to her with the same kind of care Mordon was using. Some, like Senda, were deliberately using the privacy requests, which, perhaps, a skilled stone-carrier could penetrate. Allis couldn't. It was comforting to know that the troubles she was having in learning to use the stone were not entirely due to her own stupidity or ineptness; she wasn't getting cooperation, despite Milani's orders.

Allis moved quickly, fetching the scraps of Milani's coat they'd been using to cover the lights, her own coat, which still was in one piece, and the remaining food containers. Most of the equipment in the forge was already secure, for Milani's crew worked neatly, replacing shears and other tools in stanchions or clamps every time they were done with them. The work consisted of securing the oddly piled ingot stacks as the bricks were removed to be formed into new sailcloth. In moments the work was done, and the captives filed through the hatch and into the corridor.

At the gangway that led to the axis, Milani reached for the stirrup and a guard shoved her aside with a laugh of ridicule. The stone-carrier would not be risked in the maneuvers outside the ship. Allis was motioned forward.

"Her arm . . ." Milani protested.

"Haven't seen a sailor yet who couldn't operate a pod with only one arm," the guard said.

Allis didn't hesitate, for she knew that Mordon would tell her how to operate the labyrinth controls in the pod. It gave her some satisfaction to know that Milani probably was swallowing some gall. She couldn't afford to have Allis risked any more than Dacko could afford to risk Milani. She hoped Mordon had given no sign to alleviate Milani's worries; she liked the thought of the leonine captain sweating over the welfare of an earthworm.

Mordon was a competent instructor and a brilliant pod handler. Allis knew he maneuvered to keep her pod in his viewscreen, and he silent-talked her through every move. He'd given her the job with the least risk, as line tender, which put himself and Senda in greater peril as they furled the old sails. Allis had to keep track of fourteen guy wires and two tether lines, changing tension as the pods and the furled sails moved. She had only one hand to use to control the sixteen waldoes that held the lines. Mordon and Senda had to compensate for any lack of coordination from Allis, and had to do it in a seemingly routine fashion.

Retrieval of the old sails was hazardous. The angular momentum of the first furled sail increased so much as Allis hauled it in that Mordon was alarmed that the impact against the body of the ship would be great enough to damage the sail. There was no way that he or Senda could pull it back; their combined mass, braced against the void of space, would have no effect on the steadily increasing momentum. Allis stared at the onrushing silver projectile, wondered if she could remember which of the labyrinth control faces governed her pod's jets so she could fire them in time to get away.

—Fire the thruster on the tether line.—She realized that Mordon had repeated that frantic thought more than once. His image of which glovelike waldo control to slip her hand into and which finger to squeeze and for what duration was as precise as if he were in Allis's pod with her. His thoughts were urgent but without panic, and Allis tried to match his composure. The onrushing sailbolt slowed as the thruster continued to fire. If Senda or Mordon had positioned the line with the thruster carelessly, no amount of firing would have stopped the onslaught; it merely would have sent the sailbolt atumble in its line of flight. Finally Bracha and Droganie appeared from under the superstructure to take the old sail in tow.

From her position as line tender, Allis had her first opportunity to come to grips with the vastness of the stellar sails. She knew the size of the ship, having roamed all through the *Sovereign Sun,* which was about the same diameter as a city block, but saucer-shaped. The keel, the outer rim, was slender and had a strake of ultraloy around the entire circumference of the hull. The bilge, the rounded portion inside the keel, afforded the most pseudogravity aside from the keel itself, and it contained work stations, forge, machine shop, and hydroponic farm. From there to the axis the ship slimmed again, but never to the thinness of the keel. There was a huge axle running through the axis of the rotating ship, which attached to an inner gimbal, which in turn was mounted on an outer gimbal. This superstructure also provided mounting for the electromagnetic counterforce that kept the ship from being crushed when it entered a gravity slip.

The *Dowager Sun* was smaller than the *Sovereign Sun,* though not by much, and the space in her was used with great efficiency. But the sails! Miles and miles of gleaming silver, each mile attached to the outer gimbal by a dozen slender lines. It was like seeing the sails of a fleet of clipper ships hauling one single, very tiny, and insignificant child's gyroscope. The monstrous sails harnessed the solar winds of any nearby sun—cheaply, efficiently, and very reliably. And with the availability of the gravity slips, the sailing ships were not confined to any single solar system. The sails of the *Dowager Sun* were the biggest thing Allis had ever seen made by human beings, and she and the other captives were going to double that wind-catching capacity. She wondered how long it would take.

When the sails were furled, Bracha and Droganie came out from beneath the inner gimbal where they'd been stowing the new sails, and they helped Senda and Mordon bring in the old sails. They could see the wavy lights in the stars ahead where the gravity slip lay waiting; it seemed to be growing quickly, stretching starlight like light rods run amok.

Mordon helped Allis guide the lines in. She was Mordon's dummy, a robot carrying out skilled directions. It would be a long time before she could hope to master the labyrinth controls on her own; even the sailors spent thousands of shifts learning to operate them before they were proficient. Allis had the life-support system down pat; seal the pad hatch and life support came on. But even something as elementary as the viewscreen was impossible for her to operate without Mordon's thoughts to guide her. It required

simultaneous focus and direction, accomplished by
patterns traced in the labyrinth above the glovelike
controls for the waldoes. Allis wondered what the
aliens had against dials and knobs.

When the captives returned to the ship's forge,
they found it colder than an ice cave. It had been
open to the vacuum of space beyond the hull for half
a shift, the length of time it took them to stow all the
sails. It was pressurized again, but the flow of warm
air coming from the vents did little to offset the cold
that seemingly radiated from the metal decks and bulkheads. Dressed in the same light garb of trousers and
blouses, which they'd worn since leaving the *Sovereign
Sun,* the captives huddled together near an air vent,
shivering on their feet. It was much too cold to sit
down.

Milani was returned to the forge soon after the ship
passed into the gravity slip. She was plainly relieved
to see Allis was safe, and apparently assumed one of
the crew had assisted her with the silent talk. If she
wondered who, she didn't ask. She almost smiled at
Allis when the guards left, and said in English, "If
you're rested, I want you to try again for Dacko."

"What do you want to know?" Allis said, rubbing
her hand against her thigh to warm it. "I can find him
anywhere on the ship." She didn't mention that she'd
briefly tried to locate Dacko while in the pod and had
succeeded. Ghyaspur, Mordon, and Dacko could not
hide from her. The concentration she'd had to give
Mordon, his sincerity in wanting her to succeed for
all their sakes, had revealed more to her in half a
shift than all the time she'd spent struggling with un-
cooperative minds put together.

Milani seemed surprised. "I didn't learn how to
locate people until I'd had my stone for two thousand

shifts." She rubbed her arms. The cold was penetrating her scant clothes, too.

"Your life probably didn't depend on it," Allis said.

Milani nodded. "Still," she said, "I'd not hoped for that. I was going to be content with your being able to hear. Locating will be doubly useful. You're progressing fast, Allis. Faster than any stone-carrier I've heard of."

"I have greater need," Allis said dryly.

"Perhaps," Milani agreed, "or perhaps your mind is different than ours."

"Just brighter," Allis said. "I work well under pressure."

Milani sighed. "How's Ghyaspur?"

"The kid's working," Allis said. "Dacko's suspicious of him, but he likes the, uh . . . attention." The young pilot had succeeded so well in putting aside his personal aversions that Allis had trouble finding them sometimes. It was almost like the cutoffs that Dacko had built into his mind, but with Ghyaspur it was a very deliberate effort. The moments when he failed were horrible for Allis to endure.

"Be with them as much as you can," Milani said. "Learn Dacko's habits and his schedule. We'll need it to pick a time. And learn where he keeps my stone."

Allis smiled. She already knew where the stone was, but she didn't tell Milani she knew. Allis was Milani's ace, and that was fine. The hiding place of Milani's stone was Allis's ace. Milani would need Allis to the very end. If she didn't choose to tell Milani where the stone was, she'd never find it, at least not without destroying it. Dacko was a devilishly clever man.

CHAPTER 22

They crouched and shivered behind the shields like livestock huddled in the trees of a stormy pasture. But the forces they were trying to protect themselves from were not cold wind but streams of hot atomic particles. Perhaps some were absorbed by the shields; Droganie, Allis knew, still believed they were safe. Allis also knew the blacksmith was refusing to notice the first signs of radiation poisoning that Bracha was exhibiting by thinking ahead to how many more sails they could fashion from the remaining ingots. Droganie did not actively cooperate with Allis the way Mordon did, but she did not have the skill to protect her privacy, or else was disinclined to use it. The colored circle was merely a transparent wrapper; Allis wondered now how she'd ever had difficulty penetrating it. Still, though they were easy to expose, it wasn't easy to follow the blacksmith's undisciplined thoughts; the human mind was complex, and the musings flowed off on unexpected and unrelated tangents only to scrape along some forgotten wound and smolder there, fulfilling some subconscious need.

Mordon had managed to fall asleep, even though the forge was cold and the pulls of the irregular counterforce uncomfortable as they traversed the gravity slip. His head was on Senda's lap, her thin white arms folded across her chest as though disdaining to touch him and to have him near, but too polite to rouse him. Yet the tight blue circle of thought whirling in Senda's head was not angry. Nor was that whirl completely impenetrable, and Allis believed Senda derived some pleasure from the contact with Mordon. Then Allis didn't know who felt guiltier for knowing that, Senda or herself, and Allis left the albino alone with the mate and her troubled thoughts.

For a moment Allis surveyed her fellow captives, all in various stages of repose. They were filthy, their clothes tattered from handling the rough ingots and working the forge. But none was broken or without hope. She couldn't help but admire them, even . . . like them. They were not the slaves Dacko considered them to be.

Allis caught her breath; just that brief reflection involving the pirate brought his scurrilous mind in focus. It was as if her subconscious knew her duty better than her conscious mind, or at least was more willing to perform it. She lingered there only long enough to sense Dacko's decisiveness and the strident anger that the man didn't even know had perpetrated the question put to Ghyaspur. Then she joined the young pilot in time to feel the electrifying thrill of his matching wits with the pirate as he heard the question: "Say the coded words to me again."

The pirate had been too shrewd to express any doubts aloud, yet Ghyaspur knew he was being tested, for Dacko had tested him on this very subject before. Did Dacko know how transparent he was in his repetitious tests? Did he think he could make Ghyaspur falter or misspeak some words?

Allis gasped, realizing that Ghyaspur did not really understand the nature of Dacko's tests. He'd underestimated the pirate's cunning, misunderstood intentions, and was being fooled more thoroughly than he could imagine. *Make a mistake, Ghyaspur,* she thought furiously, uselessly. *Don't interpret that code correctly. He's not just making a comparison, he's making a record. Don't . . .*

The young pilot took his ancestor's diary from the pirate's bejeweled hands, and casually wrapping his leg around a stanchion, he opened the diary to the graphs and grids of gravity-slip coordinates and began.

"I have to paraphrase, you know," he said, seemingly intent on the code that lined the leaf of ultraloy. He knew the words in the back of the diary by memory, just as he knew the annals recorded in the early pages. —Allis, are you with me? Or have you been through this enough times so that you know what I'm doing?—

"Allis, what's wrong?" It was Milani's voice, hoarsely whispering in English.

Roused, but not really leaving Ghyaspur or Dacko, Allis realized she had stiffened where she sat on the dirty chevron deck. Her hands were fisted, her eyes just coming back into focus. She shook herself out of her trance and moved closer to Milani so the captain could hear what she had to say. Some of it was going to be difficult to form into words, since the crux had not come from the linear silent talk but from eavesdropping on fringe-thoughts, and random musings, unpursued.

"Ghyaspur has a plan, and though he doesn't know it, it already has gone awry. Do you know what gravity slip we're in, Milani?"

The captain paused, her fingers worrying a smudge of grease from her forearm. She spoke more reflectively. "Not this time. There were several to choose from in the miners' solar system. Perhaps I can tell if you've located the bridge crew and can provide an ephemeris."

Allis shook her head. She knew how to find the bridge crew but they were not concerned with ephemeris while in the gravity slip.

Senda, attracted by the conversation in English, had stretched out, putting her head near the two stone-carriers and disturbing Mordon. He sat up, studied their faces, and saw the conspiratorial camp.

"Droganie, the listener," he growled.

As the blacksmith skulked off, Mordon casually nestled himself against Senda's bosom. He'd placed himself just close enough to the others to hear the conversation, and indicated he would use the silent talk with Allis, if he needed to speak. Any observer would think he'd simply repositioned himself for sleep. He was comfortable, and though he guessed that Senda was somewhat perturbed by his close proximity, he knew she would tell herself it was a necessary contribution to the illusion, should any pirate be watching. Allis did not volunteer the knowledge that no pirate was operating the visual scanner at that moment. Milani raised her brow a bit at seeing Mordon and Senda intimately close, but she said nothing. Bracha leaned against her own shoulder, too sick and tired to move and nowhere safe to go if he could.

—What have you learned, Allis?— the mate said, closing his eyes.

"Ghyaspur has been revealing the contents of his ancestor's diary to Dacko. If I understand correctly, there are some gravity slips whose coordinates are still unknown to the Watchers but which are known to gypsies."

—That's true,— Mordon said, answering in the silent talk that which any gypsy could have answered. He seemed to understand her need to piece together the information she'd gleaned, like parts of a puzzle. He continually provided as broad a reference frame as was within his ability to construct. —Some coordinates were kept . . . sacred. Others are known to the Watchers, but many are unused because the slips are too small to accommodate their large ships. The knowledge of many small slips has fallen away with disuse, though I suspect a diligent researcher could find many of the lost coordinates in the old Watcher computer cores.—

Filled in on the background, Allis continued. "Ghyaspur persuaded Dacko to use a particular slip that will take us to a system of six inhabited planets. This system apparently was known to Dan, and . . ." Here Allis was confused, for although Ghyaspur had alluded to a plan, he had not revealed it to her. ". . . I think he believes we might be able to obtain aid on one of the planets."

Milani looked expectantly at Senda, she being the only crew member in the forge who had served with the co-captain before he joined forces with Milani. The albino hesitated, tempted to use the silent talk as Mordon was; then, convincing herself at the last moment that Milani needed to hear as much as Allis did, she spoke aloud. She still was afraid Allis might learn her secret.

"I can think of only one six-planet system that Ghyaspur would deem special to gypsies. If the journey is properly planned through this system, the six planets align themselves for a continuous swing by the ship. There are small slips that might be used to exit the system at many intervals, but we generally used the outward-bound slip that was in opposition to the largest incoming slip."

—It meant a lot of time in the system,— Mordon said, quickly painting a diagram of a planetary system with a star at the center and the trajectory of the ship forming a tangential line with the orbits of the planets. —The opportunity to intersect all six planets in one sweep would be rare, since planetary alignment must be perfect. If the computer says the time is now, it's now.— Gypsies were alert opportunists, even the rogues, it seemed.

Senda went on as if there'd been no interruption; indeed, for her there had been none. The silent talk was rapid. "We left people on some of the planets to develop trading ties that would be consummated on the pickup portion of the journey, on the exit trajectory that would intersect the orbits again. One of our people didn't want to return to the ship; she'd developed ties with a landlubber." Senda glanced uneasily at Milani, but the captain said nothing.

"Perhaps it's from that person Ghyaspur expects we can get help," Allis said. She still was listening to Ghyaspur's translation of the code, but her attention was here in the forge.

Senda shook her head. "He'd know better. There are too many light years between Valerio, the one who stayed behind, and now."

"It didn't seem that long ago in Ghyaspur's mind," Allis said.

—You have a landlubber's strong emotional ties to thinking of time as absolute. It's a misconception you must abandon,— Mordon admonished, his tone tempered with the patience of a teacher. —Condition yourself to thinking of time as an effect proportional to the square of the ratio of the velocities involved to the velocity of light. We have been through many gravity slips since Daneth's shipmate was left on that planet. With the distances involved, a computer would be necessary to calculate the precise amount of time that has passed relative to the people on that planet.—

And how much time had passed relative to the people Allis had left behind on Earth? She wanted to know but said instead, "I hope a descendant of this Valerio will aid us, and that aid comes quickly, because what Ghyaspur doesn't realize is that Dacko isn't merely acting on that innate mistrust of his. Dacko's recording the contents of the diary against the time when we're dead. That time doesn't seem very distant, but I don't know for sure."

Milani shook her head stubbornly. "Finding a descendant is too remote a possibility. Ghyaspur can't be that naïve." Her bushy brows pulled together in a frown. "Though, if it's primarily a good system for trade rather than pillage . . ." The captain looked hopefully to Senda, who shrugged to indicate both were possible as she remembered. Milani sighed. "Unless that system turns out to be one where Dacko needs me and my stone to trade for him, a need which may keep us alive, it would seem that Ghyaspur has exercised bad judgment in getting us there."

Allis nodded solemnly. Dacko was not giving any thought to his prisoners' future at the moment. He only was intent on being physically close enough to his youthful victim to be certain the device he carried was relaying Ghyaspur's words to a recorder. Strange that for once Dacko's closeness was not in the least sexually motivated.

Ghyaspur, however, did not know that this time the pirate's closeness would end differently, and he

looked up nervously. Allis knew the pirate's boudoir
nearly as well as Ghyaspur, having seen it through
his eyes before. She still found it disconcerting, for
all the familiar clues to the local vertical were ob-
literated by the bizarre furnishings. Ghyaspur had
constructed new clues for himself from the pleats in
the velvety drapings. And there were glide poles and
stanchions, however padded and disguised with glitter, and Ghyaspur's familiarity with their angles and
purposes from similar fixtures on *Sovereign Sun* gave
him an advantage over Allis's disorientation.

It was best to relax completely and trust the young
pilot's instincts rather than to impose her own. Yet she
couldn't because she desperately wanted him to con-
tradict himself in his discourse with the pirate, at
least to make Dacko wonder if it wouldn't be wise
not to dispatch his prisoners too hastily. *Make a mistake, one Dacko will catch you in!* Space, it was
frustrating for telepathy to be one-sided. Flushed
and inexplicably confused, Ghyaspur turned back to
the diary.

"He's not telling Dacko about the sunspot activity,
even though that information is in the code," Allis
told the others when Ghyaspur skipped a fragment of
code.

"Space, what's he thinking of?" Milani said, greatly agitated now. "He knows it's his own shipmates
who'll have to unfurl the sails. Dacko won't much
care about our getting an extra dose of radiation in
the pods if he doesn't plan to keep us alive much
longer anyhow. Why'd he urge Dacko to try this system? Why didn't he select a nice quiet star?"

"This diary reading explains why Dacko hasn't sent
Ghyaspur back to the forge, doesn't it?" Senda said
dully. "Dacko knows that we conspire to some de-

gree, and he probably assumes, rightly, that one of us would have warned Ghyaspur against second-guessing the pirate."

"Or that I simply would have forbidden his translating any of that code for pirate use," Milani said, resentfully.

"And he's not telling Dacko about the comets' orbital planes," Allis added now.

—What was that?— Mordon's question filled her head like an explosion. He wanted more about the comets: Were they present in great numbers? Were they low-inclination comets, short-period type? Would the ship's trajectory pass through the comets' orbital planes?

But Ghyaspur had skipped the code about comets and was describing the orbital elements of the third planet *Dowager Sun* would encounter. She'd get no help in answering Mordon's questions from Ghyaspur. She lowered her head to look at the albino. "Senda, do you remember anything about the comets in the system?" Allis asked for Mordon, who still feigned sleep.

"Only that we avoided their orbital planes, of course."

"If the ancestor recorded cometary orbits in code, they must have been important in this particular system." Milani's voice was calm, but instantly galvanizing. "Do you suppose . . ."

"Shhh," Mordon said, breaking his auditory silence for the first time since the conversation began, and at the same time allowing himself a delicious sigh of relief.

Milani, suddenly smiling smugly, leaned back against the last of the ingots, and Senda lowered white lashes over bright orbs.

"No pirates are listening to us," Allis said irritably. "Will someone please tell me what's going on?" She had the feeling that the three of them suddenly were telepathic and that she was not. Obviously they shared some knowledge Allis did not possess.

"We'll have to know where every pirate is at any given moment," Milani said, more to Senda and Mordon than to Allis, even though if such information ever were forthcoming it would be from Allis.

"It won't be easy to rig the sails," Senda whispered to Mordon, her hand tightening over his for attention.

"Rig the sails for what?" Allis said, her frustration mounting. Mordon was being deliberately obtuse, reveling in Senda's closeness, his mind mysteriously at ease. It was obvious that Senda and Milani assumed he was using silent talk to fill in conversational gaps as he had done earlier. "Mordon!"

—In a moment . . . Allow me the luxury . . .— Senda had not pulled away from him even though the need for the deception of sleep never had existed, especially now, considering Allis's assurance that no pirate was spying on them. He snuggled closer to the albino's breasts, unashamed that Allis was sharing the feelings of excitement stirring in him. Allis sensed this grant of enjoyment was something of a gift from the mate to her, just as Ghyaspur's privacy request when excitement involuntarily but similarly stirred him with Dacko also was a gift.

Senda, too, was momentarily unguarded. But whatever weakness caused that . . . No! Allis sensed the opposite. Senda's insidious fear was just *now* returning, debilitating her strength and even her love for Mordon. Then Senda was impenetrable again, and she pushed Mordon away.

He didn't hide the sharp pain that caused him, but quickly resigned himself to knowing the moment was gone and that Allis was waiting.

—Comets produce small, low-density particles in sufficient quantities for debris to form in their planes. A shower of dust particles blown directly off the comet's nucleus can damage a sail, especially a sail that is already weakened by . . . mischief. Ordinarily such an encounter is a rare event, so rare as to be all but discounted. I believe that our young pilot has done quite well, if what we surmise about the extensiveness of cometary planes in this system is true. Since a comet's period is long and often erratic, its orbit is not discerned easily by a newcomer to a system. But in just a few cases, it's information a ship's captain had better know, better have gotten from an observer of the system or perhaps from an ancestor's diary. Ship's logs are incalculably valuable in that way.—

Mordon was tempted to digress, but Allis already understood that in the vast quantities of possibilities in any given planetary system, let alone in the whole galaxy, a single captain could not encounter them all. A captain could, however, share the knowledge of an individual experience, and when combined with other experiences from other captains' logs, considerable knowledge could be gained, or withheld. —Just knowing Ghyaspur's withholding knowledge from Dacko makes it important, and valuable to us. He'd know you'd report it to us, and he'd know we'd understand. Doubtless he'll give the whole of it to you when he isn't so preoccupied, which will certainly corroborate what we've surmised so far. It's as simple as that; he's a good lad.—

"He also isn't aware that Dacko is recording the

contents of that diary so he won't need Ghyaspur, or
any of us, when it's done," Allis said, tension in her
voice.

As Senda moved away, Mordon sat next to Allis.
He nodded thoughtfully, rubbing his itchy beard.
"That's true, nor does Dacko suspect we're aware of
his plan, nor that surprises are in store for him.
My guess is he'll let us finish making his sails before
disposing of us."

"But that's only eighty more shifts in his mind,
less in Droganie's estimate."

"Well, we'll have to make the work last for Dacko's
count," Mordon said soothingly, "though it's a little
difficult to know just when the sails will give. If I rig
them to rupture too soon after we've set them,
Dacko's sure to become suspicious. Yet if it takes too
long . . ." He shrugged their helplessness. "Does he
intend to space us? Or just wait until we die of
radiation or starvation?" The mate's little eyes seemed
no different than if he'd asked her direction to the
nearest sanitary.

"I don't know," Allis replied, rubbing her arms
for circulation. The gypsies were so blunt they sometimes made her flesh crawl.

"You'd best stay with him; our young pilot knows
what we need to know, and he'll do his best to provide
the information." Mordon's pride in Ghyaspur
couldn't have been greater if he were his own son.
The young man was, in fact, everyone's surrogate
son; he had a lot of expectations to live up to. For
once Allis did not feel that it would be all right for
Ghyaspur to fail.

Even if Ghyaspur did his job well, Allis still was
puzzled over the eventual outcome. "What if the

sails do fail and we're fortunate enough to be alive to experience it. What good does it do us?"

"It provides an opportunity to take over the ship, of course," Mordon said, looking at her with some surprise. "They have to let us out of the forge if we're to make the repairs for them, which we surely are. They won't send their own people out under the best of circumstances, as they've already demonstrated. With the sunspot activity, they're certain to use us. All we need is to be out of this forge."

"You're spacing crazy," Allis said. "We've been out of the forge before and never so much as thought of taking over the ship. If it was possible, why didn't we already do it . . . or plan to perform this marvelous takeover with just seven people against forty-four when they have us set the sails after we get out of this gravity slip?"

"Allis, you don't understand anything, do you? Until now we didn't really have a stone-carrier to aid us. It's only now that your abilities have developed to a point where they are of some use to us. We *can* take over the ship, even seven against forty-four, as long as we know where every one of those forty-four pirates is and that most are sleeping at the moment of our takeover. We cannot make our move before you're able to give us that information. You will need time to identify every pirate on the ship and place each one spatially at any given moment. That will take conscientious studying on your part, I'm sure. I will provide the time for you to make such a study by rigging the sails."

Allis considered a moment. She knew by following great lengths of Mordon's fringe-thoughts that he believed he and his crewmates could overpower the

pirate guards when they chose to do so. But Allis
had visions of hordes more coming to the rescue of
fallen comrades where Mordon did not. "How can
you arrange for the sails to give only when most of
the crew are sleeping?"

"The sails will give when they encounter the right
stress, and I can't know when that will be. But I
can control how long it will take us to make the repairs, and I guarantee that if most of the pirates are
sleeping when we leave the ship, the repairs will not
take long. Otherwise, restoration surely will take a
full shift . . . more if we need it. You'll tell me when."

The repairs had to be made before any insurgent
action. With only seven crew members, there was none
to spare on time-consuming activities afterwards. The
ship had to be spaceworthy. Allis knew, too, that the
success of the plan rested on her. Identifying forty-
four minds nearly simultaneously would be a difficult
feat. She wasted no time in getting started on the
challenging task.

CHAPTER 23

The sails were unfurled, a vast section of them imperfect, their belay lines frangible, but holding the stellar wind until the forces hurled at them by the angry star became too great to bear. It seemed to Allis, when they'd come through a huge comet plane, sails unscathed, that Mordon had been too cautious. Droganie was making great work of securing the last fabricated bolt of sailcloth in the stanchion, but it was the *last*. Eighty-six shifts had gone by since the plot conceived in the gravity slip was employed, and still the sails held.

The *Dowager Sun* was approaching the second planet in its swing through the system. A shuttle with a trading party had sped before it, ephemeris dictating that this trip planetside be a short one. For the first time Dacko had chosen Ghyaspur to be Milani's burden, apparently no longer caring that the boy would reveal to his captain that he'd translated the code in his ancestor's diary for Dacko. Of course the pirate didn't know that Milani already had such knowledge through Allis, but the leonine captain seemed pleased for the opportunity to use the silent talk with one of her crew and not to have to pretend any concern for Allis during the trading venture.

Allis had intended to follow Dacko and Ghyaspur

as far beyond the ship as she could, just to see what her stone's range was. She lost Ghyaspur in the planet's ionosphere, but she read Dacko long after he was on the planet's surface, until the instant he handed Milani her stone. Then contact ended abruptly. It was as though Milani's stone had amplified Dacko's thoughts, or at least had given her an especially good source to zero in upon.

The incident made her wonder about powers the stones might have that were unknown to her, perhaps deliberately concealed by Milani. That they provided telepathic contact was obvious, and she'd not thought beyond that until now. She didn't know much about the prize she carried strapped on her arm, and had heard only legends about the people who fashioned it. The stones' use as communication devices was mere speculation. She wondered how much she had yet to learn about her stone, and how long she would live to learn more.

Droganie's return from the sail stanchion was an intermittent glide through the low-gravity shop, and she settled behind the massive slitter with the other four prisoners. The tall blacksmith thought wistfully of her snug forge on the *Sovereign Sun*. She was finally openly concerned about the radiation exposure her crewmates were taking, less concerned for herself since her body was probably only now reaching the end of its antiradiation reserves.

Allis didn't realize the gypsies had any antiradiation methods, and she was immediately curious about them, but Droganie didn't give them a second thought. She was preoccupied with the foreboding that only she might live through much more radiation abuse. Bracha was getting worse, too tired and unable to keep food in his stomach. It confirmed what Droganie already feared, that Dacko had no long-range plans to keep his captives alive, not even Milani.

Droganie did not want to be abandoned by her crewmates, the only people in the galaxy whom she knew and trusted. They had to escape soon, or she alone would be left. But what if they did escape? Perhaps all of them were sterile by now, or their genes so horribly damaged that they'd wish they were sterile. She wondered what was happening to the earthworm's child, Daneth's child. She'd barely been able to conceal her joy when she heard the good news, though of course she had for Milani's sake. Any birth on the *Sovereign Sun* would have made Droganie happy, but knowing Daneth's child survived him brought her special delight. Could it possibly be developing normally, or was it dying, or mutated?

Allis shivered and hugged her knees. Mordon, sitting nearby, reached for the rolled-up coat and handed it to her, believing she was cold. Allis never had become accustomed to the shipboard temperature, which was cooler than southern California. Yet it wasn't the cold that made her shiver just now. She was more anxious than ever about her unborn child, the bulge of its growth quite evident now beneath her trousers.

Allis took the coat and set it aside. "When will the sail rip?" she whispered to Mordon. With her stone, she always knew when the pirates were eavesdropping or watching them, but Mordon, not realizing that a whisper was all she could manage, frowned warningly at her. Allis cleared her throat. "It's all right. They're not listening."

His gray-blond mustache twitched. The next big wind will do it. But no one can predict the stellar flare that will cause the big wind. Maybe we'll go through another comet's tail."

"The last one didn't do a thing."

Mordon shrugged. "We barely touched the edge of the plane. Ghyaspur explained that to you. He told you the pirates weren't even aware . . ." He stopped, knowing he was repeating himself. "All we can do is watch and wait. Are you getting anxious, Allis?"

Allis nodded and drew her knees up tight against the bulge in her lower abdomen, as if her limbs could shield the child.

"Then let's go over the *Dowager Sun*'s schedule once again. We must be certain you know where every weapons-locker is and where every crew member is at any given time," he said, scooting his tall body closer to her. Like the rest of the captives, he stank as badly as the pirates, but all of them were inured to it now.

Allis closed her eyes. "I know the schedule in my sleep. I feel them walking, eating, moving their bowels, and the part of my mind that keeps sunwatch with them becomes very irritated when they don't pay proper attention to the screens."

Allis didn't have to open her eyes to know that amusement did not show on Mordon's face except, perhaps, for the tiniest brightening of his eyes. But inside Mordon laughed to remember what a poor job Allis had done on the sunwatch when she'd actually sat at the console. He'd spent half his life with Milani and conditioned himself not to display levity on the bridge. But didn't he realize that Milani would hear his silent laughter as clearly as a big guffaw?

Next to Ghyaspur, Allis knew Mordon the best. Even so, much of him remained a puzzle that Allis could not piece together. He was brilliant, probably a genius; a strong man when he had to be, and sometimes when he didn't. The tenderness and caring in him were not always so well concealed as he'd like.

And he criticized his capacity for compassion so sharply and so thoroughly that his personal feelings never got in the way of doing a job and doing it well. He wasn't the only one filled with contradictions; he was just more aware of them than his fellows. He'd stopped laughing, and Allis saw in his mind a reflection of her own somber appearance.

"You've seen a lot of radiation effects, probably more than I've ever heard of. Tell me if my baby has a chance of living," Allis said.

Something stung Mordon, something bitter and painful. He forced the ache from his mind and thought about Allis's baby, but not before Allis glimpsed a vision of another baby, his and Senda's child. He recognized his lapse, and the thought that followed was stern. —I'll deal with that myself.— His mind shifted, leaving Allis mystified. *Deal with what?* she wondered.

"Your child has a chance, but each shift we spend in this forge diminishes it," he said honestly. His beady eyes seemed translucent windows to the appraisal of her going on in his mind. He decided to hide nothing. "You were unquestionably clean when you came to us, and Daneth worked in hydroponics or planetside, which is clean work. The probability that your baby is perfectly formed is high. But the radiation accumulates, so it's more a question of how long it can survive."

"It's not likely to be deformed?" Allis asked, refusing to consider that its life was being shortened, perhaps so truncated that it would not live to term.

Mordon smiled one of his rare smiles, a reassuring gesture. With him, as well as the other captives, there was a special hope, almost a prayer, because it was Daneth's baby. The co-captain had been planetside when the rest of the crew caught an especially bad dose of radiation that left many with short life expectancies. Others were sterile or as a result of the accident conceived only horrible mutations, lethal mutations. That had little to do with Allis and her child, but Mordon deemed it was important that she know.

"Milani was one of those affected?" Allis said, trying to confirm what Mordon was alluding to.

He nodded.

"Does she hate me because I'm having his baby?" Allis asked. It seemed that way, according to Mordon's thoughts. Most gypsies were not promiscuous by Earth's standards, yet children were so precious to them that fertile women were known to ask men for whom they had no affection but who were proven breeders to sire a child.

Mordon seemed uncomfortable, wanting to be honest with Allis but without betraying Milani. "Partly it's the baby, and partly that you're being pregnant confirms that he lay with you . . . not that such doesn't ever happen among us, especially planetside where crewmates would never be the wiser." Allis was not embarrassed by his sheepish grin nor the unbidden urge that accompanied it. She was becoming accustomed to such fleeting desires, and knew that at least for now it wasn't even serious wishful thinking.

"You know Milani is sterile. What you don't know is that it was her own . . . blunder that caused the sterility. She's taken the blame entirely upon herself.

"Milani fell into a Watcher trap. She answered a mechanical distress signal coming from a cenotaph." Cenotaph was a euphemism. Mordon's mind described the distasteful reality with the vision of an abandoned stellar sailing vessel, its hulk endlessly orbiting some alien sun.

"How do they get that way?" Allis wondered, saddened by the vision.

Mordon shrugged. "One final time through a gravity slip and there's not enough healthy crew left to unfurl the sails. Most of the surviving gypsy ships are not like this bitch of a *Dowager*, where Watcher poisons aren't contained. The Watchers fooled a lot of gypsy captains in the beginning, the best of gypsy scientists being pitifully ignorant of the workings of nuclear forges. But as you know from *Sovereign Sun*, we did eventually learn, and now we have our own cooling systems and additional magnetic shields. We don't rely only on the ultraloy containment vessel."

"Are you saying the Watchers deliberately poisoned gypsy ships with radiation?" Some of the confusion she'd experienced when Ghyaspur first told her the diary stories was clearing up.

"Of course," Mordon said bitterly. "What else could they do to eliminate gypsies from the galaxy? They were quite successful, too, until gypsies learned to rig their own shields and to ingest prophylactics as a way of life. Didn't you wonder why our diet was so high in bulk and amino acid cysteamines? There are special vitamins, too; all our foods were rich in them."

"I knew the food was high in protein, but I didn't know it had those other things. I thought the lack of carbohydrates had to do with lowering the metabolic rate because of the ship's environment—almost no gravity to use them up."

"That's a consideration, of course, but mainly our food is prophylactic. The forge workers took antibiotics, too. Anyhow, after the gypsies caught on to what the Watchers were doing, they stopped succumbing from the plague of radiation, at least outright. But you know about the birthrate, the damage already done. There're so few gypsies left you'd think the Watchers wouldn't notice us anymore, but I guess even a few is an affront to their pride . . . maybe even unpleasant reminders to their consciences, if they have them. For whatever reason, they've rigged deathtraps in some cenotaphs.

"There's something to be said about gypsy pride, too. Milani'd heard the stories, and she—all of us, but still she places the blame only on herself—thought they were merely war stories, and that the war was over for the few survivors. But we should have known just as surely as absolute motion is meaningless in space so absolute time is meaningless; peacetime, wartime, it's all the same. So she answered the distress call and led a party of sailjockeys into a deathtrap. It was Droganie's brother who became suspicious. He took a lethal dose of radiation in the time it took him to get from the axis of that abandoned ship to the forge and discovered the breached containment vessel. He died within ten shifts, of course, but the others survived."

"And there weren't really any people on the ship?"

"No." He paused a moment, grieving. When he continued, his voice was husky. "It never was spoken of, but I suspect Daneth must have been terribly disappointed when he found out. Not just for the mistake of going, but for what it did to Milani's ability to conceive. Milani knew he was disappointed; how could he hide that from her? She blamed herself."

"And he let her," Allis said with disgust. "He always was a sanctimonious—" Her deprecation was hurting Mordon and she stopped abruptly. "Sorry. I didn't mean . . . well, maybe I did. Dan was just human, after all." And that seemed to hurt Mordon even more, and for a while both were silent. Abruptly he decided it was important to his ultimate goal that

Allis understand Milani and Daneth, and he continued.

"Maybe it's as you say, that he had no right to let her feel guilty. That fits both our concepts of what Daneth was like; he never took responsibility for anyone's guilt. They felt that way, not him. He had his own burdens to bear, such as his disappointment, which he couldn't hide from the woman he loved. Daneth was clean, yet he continued to refuse to sire children with other women, never lay with anyone but Milani so far as we knew . . . until you."

Allis nodded. "I begin to see the double-edged sword. I really twisted it in her guts, didn't I?"

Mordon nodded solemnly. "Theirs was a special trust, one that was not always easy to keep, and one which, in the end, was broken."

"You mean because he gave me the stone?" Allis shook her head. "Giving me the stone wasn't a very loving thing to do. Look where it's gotten me."

"Senda said you cursed Daneth for giving you the stone, and I can understand that love can turn to hate when a person is left with a dead man's burden. But I don't understand why you hate Milani."

"You don't understand about my wanting to go home," she said bitterly. Then she could say no more, for she realized Mordon did understand. He was not gypsy by blood; he had memories and ties that never could be forgotten, even if the thread to them had been so thinned by space/time as to be meaningless.

"Your home is in the stars now, just as mine is," Mordon said with certainty. "It is whether you admit it or not. A stone-carrier selected you, just as one selected me, knowing us better than we know ourselves."

"Space!" Allis said, angry with his conviction and

reverence. "What kind of god would betray two women, leaving them miserable and having to deal with each other?"

"Make no mistake, Allis. I never believed my captains were gods. Daneth was simply more conscientious than most, and Milani more conscience-ridden. I can do nothing for the man who is dead, but . . ." Mordon's words trailed off, but not his thoughts.

Allis looked hard at him. "You want *me* to help Milani? I can't even read her. Besides, I did try to help her once," she said, thinking of her complicity in Ghyaspur's attempt to claim paternity of the child, "but she flung it back in my face."

"Yes, the secret with Ghyaspur," Mordon sighed. "Did you expect her to deny Daneth's child?"

"You knew?" Allis said, surprised.

"She told me, despite her pride."

"Then you know it's useless for me to try helping Milani, even if I were willing." Deep inside she feared Milani; the captain was powerful and intolerant, and as smug as Dan ever was. Dan's self-satisfied and egotistical aspects had been charming when he was alive. In retrospect she considered him priggish and pharisaical, and his co-captain was no different. Mordon had more to say, but Allis silenced him with a hand. She'd just been alerted by Ghyaspur that the shuttle on which he and Milani were passengers had docked in the *Dowager Sun*'s axis.

"They're back," Allis said, switching her attention to the center of the ship. She felt Dacko's mind sneer as he watched Milani and Ghyaspur shove off with the guards. "One more planetfall and we're dead," she told Mordon with horrified certainty. "The little port they just came from was riddled with signs of Watchers, and there wasn't a ground blizzard this time to keep them away. Dacko cut the trip short. He suspects Ghyaspur set him up; doesn't believe he didn't know about the Watchers. *Is* there any hope of help from them?"

Mordon shook his head bitterly.

"That sail better give pretty soon."

"It will," Mordon said confidently. "It will."

CHAPTER 24

He knew it was the beginning of the end. There could be no other explanation for Dacko's using him as Milani's burden during the planetside trading venture, allowing him in her presence while she possessed her communicator-stone after the long and lonely centishift of isolation from any of his comrades. At the first opportunity he had told his captain that he'd translated the diary for Dacko, as Dacko must have known he would do. It only meant the pirate no longer cared that Milani knew, or wanted her to know about the translation.

Ghyaspur believed Dacko's grin when he first handed Milani the stone was one of triumph, for she seemed to pale at Ghyaspur's silent exposition. Momentarily he feared all his effort had been in vain; perhaps he'd overestimated Allis's ability to use her stone, or Allis hadn't understood the significance of the cometary debris, or Milani stubbornly had refused to act upon anything relayed by the Earthling. But no; a silent and secret sign from the captain stilled his wild surmising. All was well. Maybe Milani could pale at will and had pretended chagrin for Dacko's amusement. More likely the stress of being on a planet and not being well conditioned for it had begun to tell on her at that moment. Ghyaspur couldn't imagine his captain feigning anything for anyone's benefit.

Contrariwise, Ghyaspur was having difficulty containing his joy at finally being returned to the forge where his crewmates waited, where the end was at hand. What if the guards held him back when they opened the hatch of the forge, dropped Milani in there, and took him on down the gangway to Dacko's scarlet cabin? He couldn't help the sudden perspiration that chilled him as thoroughly as the planet's wind had done. Milani no longer carried her stone and could not comfort him with a sign this time. To his immeasurable relief he was motioned through the hatch even as he stumbled atop his captain's heels as he followed her through. They'd have had to fight with him this time to take him away. He would be with his mates for the end.

He was unprepared for the deterioration his crewmates had suffered during his absence. Their faces were pinched and etched with misery, flesh withering over their bones. Some had bruises and festering sores, whether from improper nutrition or radiation effects he did not know. He'd fared much better than they, and he felt guilty for that despite knowing one healthy and able person among them was better than none. He just wished someone else had been spared.

"On whom would you wish the suffering?" Allis said, coming to his side. Her hair was in a ragged braid, fingernails broken and dirty. But her soft brown eyes, more sunken than he remembered, were bright and glad to see him. "And anyhow," she added, taking his arm to lead him to the shelter of the slitter, "we look worse than we feel . . . except for Bracha. He is very ill."

Ghyaspur felt a chill at Allis's touch. He had dreamed of her sometimes, and she might have shared those dreams with him through her stone. It would be like her to show her affection in this manner. Still, he felt embarrassment that she would touch him while his crewmates could see. It took him a moment to realize that all the prisoners were scrunched together, shoulder to shoulder, thigh to thigh, and not entirely to shield themselves behind the slitter. Did this alien-looking contact among them mean they no longer cared about propriety? Were they defeated even as he'd planned and implemented their escape? Confused, he looked at Allis, only to see that her fingers were twisted in a meaningful sign: *beware.* She'd been carefully coached in *Sovereign Sun* secrets during his absence, and he guessed that the pirates were spying. The sign changed: *affirmative.*

He extricated his arm from her fingers as he sat down in their midst, impatient because he'd waited a hundred shifts for this reunion and somehow hurt because he felt like a stranger among them. And why was Milani looking at him with that unexpected vehemence in her eyes? His shoulders rose in interrogation.

"Did you think you could buy your life with the diary where you could not with your favors?" Milani said, her tone accusing and cold.

Shock left Ghyaspur speechless. Would these people he loved never understand him? If Allis hadn't been able to grasp that he'd planned the destruction of the sails, surely experienced sailors could figure it out. He would have, if he'd been in *their* place. And he wouldn't have suspected any one of them of acting selfishly and childishly in *his* place. There was no flicker of understanding in his captain's eyes, but finally he noticed her fingers: *beware.* An act then for an audience of pirates. But he could not participate now that he'd felt self-doubt. He couldn't help wondering if some remote part of him had indeed been trying to curry favor with the pirate.

He shuddered. There couldn't be any other reason for his impulsive errors while making those translations for Dacko. A personal survival mechanism working against his better judgment, something unbidden making him say the wrong words, but knowing full well that Dacko would recognize the errors and keep him alive and well to straighten out the records, at least for a while. Worst of all was that Allis must have known, and must know even now how weak and self-centered he was. Anguished, he put his head on his drawn-up knees and closed his eyes, not wanting to look at any of them.

Space! He wouldn't even lift his head. He'd come in blushing heroism and in moments dissolved to needless shame that Allis was helpless to prevent. Milani looked irritated that he wouldn't feign a fight with her, but if her concern went deeper, her face didn't show it. Allis didn't have to look at the other prisoners to know what they thought. Mordon wanted to know if the pirates had stopped watching, if something had transpired that he'd somehow overlooked, for he thought Ghyaspur's behavior quite strange. Even Senda chanced a puzzled query, something in Ghyaspur's last anguished look extracted some sympathy from a place in her that she kept covered and untouchable. Allis only could rock restlessly in her little niche by the slitter, mind locked onto Dacko's while he watched his prisoners from a screen on the bridge. Milani's bitter accusation had given him some satisfaction; he liked knowing Milani felt betrayed, and Allis had no doubt that Milani'd planned a little scene for his amusement. Too bad she hadn't fore-warned Ghyaspur.

The pirate's nub of satisfaction was getting no additional stimulation from his viewing the quiescent prisoners. How to stir up . . . But some budding thoughts of humiliating Milani were interrupted by queries from his crew. Ah, yes, the slave girl with the yellow eyes like Milani's. He was only vaguely aware that the poor girl was merely a substitute for the woman he feared, just as Ghyaspur had been. The power on the viewscreen faded with the movement of Dacko's hand, and Allis left him just as soon as she was certain the newly acquired slave had commanded his complete attention. She was afraid of the pirate in a way that Ghyaspur never was. Odd that Allis only felt gratitude to the unknown girl and very little sympathy. She didn't stop to ponder her callousness. She was free to speak now, even if she didn't know what to say. She leaned back, using the silence still enforced on the others to think. Milani looked at her suspiciously, but said nothing.

Finally Allis leaned forward. "Milani, can a stone-carrier put a suggestion in someone's mind while in contact with that person?"

"Those are nothing but legends, stories told to amuse children," the captain answered, giving Mordon a reproving scowl.

"I've heard a lot of stories, but stone-carriers planting suggestions wasn't one of them," Allis said, defending Mordon before he even realized he'd been hurt. She didn't want to have to deal with two wounded gypsies. "We all know how complex this escape plan is—conceived by Ghyaspur in one place, and acted upon in another by us. Considering that, it's gone well; no errors on either side. I wonder if that is because of some, uh . . . hints he picked up from me?"

Ghyaspur raised his chin off his knees in time to see Milani dismiss Allis's suggestion with a disgusted shake of her head, but knowing that all was well was not without some positive effect. He brightened considerably.

"What about this feeling . . . no, this knowing that sometimes I'm in someone else's head. It's not the same as when I hear the silent talk, and though I'm certainly not disembodied, I believe something of me is with the other person, spatially away from me, yet somehow linked."

Milani cocked her head, still frowning. "It's not like that for me . . . except, perhaps, when I'm experiencing the burden. I'm closer to the other person at such times." She looked softly at Ghyaspur. "How are your neck and shoulder?"

"A little numb," he said, shrugging without a wince. "I'd forgotten it," he lied.

"If you'd wanted to communicate something to Ghyaspur, could you have left a thought of it in his mind during that intense sharing?" Allis said, refusing to be sidetracked by Milani's sudden solicitousness. Ghyaspur was brooding less now, spirited by the absence of any condemnation save his own. But Allis had new concerns. She would have given much to know if this mental suggestion stuff was a subject Milani considered taboo within hearing of her crew, or if she merely thought it was not worth pursuing. But the void in perceiving the captain's innermost thoughts was absolute. And kept that way by whose hatred? Allis wondered. Milani seemed to be considering her response with abnormal care.

"If it could be done, don't you think I would have

put thoughts of freeing us in Dacko's mind when I had the opportunity?"

"Maybe," Allis said. "Or maybe you're reluctant to discuss it because I can do it and you can't."

Milani looked at her coldly. "Your imagination exceeds your abilities. What you suggest cannot be done."

It wasn't the rising hostility in Milani's eyes nor the tone of finality in her voice that made Allis back off her quest. It was the dread in Mordon's very soul that such power existed anywhere in the galaxy, the astonishment that he might not be the master of his own life. Maybe the stone-carriers *were* gods, and he was not alone in his opinion. Ghyaspur was outraged at the thought that he might have been manipulated once again. Even Droganie, who paid little attention to practical or philosophical aspects of the mind reading, was thrust into a quandary. What spirit had possessed her brother when he heeded no one but went directly to the heart of that cenotaph to expose the Watcher trap?

Their reactions took Allis by surprise, and she berated herself for not thinking beyond trying to squeeze some sort of admission from Milani. Of course, if Ghyaspur had acted on Allis's silent suggestion, sent however desperately and for whatever good, then he was already in bondage. And if Dacko could be convinced to free them with just a little hard thinking on Allis's part, what meaning was there to any trial in life? What good the triumphs or heroics that were hollow echoes of a stone-carrier's whim? Now she must say something to assuage their fears and reestablish their trust in the stones. Odd that knowing the very depths of their suspicions did not provide a foolproof response. Fleetingly she credited Dan more for true insight than for the simplicity of a commanding position. She had that advantage now but the right words were not easy to find, not even for a glib tongue.

Milani, even without her stone, was aware of the tension around her. Her eyes did not move, yet Allis had the feeling she was being scrutinized along with the crew. Then Milani's gaze did move and came to rest on Senda, who was relaxed by comparison to the others. Until now, Allis had not noticed that Senda, within her stationary privacy request, emanated no pulse of alarm, did not join the chorus of doubt.

Having pointed out to Allis where the convincing argument must lie, Milani edged back, leaving to Allis's discretion how to reveal it. The captain apparently was unaware that Senda always used the privacy request, or she wouldn't have backed off so easily. But Allis immediately decided she wouldn't let anything so intangible as a privacy request stop her. She'd had small glimpses of Senda's thoughts before, so she knew exactly how to go about getting more.

Ruthlessly Allis probed through the outer thoughts, that layer of nearly nothing that only concealed if Allis chose to allow it to conceal. There was no single line of action or thought, merely a fragment that told Allis she would be dead if Milani could have commanded it. The knowledge was not shocking; Allis already knew from that single blinding exchange with Milani when she first boarded the *Sovereign Sun* that the captain's wishing her dead was about the kindest ill she had threatened. Nor did the unfulfilled death wish reveal why Senda alone was convinced that a stone-carrier could not manipulate a person unnaturally. But the reason was there, somewhere in

Senda's head, if only Allis could make her think of it. She didn't care that she'd have to continue invading Senda's privacy to learn what it was.

"If it isn't possible to do, I want to know from someone other than you, Milani," Allis said stubbornly.

Milani raised her brow a little, but remained silent during the moment it took for the albino to realize she had been addressed. Senda struggled to escape Allis's intense eyes, and inside she fought an even more intense battle.

"Try it," Senda said, furiously throwing up wild and disconnected musings in her mind, momentarily more fearful that something untoward would involuntarily escape her than that her mind would be invaded. "Try to control Dacko and you'll learn it cannot be done." The why of it was protected from Allis's prying by a mental fencing skill she hadn't realized existed. A maelstrom of thoughts, a potpourri, even silly ditties dredged from childhood protected one bottom line. How different this was from the stream of consciousness Mordon used to communicate with her; how much more disciplined this mind.

"Senda, you know I can't go beyond your privacy request," Allis said, disarmingly pleasant and blunt and dishonest. "But I do feel your mood. You're the only one who has no curiosity in this matter. Why not? Are you aware of something no one else knows? If you are, please share it."

It was quick. The albino had buried her fear deeply, but the human brain was too well conditioned to respond in predictable patterns. The verbal stimulus referring to what Senda feared to expose led Allis directly to the fear. Senda had not stabbed Allis in the Watcher antechamber as Milani wanted her

to do, as Milani would have willed her to do. The
incident was replayed for Allis in a breath of time,
the pain and the fear was concentrated around
Senda's realization that she had deliberately misread
a silent signal from her captain to carry out the deed.
From this painful knowledge, Senda also had learned
a stone-carrier's will could not be forced on others.
If it could, Milani would have taken control of a
too timid or too selfish crewmember, and Allis would
have been killed.

"And I thought I was in danger from the Watchers," Allis said quietly. But Senda heard. She knew
Allis abused her privileges as a stone-carrier.

"I do not willingly share with dirt eaters," Senda
said, her voice brittle with rage, "not my thoughts
and not my knowledge. I leave that to other dirt
eaters."

Mordon was stung, his patience at an end. He made
no attempt to forgive Senda this time, even if the
forgiving always had been for his own satisfaction. He
rose gravely. "When Ghyaspur was taken from us,
there were only two people left to teach the silent
talk to Allis—you and me. As a linguist, a person
whose entire life was spent communicating with people, the burden fell more logically to you. When I
realized you hadn't taken it up, I did so, just as I
had picked up the burden of keeping our love alive
for so long.

"I thought to provide a refuge for you because I
believed your peculiar behavior was my fault, just
as the baby may have been my fault. But all this
blame I've taken on myself is crazy. You're the one
who is albino, the one with the damaged genes."

"You think I blamed you for that?" Senda said, in-
censed by his stupidity.

"What else? If I have somehow wronged you, tell me how now so that I may explain or beg your forgiveness, whichever is needed. If you don't speak, I'll hold you in contempt forever."

Too strong, Allis wanted to tell him. Senda's conviction that any manipulative attempt on Dacko would fail had put her crewmates at ease, for they trusted her, and now they were further distracted by the confrontation between her and Mordon. Allis wanted to warn Mordon that his ultimatum was untimely, considering Senda's mood, but any warning she'd give might reveal to the others that she'd invaded Senda's privacy. Having just repaired one breach between herself and the crew, however clumsily, she did not want to create another. Then, too, Allis remembered Mordon had said he wanted no interference from the stone-carrier in his relationship with Senda. He gave no indication that he'd changed his mind, so Allis decided she'd better honor his request. She settled back against the slitter and tried to be a spectator, like the rest of the crew. That attempt was quickly thwarted by an angry tirade.

—Shall I tell him how far you must have gone into my mind against my will to know what I was hiding even from myself?— Senda's pink eyes blazed like embers in a fire just stoked, and not by Mordon. —Shall I shatter what little trust you've established with him? Space take you for reminding me of my shame. But know as he cannot know that I won't jeopardize my crewmates' only hope for escape just to keep Mordon bound to me. And beware, earthworm. I know what Milani has known all along. You are not worthy to hold the stone.—

"So be it," Mordon said to Senda's apparent silence. His eyes didn't so much as water, but a flood washed through his heart and mind, and he thought the treasure that was Senda was carried away. Allis knew better. His decision to stop torturing himself over Senda had cleansed the wound. It would close right over his love for the albino, never to be raw or sore again, but not without leaving its mark. He would never be able to look at Senda without feeling it, but the pain would be gone.

Senda was not faring as well as her ex-lover. She was recanting her love for Mordon, all feelings she'd ever had for the dead babe, knowing full well that if she did not deny her loves there'd be so much hurting there'd be no room for anything else, no room left to trust her captain to keep alive the gypsy way. Allis knew this, indeed she felt it as strongly as Senda, yet she knew not what to do.

Allis trembled as she tried to rid herself of the albino's thoughts, but she couldn't fight the tendency to share Senda's agony. Only when Senda got hold of herself did Allis feel able to break away, and even at that she found herself groping for the albino, wanting to touch to see if she were all right.

Everyone else was calm. Mordon was no longer concerned about stone-carriers being gods. Ghyaspur displayed his inimitable resilience in overcoming any lingering suspicions of his cowardice. And Senda, despite her outrage, would not change her passive attitude, no matter how much more it hurt her. She'd martyred herself long before Allis came along.

Allis knew she must keep silent. Keeping silent must have been what Milani had done. With her stone the captain must have known how deeply ashamed Senda was, how terribly frightened and hurt, when she believed she'd betrayed her shipmates and captain by not killing Allis. Silence had served Milani's purposes, and silence could now serve Allis. Did that mean that Milani had been afraid and confused like Allis was? Or did it simply mean they both were self-centered? The answers to these questions weren't in anyone's head but her own and perhaps Milani's; the stone was useless now.

It was easy to keep silent—safe. Mordon might never understand that he'd just realized Senda's greatest fears, repaid her love, however hidden, with contempt. Not much worse than losing him when he discovered she'd failed to carry out a command. Allis tried to console herself again with the knowledge that Mordon specifically asked her not to meddle where he and Senda were concerned. Easy to oblige him. Too easy. Too safe. Too hard to live with. Allis sighed unhappily.

"Senda, only a fool would have given you that signal, or someone so blinded by hate that she didn't consider the consequences. You displayed good sense. She should thank you," Allis said.

It took a moment for Senda to understand, and when she did she stared at Allis. —She is my captain.—

"She was wrong," Allis said. But Senda only stared at her through pink eyes. Senda knew the earthworm was not trustworthy. Senda knew Allis raped minds. Yet the gift of silence Senda had given was not going to be withdrawn now, not when she'd paid for it so dearly.

Allis sighed. This stone-carrying business couldn't have been easy for Dan either. Knowing when to keep silent and when to speak required more than a mind-reading ability. At least this time Allis felt she'd made the right decision.

CHAPTER 25

Allis had awakening down to a system. The first sense of consciousness brought with it a compelling urge to touch Dacko's mind and learn his whereabouts. It was a much stronger urge than morning ablutions ever had been, but it was possible Allis didn't remember correctly since the luxury of washing was somewhat low in realistic priorities and, being slightly dehydrated, she sensed her bladder infrequently now. When the pirate leader was placed in a memorized blueprint of the *Dowager Sun*, her thoughts turned to the bridge to take a head count and to learn what she could from the sunwatcher and navigator. This particular mental journey was short, for Dacko was on the bridge, at the navigator's console, but giving no thought to navigation.

A quick shift to the ship's communication console told her no one was spying on the prisoners at the moment. That was a red flag area that warranted constant surveillance. At this stage she could no longer be said to be the least bit sleepy, but her eyes did not open until every pirate and slave on board the ship had been found, location and current occupation duly noted in her mind. When all forty-four had been accounted for, she spent another moment noting the texture of their arrangement in her mind so that any spatial change among them instantly attracted her attention.

Mentally chaperoning forty-four people would have been impossible for the Allis who used to have difficulty remembering more than seven items on a list and was a total failure at Clue. But the minds of the pirates and slaves had actual form and substance; the only artificially imposed structure in her head was the *Dowager Sun*'s blueprint. That had been constructed from Mordon's knowledge of gypsy ships, and she'd filled in singularities like the weapons-locker from the pirates' own minds. For the rest of her waking hours, the *Dowager Sun*'s crew would move like figures on a game board, which she'd follow with celerity. And Allis, satisfied that the awakening ritual was complete, finally opened her eyes to a collage of boxcars, the all too familiar forge equipment set at angles and heights that were impossible on Earth. She glowered at them resentfully, unable to make a mind that followed minds through an invisible diagram accept that the impossible arrangement of equipment was spatially economical and convenient in the nearly gravityless environment. She wanted the equipment on the deck.

Stretching her legs between the sprawled limbs of her companions, Allis flexed her muscles rhythmically, hoping to keep them toned so they would serve well enough when she had to call on them to carry her again. Her legs touched someone—Ghyaspur, she noted as she allowed the awareness of the prisoners' minds to attend her. He was the only one awake aside from herself, though Senda was stirring. Ghyaspur cringed from Allis's touch, and she turned to see him pulling up short from sit-ups he'd been diligently executing. The quick movement in an environment where an unexpected sneeze could knock one over was not without consequence, but he recovered by bending his knees and grabbing the stanchion in which he'd jammed his feet, leaving him cantilevered but secure.

Had this been anyone else, awake and exercising, Allis would have offered to add her mass and muscle to strain against and would have received like treatment in return. This form of touching was commonplace among the captives now; indeed they were elbow to elbow nearly every moment in order to keep their bodies behind the slitter, the only solid protection from the white heart of the forge since the ingots had been consumed. Some, like Mordon, had shed the touching taboo spontaneously as soon as the need arose. Others endured the necessity of physical contact as a practical matter. Yet Ghyaspur, who'd once demonstrated an ungypsylike proclivity for touching Allis, touched no one, despite the cramped quarters.

He was flushed and angry, though not with Allis. He knew he had not flinched from her touch, not from her who represented all seasons to him, a bird on the wing, a long winding trail. He'd flinched from the memory of Dacko's touch and from knowing that even if he learned not to shrink from being touched, he could never forget how he had endured Dacko. It angered him to know how much those evil times were a part of him.

"If you must keep thinking of him, let it be about how you outsmarted him and led him into this solar system," Allis said quietly.

Ghyaspur's brows rose suspiciously over rainblue eyes. "Did I? Or did you?" His question was not accusatory, but slightly admiring. Stone-carrying goddess.

Allis shook her head, confused by the shock of

pleasure she felt at being held in such high and mystical esteem. But the god role was a trap, and she knew it now. "I'll tell you now while the others are asleep that I only hoped you would make a mistake, one that Dacko would catch. I was afraid that if he believed he'd received a completely accurate translation of the diary he'd do you some harm . . . kill you, probably. It was in his mind that he had little or no use left for you. But the overall plan, I confess that I came on it late. You'd already brought it into being before I even realized what was going on."

"Which proves how honorable you are, since I mostly whispered the plan in the black one's ear," Ghyaspur said, his voice bewilderingly bright, considering how much he hated those private times with Dacko. She sensed his determination to inure himself to the unforgettable.

"I learned early what a privacy request was," Allis said. "You sent me away with yours."

"Not always," he commented huskily, his eyes lowered. He was thinking of the times he went willingly to Dacko, though dreaming of Allis, pretending through a cloud of drugs and liquor that the pleasures he gave were for her to know.

His thoughts, plainly there for her to share, jolted her. It had been easier for her not to participate in the sordid acts, and she'd responded honorably to his privacy requests, leaving him alone to lessen his embarrassment and pain. She'd known about the drugged liquors and had assumed his occasional failure to request privacy had been because the chemicals in his bloodstream made him forgetful. She'd left him of her own accord.

Now she remembered the beautiful dream she'd been caught up in; she should have guessed it was not her own. The stone had fed in Ghyaspur's interpretations of a desert wind as a sensual, enveloping heat, the indigo sky was his backdrop for an orgasm of stars. Through the drugs, indeed, because of them, she realized now, he'd understood and used the power of her stone to bring her joy in this desolate and lonely place.

Profoundly touched, Allis put her hand on his, and felt him press it fiercely to his lips. His reckless and flaring heart had somehow emerged unscathed by all that he'd suffered, his love undampened. Glad that he'd survived, she found it impossible to be honest with him, to tell him that he didn't love her but only what she represented to him—the rich foliage in verdant planet valleys, the swell of waves in an energized sea, the breath of life borne on the wind. She epitomized his dream of planet life, and one night's adventure and brief trading stops were not enough to satisfy him.

"We'll get there together," Allis said, more hopeful than certain, considering the circumstances.

A crack of laughter was his response, and it was aimed at shooting down her patronizing words. "I think you can love me, too, Allis, if only you'll stop being afraid."

Bewildered, Allis sat back and would have pulled her hand away if he'd loosened his grip. "I don't know what you mean."

"Of course you don't. You have the stone and so you think you must know everything about me, and since you're so wise and well informed you've concluded that I must be confused in thinking I love you. More likely you simply don't know what love is all about; certainly there's been none for you to witness except mine, and you don't trust me because you think I have so little experience with it. And if you've looked for love in my mates' minds and believe you've found it, you're wrong. They're weary and dull and fearful, and you've been caught up in it."

His description of their companions was all too accurate. Allis defended them haltingly. "It's the imprisonment, the shame and the loss."

Ghyaspur shook his head. "If you'd taken up the stone when you first had the chance, you'd know that they've been tired for a long time. It has nothing to do with our present circumstances. With the death of every babe, with the sadness of bodies joining but never quickening new life, with the fear that each of us here might be the last of the gypsy race, the ability to love died. I give them credit for having the courage to carry on as if it were not so, some longer than others. But life without love for life is meaningless."

"Our lives are near ending." It was Senda who spoke so resignedly. Allis had been aware of her awakening for a few moments.

Ghyaspur wasn't the least bit startled by her words, nor did he ponder them long. He knew that Senda was not referring to death by Dacko's hand. He scoffed. "You came from Daneth's ship and should remember how well we overcame even the greatest adversity and that we were happy while doing it."

Senda's scowl brought him up short. "Childhood memories are inaccurate."

"You can believe that if it comforts you, Senda," Ghyaspur said, refusing to be put off. "But Daneth didn't become jaded in his worst moments. If you doubt me you have only to look at Allis's belly; it's big with his child gotten even while he was dying. That's not the work of someone who's afraid of the future."

Allis put her hand thoughtfully on her belly. It

was huge, though not so large as it would be in just two more months, if she had two more months of life.

"He's right," Senda said, reflectively. "At least I for one am afraid." Of life, Allis knew, but that didn't eliminate Allis's bewilderment.

"And this is what I'm expected to lead on a raid?"

Again Ghyaspur laughed. "Don't worry about that. People afraid of life have nothing to lose on a raid to regain control of those lives. Odd as it may seem, there's not a coward among us, not for what must be done."

"I hope you're right, because it's too late to change our minds," Allis said, stiffening with alarm. "Better waken Milani."

Ghyaspur wondered why he should disturb the captain, who was known to sleep only fitfully. When they felt the *Dowager Sun* begin a huge pendulum swing, he understood why he must waken Milani, but he didn't have to. The captain awoke with a start, knowing instantly as Allis had that the sails had split.

CHAPTER 26

Once he saw the rent in the sails displayed by telemetry on the viewscreens on the bridge, he'd rushed down the gangways and corridors, knowing whom to blame. It seemed to take an eternity for Dacko to reach the forge, but in reality the *Dowager Sun* had just completed the first pendulum sweep, which the loss of sails had precipitated.

"You've sabotaged my sails," Dacko shouted, bursting through the hatch. Guards were at his heels, but rage had caused him to forego his usual caution. His anger was as visible on his face as it was in his mind. Yet Allis felt safer looking at his face this time, ugly with anger, which was a clear change from the past when he seethed and boiled behind smooth features and outward calm.

"Ridiculous," Milani said, standing to face him. "I've nothing to gain by foundering the ship I'm sailing on."

"It's probably the old sails, Captain," Mordon said, holding a stanchion against the change of sway. "My riggings are always faultless. No telling what kind of ignorant fools worked on his old ones."

"No doubt," Milani agreed with alacrity.

"It's in the new sections," Dacko insisted, his mind running riot. He hadn't believed they'd dare try sabotage. "The tear is miles long, and the lines have failed."

Milani shook her head unperturbed. "Morton always rigs them stoutly. The fault must be in the old sails. If it's not, I'll space him myself," she said, cold-bloodedly convincing. She crossed her arms across her chest and stood firmly on her heels, and just a little aloof from her own crew.

Dacko noted her poise and that the mate looked appropriately chagrined, both of which pleased Dacko immensely. The thought of watching Milani blow the rodent-faced man from a torpedo tube was exciting, even more exciting than doing it himself. She'd have to be very frightened of her captor to go through with it; a stone-carrier afraid of him! "It's in the new sails," Dacko repeated firmly, sneering as he looked at her disheveled hair. How had he ever thought this stone-carrier looked stately?

"If it is, Milani, it's because of defective extrusions in the rigging, not in my work," Mordon said with the cleverest trace of whining in his voice.

"Then it's Droganie to blame?" Milani said, raising one disapproving brow.

"It must be," Mordon insisted frantically. "You'll see. Watch the repairs from the bridge. I'll prove it to you, I swear."

Droganie crept forward, shaking her head as if she couldn't believe what she was hearing but saying nothing. Milani looked from Droganie to Mordon, appearing to be unmoved. "The damage had better be in the old sails," she said finally. "If it isn't . . ." As the warning in her voice trailed off, she turned to Dacko. "With your permission, I'll watch the repairs from your bridge."

Dacko nodded, pleased with the prospect of tormenting her with proof of her crew's inadequacies. Would she submit with good grace? Or twitch like a trapped animal? His anticipation of seeing the leonine captain defeated in one way or another actually prevented him from realizing that it was he who followed her through the hatch.

They hadn't expected to get away with that part of the plan; it put one more captive out of the ship's forge when they made their move against the pirates. Exhilirated by success, Mordon tried for the rest. "Come on," he growled, and as was prearranged, everyone, even sick Bracha, queued up to the hatch.

"Not all of you," one of the guards said. "You'll only need three beside yourself."

"It will only take that much longer," Mordon protested.

"Three," the guard repeated stubbornly. He was suspicious even if his captain was not.

Mordon beckoned to Senda, Allis, and Droganie, leaving Bracha and Ghyaspur behind.

"Why her?" the guard said, pointing to Allis's arm, which was still bound by the castlike covering.

"She's my best line tender, even one-handed," Mordon said in a tone that brooked no nonsense. Allis hurried along to get through the hatch before the guard protested again.

The rip in the sail was a big one, but not so large as Mordon had planned, and it was a clean rip, too. Repairing it would be short work no matter how they hedged. Still, he knew they needed only part of a shift until many of the pirates would retire to sleep, if they kept to their normal pattern. He was not unduly disturbed. Allis was. Since the talkways in their pods were monitored by the *Dowager Sun*'s bridge, she had

no way of telling him that the pirates weren't preparing for sleep but were placing bets on whether the
blacksmith or the mate would be spaced by Milani.

It was prearranged that he would wait for the inno-
cent-sounding "Come in" command from Allis in her
role as line tender, so she wasn't worried that he'd go
on the assumption that the normal schedule prevailed
and come in on his own. But she did wish he wasn't
so efficient. The three gypsies had the torn sail furled
and replaced much too soon. The holiday mood on
the ship just didn't lend itself to thoughts of sleep;
they should have known that any exception to the
monotony of ship life was always accepted gratefully.

When only a little makework remained to the repair
job and the signal from Allis still did not come, the
three gypsies began to realize something had gone
awry. In desperation, Mordon arranged a line accident
to prolong the time they'd spend in the pods. For a
while Senda had a bad time of it. Allis was privy to
Mordon's plan, but Senda and Droganie were not.
First Senda was helplessly snarled, and Allis was surprised but glad to realize that she actually understood
her line-tending job this time. Mordon's relentless
drills on how to operate ship equipment had paid off,
for she'd never have managed to stress the right line
while Mordon's eyes and attention needed to be elsewhere if she hadn't some sailjockey sense of her own.
Within moments the strained line snapped, and Senda
was drifting freely toward a clot of alien stars. The
chase, securing a new line and the return, unsnagging
the old line and reeling it in, all took time, but not
enough. The better part of a shift had gone by since
they left the ship, but Allis knew they had used up
all the time they could safely take. She forestalled
Dacko's decision to order the repair crew to return

to the ship by giving the "Come in" just as he reached
for the microphone. The gypsies made short work of
stowing the outside equipment, then all returned to
the axis.

The plan was upset by the pirates, yet Senda,
Droganie, and Mordon were unaware of the problems,
and so they continued with their charade the moment
the pod hatches were unscrewed. Senda floated into
the axis shouting, "Stupid line tender. Idiot daughter
of disreputable parents." She wasn't certain that her
accident had been arranged, but it was her job to get
the guards' attention and she knew a good opportunity
when she saw it. "You could have killed me out there."

Allis was grateful that sound didn't carry too far;
still, she didn't shout her reply. "It was your own
fault. If you'd watched where you were going you'd
have seen your mistake." She'd picked the proper
retort from Senda herself. She gave Senda a warning
glance, trying to alert her that something was amiss,
but Senda didn't see it.

"You're supposed to watch. You can see where we
can't."

"How am I supposed to see your line when it gets
behind a sail?"

"Stop!" Mordon said. "That's not important. Get
that extruder I brought in. I must show it to Milani."

"You'll show it to me first," Droganie said, pushing
quickly to Mordon's empty pod where one of the
waldoes still gripped the silver rigging. But Mordon
reached it first and soared easily toward the guards
who were holding stanchions and watching with interest.

"Take us to the bridge so I can show the captains
that the rip in the sail wasn't my fault," Mordon said,
coming to a controlled halt before the guards. He

held out the piece of rigging. "Here, look for your-
selves." One of the guards lowered his gaze to look and
Mordon alerted Allis silently. —Now!—

Allis had no time to warn him that two more guards
were about to enter the axis and that the second guard
was suspicious of Mordon's excitement. Allis flung herself at the suspicious guard as Mordon rammed the
extruder into the curious one's gut, shouting for Senda
and Droganie to be ready for the two who were about
to come through the hatch from the gangway.

A waldo, hidden in Senda's sleeve, smashed the skull
of the first pirate who came through the hatch.
Droganie garrotted the other with silver wire before
he could back down the gangway. Allis managed to
keep the guard she'd tackled engaged with trying to
get loose of her; without any leverage the freefall in
the axis kept them spinning and tumbling until Mordon put an end to it with a well-placed blow to the
pirate's head. Allis grabbed for a stanchion, breathing
heavily and badly frightened.

"You almost sent us all down the tubes," she said
angrily to Mordon. "I knew those other two were coming; you didn't. It's luck that I had time to get off a
warning, and believe me, this mission is already out
of luck. Wait for my command."

Mordon reacted instantly to the snap of authority,
but Allis realized it was going to be hard to hold back
her companions now. They were stimulated by adrenaline and success, quite ready to take on more.

Allis was tearing the bindings from her arm.

"The crew's wide-awake," Allis told them, "but
we're committed now." As she expected, the news
sobered them quickly. She flexed her arm. Despite
secret exercising, it hurt horribly.

Mordon assimilated the implications of Allis's information and chastised himself for not trusting her judgment and for moving too soon. Had it not been that Senda and Droganie, two of the most nimble free-fall movers, were backing him up, the second set of guards probably would have had the split second needed to draw their weapons, and that would have ended everything. —I'll not make the same mistake again. But you're right. My haste has committed us now. What is your plan?—

"The plan is the same. Most of the pirates are drunk or high on something, so they're not moving about too much. We just can't depend on their staying put. The only difference is that we'll all be armed, no need to stop at a weapons-locker," Allis said, removing a laser from the hip of the garrotted sailor. Blood was floating in sanguine globules and she ducked under them. Mordon had detailed the use of the laser guns to her. They were not much different from handguns, having finger rings for gripping, thumb-operated triggers, and firing in the direction in which they were pointed. They had little mass, and Mordon said there would be no recoil to compensate for.

"These clothes will fit Mordon and me," Senda said, looking critically at the bodies of the two smaller pirates. "It might delay someone's shooting us if they see familiar clothing."

"We won't be surprised if you'll follow my lead," Allis said, angry that at this late moment someone wanted to change the plan. Senda seemed surprised at Allis's curtness but protested stubbornly that taking the clothes was a good idea. "Do it," Allis said, resigned but wary.

"You are the leader," Mordon said with warning looks to Senda and Droganie.

"Hurry up and change clothes. Those two guards who popped in on us were supposed to determine who won the bet. When they don't return to the armory, someone will come looking for them."

"What bet?" Mordon said, pulling bright trousers over his own dull and dirty ones.

Allis didn't answer; she was concentrating on the corridors that opened into the gangway they must use to reach the corridor along the keel of the ship. Momentarily the way was clear, and just as soon as Senda and Mordon were dressed she shot feet first into the gangway, pushing herself along the rungs as fast as she could. They had a long way to go to reach the bridge, for it was on the other side of the ship.

There were shortcuts, but those were too dangerous, filled with pirates who were drunk or exhilirated about the prospects of winning large sums from their fellows. They'd have to stay in the outermost corridor, which provided little more than a horizon to hide behind. The hatch between the gangway and corridor was clear, and then they were passing under the cabins where pirates were gathered in groups for gambling and other diversions. Any one of them could be summoned to the freshener or decide to go to the galley.

Suddenly Allis turned her companions around, urging them quickly and silently to retreat behind the horizon. Allis stooped to watch the legs of a pirate come toward them, then, as she expected, the legs lifted as the pirate leaped for an overhead gangway without seeing them. But from directly above there was a new danger. Allis had been aware of the man and woman in the cabin over their heads, but he still managed to surprise her by dropping into the corridor, nearly blind with rage. There was no time to retreat from sight; indeed, Allis wouldn't have known which way to tell them to run, for the angry pirate had no particular destination in mind. His only concern was to leave the presence of his companion.

Allis hissed a warning, and Droganie and Mordon reacted quickly, taking the startled pirate even before his hands were clear of the hatch. They left him securely trussed in another cabin that Allis knew was empty, and took a moment to rest there while another pirate walked along the corridor below them. For a while the corridor was clear, and the four of them hurried down-spin until they reached the ladder leading to the bridge's hatch.

"How many inside?" Mordon asked, his hand already on the ladder.

"Seven," Allis replied, eyeing the hatch. They had to climb the short ladder, open the hatch, and only then could they poke their heads through.

"Remember to go in blasting," Mordon said. "If any of them has time to put a finger on the alarm, we're surely dead." Allis knew they had to gain control of the life-support systems from the bridge before the pirates had the presence of mind to override them manually. Her mind was cluttered with details of what to shut down and where to leave air circulating; most especially she knew how to keep the locks on the forge from being blown so that Ghyaspur and Bracha would be safe. But this thinking was premature, for they still stood in the corridor beneath the bridge, and Mordon was demanding her attention.

"Where are they in there?" he said, gesturing toward the bridge. "How do they stand? We can't waste time with misses."

Allis nodded and stepped forward so all three could see her, and certain from the feedback of her stone

she constructed an airy diagram of the bridge with
her hands, placing Dacko and his crew while the three
gypsies watched her intensely.

"Good," Mordon said, fixing the positions in his
own mind. "Now where's Milani?"

"I don't know," Allis said honestly. Milani had no
circle of thought, no pulsing emotions, nothing. She
was a void and had been ever since Allis took up the
stone.

"Surely you can place her," Mordon said, aghast.

"No."

"She'd be near Dacko, if she could," Senda ventured, trying to fill in what Allis could not.

"Yes, but if she's between Dacko and the hatch, we
might blast her down!"

"She knows we're coming," Senda said. "She'll take
cover at the first sound."

"And she may not be close enough to hear, or if she
is, she may dive right into the line of fire," Mordon
said. He'd not realized that Allis's hatred made Milani
invisible to her. He'd assumed some kind of barrier,
a tangible one. "Do you hate her so much that you'd
risk her life?" Mordon was completely dissatisfied
with the prospect of not knowing where his captain
was when he was going to be blasting for a quick
kill.

"I don't seem to have control over it."

"Space, woman. Try!"

Grimly Allis nodded, and felt Mordon's subliminal
encouragement. His mind was filled with worry and
self-deprecation. He didn't like surprises and felt he
should have known Allis's limitations.

Allis limited her reception to the space around
Dacko, hoping at least for a shadow of another
mind. But she was blind to Milani, and knowing the

blindness was caused by her own hate and anger didn't make it any less real. Deliberately she tried to put the anger aside. She thought of the captain's gentle touch when Milani woke her from Ghyaspur's gripping terror. It was the only time Allis could recall even a moment of true sympathy, but it was enough to check her anger. For a moment, just for a tiny mote of time, the hatred slipped away and was replaced by Milani's thoughts. Then Dan came to mind; whose mind she was not sure, but with the memory of him Milani's presence was voided. It was as if she hated Dan, not Milani, and that the pensive and wistful recollection of him was so much a part of Milani they were inseparable. Allis didn't dwell on the realization, but she knew she couldn't ever forget it.

"She's standing here, by Dacko," Allis said, referring to the airy diagram again, "and she's ready. She'll jump the man in the communication console as soon as she senses our move. He's the closest to the ship's alarm."

Mordon was not studying Allis's signs as much as he was studying Allis. He didn't know if the Earthwoman had just saved his captain or set her up for a kill.

"Let's move," Allis said, knowing it was useless to argue with him. "If we wait too long she may change her mind and jump another way."

Mordon nodded. "Allis, you take the one at the sunwatch. Senda, the navigation console. Droganie, the helm. I'll take Dacko," Mordon said, not trusting Allis to fire into the area where his captain was standing. He hoped she hadn't lied. If Milani was in another part of the bridge, she could easily be caught in crossfire. There would be room in the hatch only for him and Senda to spring through, but Droganie and Allis, just under them on the ladder, would be ready to fire beneath their feet. If they got their first shots off as planned, the pirates wouldn't have time to draw their own weapons, and they could spread through the hatch. If not, just one wide beam from a single laser would drop all four of them.

"Get ready," Mordon said through stiff lips. He and Senda mounted the ladder and felt Allis and Droganie crowd on, too. "Now!"

When Allis had her head and shoulders through the hatch, she did not take the sunwatch target assigned to her. She aimed past Mordon's ankle at a pirate who'd turned his head toward them the very second the hatch flew open. Only Allis knew of his alarm at seeing the hatch cover move without an entry signal, and the pirate assigned to her still had his back to them. She hoped to get the moving man with her first shot and still have time to fire at the seated figure in the sunwatch console. But she didn't. The laser had no recoil as Mordon had promised, but aiming accurately over the edge of a floor while supported by elbows and a foot still jammed in a ladder rung was impossible. She only singed the moving man's hip and had to take a second shot. By then Senda and Droganie were standing on the deck, the pirates at the consoles already dead. Senda had reflexes like a cat, and she downed another pirate and Allis's assigned target just as he turned.

At the first sign of violence, Milani jumped the way Allis said she would, disarming her victim expertly. By the time she was done, the attack was finished. The only sounds were the ones in their minds as pirates slumped and fell with amazing grace. The air stank of burned meat and charred clothing. Dacko was sprawled over his console, quite dead.

Senda slammed the hatch shut from a console, and Milani was giving orders as if she'd stepped onto her own ship's bridge. Allis couldn't move. Feeling six sets of thoughts disintegrate was worse than seeing the bodies, limbs asprawl, heads and torsos all horribly burned. Only the man Milani had tackled was still alive, and he was terrified.

"Life support in the corridors is shut down, Milani," Allis heard Mordon say. "It'll be just a moment until the air is gone."

"I hope that's not too long," Milani said anxiously. "How many pirates have made it into the corridors? Did a silent alarm go off?"

Allis shook her dazed head trying to understand what was required of her. Four minds were being consumed by the agony of suffocation, and Allis could not disengage herself from them.

"How many pirates are in the corridors?" Milani demanded again.

"Four," Allis said, breathing deep and hard. Air slid easily into her lungs but seemed not to nourish.

"We'll wait until we're certain they can't get through the corridors before our next move," Milani said. "Allis, are any of the pirates within reach of warheads? I don't want some fanatic blowing the ship apart."

The struggles in the corridor were over and the last awareness of four minds came to nothing. Allis was vaguely aware of Senda and Droganie pulling bodies out of the consoles and stacking them against the bulkhead. Dacko was heaved atop with no special ceremony. Allis supposed it was like war must be, and these pirates were the enemy. But she'd never been in combat, never known her enemies' minds. It was anticlimatic for minds to end like this, just six vacant flesh heaps awaiting disposal.

"Allis! Allis!" It was Milani shouting and shaking her roughly. Allis focused her eyes on the amber ones in Milani's dark face. "Where is my stone? Space, she's caught up in the dying." Shaking again. Something sharp against her cheek. A slap? "The stone. Where is my stone?"

The man who'd lived through the fracas lay on the floor, all limbs in easy view. He trembled before Allis's eyes and shrieked the fear of death in her mind. But he was alive, not dissolving. Yes, a slap. The stone. Milani's stone. Again she saw the captain's amber eyes.

"In that caisson . . . there." Allis pointed to a small pyramid bolted to the console on Dacko's dais. Three controlled strides took Milani across the bridge, and she'd mounted the dais before Allis shouted, "Don't touch it, Milani!"

Startled, the captain looked at Allis.

"The opening mechanism is tuned to Dacko's touch. If anyone else opens it, it will destroy the stone."

Mordon spat. "Why didn't you tell me? We'd have taken Dacko alive if we'd known." He gave Allis a long questioning look. "Or is that why you remained silent? Are you nothing but a miserable miscreant, after all?"

"He'd never have given it up," Allis said, fully convinced that she spoke the truth, but unable to tell the full truth that she had held back the stone's location as some kind of insurance for her own safety.

"Perhaps she's lying," Senda said, wondering if the caisson would open safely.

"No," Allis said. "I'm not lying."

Milani seemed hesitant. "You must have known about the caisson all along. You never intended for me to regain my stone. Or are you merely toying with me, waiting to see how long I will wait before I take the stone from the caisson, whatever the risk?"

"If I didn't want you to have your stone, I would have let you open the caisson and destroy it," Allis said wearily. "I simply saw no other way. Dacko would never have returned it to you, not even if his life depended on it. He feared its power. If he couldn't control the stone, no one else would either."

"Or is it that you wanted control of the stone?" Milani said suspiciously.

Allis shrugged. "Once, perhaps. But no longer." She looked at Milani steadily. "I'm not afraid of being in its control anymore. In itself, it controls nothing, no one."

"We'll leave it for now," Milani said, stepping off the dais. "Later Mordon will examine the caisson to see if anything can be done with it. Has anyone looked in on Ghyaspur and Bracha?"

They didn't believe her, and Allis couldn't blame them. Every time their state of mind reflected some confidence in her, she promptly provided grounds for doubt. She didn't like finding herself doubted by her peers, her pride shattered by injustice, even though she recognized that she brought it on herself.

She wanted to restore herself. She wanted Dacko alive and willing to open the caisson and retrieve the stone. She wanted it so much that she could see the pirate captain walking to the console on which the pyramid-shaped caisson was resting. He was stumbling and hesitant, his eyes opened in a horrible, vacant expression.

Only when Senda's mind froze from shock did Allis

realize the vision was not a fantasy or wishful thinking. Dacko was indeed standing over the caisson. He put his hand on the labyrinth side of the triangles, tracing a pattern until the caisson opened. Then Dacko crumpled onto the deck.

Allis gasped. He was dead; he had been dead. His back was half burned away, yet she knew she'd caused him to walk nearly the entire breadth of the bridge to open the caisson. She stared in horror.

Milani was the first to move. She paused to examine Dacko's body, feeling for a pulse and looking into his dead eyes. "You compelled a dead man," she said, breathing hard. "I've never heard of a stone-carrier who could do that."

"Space," Allis muttered. "Space, space, space."

"Are you all right?" Mordon asked, still awed but growing concerned for Allis.

Allis shook her head. She wasn't all right. She had regained some measure of trust . . . no, it was something tinged with reverence. It would do if she could stop being dizzy, if she could tear her eyes from Dacko's lifeless hulk . . . if she could stop being frightened of the power strapped to her arm. Not given to hysteria, she blacked out the universe.

CHAPTER 27

The earthworm had fainted. She lay where she fell, exhausted and drained by the feat she'd performed. It had stunned Milani, too, but she hadn't allowed her crew a moment to contemplate what Allis had done. The job of taking over the pirate ship was only half-done when Allis gave out.

The gypsy ships were not designed for battle or as battlegrounds; they were nothing more than freighters, though jury-rigged for longer journeys than the original designers envisioned. The fact that invasion of the ships had never been contemplated made securing one a simple task. The designers had provided the means for sealing the ship in sections in the event that the integrity of the hull was violated, whether from the outside by a meteor or from the inside by a volatile cargo.

It was this very feature that had made escape from the *Sovereign Sun* possible, for the undamaged bridge section had been sealed off from the ruined portions of the ship. Now *Dowager Sun*'s bridge was sealed off from the rest of the ship by the same mechanism, activated by Milani's people on the bridge. There were internal life rafts, compartments within sections that were provided with emergency oxygen that could be manually activated by anyone capable of reaching them. Most of the pirates had survived by this means, and since the emergency oxygen was nearly inexhaustible—also by design that didn't foresee their use in battle—they were inaccessible to Milani's crew. But with the communicator-stone in her possession once again, making prisoners of the surviving pirates would be simple, though time-consuming.

They pressurized the first section of corridor along the keel, then Mordon patterned up a communication link to the first cabin full of pirates. "Throw your weapons into the disposal and come out peacefully," he ordered. "Milani has her stone and we will know before you near the hatch if you have complied with my order."

The hatch opened and Milani stepped into view of the opening, ignoring Mordon's protest as she exposed herself. She knew she was safe. One mind up in that cabin could not bring itself to believe anyone's words, but was satisfied there was no alternative to surrendering just as soon as its own eyes beheld the stone on Milani's neck.

They took those first three pirates to the ship's brig, where security alarms would alert the controlling crew of any attempt at mischief. The holding area was large; not large enough to keep Dacko's entire crew, but quite adequate to have kept Milani's small band— had Dacko chosen to use it—safe from the radiation in the forge.

"Don't know what we'll do with them all," Mordon said, closing the transparent hatch on the three doleful pirates.

"It's only temporary," Milani said.

"Do you mean to dump them planetside?" When Milani nodded, Mordon smiled. "Just let me pick the place."

"Yes," Milani said, "and I shall select the other."

Mordon seemed not to have heard her, but Milani sensed a fear in Senda that nearly riveted the albino to the deck. For a moment Milani felt an overwhelming pity for Senda. How could she have known this woman for so long yet not know she was terrified of the planets?

Milani shook her head in disbelief, but Senda took that gesture to mean her fears were unjustified. Unable to tell her the truth, Milani walked briskly back to the corridor, more willing to deal with pirates than with her own crew.

Most of the pirates gave up easily, and after many tedious trips through the corridor, the brig was filled. Milani ordered isolation seals installed over the hatches of hesitant pirates, leaving them in their cabins where the certain pangs of hunger would likely cause most to reconsider a few shifts hence.

Had there been more of her own trusted crew, they wouldn't be so tired now. The toll of their long confinement was being paid in exhaustion, for even though they had stopped at the galley long enough to stuff their pockets with food, they were too tired to eat it. At least they were safe; all of them, Ghyaspur and Bracha included, were back on the bridge. The pirates were trussed in the brig or in cabins with isolation seals over the hatches. There were some among them, mercenaries and slaves, who probably had no special loyalty to Dacko and who might be used to augment her small crew for a while, but Milani was too drained to interrogate them properly.

Mordon was at the helm, trimming the sails and bringing about the ship's attitude to his satisfaction, grumbling happily about having to do it manually. He'd be reprogramming the computers and having the ship cleaned if Milani didn't put a stop to it. She started to move toward him but instead stopped to look over Bracha's shoulder to study the sunwatch screens and satisfy herself that he was not yet too ill to stay alert. She would have relieved him if there had been someone with whom she could do so, but as it was, she counted herself lucky that he was performing as well as he was.

"We are victorious," she heard Mordon say as he stepped away from the helm, finally satisfied. "We have defeated the vilest mind ever to command a stellar sailing vessel."

He was crowing and he expected Milani to join in. But for Milani the victory was a hollow one, for her crew numbered only seven; not enough to crew a ship. It was futile to worry about that. In all the galaxy there were perhaps one hundred other sailing vessels. The crews of one hundred ships could not support a race; genetic drift and radiation damage had already taken its toll. The gypsies were a doomed race, as they had been from the beginning.

She saw Mordon and Droganie exchange worried glances over their captain's refusal to show some joy or satisfaction, but they followed her lead, and Mordon asked in all seriousness, "Shall I lay a new course into the helm controller? Or do you want to continue on Dacko's course and finish calling on the worlds in this system? We could rid ourselves of some of those miscreants in the brig."

They thought she was deciding as she walked silently to Dacko's console and sat down. When she touched her stone, now fastened properly around her neck, they were sure she was deep in thought. She'd been without the stone for a long time and should have been comforted by its return. But with duty behind her, the *Dowager Sun* secure and trim, Milani willed a renewed telepathic silence. She did not want her own bitterness enhanced by the crew's when she told Mordon what course was the only one left to them.

She looked at them, one by one. Droganie shambled between the communication console and the forge monitors where once she walked proudly. Droganie mastered the forge while Milani mastered the helm. They had been children together; they'd worked together most of their lives. Milani wondered if now they would face doom that way. Droganie thought so; Milani could see it on her face. Senda never looked so old, so wraithlike as she did now. And Ghyaspur, a boy so handsome that he turned the heads of men and women alike, already had blood on his hands.

He'd carried a full burden during the captivity; one heavier than any Milani would have wished on him. Small, wiry, efficient Mordon was piloting the ship. He was a level-headed man, except now, as he was consumed by anger. He knew from her silence what the others had not yet guessed; this was the first time Milani felt certain his anger was not for himself, and she felt rage rise in her.

"Look at Bracha," she said angrily, "attending to duty even as he dies. You should do no less."

But the mate just shook his head, his beady eyes holding her in contempt until she had to turn away. She saw Allis stirring now from her place on the deck. Her elfin beauty was enhanced by her belly bulging with Daneth's child.

Allis sat up, looking confused at first, but finally smiling as she saw the one-time prisoners working, however tiredly, over the consoles. Involuntarily Milani remembered what she'd seen when she first looked into the earthworm's mind. She'd relived that horror a thousand times; Allis standing before her in the corridor in a stupor of hatred for the man Milani loved, blaming him who must be held faultless. The worst was knowing that Daneth had loved the ungrateful little creature. Every synapse in Milani's brain had screamed denial, but there was the stone, resting softly between Allis's breasts.

How could he have traded the deep love that only two stone-carriers could know for the primitive, one-sided affair it must have been with Allis? How could he have died—Daneth who was so free of radiation damage—while Malani, who'd taken a nearly fatal dose, lived on?

Allis had misunderstood. She was inexperienced in using the stone, and she completely misunderstood what transpired. In the moment of confrontation with Milani, Allis had learned that Daneth loved Milani. Allis didn't try to deny it, couldn't, for the imagery of their love was too strong in Milani's mind. Then Allis assumed Daneth had been planning to return to the ship and to Milani, and she felt betrayed. Moreover, she hated Milani's power over Daneth, and hated him for being so weak as to succumb to it.

In that moment Allis's mind, like Milani's, had darkened, and all thought transference between the two women ended, but not before Milani sensed Allis's fear of succumbing to the power of Milani's stone. Milani hadn't cared about the earthworm's fear, except perhaps to make a subconscious note of it, and later, perhaps, some use of it. She was too hurt by knowing Daneth had loved another woman, however briefly. Milani could have killed Allis with her own hands right then. She was only slightly glad that she hadn't; without Allis she knew they could not have overcome Dacko and his crew.

Was it her Earth blood that caused Allis to leap past rudimentary abilities and to excel in using the stone, as if she'd used it for thousands and thousands of shifts? Or was it merely as Allis herself had explained, that she had a greater need to learn, greater than any other stone-carrier before her? Milani had seen people accomplish what was said to be impossible in times of need, and what could have been a darker time for the *Sovereign Sun*'s crew and even for Allis than to be captive on a pirate ship? Even so, Milani found Allis a dark savior. They'd finished their task, had their revenge, but they were dead. Seven gypsies could not crew a sailing vessel.

"Don't smile, Allis," Milani snapped, needing to lash out now and finding her old target. "After megashifts of hope extinguished bit by bit, our race is dead. Your joy is intolerable."

Allis stood up, her smile fading as she felt the crew's thoughts and absorbed their anguish. She met Mordon's eyes briefly, her eyes coming away from the exchange as narrowed as his. Then, turning on her heel, she crossed the deck to Milani's console. "This isn't the end. It's a new beginning. Listen to your crew!"

Milani shook her head. Seeing her crew's faces was enough; she didn't want to feel more bitterness in her mind, too. "It ends here with us, they know that," Milani said, feeling gray with weariness. "Our ancestors dreamed of a beginning, but it was only the beginning of the end."

"*Space*. Even when you have your stone you won't hear. Milani, for once really listen to them. They are your crew."

"It is they who must hear me. This is the end. There is no other way."

"What of Dan's child?" Allis demanded. "Is his

child supposed to live on some planet so backward the Watchers don't even want it? Or do we try a place a little more advanced where Watchers will get our stones from us, and probably our lives as well?"

Milani's fist tightened and her heart lurched at hearing her lover's name anglicized. Allis didn't understand that they would have to go planetside, as their ancestors should have done when the first ending came.

"I understand, Milani. I understand a lot more than you've ever given me credit for. I understand that you're giving up and you think you've got the right to take the rest of us down with you. But you'd better understand right now that I have no intention of going to any planet except Earth."

Milani looked at her, not believing what she heard. It seemed as if Allis had answered her subliminal thought; yet she could not have heard Milani's thoughts.

But Allis nodded. "It's gone," she said simply. "I just couldn't get at Dan. There was no point in hating a dead man, but his memory was so alive in you that I blamed you instead. I don't hate you anymore. I'm just as angry as hell to know you think you've got any control over what happens to me, but I don't hate you anymore."

By the look on Allis's face, Milani knew she said more in the silent talk, and by the frustrated shake of her head she knew Allis realized Milani couldn't hear her. Allis spoke aloud again, not caring if the crew heard her. "Stop punishing yourself for things you can't control. Take comfort in knowing he loved you."

"Don't," Milani said. "If you can forget him, then do. But I can't."

"I can see that," Allis said, pointedly reminding her

that she had read Milani's thoughts. "I don't want to talk about Dan, but you leave me no choice. He's so much on your mind that nothing crowds him out. How can you forget while every breath you take reminds you that you're alive while he is dead? Can't you see beyond your guilt? He wasn't the strong one after all. He got sick and he died. You have survived."

"I should have been there," Milani said. "I should have been the one to die."

"How would you have arranged that? Could you have held back death with your stone or with your love where all of Earth's medical knowledge couldn't?"

"No," Milani said, slowly realizing that neither saving Daneth nor trading places with him had ever been within her power. It wasn't a new thought, but it was the first time she didn't feel at fault for not having such powers. "I couldn't have prevented his death."

"Is that why you hate me? Because on Earth Dan got something you couldn't give him . . . time? A little time to love an earthworm, time to give the stone so that it wouldn't die with him, and even time to make a whole and perfect child."

Milani sighed, and with the next breath felt less pain in her heart. Daneth always lived in the present, putting aside the past as best he could and enjoying the moment at hand. It would be like him to take gleefully that which was given—love, a child, and time. She knew he could do these things and love her no less while doing them. But what purpose did it serve to know? How could she survive without him—especially now when the gypsy race was dead?

But hope niggled. Visions of a rejuvenated race of gypsies persisted in her mind when she thought she had banished all hope. Suddenly Milani realized they were not her own wishes. She looked at Allis in surprise. Beneath the dark and glittering curls the Earthling's mind was as much a void as before, but Allis was smiling wickedly. —Putting thoughts in my head won't work,— Milani said subliminally. —And don't smile. This is a time for laments.—

"You don't think of me as earthworm anymore," Allis said, her eyes widening in mock relief.

"It doesn't matter what I call you. It may have been my own guilt between us; I believe that now, yes. But knowing doesn't change our fate. We must go planetside."

"No!" It was Ghyaspur who spoke aloud what all her crew must be thinking. "No, please, not like this."

Milani raised her eyes to the boy's tragic face. He wanted planet life, but on his terms and she could not give him what he wanted. She didn't mean to shout, but the horrible injustice overwhelmed her self-control. "We must go because we cannot survive in space with this small number."

"The Watchers. We saw signs of them," Ghyaspur protested desperately. "We . . ."

Allis cut him off with an authoritative wave of her hand. "We can survive in space." Her voice was calm but galvanizing as she faced Milani. "Dan took one small step in preserving the stellar sailors by giving me his stone. We can do the rest, Milani. Men and women from Earth will be your crew."

Milani frowned because Allis was so sincere, but the crew didn't frown. "You've forgotten the Watchers. They won't allow us to impress from your planet; they have laws against it and they enforce their laws. You saw what it was like at Crossroads. I cannot hide a whole crew from them. *Space*, I couldn't even hide one determined Earthling! An alien crew would be detected and removed when we came to refurbish the nuclear generators. Space knows what they'd do to the rest of us, but it's certain they'd take the opportunity to rid the trade lanes of one more gypsy ship."

"The hell with the Watchers," Allis said savagely. "Are you going to cringe before them forever?" Then, more reasonably, "But we won't be impressing crew. We'll hire them. We'd be secretive about it while on Earth so that if there are Watcher spies there . . ." She looked at Milani and received a shrug; there were no Watcher signs when Daneth was there, but time had passed. Watchers came to all planets eventually, even the ones in this little-known system through which they were traveling. "We'll hire secretly," Allis continued still undaunted. "A work contract for a specified time, after which we'll return them to Earth. Is that against the Watchers' law?"

Milani considered. "Not the letter of it, but yes, it is against the spirit."

"Then we'll add lawyers to the crew's roster," Allis said resolutely.

"What?"

Allis shrugged. "Where there's law, there're lawyers, and I used to know some of the shadiest scoundrels on Earth!"

Milani had a healthy respect for Watcher power, but no faith in their laws or customs. If she could bend or break their laws, she'd willingly do it. But there was a more basic problem to solve. "Planet people do not like to leave their lands for the unknown, as you well know. It takes a special breed, one that has developed slowly over centuries."

Allis's eyes glittered. "You haven't been on Earth for a long time, Milani. Dan was, and he saw a nation

of technologically competent adventurers who are
forced to satisfy their curiosity with meager nibbles
of the stars—moon walks and unmanned flybys. There
were thousands who'd have given their lives to know
what lies beyond Jupiter."

"You haven't been on Earth for a long time either,"
Milani pointed out.

Allis shrugged. "It doesn't matter. There still will
be astronomers with pet theories on the origins of the
universe and they'll clamor for berths on *Dowager Sun*
and an opportunity to do more research. With our
communicator-stones we won't have any difficulty finding willing Earthlings to crew this ship . . . *Sovereign
Sun,* too, if it's salvageable."

Two ships with full crews was an infectious thought.
Milani couldn't help raising her eyes. The golden
flecks in Allis's brown irises glittered, and their excitement infected her even more. "The Watchers . . ."
she said, struggling to remain calm and to think
logically. "They may arbitrate the issue of Earthlings
as crew, or they may unilaterally decide the issue.
Whatever they do, it won't be good. The law is explicit about trading technology."

"We won't trade technology, not stellar sailing
technology nor the Watcher's. We pay the crew with
gems. No law against that, is there?"

Sadly, Milani shook her head. "Unless we impress
. . . keep the crew for all time . . . Earthlings who
return to your planet would take our technology with
them. The Watchers disapprove of accelerating a planet's technology even more strongly than impressing."

"Hell, they can pass laws until the sun goes nova,
but they can't control people's knowledge. Besides, we
have many years . . . thousands of shifts before this

ship's nuclear generator needs new fuel rods or any kind of attention from Watcher technicians, isn't that so?"

Absently Milani nodded.

"You managed to develop your own shielding system without Watchers; with a few nuclear physicists we may be able to solve the other problems, too."

"But I have a duty to my crew—what's left of them. Whatever I can do for their safety and for their welfare, I must do."

"They're not colonists," Allis said with disgust. "Listen to their minds for a moment and see what they think your duty is. I already know."

Milani looked at them, six faces with hints of hope burning in their eyes. She turned to Allis, hovering at her side. "I'm still blind to your mind," she said, "and since I can't know how sincere you are nor how much knowledge you really have, I am reluctant. And there are your . . . special powers to consider. How have you learned to use the communicator-stone in such a short time when every other stone-carrier I've known, including Daneth and myself, has taken thousands upon thousands of shifts to learn its intricacies? How did you compel Dacko? And how have you learned to break through the shadow of hatred? You see, Allis, there still remains the question: Are you savior or serpent?"

Allis shrugged. "You know how to find out."

Milani hesitated. She didn't want to see the gloom of her crew if Allis had lied. She didn't want to pick up the burden of her stone again; it was too heavy.

Suddenly Allis's hand was on hers, and she dropped to her knees to whisper close so the crowding crew could not hear. "Don't be afraid, Milani. It's the privilege awaiting you. I swear I'm telling the truth."

Milani wanted to believe her. She wanted to take up the banner Allis was offering: A chance to captain a healthy ship and to defy the Watchers intrigued her to her very soul. But once she opened her mind to Allis, she'd know, once and for all. What was there, good or evil? "It cannot all be privilege," Milani protested. "It never was."

"But I will be with you to share the burdens," Allis said. "If you will only believe in me. It will only take a moment of trust . . ."

Ignorance was a shelter. In it, Milani didn't know the fears or sorrows of the crew.

"The joy of life awaits you. I promise you that," Allis whispered, imploring her.

Milani wanted to believe. She wanted to see her people have a new beginning. . . .

Allis lied!

Her mouth spoke grave words, but she was afraid. She feared the Watchers whose power she'd badly underestimated. And now Allis knew that, too, for Milani had involuntarily but instantly described the danger awaiting them. Allis wondered if she was planning slaughter for her fellow Earthlings by putting them in the reaches of Watcher "justice." She feared she'd spawn a mutant child and that her own genes were irrevocably damaged during their captivity. But there was something else. Allis could not lie to Milani now, not while they both used their stones, and all the fears that Milani perceived were important only in that they served in making Allis's courage a rational choice; something deliberate and thought out, and reasonable because the fears were acknowledged.

Milani watched Allis get up from her knees, then looked at her crew with their perplexing minds grasping at the dust Allis had flung to them, each of them building dreams with positive faith. And she knew Allis was determined to carry through everything she'd suggested and more, as if there were nothing in the galaxy that could stop her. Already she was detailing to Milani just how they would go about selecting crew on Earth, doubling the number so that they could return to the place where *Sovereign Sun* endlessly orbited a distant sun, no cenotaph in Allis's mind.

—A ship for each of us, is that it?— Milani said. —It's a bold plan.—

Allis grinned. —You're learning, Milani.—

—Your skills with the stone do exceed mine. I think you can compel live people, too. Or am I as bewitched by your love of life as Daneth was? Did he choose you knowing you'd one time have me contemplating a whole new era, a viable race competing in the galaxy for its rightful place? Another moment and you'll have me calling you friend and sister.—

—Just tell me how much time has passed on Earth. I never was good at figuring relative time, and it will help me to make plans.—

Inwardly Milani chuckled. —Don't try to hide the real reasons, not from me, my friend. You're wondering if we can return to Earth before the birth, so your daughter will know the thrill of that blue, watery world. You still have a lot to learn. A woman who has spent her pregnancy without the restraints of gravity would find giving birth planetside an unpleasant experience. But, don't be disappointed. There are compensations; consider the joy of the child moving from one weightless environment to another, not so different.— There was more to tell, more to share, but for now Milani turned to her waiting crew.

"Mordon, I need six orbital elements to plot trajectory to the nearest gravity-slip system that will take us to Earth. Our crew awaits us."

EPILOGUE

Ghyaspur stood on a rise of earth, watching the faint blue flame of the shuttle's cold-jets fade into the starry night. Before it was even gone, the moon caught his eye, a fat yellow disk with little noticeable depth, its craters hard to see through the atmosphere. It illuminated the planetary darkside quite well; he could even make out the jagged purple line of distant mountains on the horizon. Closer in there was a black silken strip running through the desert. He'd thought it was a river at first, but then recalled how unlikely it was for a river to be running through an ecosystem like this. Then he saw the first set of twin lights skimming over the shiny road, a *car* or a *truck,* he thought, and whispered the words Allis had taught him.

Allis had told Milani that Ghyaspur was the best choice on the *Dowager Sun* to go to Earth to choose a crew. He was young enough so that the time lost between the stellar sailing vessel's departure and return would not be as significant to him as it would to an older crew member. He did not hold the prejudices against planet folk, and he was more willing than any other to adapt to planetary ways and to discover the means of securing a good crew without arousing local suspicions.

Milani had agreed without protest, but Ghyaspur

believed that was only because the captain could send no other. She could not spare Mordon or Droganie; Bracha was too ill, and now that Senda's fear of the planets was known, Milani would not subject the albino to centishifts ... *years*, he reminded himself, of torture. No, it was between Allis and himself, and Allis had decided to have her baby in the weightless environment of the ship. Milani bowed to Allis's wishes, even seemed pleased to gain some time with her new stone-carrier friend. There was talk that she was eager now to teach Allis some fine points on how to use the stone, but Ghyaspur, remembering how Allis had compelled a dead man to move and suspecting that he himself had been compelled to do something extraordinary, believed it was Milani who should be doing the learning.

Allis's confidence in Ghyaspur aside, he was resentful to know he'd been assigned this important burden, once again in his lifetime, only by default. Still, he'd eagerly taken the opportunity. Not even the stone-carriers could fathom the reason why, since he chose not to reveal it.

It was simple, really. Before his imprisonment, he'd fallen in love. Allis might prefer to believe it was infatuation, some confusion in his mind about her being a symbol of planetary life. She could think what she liked, but he knew his own heart, and he loved her with all of it. But it would have taken a simpleton not to know his love was not returned.

The solution to that problem was not an easy one, but he believed he had found it when Allis suggested him for the Earth mission. If Allis could not love the boy he was, perhaps she would love the man he would become in these intervening years. Time dilation would keep her largely unchanged; there was little danger that she would not be the woman he remembered when they met again.

Ghyaspur took a last glance past the moon. There was nothing but stars to see. A scented breeze passed over his face, tickling his nose and eyes. It felt like Allis's hair. He took a deep breath and closed his eyes; her presence surrounded him and his heart seemed to swell most pleasantly. He sighed a final sigh and opened his eyes.

When he took a few steps toward the distant road, he discovered that the bones in his feet were already aching despite his exercising vigorously during passage through the series of gravity slips to Earth. His knees became points of pain before he was off the rise and on the flatland. He gritted his teeth; nothing could stop him now, certainly not physical pain. He'd known much worse than aches in his limbs. Besides, he had only to make it as far as the road before the world finished its turn out of shadow, and at the edge of the road Allis had told him he had merely to hold out his thumb and presently a car or truck would stop, its driver offering a ride.

He clenched his fist and thrust out his thumb in the fashion Allis had demonstrated, practicing conscientiously. He laughed inwardly. There were more important things to learn about this huge biosphere than how to stop a car or truck on the roadway. He would learn them before Allis came back to him.

Award-Winning
Science Fiction